I0699533

Aris and the Obsidian Door

Game of Gods: Book 2

E. M. Leander

First edition
ISBN ebook: 979-8-218-26356-0
ISBN hardback: 979-8-218-29427-4

Editing by Ben Gibson and Leonora Bulbeck
Cover art by Salome Totladze (@morgana0anagrom)
Cover design by Giessel Design
Map Illustration by Foreign Worlds Cartography
(https://foreignworlds.net)
Latin translation by Joaquin Dominguez Arduengo
(https://www.signatranslations.com)
Chapter Illustration by Gabrielle Ragusi

For you.

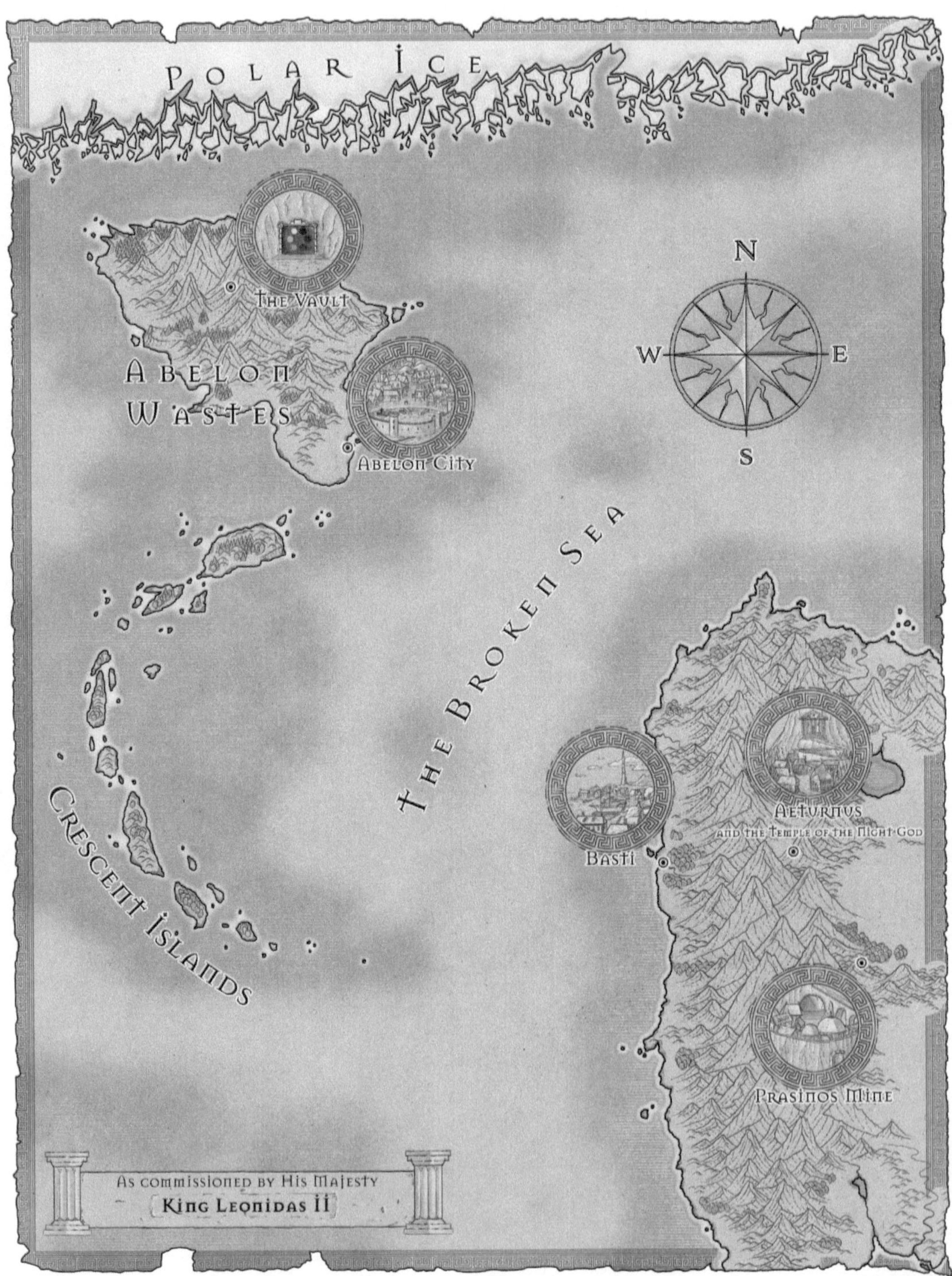

POLAR ICE
THE VAULT
ABELON WASTES
ABELON CITY
N
W
E
S
THE BROKEN SEA
CRESCENT ISLANDS
BASTI
AETURNUS
AND THE TEMPLE OF THE NIGHT GOD
PRASINOS MINE
AS COMMISSIONED BY HIS MAJESTY
KING LEONIDAS II

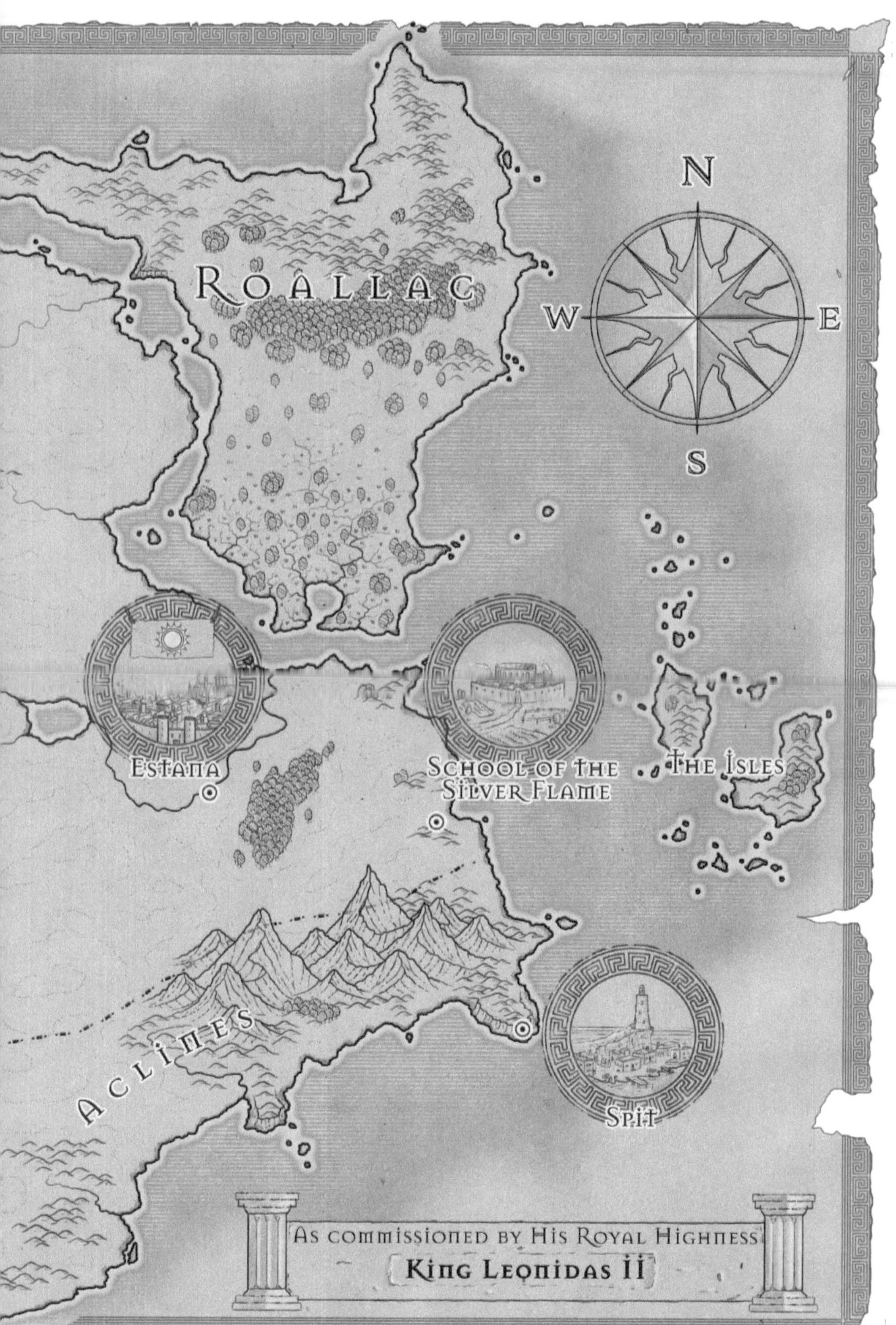

ROALLAC
N
W
E
S
Estaña
School of the Silver Flame
The Isles
Aclines
Spit
As commissioned by His Royal Highness
King Leonidas II

POLAR ICE
THE VAULT
ABELON WASTES
ABELON CITY
N
W E
S
THE BROKEN SEA
CRESCENT ISLANDS
ROALLAC
OCRON
Basti
AERURTUS
and the Temple of the Night God
PRANNES MINE
Estana
ACLINES
SCHOOL OF THE SILVER FLAME
THE ISLES
SPIT
As commissioned by His Majesty
KING LEONIDAS II

PROLOGUE

"You're going cross-eyed. Did you know?" the goddess asks.

Aenon looks up from scrying, his gaze for a moment unfocused. His sister comes into view slowly, as if he were emerging from underwater. Her pale face is stern, her posture flippant. But there is curiosity in her sky-blue eyes, even as she pretends to ignore him.

"Anything different today, brother?" Cephus asks. The least hated of his siblings, Cephus is as solid as the earth, as imperturbable as granite. His is the slow patience of growing things, the strength of metal and rock. Aenon has always found his presence to be soothing compared to his own moodiness.

The bland features of their immortal prison are made of mist and cloud. Not even Cephus's flowers last long. They crumble within a mortal day and dissolve into the nothingness from which they were formed. After hundreds of years, though, he still tries. He still brings forth carpets of moss and curtains of vines each day. It has been hard for him, not to be able to feel real dirt beneath his bare toes. He—like the others—can only minimally influence his elements on the mortal plane, or through one of his creatures, left behind when the gods accepted their exile. It pleases Cephus to bring forth new growth there each spring, to see his metal and stone crafted by man into objects of strength and beauty, even if he cannot experience it himself.

Mortals rarely fathomed the depths of Aenon's realm.

"Nothing different today," Aenon admits. "But soon."

"You've been saying that every day for the past century," Helene remarks, for the ten thousandth day in a row, flipping yellow hair over her shoulder. Stray wisps of breeze keep her long hair floating softly around her, free of the snarls that have caused Aenon's to twist tightly, wrapped in seaweed and studded with shells and barnacles.

"What is an eon compared to your immortal life, little sister?" Aenon asks.

"The humans forget about us more day by day," Ignatius says. He sits opposite Aenon—his opposite in every way, with wings of flame crackling about him.

Aenon does not let the smirk reach his lips. While his siblings complain and bicker, he bides his time. He has set his plans in motion, and soon they will be as inescapable as a whirlpool—and as deadly.

So he merely ducks his head and responds, "Perhaps."

"You gave them the power of the gods, Ignatius. You cannot still be surprised that they don't need you anymore," a voice drawls from the shadows.

"If we'd had your help, we wouldn't have lost the strength to cross back to the mortal realm and so remind them of their place," Cephus says.

The darkness coalesces. Caladrius, the god of night, forms before them, his skin as white as the full moon, his hair and wings forming a cape of blackness around him.

"Then why do you still watch them so intently, I wonder?" he says, arrogance dripping from his mouth like venom. He turns his focus to Aenon. "Is it not enough for you to be master of the seas and the storms? Is it not enough to bring rain or drought at your whim? Must you have their obeisance also?"

"It helps to pass the time. Perhaps I find some of them interesting," Aenon says, trailing a finger down his scrying shell. "As have you."

Caladrius raises an eyebrow. "Just the one, brother," he says, a hint of sharpness in his tone. "And I'll thank you to leave my pet alone, if you want your own left ... intact."

Ignatius surges to his feet, his wings flaring, his hands clenched at his sides. "How dare you threaten him!" His voice is as terrible as an inferno, as dry and fierce as a wildfire. His eyes blaze with frustration and fury.

Aenon is surprised at his brother's defense of him. But then again, the elementals have never much cared for their dark brother.

Caladrius does not flinch. "It is not an idle warning," he says, his gaze finding each of them by turn. "It is a promise."

CHAPTER 1
ARIS

I am so fucked.

The early morning sunshine does nothing to take the edge off the chill in my mood. If Wren notices, I hope she thinks it is due to nerves. That the journey to the west, where uncertainty and likely our doom are awaiting us, is making me—the white tiger, the fiercest Shield in the country—nervous.

But I'm not nervous. I don't get nervous. I can't afford to be. Fear is for fools and weaklings, not Shields—but I'd rather Wren think I'm nervous than guess the real reason behind my mood.

Anger is much more useful than fear.

My hands are starting to ache from clenching the reins, when what I really want to do is wrap them around Leo's neck. King Leonidas III, royal pain in my ass. He thinks he's so smart, sending Wren out with his handpicked entourage. The best in the realm to keep his beloved Night Mage safe, he claimed. She, of course, felt nothing but gratitude (and possibly affection) for him and his thoughtfulness. She missed the smug look on Leo's face when I realized that two of my ex-lovers were joining our group—lovers that Wren is not even aware are a part of my history.

And now Wren, my fearsome, naive Wren, is riding along with them, oblivious. On her left side is Dimitra, one of the highest-ranking Shields at the School of the Silver Flame, outranked only by Commander Markos and a handful of others. On Wren's other side rides Mariana, a powerful Water Mage, who thought I'd claim her at my last games in the arena. I've disappointed both of them, in more ways than one.

I swear Wren knows I am thinking about her. She turns, flipping her long braid over her shoulder, and gives me a warm smile that goes straight to my groin, before going back to making small talk and laughing with the other women. *What are they talking about?*

At my side ride Caelus and Rafael. Caelus attempts to read as we go—I've never known a Shield to be so invested in books. I almost pity his horse for having to carry them all. Rafael tries to engage me in conversation, to relive our past adventures and to find out more about the enigmatic Night Mage he's been entrusted to guard. I ignore him, and after a while he finally shuts up—and then the bastard starts whistling. I'd gotten used to Wren's quiet companionship – Rafael is already grating on my nerves.

I watch Wren sway in her saddle, reaching out to let a passing bird land on her finger for a moment. She strokes its breast, whispering something softly to it that I can't hear. I'm immediately jealous of the attention it's getting. The bird answers her by fluffing its little brown feathers and offering a snippet of song before flying off. She watches it wistfully as it disappears into the grasses. She has not yet come to terms with the power she wields over animals, the influence she has over the elements, given to her by the god of night himself.

On top of that, I've gone and kissed her. Thoroughly, and at every possible opportunity. While I'm positive she reciprocates my feelings, she is as unexperienced with them as she is with her powers. The last thing I need is for Dimitra or Mariana to say something—*anything*—about our past and ruin whatever chance I have. I want Wren—I want her like I've never wanted any woman before.

Gods.

How am I supposed to defend this woman as we march toward a den of monsters if I can't keep my focus off getting into her pants a mere handful of miles into this journey?

The odds are not in my favor.

CHAPTER 2
WREN

We are not an inconspicuous bunch.

Three heavily armed Shields—essentially bodyguards—and their three Mages. The Shields bristle with weapons. Until recently, I had no idea what a Shield was, or just how lethal they were. Still, you only have to take one look at them to know that they are not just average warriors. They've been gifted by the god of day, Rigrasil, himself with speed, strength, and endurance far beyond what any ungifted person could claim.

We Mages stand apart too. My own black Mage robe flows softly around me, hanging in elegant silken folds—a gift from my tutors, Ismini and Panos, formidable Mages who work for the king, and who were staying in Estana. I wish for the tenth or thousandth time already that Ismini was coming with us. Her strength, kindness, and steadiness (and scones) are hard to leave behind.

Then there's Mariana in bright blue, riding an elegant white mare, and Rafael, chatting to Aris in the back, wearing a robe so blindingly red that there's no doubt it can be seen for miles across the flat countryside. These robes are a signal to anyone in Ocron that the wearer is a Mage. As such, Mages are tasked by the king himself with protecting the people and the land. In my case, that means riding out west to see why the god of night felt he had to go and create *me* when there are elemental Mages.

Especially since now all kinds of foul things are coming after me. I'm glad to have the Mages' protection, even if Aris is not. Not even Aris Valorius can take on the whole world alone.

Caelus—Mariana's Shield—rides out in front, scouting the way through the grasslands, though we've barely left Estana. He's lean and weathered, wearing clothes as gray as his rangy gelding. His swords, two gladiuses crossed over his back, as they are on the other Shields, are contrastingly well kept. His round shield, too, is immaculately cared for. He pays less attention to his wild brown hair. He's such a contrast to the prim Mariana that I wonder why she agreed to be his Mage.

I glance over my shoulder at Aris, riding grim-faced next to the last member of our group, Rafael. Aris was supposed to pick Mariana at the games. Everyone thought he would. It is the natural order of things. The best Shield picks the best Mage, the second best picks the second best, and so on. Until I came along. Mariana has two years of training on me, and still, Aris picked me. At the time, I didn't realize that I already knew him—only as his shifted form, a glorious white tiger who'd felt my magic call to him weeks before. He'd believed in me before I even believed in myself.

I turn to look at Aris, drinking in the sight of him, the width of his shoulders, the soft fall of his black hair. "Pretty boy," Zale called him once—a beautiful facade hiding a honed weapon. Aris can distract me with his kisses and flirtations all day, but underneath he is a warrior, a force to be reckoned with. And that tiger-shaped helmet he carries—when he puts that on, Aris the Shield would intimidate the gods themselves.

And *gods*, how did I get so lucky? To have found such an ally, by chance or by fate. Someone so incomparably skilled, someone who defied his own past to become my future.

Not to mention he's extremely handsome—as he reminds me, often.

I must be smiling like a fool, because Mariana lets out a delicate snort before fixing her eyes ahead again.

Dimitra, on my other side, is the complete opposite of Mariana— she is quiet and fierce, a little like a teakettle just getting ready to boil, whereas Mariana is as cold as ice. Dimitra wears the traditional round wooden shield on her back, like the other Shields do, and carries more knives than I could begin to count. Every time I look, she's fiddling with a different one, sharpening or cleaning them as we go. They're strapped to her arms, to her waist, in her boots, and I think there's a small one in her hair too, which she uses like a pin to keep the twists of black hair off her face. She is so poised, so graceful. Next to her, I feel like a wren next to an eagle.

My good mood fades as we approach the Golden Crown Lodge. Or rather, what's left of it. I've been worried that our little band is going to be too noticeable in the featureless continent before us. So how have trolls—which are giant, and stupid—snuck up on the only building around for miles?

Our party is silent as our horses drift past the smoking husk. Not so very long ago, Aris and I spent the night there. Heat rises to my cheeks as I remember that evening, the way I spied on him in the bath, the way he carried me to bed in his arms—before drop- ping me abruptly onto the cold mattress. I had spent the night alone and confused, while he tossed and turned all night on a small cot by the fire. Tension increased between us then, raising sensa- tions I couldn't have begun to understand, that I am only now starting to.

Seeing that lodge now turned into a smoldering ruin cools down those memories fast.

The stone foundation remains, mostly. The small stable is nothing but a pile of ash. The stone fireplace is scorched almost entirely black. A few people wade through the wreckage. One I recognize as the innkeeper, though his eyes are reddened and his ruddy face streaked with soot and tears. He meets my eyes, and I have to avert my gaze.

This all happened because of me. He's lost everything. It is a miracle that no one was killed.

All because of whatever gift the god of night has given me, which calls monsters to me like moths to a flame—or like trolls to a lodge, where apparently they were tracking me. I want to offer some comfort to the innkeeper, but what good would words do? I'll write to Leo, I decide, and ask him to donate whatever I have in terms of my Mage allowance to the lodge, as penance. I scribble my note on a paper I tear from a notebook, and give it to one of the stableboys to deliver for me. The boy wipes his streaming eyes on a soot-stained sleeve before accepting the note and payment and scurries off.

I think back to my lighthouse on the Spit, where I grew up. The life I was forced out of when magic—and Aris—found me. The flame I carefully tended through the years.

Now it, too, is nothing more than another pile of rubble and ash, torn down by some great sea beast, if the rumors are true. Is this to be my legacy? Piles of destruction and ruined lives? Leo told me that the rest of Spit was left intact, though a number of the residents decided to leave in case the kraken came back. I am being hunted, and anyone I come in contact with is now at risk.

I square my shoulders. Leo has entrusted me with this task, to find out why magic is changing, why krakens and trolls and other beasts of legend are once more finding their way into human territory. Why the god of night has decided to grant me his power, magic that I can only access, infuriatingly, at night. *Why, why, why?* I can only hope that the god of night's temple will have the answers I seek, but somehow I doubt it will be that simple.

I glance over my shoulder again, back to Estana, shining golden in the distance, its banners—red with a golden sun—flying high. I wonder at the ache in my chest, seeing it diminish behind us. As ridiculous as it sounds, the palace was starting to feel like home. Part of me, though, wonders how much of that ache is due to leaving Leo and Ismini and Panos behind. They've become more dear to me than anyone else—my teachers, my mentors, my friends.

I have to leave. If monsters want me, then I can't stay in one place, and certainly not one like Estana, where the casualties could be catastrophic—*have been* catastrophic already, at the Golden Crown. No, this is the right decision, I tell myself, over and over. Heading west, to seek out the Temple of Caladrius, the god of night. It is—conveniently—located in the wilds of the formidable western mountains, along with more trolls, winged beasts, and things so foul that names for them don't even exist. I've seen the refugees from there come and plead their case to Leo at court, to beg for his help. Their homes have been destroyed—their families and friends killed —by those winged, spiked creatures and by bands of heavily armed trolls.

All of which are still hunting.

And I am their prey.

CHAPTER 3
LEO

*M*y Wren,

I know you'll likely get this before you've even been gone a day. Ismini has insisted that I remind you to never take off your robe, and that she and Panos imbued it with every charm and spell they could think of to keep you safe. Do not worry over Estana while you travel—we will all be awaiting your swift return.

On that note, please do stay safe out there. The palace has already become a far more boring place since you left.

I have sent your wages to the Golden Crown, as you requested—and multiplied them a few dozen times over, for good measure.

Yours,
Leo

CHAPTER 4
ARIS

Just before we break for camp near a small copse of trees, a messenger hawk arrives for Wren. He's not one I recognize—most of them are unpaired Shields who work running errands like this for the king and other nobles. A waste of Shield talent, but not everyone is cut out for claiming a Mage. Not everyone wants to risk going gray someday, trading that risk for glory. But no one will ever remember a messenger hawk; no one will ever sing songs about their adventures. Their story will fade after their death, like smoke dissipating from a candle.

The story of Wren and I will be a bonfire, so large and fierce that it will be a legend, told for generations. Our flame will never go out.

The bird circles Wren before alighting on her outstretched wrist. She strokes his chest before untying a small scroll from his leg. The flash of gold wax on the seal tells me that it is from the king.

The flush that warms Wren's face tells me I wouldn't like the contents very much. Gods, we haven't even been gone a full day. I am grateful, at least, that she's getting some distance from him.

"You're going to need new tack in a week if you keep that up," Dimitra says, eyeing my reins before dismounting.

I look down—the leather is already cracking from the strain of my grip.

"What's got you so tense?" she asks.

Dimitra removes her mount's saddle with practiced ease. She shoots a glance over at Wren, who is fumbling with Jasper's saddle. If the horse wasn't so dumbstruck by Wren's magic, no doubt she would end up getting nipped or kicked with the way she is yanking on the girth. Dimitra sees me watching Wren, sees the exasperation on my face.

"Good luck with that." Dimitra smirks and hands me the halter of her own mount. "Here. Hold this. I'll get a hitching rope strung up."

Getting camp set is a quiet affair. Quiet seems to be Caelus's modus operandi, which the gods know I appreciate. Even Rafael senses the tension and has the good sense to keep his mouth shut, which I have previously thought impossible. Wren's eyes flit between our companions, deciding whether to stay and risk awkward conversation. She decides she'd rather go and gather firewood.

We stand on a small cleared space where the grasses meet the small grove of trees. There are remnants of many prior groups having used this place—hells, maybe I have at one time too—and Wren neatly arranges the twigs and branches over the old firepit.

"Anyone have a flint?" she asks, rocking back on her heels.

Mariana barks out a laugh. "Seriously, Night Mage? The sun is down. Do your thing," she says, gesturing toward the wood.

Wren glares at her but bites her tongue—a minor miracle.

Wren looks at the wood, gaze flicking up a few times to note the position of the setting sun, the stars winking into life overhead. Her magic rises as the sun sets, though she is just starting to figure out how to access it. As a Shield, I have generations of warriors to learn from and have been training since the day I was born. I know my strength and my place. Wren ... well, she's trying to figure it all out. She'll have to make her own way, and if that throws everything else into chaos in the process, then so be it. I'll be by her side through it all. That's what a good Shield would do—and I am the best.

Wren continues to stare at the gathered wood, concentrating, but nothing happens. She whispers under her breath, twists her fingers as she says words to try to bring forth the flame, but still there's nothing.

Wren sighs and stands. "Unless you all want a cold supper, Rafael, could you show me?" she asks, looking to the Fire Mage. Her cheeks are flushed—she's angry, maybe embarrassed. I've seen that look on many a recruit after I've knocked them down in the arena. There is no shame in asking for help when you are learning—the only shame comes if you decide to give up.

Rafael shoots her a broad grin, rolling up his sleeves like he is ready to put on a show. Wren's gaze flickers to the waxy scars on his hands and arms, stark white against his otherwise tanned skin. Control is everything to a Fire Mage—I don't want to admit that maybe Leo was right in sending Rafael along with us, but Wren can actually learn a lot from him. I don't feel like being put through another one of her magical tornadoes every time something pisses her off.

"Well, that's disappointing," Mariana says, crossing her arms. "Don't like being put on the spot, Night Mage?"

"Her name is Wren," I remind Mariana with a growl. "And you know damn well her magic's been tricky, especially since she battled the strongest Wind Mage on the continent and *won*."

Wren shoots me a glance that is equal parts mortified and apologetic—but she has nothing to apologize for. It's not like she'd asked for Saroya and Nestor to kidnap her and clap a manacle back on her wrist. As far as I'm concerned, they both got what they deserved.

"Yes," Mariana purrs, looking at me through narrowed eyes. "Let us not forget how dear *Wren* pushed our Head Mage into burnout. You may as well have killed her."

Burnout is the ultimate fear of any gifted person, usually a Mage —an irreversible state, reached when a gifted person pushes too far, too hard. "Going gray" is the other term for it. It can also happen when one of a claimed pair—either the Mage or the Shield—dies. The other simply fades until they stop altogether. The bond between them is so strong, so absolutely vital, that one cannot end up living without the other. So they stop. Stop eating, stop talking, stop breathing. I mean, as far as I know, Saroya is still alive, whatever that life is worth now, and she didn't ever bond with a Shield, so it is just her own life at risk. She and Nestor, my father, kidnapped Wren after realizing—partially—her significance, on the misguided notion that she is dangerous, or drawing in evil creatures. A beacon—or a harbinger.

"Well, you can put a Mage's robe on a pig, but in the end, it's still just a pig," Mariana says, inspecting her fingernails.

Wren's hands clench at her sides as she glares at Mariana. Her eyes flash with jade fire, and a whirl of wind stirs her robe.

I know that look. Nothing good comes of that look.

Shit.

I move to her side and put an arm around her shoulders. Even now, after all that has happened, the intimacy of this kind of contact startles her, and she glares up at me, that smoldering magic ready to boil over. Mariana grins smugly, but I barely register it. Wren's eyes —usually a cool gray-green—are glowing. The wind is whipping around her now, but only her, sending her long braid flying like a whip across my face.

The last time I saw her look like this, she turned my gladiuses into glowing weapons of doom, sharp and strong enough to cut stone—while simultaneously battling Saroya with a whirling vortex of pure elemental magic.

It's not even been a full day out on this journey, and Wren's ready to unleash the same power on Mariana.

"You can do this," I tell Wren, wrestling down her braid. "You can light fire, remember? Just like you practiced on all those candles."

She tears her gaze away from me, back to the wood, her face screwing up in concentration, but still nothing happens.

"Oh, for fuck's sake, just light the fire, Raf," Dimitra says. "It's getting cold." She sits on one of the old logs around the firepit, like nothing unusual is going on.

Wren's eyes return abruptly to their usual gray-green, and she looks away. I pretend not to notice the dampness gathering in them.

Rafael whispers, "*Flame,*" and points his index finger with unnecessary flair. The wood bursts into fire.

"Nothing like a roaring campfire to turn traveling companions into friends," Rafael says, sitting by Dimitra.

Usually his perpetual good humor is annoying. Now I am oddly grateful for it. It seems to defuse the situation a little. Gods, I wish Wren and I were traveling alone, just the two of us—for so, so many reasons.

"Thank you," Wren mutters as she takes a seat.

Rafael dips his head, watching her more carefully than I like.

I sit at Wren's side, and eventually Mariana joins us too. Caelus remains alert, standing back from the fire, standing guard. He scans the darkening horizon like he is expecting an attack at any moment, even here, so close to the capital, on a main road.

Maybe that makes him the smart one. After all, no one expected the trolls to so blatantly attack the Golden Crown.

"So, I thought maybe we could all review the plan," Wren says, reaching for a knapsack.

Mariana snorts, crossing her arms.

"What is it?" Wren snaps.

They glare at each other over the flames, which suddenly jump to three times their height.

"Hey," Rafael says quietly. "Let's not burn all the fuel at once. Pace yourself."

Wren doesn't take her eyes off Mariana, though the flames do quiet back down.

"Get yourself under control," Mariana says, tossing her hair back over her shoulder. "Or you're as much of a danger to us as the beasts on the road."

"Oh, get over yourself," Wren grumbles. She plucks pieces of grass and tosses them into the flames, though her lips are drawn tightly.

"You should be beside yourself with gratitude that I'm even *here*," Mariana says.

"Why *are* you here?" Wren asks, glaring at Mariana.

Mariana glances at me, and I freeze. What is she going to say? That Leo asked her to accompany us to Aeturnus and the Temple of Caladrius because he thinks she's talented and will keep Wren safe? Or that Leo isn't giving up on having Wren for himself and so sent my ex-lovers along to help her make her choice?

"The same reason Dimitra's here, I'm sure," Mariana says sweetly.

Wren looks confused, glancing toward Dimitra.

Dimitra is as still as a statue, arms crossed.

"Because the king commanded it," Caelus says simply, oblivious to the building tension.

Wren accepts this, and relief floods through me. For the moment, at least, it's still my secret to tell.

"Also, because Caelus knows more about the gods than anyone," Rafael offers. "The man's practically a living saint. I'm pretty sure King Leonidas just wanted Caelus on this trip, and Mariana got thrown in for fun."

"He's *my Shield*," Mariana hisses. "Where he goes, I go. And I'll have you know I was top of my class. Wren should be thanking the gods that I even agreed to come on this trip."

"So you're beautiful *and* smart," Rafael says, a grin spreading across his face. "Today must be my lucky day."

I groan—this trip can't end soon enough.

"Look," Wren says, "if you're still mad because Aris picked me over you, just say so. This is a long trip, and I don't feel like looking over my shoulder the entire time to see if you're going to stab me in the back."

Mariana cackles, shooting me a smirk. I shake my head slowly, and Mariana arches an eyebrow. She knows, then—that Wren doesn't know I've slept with her, that this spat is more than just the fact that I embarrassed Mariana at the games by choosing someone uninitiated over her.

To be fair, I've never promised her anything. If she assumed I'd claim her just because I was sleeping with her, then that is on her. We were two consenting adults enjoying our brief time together, and that's all. I owe her nothing.

Mariana does not feel the same, apparently. Women rarely do.

"It is a shame that Panos wouldn't let me bring the manacles," Mariana says, picking at her fingernails.

Wren jumps to her feet, and so do I. She's had enough.

The fire goes out.

In its place, the embers glow an eerie jade green. Raw energy crackles from Wren's fingers, circling her wrists, waiting to be unleashed into the gathering night.

"So your magic *does* work after all," Mariana purrs, unperturbed. "Interesting. Though we've got to work on your control. Tomorrow. I can give you lessons as we ride. I won't be left at the mercy of your *moods* when we run into trouble."

The green glow flickers uncertainly and dies. The fire comes back its usual orange. Wren sits back down hard, close enough that her leg brushes mine. I sit and put my hand on her knee, squeezing it, in a way I hope is reassuring. Wren gives me a small smile, but it quickly fades.

"Gods, can you at least keep your hands off each other until I'm asleep?" Mariana groans.

Wren colors and scoots a few inches away from me. She has lived in a tower by herself for years—physical contact of any kind leaves her flustered. I've made some headway, sure—not as much as I'd like, but still.

And I've had it with Mariana. However, the frequently ignored rational side of my mind argues, I can't push her too hard. I have no doubt if I did, she'd be thrilled to tell Wren about our past exploits.

In vivid detail. And then Wren will clam up, and we'll be back to where we started.

"Honestly, I have no idea how Caelus has been able to put up with you," I say.

Mariana lets out a laugh.

Good. I've managed to shift Mariana's attention away from Wren for a moment.

"Caelus is a serious Shield. He respects our professional boundaries, unlike some," she says, glancing down at me.

"Keep pushing my Mage, and you'll see just how serious I can be."

"Oh?" Mariana's mouth twists into a cruel smirk, and I realize, *Shit, this is it. This is how Wren finds out that I slept with Mariana.* I've never pretended to be celibate, but I think that this bit of news might just make Wren lose what slight tether she does have on her magic right now.

Overhead, storm clouds begin to gather, swirling, as Wren's frustration with Mariana grows. Her eyes take on that green glow again.

"Well, this is going to be fun!" Rafael says, breaking the tension, clapping his hands together. "Mariana, your methods *are* a bit … pointed. We can talk about how we're going to instruct Wren later. Let's just eat. We're all tired."

Mariana glares at him but doesn't retort.

Wren blinks and looks down at her hands, which are trembling slightly in her lap. The clouds above dissipate, and again we're left with a clear evening sky.

Gods, it's going to be a long trip.

"I'm starting to wish it was just the two of us," Wren whispers, letting the others sort out the evening's rations.

I let my hand find hers, taking her shaking fingers in mine. I contemplate leaving them all—taking Wren and going off into the west by ourselves.

And then I remember how it felt to have Nestor shackle me, clapping that damned manacle on my wrist like *I* was the villain, not him. How my muscles atrophied and my strength ebbed in the matter of a moment, rendering me completely useless.

No. As much as it pains me to even think it, it is the smart move to go with a group, especially one as highly trained as this one. Dimitra could take on an army by herself, and I've seen Caelus's technique personally in the arena—the man is calculating, cold, and deadly. And Rafael has saved my ass more than once.

We need them. I'm going to have to find a way to deal with Mariana—and Dimitra too, I guess, though fortunately she's remained quiet until now. I don't know if I'd even survive all three women turning on me, or if I'd emerge from such a fight with my manhood still attached. And I am rather attached to it.

"I wish we were alone too," I say absently, rubbing my thumb against the back of Wren's hand, glaring daggers at Mariana.

But deep in my gut, a guilty thought worms its way through me —for entirely different reasons.

I barely sleep that first night. Aris insists on taking the night's watch. As a Shield, he can stay up for days without resting, but I have a feeling he wouldn't be able to sleep, even if he had the opportunity to. Something about this group is chafing him. If he were in his tiger form, his tail would be swishing, his ears back, his hackles raised. As a man, he is harder to read, but only a little.

I lie on my side, watching the fire, snug in my bedroll. A pair of field mice find me and curl up near my head, keeping me company. I smile watching them. They remind me so much of the little dormice I used to have back at my lighthouse, tiny things that I watched grow and have babies of their own over the years. Gods, I never knew I could miss a place so much.

I can barely make out the shadow of Aris at the edge of our camp, just beside the horses. He stands tall and broad, as immobile as a statue. I'd much rather he were here beside me, keeping me warm. The thought brings heat into my cheeks—I guess we won't have a lot of privacy out here, which makes me feel strangely conflicted. A little tingly, a little regretful—and a little grateful.

Aris is just ... a very physical person. And I am not. In fact, I nearly jumped out of my skin when he put his arm around me earlier, like he was staking some sort of stupid claim. And though I know he wants further intimacy, I am not quite ready for that leap—which he respects. He doesn't like it, but he doesn't push. I mean, I lived on my own for *years*. Gods, days or weeks could go by without my even seeing another person. I can't imagine what it must have been like for Aris growing up, with so many siblings, enrolled in training with his peers from the time he could walk. Never without someone to talk to. He rarely speaks of them, but still, I envy his large family.

Even when my father was alive, well, he wasn't really a physically affectionate person. Valeri liked to show his love by taking good care of me, by working hard, by sharing the things he loved with me—by sharing the lighthouse's legacy. That was all he had to give, since he poured his entire life into it.

And now it is all gone because of me.

I sigh and roll onto my back. The stars are out, and the moon is nearly full. I still have some of my bruises and scrapes from when Aris's father and the Head Mage drugged and kidnapped me. If Panos is right, then when the moon is full, I will be healed, like the way Shields can heal, the way I healed after the trolls attacked us in the woods and I was injured. The same power that the god of day, Rigrasil, granted Shields reflects off the moon when my own magic is at its peak. The one large bruise down my flank has faded to a ghastly greenish color, and the abrasions on my wrists and ankles are still pink but no longer raw.

Night Mage.

The name still sounds strange to my ears. Mages are supposed to be elemental—like how Mariana is a Water Mage and Rafael is a Fire Mage. I am still a little hazy on exactly how the elemental gods and the two main gods are related—I grew up in a country where those gods are not worshipped. Even here in Ocron, they haven't really been heard from in centuries. It seems they just vanished. Here one day, meddling in people's lives—and then gone. And after a while, since magic continued, people stopped caring about the gods at all.

Until magic started fading.

And until I came along. The Night Mage, the herald of doom.

I watch a wisp of cloud drift through the blackness overhead, the stars twinkling behind it.

And somehow, despite everything, I fall asleep.

I am dreaming. I know I am dreaming—which is strange. I've never really been able to tell before. It is the same dream I've been having for days now, of a winged man on a great black horse, the rest shrouded in mist.

But he is clearer now. It is night, like always, but now he glows like a star, like starlight makes up the white of his hair and the alabaster of his skin. He is shrouded in a cloak as black as the space between the stars, and it moves on a breeze that I can't feel.

And then his head turns, and his gaze is fixed on me, and I can feel my skin charring under the intensity, can smell my hair burning as I scream, invisible flames consuming me. Even in the dream, my consciousness rapidly fades, giving way to nothing but pain and darkness.

I wake, sitting bolt upright, the scream still ringing in my ears.

But it is not my scream.

Aris is at my side, one hand on my shoulder, the other holding a gladius, like he thought I was in real danger.

"Are you all right?" he asks.

I nod, putting a shaking hand on his, drawing strength from him, grateful for him. The strangeness of the dream, the burning sensation on my skin, is fading. It was just a dream. Why, then, did the pain seem so very real? I shudder, and Aris plants a soft kiss on my head.

That's when I realize—someone is *still* screaming. A voice shrill with fury, punctuated with the sound of heavy thuds and splashing.

I stand up and am greeted with the most glorious thing I've ever seen in my entire life.

A dozen snakes pour out of Mariana's bedroll. She is dancing around them, hair and eyes wild, trying not to step on them as they slither and hiss away into the grasses. Some are impressively large specimens, laced with beautiful green and brown designs on their backs. I'm not familiar with the species, but I know instantly that they have a special place in my heart now. I didn't intentionally set them on Mariana, but I'm not exactly upset about it. Not that they are attacking her—more like they chose her cozy bedroll as a nice place to take a nap themselves. I would say that they recognized her as being as cold-blooded as they are, but that would be insulting to the snakes.

Mariana's pale hand claws at the air, and I watch as water condenses in her palm, like a small marble. She flings it with a word, and I watch a snake fly into the air from the impact before hissing mightily and retreating. I can see mud spatters on the ground where her other attempts have hit their targets.

I stifle a laugh. Mariana hears and whirls on me. She looks terrible, which makes my mood even better. She is usually annoyingly beautiful, as sharp and cold as ice. Now her hair is wild and tangled, and her cheeks are a splotchy pink.

"YOU!" she screeches, and another orb of water—much larger this time—shimmers into her hand. She raises it, like it is a ball she is about to heave at me.

I look up. The sun has risen completely, bathing the grassland in a pale rose glow.

I have no power against her now, not when the night has ended. I can only hope that the water will soak me and not fling me into the air the way it did the snakes.

Aris places his body and his shield between us, meeting Mariana's wild eyes with his own furious gaze.

From nowhere, Caelus appears. He grabs Mariana's wrist, speaking quiet words to her.

The orb of water splashes to the ground, soaking her shoes. Mariana appears not to notice. By now, everyone else is up and watching her. She sniffs, raising her head, and turns her back on me like nothing has happened.

She doesn't see Rafael wink at me, or Aris run a hand through his hair as he whispers a sarcastic prayer to Rigrasil for strength and sanity.

Yes, I decide, the memory of the painful dream already fading. Today is going to be a better day.

"Come on, princess, time for lessons," Aris teases. He's flipping his dagger end over end in his hand, a wicked grin on his face.

I groan but pull my own knife from my boot—he checks several times a day to make sure I have it on me at all times—and follow him to the edge of camp. The grasslands still remind me of home, though we've stopped near a convenient copse of trees for the night. The rippling of the grasses reminds me of the waves back home, on a rare calm night. The thought of "home" makes an ache start in my chest, and I get a sense of coming unmoored. I don't have a home, really.

Not a place, anyway, but I do have a person. A very handsome, arrogant person who is currently pacing, impatiently waiting for me to get ready. He prowls like the tiger he is, his blue eyes flashing in the twilight.

"Knife up," he growls—and without further warning, he attacks.

He's moving slowly by his standards, but still too quickly for me to block his assault entirely. He persists, stabbing and whirling, each time the knife halting just a hair's breadth away from touching me.

My legs ache from riding all day, and it takes some time for me to get limbered up. I'm getting used to his training style by now—relentless, disciplined. He shows me a new way to disarm an opponent and then reminds me again of my obscene lack of skill.

"You fight to get away, princess, not to win. You fight to buy time for me to get there, or for you to escape," he says, raising a finger to emphasize his point.

I massage my wrist, which is aching now from the force of blocking his blows. I hear a snigger from behind us—I can't tell if it came from Dimitra or Mariana. Maybe both. Compared to them, I have the skill of a toddler.

"And you think too much," Aris says, breaking into my self-pity.

He attacks with both hands now—the dagger in one, his other a fist. He moves slowly again, so I have time to figure out the best way to block him, or duck.

"And you don't think enough," I retort, spitting the words out hastily as I dodge the knife.

He grabs me with his free hand, spinning me until my back is hard against his chest.

"That's not true. I think about you *all* the time," he whispers, giving the shell of my ear a playful nip.

I can't deny the sensations he's causing, heat and butterflies all at once, flooding my face with warmth.

I drive my elbow into his sternum, and the air leaves his chest, followed by a grudging chuckle.

"Not bad," he says, rolling his shoulders and giving me a feral grin, his teeth very white against his tanned face.

A flicker of pride warms me.

"Think I could ever take down a Shield?" I ask, emboldened, switching my knife to my left hand, my weaker side.

At this, Aris laughs, and I feel a spark of indignation. I yell and attack him this time, instead of merely defending. I have no doubt that if it were truly nighttime, my blade would be green with magic. My magic seems to flare when I'm emotional, rather than when it is summoned with words, like with the elemental Mages. And the way Aris is toying with me is starting to irritate me.

As it is, he disarms me in a moment, grabbing my arm and wrenching it behind my back. My eyes water at the sensation, though the pain isn't that bad.

Aris eases up immediately, and I step away, rubbing my shoulder.

"You're not a Shield, Wren," he says. "In a physical battle, you'd have no chance at winning, but that's not the point."

I frown.

By the campfire, I hear another laugh—this time I know it is definitely coming from Dimitra.

"So what is the point?" I mutter. "I'll never be as strong as Dimitra, or Mariana. I'll never be as good."

In a blink, Aris has closed the space between us. He hooks my chin between his thumb and finger, raising my pouting face to his. He kisses me soundly, and though he's only touching my face, I feel it like wildfire through my entire body.

"Words have power," he reminds me, and I can feel the touch of his words, his lips are still so close to mine. "If you say you will never be as strong as they are, then you won't. Your magic will make it true. If you say you are *stronger*, well ..." He kisses me again, gently this time.

Then he steps away and levels his dagger at me, a wicked glint in his eyes. "New rules," he says.

I roll my eyes. Honestly, I am so focused on wanting to kiss him again I barely recall what we were talking about.

"Repeat after me," he says, and he slashes his blade down toward me.

I rush to block it, knocking my forearm against his with a jolt that reverberates through my shoulder.

"I am the strongest Mage the world has ever seen," he says, grinning.

I roll my eyes again, but then he's attacking me again, and I struggle to block his moves. For a moment, all I can focus on is the movement of his body and the response of mine. It's like a dance, I imagine, though I must look so clumsy to him.

"Say it," he says, pushing me back against one of the trees.

The air leaves my lungs in a grunt of effort as I push back against him. I bite my tongue.

"Say it," he says again, now pinning me to the tree, his hard body pressed against mine.

My mind goes completely blank. His knee is pressing against my thighs, and I'm panting so hard from the exertion that my chest is heaving against his.

"What?" I ask. The word sounds dazed, even to my own ears. All I can see, all I can feel, all I want is Aris, in a way I've never wanted anyone before in my life.

"Say it. Say you are the strongest Mage," he says. He buries his knife into the trunk beside me—not to intimidate me, but to free his hands to wander down my hip and to trace my flushed cheek.

"But I'm not the strongest Mage," I say, and though I try to keep the worry from my voice, it wavers. I am the girl from Spit who befriends animals—that's all. This whole thing is so very much bigger than me.

"Not with an attitude like that you're not," Aris says. "Say it, the right way this time."

"Maybe I'll use my magic on *you* instead," I grumble, looking him up and down. I don't want to do what he's asking. In order to *make* someone do something with magic—even myself—I have to feel it, believe it. And I just ... don't.

Aris bends, touching his forehead to mine. "Oh? What kinds of dirty things do you have in mind, princess?" he whispers, and his low tone sends shivers down my spine.

I swallow hard. "I could *tell* you to kiss me. You'd be powerless to resist," I say. Not that I'd ever do such a thing—the idea of *making* Aris do anything, intentionally or not, is something that has weighed on me ever since Saroya. What if I get angry and say something stupid, some curse that previously would have held no threat? *I hope you break your neck.* Or worse, *Go away.*

Aris drags the tip of his nose across my cheek to my ear and plants a kiss on the sensitive skin there.

"I'm already under your spell, Wren. Your powers have no effect on me," he growls, and heat rushes through me—relief, or something else. Then, with an immense show of reluctance, he pushes himself back, just enough so there's a hand's breadth of space between us, just enough so that I can catch my breath.

"Now. Say it. You are the strongest Mage."

"I am the strongest Mage," I repeat quietly. It sounds pathetic even to my own ears.

"Louder," he urges, baring his canines in a wicked smirk.

I narrow my eyes at him.

"Louder!"

"I am the strongest Mage!" I say, and—magic or not—yelling it brings a true smile to my face, and to Aris's too.

"You are a force like no one's ever seen," he prompts. "You are remarkable. You are the first and greatest Night Mage in history."

I echo his words. He kisses me after each sentence, deeper each time, a reward for good behavior, I suppose.

"You are the claimed Mage of the greatest Shield in the history of the world," he teases. "You really think I would have chosen you if I didn't see your potential?"

"Fortunately, I have enough humility for both of us," I say.

He smirks. "Gods, you are frustrating sometimes," he says, and he kisses me soundly, pushing me back against the rough bark of the tree. "And magnificent. I wouldn't have it any other way."

CHAPTER 6

LEO AND ISMINI

M*y Wren,*

I am so pleased to hear that the first few days of your travels have been uneventful. I'm afraid civilization will become sparse as you continue west, until you reach the mountains. At least there are some mining towns there, and some farms in the foothills. I've instructed the temple to prepare for your arrival. It seems there's a bit of superstition about the place, rumors of a monster that has taken up residence. I asked Panos to investigate. He assures me that the temple's guardian—not a monster but a man named Tekton—is awaiting you. I can only pray to the gods that you stay safe, little bird.

In the meantime, I must make a trip to Roallac soon, a political necessity, to assure them and their queen of our continued wish for peace. They wish to send some of their Water Mages—they have quite good ones, I hear—to the School of the Silver Flame to learn. You'll be happy to hear that the senior Mages have elected a new Head Mage to preside over their council and the school, an Earth Mage named Iraklis. Ismini is thrilled—

by the way, she sends her well-wishes. I do like Earth Mages. They are such solid, practical people.

Though Night Mages will remain ever my favorite.

Yours,

Leo

Dear Wren,

Don't forget to practice finding your center, your core, while you travel. We know you have power—have Rafael help you with control. His mastery over fire magic is impressive, to say the least. I always thought of working with fire magic like dealing with a toddler you might think you're the one in control, but don't let down your guard for a moment!

And do be careful out there.

Aleka would skin us both alive if anything happened to Aris.

Stay safe!

Ismini

PS Don't ever take off your robe!

PPS I was going to send scones along with this letter, but the king ate them!

CHAPTER 7
ARIS

We are falling into an uneasy pattern. During the day, Wren rides abreast of one of us, learning as we travel.

Caelus, it turns out, is something of a religious zealot. He prays to each of the six gods several times a day and knows more about their history than I'd wager even Panos does. He's got a book of the saints that he carries with him, and he tells their stories to Wren, explaining the lessons to be learned by studying their lives—in summary, don't be a dick. I listen when he mentions Rigrasil. Otherwise, I focus on riding and definitely not on Wren.

The days Wren rides by Rafael seem to go relatively well. She'll often laugh at his jokes. Fire is by far the most fickle of gifts—as Rafael has discovered, over and over again. As a result, he mastered control over the heat and light and flame until every scar he bore became a testament of what he'd overcome, instead of something to be ashamed of. He makes no attempt to cover his scars, which cover both hands, half his chest, and his neck. Though his gift is nothing like Wren's, I know she can learn a lot from him.

I just wish he didn't need to show off so damn much.

"Where did you grow up, Rafael?" Wren asks.

"The Valley of Vines."

Seeing her blank look, Caelus says, "It's in the southwest of Ocron, the part that seems to bear out the fullest blessing of the Book of Gold. They say that even wildfires bloom into flowers there, and gold litters the streams and rivers."

"Why did you leave?" Mariana asks, with what seems to be genuine curiosity. She's pulled her white mare alongside Rafael.

"Because that bit about the wildfires isn't true," Rafael says lightly, with a smile that quickly fades.

Wren shoots me a glance, and I shake my head. It's not a good story, and there's no point in causing him the pain of reliving it.

"The bit about the gold isn't true either," I offer. "It's just a myth."

Rafael is quiet for a while, clearly uncomfortable. Mariana shoots him a worried look, then rides up beside Wren and immediately starts a lecture about how to focus her magic. Rafael barely notices the reprieve, and for the rest of the day, he is quiet.

At night, we mostly camp outside. We trade for food with other travelers and small farms, who are all too grateful for the king's coin. We do manage to stay at an inn once, but we all share a room filled with bunk cots, so privacy is not an option.

Gods, I want to be with Wren, but the way Mariana smirks at me when she catches my eye, enjoying the game, enjoying this truth hanging over my head like an axe, and the way Dimitra still casually offers to share the night's watch with me, all of it is infuriating. I have to tell Wren, but there isn't a chance to bring it up privately. Anytime we get a moment alone, inevitably something comes up. Dimitra suddenly wants to run some drills, or Mariana wants to run a special training session with Wren.

And despite her acting like a complete ass sometimes, I have to admit that Mariana is taking her role as teacher quite seriously. She drills Wren relentlessly, and Wren's control *is* improving.

And so I am relegated to stolen kisses and nothing more.

"You have to *see* it, in your mind," Mariana is telling Wren.

I prowl the edges of the camp. Mariana catches my eye and shoots me a wink. My hand clenches around the sword I'm holding, but I do not otherwise respond to her taunts.

Wren doesn't see the silent battle between Mariana and me. She's too focused on her craft—her hands held out before her, sweat beading on her forehead as she tries to draw a droplet of water up from a mug, as Mariana demonstrated. Mariana's droplet hovers in the air a few inches above her palm. She keeps one eye on it as she coaches my Mage.

"Maybe it would be easier if you used words, like we do," Mariana says.

Wren frowns, concentrating. "I've never had to before."

Mariana shrugs. "The gods only know why your magic won't behave properly," she says. "Say it anyway. Even if you don't *need* it, it will help you focus."

"My focus is *fine,*" Wren says. A split second later, the entire contents of the mug fly into the air—and land in a splash on Rafael's head.

Rafael splutters and grins, wiping his long hair back from his face. Whatever thoughts he was lost in earlier, they seem to have passed.

"I'm sure you meant to do that." He chuckles. "*Heat.*"

With that, his hair and robe flap, as if caught in a breeze no one else can feel. Heat rolls off him, and he is instantly dry.

Sometimes I wish I were a Fire Mage—that is, if I couldn't be a Shield. Their magic seems to be the handiest, out of all the elementals. I'd never be without a weapon, never have to deal with cold feet. I slept with a Fire Mage once—I was nearly incinerated, but *gods,* the things she could do with that heat.

I wonder if Wren could do that.

"Go fill it back up," Mariana commands, pointing at the mug, and I am shaken from my reverie. "And we'll do it again, until you get it right."

Wren grumbles a curse under her breath but gets the mug. I

consider offering her a word of encouragement as she passes by, but as soon as I open my mouth, her murderous gaze meets mine, and I snap it back shut so hard that my teeth clack. She is not in the mood to talk, and I'm not in the mood to be drenched by her errant magic. She gives me a scowl, reminding me just how good I am at pleasing women *outside* of the bedroom – which is to say, not at all.

By the time we all settle down to sleep, though, she's managed to pull a ragged droplet from the mug and keep it hovering for a moment. Mariana scoffs, but I can tell she is pleased.

I still run drills with Wren myself, working on her skill with a dagger—which remains alarmingly poor. Sometimes Dimitra joins us, and we teach Wren how to block multiple assailants. Dimitra offers to teach Wren on her own as well, which I shut down with such vehemence that Wren stares at me oddly after. The last thing I need is for Dimitra or Mariana to break the secret to Wren before I do. She'd never forgive me if they did.

I'm not ashamed that I find joy in my body. Many Shields do. I will not apologize for past liaisons. I have no regrets.

So why am I finding it so hard? To simply tell her, yes, they are a part of my past but not my future? I am the White Tiger, after all, and I fear nothing and no one.

Except, apparently, the scorn of one modest, tantalizingly curvy, spitfire little Night Mage.

We are just over a week into our journey when we start passing the bodies.

There are fewer travelers on this stretch of the Western Road. Some farmers, but that is all. Nothing and no one for miles. Nothing but boring stretches of grass and more grass.

And the mangled remains. Some are days or even weeks old. Others could be less than a few hours. Men and horses and cattle, mostly. Bloated and rotting, abuzz with maggots and hordes of black flies. Ripped open, their entrails spewed across the road for hundreds of feet. They mark the road every few miles, like a grisly trail.

Wren turns a sickly pale color, but she doesn't look away. Mariana does, closing her eyes each time with a shudder and occasionally wretching. Rafael rides at the back of our pack, lighting each body with his flames. He waits for a few moments as his magic grants each one a funeral pyre worthy of royalty, before he snuffs them out, leaving only ash behind.

"They're not being eaten," Wren says.

I am riding by her, slowing as Dimitra calls out that she's found a good camping site ahead.

"What?" I ask, looking at the most recent corpse. It is an old bull, one horn broken, its spine severed and exposed, long rents through its abdomen spilling foul guts.

"Whatever it is, it is killing, but not for food," she says.

I've noted the same. I have no idea what could cause this kind of carnage. A wild bear or wolf pack would have consumed them, not displayed them. These bodies have been left as a warning—though by man or foul beast, well, I'm not sure which I would prefer. Something evil is at work here.

"Aris," she asks, and I look toward her from the mess. Her eyes are wide and pained. "What is doing this?"

I shake my head. I find myself wanting to offer comfort, but I have no idea what we're up against here. "Whatever it is, it might be able to take down an old cow, but it wouldn't stand a chance against a Shield," I tell her.

I look over my shoulder, glancing at the rest of our group. Yes, any man or beast would have to be suicidal to want to come up against us. As much as I hate to admit it, Leo was right in sending the others with us.

Wren nods, but her lips are thinned, tight. I have not succeeded in reassuring her. We are barely halfway across the continent, and already the horrors are becoming more and more common. This is not the work of trolls, or any wolves or other mortal creatures I've ever seen before. At this rate, by the time we get to the Temple of Caladrius, well, the body count could be tremendous.

"They're being dropped," Dimitra says as we approach her. She's found us another previously used campsite, this one by a small, clear stream—thank all the gods, because we stink.

I am so focused on thinking about Wren bathing that I nearly run into her horse. I shake my head, dismount, and offer her a hand down.

"What?" Wren asks Dimitra, sliding down into my arms. She doesn't linger there but steps from my side, wrapping her arms around herself.

"From a height. The bodies are being killed elsewhere and dropped along the road, as a warning," Dimitra says.

"For me," Wren says.

She doesn't say more, but I can see the color fading from her face as she tallies each body in her mind, each one another strike against whatever force is waiting for us. Whatever pleasant thoughts I had about bathing together are gone, replaced by concern. Mostly.

"This is not your fault," I remind her, earning a small smile in return.

Mariana rolls her eyes.

"Caelus," I call.

He turns, surprised, as if I've never actually initiated a conversation with him before—which may be true. "Feel like hunting tonight?"

His strange yellow eyes light up, and his lips curve, revealing elongated canines.

"Thought you'd never ask," he says.

There is nothing like hunting in shift form. We leave Dimitra, Rafael, Mariana, and Wren at the campsite, and Caelus and I patrol the area, roaming ever farther as the night falls. At night, my tiger eyes can see almost as well as my human eyes can during the day, especially with a moon that is full and bright. Caelus, a lean gray wolf, howls in the distance. He seems to enjoy his shifted form, in a way that he doesn't seem to get enjoyment from anything else in his life. He is so serious —what *was* it that Mariana saw in him that made her agree to such a claim? He is the oldest of our band too, somewhere over thirty. He is a good fighter, sure. I'll give him that.

We keep our eyes to the sky—Dimitra was right about the bodies being dropped. We are dealing with some kind of airborne horror. Nothing stirs in the night sky though—there's not so much as a bat or an owl. Just as I'm about to suggest one more wide loop around the camp, an inhuman shriek fills the air. The distant glow of the campfire suddenly flares, stirred to life by a great pair of wings. A single thought consumes me and a roar tears from my throat.

Not again.

CHAPTER 8
WREN

It attacks around midnight.

Theoretically, my powers should be at their strongest—but I am sound asleep, and the shouting is as disorienting as my dream is.

Again I find myself facing the starlit man on the black horse. Again he turns toward me. His brilliance fades and then flares again, as if some object has passed between us, though I am in too much pain to see it clearly.

This time the pain comes in the form of his voice, booming and terrible. I feel my head thrum with the strength of his power, feel eardrums rupture, feel blood leak from my ears, feel myself go deaf with the force of his words.

Waking up is even worse. Rafael is hauling me by the elbow from my bedroll, a ball of flame flickering in his other hand. Everything is dark, illuminated only by that flame and the smoldering campfire.

"Stay behind me," he says, placing his tall frame between me and ...

Gods, what is that?

Looking up at the sky, I can see a vast darkness where the stars are blotted out by a great figure, something winged like a bat, but a hundred, a thousand times the size of any bat I've ever seen.

I look for Aris. He and Caelus went on a patrol. They can't be far, but as I whirl around, I can see no sign of either of them.

Dimitra steps to Rafael's side, swords drawn, crouched and ready. Mariana has twin orbs of water spinning in her palms, waiting to strike. I take the knife from my boot and summon a sputtering green glow in my other hand. I have no idea how to handle an airborne assailant—I can barely hold my own against a human one. Whatever it is, it's got to have weak spots just like a human. I adjust the grip on my knife and try to give it the green glow I'd given Aris's blades before, the glow that makes the edge magically sharp and strong—but I'm unable to focus with my heartbeat racing in my ears, and all I succeed in doing is giving my body—and my hands—a sheen of sweat from the effort, which makes my grip slick. *Great.*

For a moment, the night is silent. The full moon shines across the grass like it is water, light breezes rippling across it. I can almost imagine I am back by the sea.

And then all the hells break loose.

A creature twice the size of a horse appears out of the darkness and sweeps through the camp, screeching as it goes, scattering the fire with a spike on its tail. Embers fly through the grass, flaring with the wind from its wings, surrounding us in flames. The grasses are dead, not yet green with their new spring growth—and they go up in the space of a moment.

Mariana and Rafael spring into action. I pull the edge of my robe over my nose and try to squint through the billowing smoke.

"*Out*," Rafael says, his hands splayed before him, impervious or oblivious to the heat and smoke. He touches each finger sequentially to his thumb, and with each touch, another section of flame dies.

Mariana uses some similar tactic, attacking the blaze from the outside in with blasts of water she pulls from the moisture in the air.

I try to mimic Rafael and succeed in smothering a few areas of flame myself. If I weren't so terrified, I'd feel a smug sort of pride at that.

Only Dimitra remains poised, coiled, her eyes scanning the sky.

For a moment, we have the flames under control.

But it is a diversion. As we are distracted by the blooming wildfire, the thing sweeps down again.

This time, I turn just in time to meet a wall of matted fur, which crushes me beneath it as claws the size of daggers circle my rib cage, squeezing, sharp talons unable to pierce my enhanced robe – but that doesn't stop him from crushing me. I scream, dropping my knife, grabbing at the thing's claws, but it is too strong, too big, and I can't breathe. I am being smothered by this thing that smells of rot and blood. I can see nothing other than the beast, can hear nothing but its roar and the sound of my own heartbeat pounding in my skull. It presses me into the ground, then clenches tighter as great wings flap, trying to get airborne.

I grasp at its claws again, willing my magic to work, to summon the green fire as I have before—to burn this thing away from me.

Nothing happens. I can't focus enough to get the magic to do much more than flicker. Green lightning snakes down from the sky, striking the ground too far away to be of any help.

My strength ebbs. I can no longer take a breath, and my vision darkens at the edges. I fight to remember the core that Ismini taught me about, to picture my magic at the center of myself, a dark void from which I can draw forth magic—but my body slams back into the ground, my head rattling against the packed earth, and I can focus on nothing except the pain.

The beast stands, roaring in rage, and blessed air surges into my body. Dimly I register a whirl of black-and-white fur slamming into the creature, ivory fangs aiming for its neck.

The thing screeches again, and if I could free my hands, I would clasp them over my ears. It is a hideous sound, like the screech of an eagle and the grating of metal and a clap of thunder all at the same time.

The beast crouches down again, and Aris—my Aris, my tiger—is flung across the grasses. He lands on his feet and is already sprinting back to me. Hot black blood dribbles from the beast's neck onto my face, putrid as oil.

The beast springs into the air, great bat-like wings pumping hard to get us airborne. Aris leaps and catches the edge of one wing, shredding it—

Before he falls back to the earth, growing ever smaller as we rise into the sky.

This is it. This is my ending. I am to be dashed on the earth like all those other bodies we passed. I'll be just one more maggot-riddled corpse for Rafael to torch.

At least the pain will be over soon.

I look down, watch Aris roar. I swear the air shakes with the sound, but it is no use. We are too high. The claws around my ribs tighten, cracking bone after bone. If there were breath left in my body, I would scream. Instead, silent agony shoots through me, and if I could choose to die now, I would. I would, *gods*, I would – anything to stop the pain.

Abruptly the creature drops, falling nearly ten feet, before it recovers and bellows into the night sky. A fresh trail of blood oozes down the crevices of loose fur on its neck, the hilt of a knife just visible.

I look down.

Dimitra stands, arm cocked back, another knife ready. She must have been fifty feet below me now. She does not falter. It is an impossible throw.

But Dimitra's aim is true. The next knife launches from her hand with such force that my stunned consciousness cannot track its flight—until it buries itself in the eye socket of the malevolent beast.

There is no bellow of rage this time. The beast plummets in silence, its grip on me loosening, until I am also falling, falling, feeling the cool air whip past me—until I know no more.

"Be grateful this happened on the night of the full moon," a soft male voice utters. "Without the healing that Lord Rigrasil's power has given, reflected into the night, she may not have withstood the damage to her body. The robe, too, protected her from being pierced. The gods smile on us tonight, brother."

"Thank you," a deeper voice growls.

That one I can feel all the way to my aching bones, and I groan as I try to bring myself closer to it. *Aris.* I would recognize that voice among thousands. Warm arms grip me tighter, and soft lips brush my forehead.

My eyes won't open, not fully. They are so swollen that I can barely crack them apart. My throat won't work at all—I cannot make even a whisper of sound. But I can feel my arms, and my legs, if only because they hurt so much. I try to remember what took place— there was the attack, my chest was crushed, and I fell from a great height. The blinding pain makes any other thoughts impossible. It comes from everywhere all at once—my back, my legs, my arms, my face. I feel like flotsam dashed against the rocks at my lighthouse.

My lighthouse. But it is gone, and I am alive. I think. I'm in too much pain to be dead.

As I lie here, feeling strong hands tend to me, pulling hard on my leg to pull some fractured bone back into place—I'd scream if I had the breath—my breathing does grow easier, and the swelling on my face diminishes. My eyes are able to crack open at last and make sense of my surroundings.

I lie on Aris's lap, his arms around me, as Caelus tends to my wounds. He pulls a bit of my shirt off my arm, where the flesh lies mangled and bloody, shards of bone poking through. I've seen an injury like this one once, on the arm of a sailor who'd been crushed by falling rigging. The town healer in Spit—who also served as the butcher—had to amputate it at the shoulder. A violent shudder goes through me, the motion making me moan with a flare of pain.

Even as I watch, though, the bleeding ceases, the bone disappears, and the muscle and skin knit themselves back together. I look up at Aris, to see if he is seeing the same marvel, but his gaze is fixed only on mine, his blue eyes flickering with the glow of the campfire, something unreadable there on his face. My Aris. My defender. I flex my bloodied fingers, scarcely believing they work, and raise my hand to his face. He closes his eyes at the touch, leaning into it, placing a kiss on my palm. There is a trail of moisture down his cheek, and I wipe it with my fingers, leaving a red smudge behind.

"What happened?" I croak. I might be healing at an unbelievable rate, but my voice makes me sound like I am about a thousand years old. However, with each passing moment, the pain eases a little more.

"Most of the bones in your body were broken," Aris says quietly. "Your ribs were crushed. For a moment …" He stops and swallows hard. "You stopped breathing. I couldn't … well …" He clears his throat before continuing. "You lost a lot of blood. If you heal anything like a Shield, it's still going to take days before you get back your strength, or longer." He says this last statement calmly, in a detached, emotionless voice.

"Thank you," I say, looking at him, wishing I could say more.

He looks away. "Thank Dimitra, and her throwing knives," he says.

I follow his gaze to the Shield across the camp, watching us from a distance, her arms crossed.

She turns and walks away into the night.

CHAPTER 9
ARIS

"I've been trying to find the right moment to give it to you," Dimitra says, eyeing the tooth.

My jaw is clenched tight, knuckles blanching where they grip the leather strap. I haven't seen this in ages. I'm still on fire after what happened to Wren tonight—seeing her fall, holding her broken body in my arms. I was so enraged, so caught up in anger and terror that I nearly bit Caelus's head off when he knelt beside me to tend to her.

"Breathe," he whispered—to the both of us. "Just breathe."

He was kind enough to look the other way when a tear trickled down my face.

Gods, I cannot lose her.

"You had no right to keep this from me," I whisper.

Dimitra crosses her arms. "I was waiting for the right moment. Surely you understand that," she says. "I meant to give it to you as a reminder."

I put the necklace on. The ivory is smooth and warm; a pang aches in my chest where it lies against my skin. I remember the battle like it has just happened, the two of us against a horde of hungry wolves. My first Mage took a fang from their alpha and wore it proudly until the day he died.

"I am ... grateful, for this reminder of Stefan," I growl through clenched teeth.

"A reminder of what it was like when you worked with a proper Mage, one who wasn't helpless," Dimitra says.

We aren't far enough from Wren that she is unable to hear us. I look over my shoulder and catch her gaze. Caelus is removing the last of the bandage from her leg. Wren swallows and looks away from me, a veil of tangled hair hiding her face.

"When you knew who you were," Dimitra continues, lower.

"I know who I am. I am the Shield of the Night Mage. I know my duty."

"Duty!" Dimitra hisses. She draws herself up on her toes, her face so close to mine that she practically spits the word in my face, one finger jabbing my chest. "Do not speak to me of duty. I searched for you for *days* after you lost Stefan. When you returned, not gray but still lost, *I* was the one who consoled you. *I* was the one who convinced Markos to give you another chance. *I* was the one who defended you when Saroya wanted to kick you out after you chose that girl. You dishonor Stefan's memory. *She* is not worthy of you."

"I never asked you for that, Mitra. For any of it," I say, quieter, hoping my voice won't carry to Wren, but I am unable to keep the building rage from my tone.

Dimitra glares up at me with all the ferocity that first drew me to her years ago. "That's what friends do, Aris," she says. Her gaze softens, her eyes flicking to my lips. "You'd know that if you gave a damn about anyone but yourself."

I look back at Wren. She is lying quietly by the fire, pretending not to listen. Her clothes are shredded and bloodstained, but even from here I can tell that the worst of her physical injuries have healed. Relief floods me again, like a physical force. Gods, I am never leaving her side. Every time I do, something terrible happens.

"I do know that," I say. "And I trusted you to watch over her. You nearly got her killed tonight."

Dimitra looks like I've punched her in the gut. All the fight goes out of her face and—gods, I think she might actually cry.

Then she slaps me. Hard. Hard enough to make my ears ring and the firelight dance before my eyes.

"I saved her life, you fucking idiot," she growls. And then she pushes past me and walks over to where Caelus is inspecting the *thing.*

I run a hand along my jaw—she nearly cracked the bone. If it weren't for being a Shield, I'd be eating through a straw for a month. *Fuck, that hurt.* Even so, it is swelling and will probably turn purple by morning.

I run a hand through my hair, then move to Wren's side. She lets me help her change and clean the worst of the blood off her, too tired and in too much pain to care about modesty, and then I get her into her bedroll. Even in the flickering firelight, I can see her skin is mottled with bruising. She is quiet, but every time she winces, every time her breath hitches in pain, my blood boils. I came so close to failing again, to losing another Mage, and fuck, we've barely gotten started. I sit beside her, resting her head on my lap, and my fingers trail in her curls as we watch the campfire, now built into a bonfire so big nothing will be able to sneak up on us again tonight. I cannot lose another Mage. I would not survive it. And to lose Wren? Fuck, I might not even *want* to survive that.

We sit in silence, watching Caelus inspect the beast. The thing before us is massive, maybe twenty feet long, like some nightmarish cross between a bat and a lion and an insect, and it smells like it has been dead a week instead of a moment. It has a lion's head and a wild mane, bat-like wings, and a chitinous, segmented tail tipped with a bony spike two feet long at least. Its scaled legs end in massive talons, black and lethal.

Legs that Caelus is currently hacking off with his gladius. Or one of them, anyway.

"Not sure that thing's edible, friend," Rafael calls.

Caelus lets out a huff of air, almost a laugh. "I'm not planning on eating it," he says between swings of his sword.

The leg comes off, a three-toed thing that is a dull, scaly yellow, as opposed to the dun fur of the beast's hide. I've never heard of a creature like this.

Dimitra retrieves her knife and wipes off the gore of the beast's ruined eye on the grass. She gives its head a kick for good measure.

"A trophy, then?" Rafael says, one eyebrow cocked. He is walking around the beast, one hand raised like he is worried it's going to reanimate. "Gods, do we even know what this thing is?"

"Whatever it is," Caelus says, wiping off his blade. "It cannot be of the gods."

"You haven't come across something like this in all your devout studies?" Rafael asks.

Caelus glares at him. He doesn't like us joking about his faith in the gods.

"Just tell me you aren't planning on taking that thing with us," Mariana says, wrinkling her nose. "It reeks."

"That's the idea," Caelus says.

He drags it closer to the fire, and Wren shrinks back against me. When I think of those talons grabbing her, taking her from me— gods, I want to kill it all over again.

"You think the smell will keep other foul things away from us?" Dimitra asks, running a finger along the length of the tail spike.

"It'll keep *me* away from us," Mariana says.

Wren stifles a laugh, and the motion makes her wince, holding a hand to her side.

Rafael is not so discreet. "I'd be happy to keep you company, if you want," Rafael says, giving her a wide grin.

Mariana huffs, crossing her arms. "You're riding at the back of our little parade," she says, pointedly ignoring Rafael.

Caelus shoots her a fond smile, seemingly immune to her venom, and sits beside the claw.

"And stay downwind the rest of the time," Rafael adds. "Or I'll be forced to incinerate that thing."

"You'll be thanking me when we reach the mines without any more attacks," Caelus says, unperturbed. "If *you* think it smells bad, I bet that other malevolent creatures will stay away too."

"Are we close, then? To the mines?" Wren asks. Her voice is so soft. She needs sleep, to rest and recover. Injuries like these are going to take their toll.

I silently thank Rigrasil for reflecting his light down on her tonight, the light that allows her to heal. At least that is one part of Panos's predictions that is true. *Gods help us.* I drop a kiss on her head. I've never been a pious sort of man, but I've already prayed to the god of day more on this cursed trip than I have in my entire life.

"Another day or so," Rafael says. "It's been ages since I've seen Stathis—and Aris, when was the last time you heard from your brother?"

Wren looks up at me, her eyes suddenly wide despite her fatigue. "Brother?"

I shrug. Spyridon, oldest of my brothers, most like our beloved father and the second-biggest asshole of the family, has been stationed in the mines with his Mage and lover, Stathis, for a few years now. I've lost track. Honestly, I really don't care.

"I have no idea," I say. I am not particularly looking forward to that potential reunion—especially since Nestor tried to kill me. Tried. He ended up in shackles, defeated by his least favorite son. And hells, he might even have been executed by now. The law of the Shields is nothing if not efficient.

"Just rest," I tell Wren, smoothing the wild hair back from her face. "I'll keep watch."

"All night?" she asks, but her eyes are already closed.

I watch her breathing deepen, her lips part slightly. She's already asleep. Gods, but I am a fool for this woman.

"All night."

CHAPTER 10
LEO

My Wren,

Despite your insistence otherwise, I'm convinced that sending four of our finest—in addition to your own Shield, of course—is insufficient for your protection. I'm sending a regiment to join you at once.

Fine, I won't—if only because you'll be safely in the care of the Earth Mages at the mines by the time the regiment could reach you. As I've said, Earth Mages are good, dependable people. The only way you'd possibly be safer is if you were back here at the palace with me—which I dearly wish you were.

I've never heard of the beast you described, and neither has Panos. He's sent his students off to the archives to do more research. I shall inform you immediately if we find anything.

Stay safe.

. . .

Yours,
    Leo

WREN

Gods, I've never hurt so much in my entire life. Between my broken body and my nightmares, I am in near-constant torment. Aris is watching over me like a mother hen, which might be amusing if he didn't look so serious. I am aware that I came dangerously close to dying, to ending this mission when it had barely begun. I just have to get to Lord Caladrius's temple. It's a litany I repeat to myself over and over and over. I'll find the answers we need there, about why the god of night has decided he needs his own magically enhanced human, and then this will all be over.

Right?

Aris makes us wait an entire day for my body to mend before he lets me back on a horse. The shadow of the beast casts a pall over the day, and though I sleep through much of the morning, I start to get antsy by the afternoon, if only because I need something to distract me from the pain. It's changed now from blinding bolts of pain, like lightning along my limbs, to bad itches, like I've been bitten all over by the midges that haunt Spit in the late summer.

I talk with Caelus as a way to pass the time—and to keep from scratching myself to death. He is quite the scholar, it turns out. He was raised in the eastern part of the continent, and his father was a Shield. His mother was some sort of academic, and though they didn't worship any of the gods in particular, she made sure that he knew their history. What's more, he took an interest in it and now takes any offense made against them—particularly Aris's swearing—as a personal slight.

"So if Lord Caladrius and Lord Rigrasil made the earth, why make the elemental gods at all?" I ask, stretching my legs. It seems unbelievable that mere hours before, my right knee was bent at an unnatural angle, the toes purple and swollen. I don't even have scars now. I watch Dimitra carve a wicked tooth out of the beast's maw as Caelus talks. Though quiet by nature, this is one topic he has no problem discussing—at length.

"The downfall of any being, Night Mage—pride. Lord Rigrasil and Lord Caladrius had made day and night, but until the elementals there was nothing else. And they wanted to be worshipped, adored. The elemental gods and goddess were made in their image, like children. All of this around us —the sky, the earth—then came from the elementals. And they in turn, the six great gods, made men, for the same reason, gifting them with magic made from their own divine sparks."

"But no one worships them anymore." I pluck a piece of grass and weave it with another, making a simple bracelet in a way I haven't done in years. I used to make them for my father, and he'd wear them—sometimes a dozen or more—until they fell apart.

"Some do," Caelus says defensively.

"And what about Prasinos? Have you been there before?" I ask, sensing I am going to upset him and changing the subject. I pluck another blade of grass. The mine is one of the entrances to the great tunnel system that the Earth Mages made to traverse the western mountains, which are nearly impassable otherwise. I am excited to see it. The idea of descending into the tunnels there, into constant darkness, makes a shiver run through me. Out here, at least, we can *generally* see trouble coming.

I look back at the carcass of the beast that nearly killed me and shiver again. Maybe the mines wouldn't be so bad—in a tunnel, there are only two directions you can be attacked from. Aris's training must be rubbing off if I am considering the strategic advantages of a place—or maybe the open sky is making me nervous, making me wonder what is going to drop from it next.

"I have not. Lord Cephus himself is said to have made the first tunnels there. I have always wanted to see them."

I glance back at Caelus. He has a well-worn book in his hand, in a language I don't know, and when he sees that I'm not going to keep asking questions, he flips it open to a random place and goes back to reading. I've never known a Shield to be so pious, so ... academic. Though I guess I don't know many Shields well.

I catch sight of Dimitra. She holds up the beast's tooth in her hand, black blood that still hasn't congealed dripping from it. It is the length of her hand, and then some. *She* is more like what I expect from a Shield.

"What do you intend to do with that?" Aris asks, arching an eyebrow.

Dimitra's gaze flicks to the wolf's tooth he is wearing around his neck. It was Stefan's, he told me. He didn't want to share more than that.

"Bit big for a necklace," Aris observes.

"I was thinking a dagger," she says, hefting it the way she wields her knives, and ignoring the inky blackness oozing down her arm. "No one in the world would have one like it."

"If you were better with your gladius, you wouldn't have to resort to throwing knives," Aris taunts.

She looks at him, startled—but then she grins, eyes narrowing. I gather this sort of thing is a kind of friendly banter between them.

"Come on," Aris says to her, stretching long, muscled arms over his head. "Let's get in some sparring instead of sitting around, getting fat."

"Hey," I say.

He shoots me a grin. "Not you. You rest. I'll put you to work later."

I grumble but comply.

He pauses briefly to kiss me, then grabs his swords, a spring in his step. Nothing exhilarates Aris like a good fight.

"Do you want to join them?" I ask Caelus.

He seems grateful for the reprieve from answering my stream of questions and leaps up immediately.

Watching the three of them together is a treat. I've watched Aris spar a bit before, watched him do his exercises alone, but to see them together—it *is* like a dance. After a while, Caelus leaves to do another one of his endless patrols around our camp. I keep watching.

The way Dimitra moves—it is indescribable, like trying to capture the way a sea hawk wheels through the sky, or the way a flame dances. She is in continuous motion, fluid and grace and a whirl of steel. I can see why they made her a leader among the Shields—she is magnificent.

Aris matches her, though, move for move, his gladius swirling faster than my eyes can follow. Despite the chill, he's removed his shirt. He claims it restricts his movement, but to be honest, he likes having us all watch him. The light plays on the tanned muscles of his chest, and though the scar on his left shoulder remains puckered and pale, it doesn't seem to limit him too much. He looks like the god of day himself, brought to life. He is larger than Dimitra by far, but she keeps swinging, keeps pushing, using her smaller size to her advantage, being even quicker than Aris. Every time she swings, my heart leaps into my throat—any one of those cuts could cause serious damage, Shield healing abilities aside. I've already stitched Aris up once. I don't relish the idea of doing it again.

Metal clangs against metal as they parry, duck, spin, and swing again, in ever-widening circles, flattening the grasses underfoot.

And then Aris whirls, knocking Dimitra off-balance, and she goes down hard on her back, the tip of Aris's sword glinting a breath away from her throat. She lets out a huff of air, and I can see the confident grin on Aris's face as he looks down at her.

Then she sweeps her legs back, catching him hard behind the knee, and somehow springs up, knocking him down. A second later, and he is the one flat on his back—as she straddles his chest, her own blade at his throat. They sit there, motionless except for their breathing, regarding each other, for far longer than I think is necessary. Heat courses up my neck.

Rafael clears his throat. Dimitra leaps up immediately, extending a hand to Aris. He brushes it aside and gets up on his own, laughing, and then swings an arm around her shoulders. It is such an easy gesture, one she seems used to, like it is something they've done countless times before.

"I can't believe I fell for that one again," he says, still grinning. "Knocked me down like a recruit."

"Steel sharpens steel," Dimitra says with a soft smile. She catches me looking at her and shoves Aris's arm off her shoulder. "If you were my recruit, I'd make you run twenty miles before I let you back into my training arena for that lapse."

Their easy camaraderie stings. They've clearly been friends—or more?—for a long time. I've never asked Aris much about his past. I know there have been other women—many. Who am I to think that *I* can change him? A wave of self-pity washes over me. Some Night Mage I've turned out to be, mooning over my Shield like some love-struck adolescent. I have half a mind to unleash a storm tonight, just to remind them that I am strong too. Maybe strength is what Aris is attracted to.

If only I weren't so damned weak at the moment. Even sitting up hurts.

"How are you feeling?" Aris asks, plopping down beside me. He's worked up a sweat and glistens in the afternoon light like his skin is gilded.

I look away, down at the woven grass bracelet in my hands. I tear it in half, letting the pieces fall to the ground.

"Fine," I say. "Just ... tired."

"Get some rest. I'll get you something to eat," he says, tucking the blanket back around my legs, like I am an invalid.

I give him a smile, which fades as he walks away from me, laughing at something Dimitra says.

CHAPTER 12
ARIS

Wren is quiet the rest of the day, and into the next. She talks to Caelus a lot about Prasinos Mine. I haven't been there before, though I am familiar with it. The mountains loom larger and larger, hour by hour, until we are finally at the entrance to the great mine itself, a long, winding stone pathway up to the semicircular wall that surrounds the mine and town.

The mountains are basically impassable—not that there is much beyond them to get to. There are a few towns on the far shore that trade with some of the scattered island communities, but that is it.

Underneath the mountains, however, is an entirely different story.

The wall around Prasinos Mine would put Estana's to shame. Of course, Estana didn't have mountain trolls to deal with. The Earth Mages have erected a wall of solid granite nearly fifty feet tall, the only way in through a single gate with a spelled wooden door. Over the gate, carved in large letters, is the motto of Prasinos: SEMPER ALTIUS CONFODE.

As we approach, I recognize the strips of metal crossing it as the same silvery metal that Wren's manacles were made of. She notices it too and shoots me a glance, though she is silent. She doesn't complain, but I know the travel is wearing on her. Her body is still trying to heal, but she insists that we push forward. My brave Mage.

Before we get to the gate, a tall woman in a soldier's leathers with a golden sun on the chest strides out to greet us. She is unsmiling, with a face as weathered as the mountains, and her black hair has been pulled back tightly.

"Night Mage," she says, addressing only Wren.

Wren steps her horse forward and dismounts.

"Just Wren," she says, extending her hand.

The woman blinks, staring down at Wren's hand like she is afraid it might bite. She shakes it quickly.

"The king told us of your impending arrival, Night Mage," the woman continues, loud enough for us—and any one of the guards listening on the wall—to hear.

"I am Nerida, governor of Prasinos. You are welcome to spend the night, but I would appreciate it if you did not otherwise linger. We've had too many unwelcome guests as it is." She nods toward the wall.

We all turn to look and note a pair of Earth Mages and their Shields at work repairing a section that has nearly been toppled. Long streaks of dried blood mar the stone, and some blocks have been reduced to nearly gravel. Wren turns pale.

"By all the gods," Caelus mutters.

Nerida snorts. "If what they say about you being a beacon for the fouler beasts is true, I'd recommend expediency here," she says. Her hand tightens around the sword hilt at her waist, a wasted gesture. I have no more wish for us to stay here than she does. Still, it is late, and staying the night is a reasonable request. She cannot deny the will of the king's favored Mage. I may not particularly like Leo at the moment, but throwing his name around does come in handy—even if we *are* "unwelcome guests."

"I'll have the mine commander escort you to your quarters for the night," Nerida says. "Your horses, of course, will not be able to accompany you into the tunnels. I'll see they are well cared for."

Wren strokes her horse's nose fondly before handing his reins to one of the men who have come out of the gate. Jasper goes to take a bite out of the man's arm, only stopping when he catches Wren glaring at him. He tosses his head at that and follows the man without further complaint, his tail swishing like an angry cat's. He doesn't want to be parted from Wren, a sentiment I understand.

"Good to see you, little brother," a man calls, striding forward from the gate, his voice grating. He is as big as I remember, the passing years somehow making him look more and more like Nestor. He smiles, but his black eyes are cold and flat like a shark's.

His gaze flicks to Wren. I dismount and move to stand by her side.

"Well? Aren't you going to introduce us?" he says, hands on hips. "Is this the bitch who got our father killed?"

CHAPTER 13

LEO

M*y Wren,*

You should have reached Prasinos Mine by now. How I wish I could see it with you and show you the great statue of the god of earth. Did you know over a thousand gems make up the base of it? The light is meant to reflect off them, lighting him up like a beacon of green. Make sure you see it at dawn—it's a sight you will never forget.

Things here have gone on mostly as usual. We held a tournament in Estana's arena as a way to get people's minds off the monsters raiding on the coast. Yes, I am saddened to report that the frequency of attacks has increased. Do not fret. I hope you travel swiftly and find the answers you need at the Temple of Caladrius—not least because it will mean you return all the sooner.

The tournament was won by a Shield named Zale, who I believe had his games at the School of the Silver Flame at the same time you were chosen. He's a good fighter, and his Mage is a rising star among the Fire Mages. As a prize, they are to accompany me on the trip to Roallac as the king's champions—I know if you had been here, your Shield would have won, and it would be you by my side instead of them. Though I'm sure they will be good company and do their job admirably, I would much prefer you.

Yours,
   Leo

CHAPTER 14
WREN

The ringing of steel fills the air as Aris draws his swords, their edges shining in the fading light. I can't believe my ears. Did this man, who looks eerily similar to his father—Spyridon, I'd guess—just say what I think he did?

I look at Aris, at the murder in his eyes.

Yes. Yes, I guess he did. *Idiot.*

Green light begins to coalesce around my hands. I'll show *him* who he's talking about, just like I showed his cowardly father. The bastard grins, reaching for his own sword, like he's just waiting for an opportunity to fight.

"Aris!" a cheerful voice calls from behind the giant man. A shorter, lean man with a patch wrapped over one eye comes out to greet us. He wears a green Earth Mage robe and seems genuinely happy to see us. He ignores the blades in Aris's hands, instead throwing his arms around my stunned Shield and hugging him tightly.

Aris doesn't take his eyes off his brother, but he does lower his weapons. I let my own magic go out. This Mage does not seem to be a threat.

"Stathis," Aris says to him, nodding.

The Earth Mage beams, clapping Aris on the shoulder. "Don't mind Spyridon. He's grieving," he whispers to me before wrapping me up in a hug that nearly cracks my ribs. Again. "We're all happy you're here." Short blond hair flops over one ear, and his hazel eye sparkles.

For the life of me, I can't see what makes Spyridon and Stathis partners, much less lovers. Spyridon looks about as approachable as a sea urchin.

"New eye patch?" Aris asks Stathis, cocking an eyebrow. He stands close beside me, our arms touching, though I can't tell if the movement is meant to reassure me or him.

Stathis touches the black cloth over his eye with a rueful smile. "Mining accident. Not to worry. I don't really need to see where I'm going, anyway. I can feel it," he says, stomping his feet—which are covered with thick boots, their toes reinforced with metal.

"Commander? Their quarters," Nerida says irritably, crossing her arms. She is eager to be rid of us.

Spyridon turns, gesturing with one finger for us to follow. The others dismount, and we gather our supplies before following Spyridon and Stathis through the gate into Prasinos.

I haven't been able to see much of the city from the road. It is set at a higher elevation than the rolling plains we've left behind, and the wall did its job concealing it. Inside, the city is like nothing I've ever seen.

Gray granite colonnades support peaked porticos, and domes are plated in green copper. The city itself is carved directly from the mountain, and it looks to be all of a single piece of stone rather than cut blocks, like the Earth Mages simply willed the structures forth. Down the side of the mountain on the right is a long series of arches supporting a channel down which water flows. People walk about, mostly with dark hair and tanned skin, like Aris, I am startled to see. I wonder if his family is from this area, if we are close to his home, if he even considers it a home. There are mostly Earth Mages here, a startling concentration of them, along with the occasional red-, yellow-, or blue-robed Mage. Caelus gave me a little background on them—the Fire Mages smelt the ore as it comes up, or use their heat to crack open the rock. The Wind Mages keep the mine shafts filled with breathable air, and the Water Mages sluice the ore down the aqueduct. It is a city built around magic and a single purpose—mining.

And directly in front of us, open like the maw of some great beast, is the entrance to Prasinos Mine.

It is a massive hole, a half-moon some hundred feet across. Men and women carrying tools, lanterns, and supplies walk in and out. There is a series of blacksmiths to the left of the opening, where weapons are being forged and stored in great racks. Aris's eyes go to these almost immediately, a sparkle in his gaze.

"Come on," I say, shoving him along. "I'm tired. You can go shopping later."

He grins, putting an arm around my shoulders and following Spyridon into the mine.

His brother does not say another word to either of us, does not glance back once. Stathis tries to keep up a light conversation, showing us cut green gems the size of chicken eggs at one workshop, another where a Fire Mage is creating massive lanterns just like the spelled candle I brought from the school—just light, no heat. I could spend days looking at the place. The forges and smiths are the shops outside, in the open air, and inside the cave are the smaller workshops, the ones dedicated to finer work. Light comes shining down through a spectacular roof that spans the width of the cave, a massive dome that is constructed of light green glass supported by rays of metal. I've never imagined such an incredible feat.

Aris catches me staring and has to nudge me along, just as I pushed him along at the blacksmith's shop. Prasinos is wonderful, and I lament that we'll only be here a short time.

"We'll have supplies ready for you in the morning," Stathis says, "and the guides will meet you at your rooms at dawn. Nireus will take you through the tunnels to the Temple of Caladrius, and his Shield Petros."

"Why do we need a guide?" I ask.

Stathis grins. "The tunnels are quite a maze, Night Mage, and as we chase veins of minerals, they are often collapsed or redirected by Earth Mages—like me." He puffs out his skinny chest a bit. "I'm afraid no current map would be sufficient. In the event of a cave-in, you'd want an Earth Mage with you to sort things out."

"Are cave-ins a frequent occurrence?" Mariana asks, a slight tremble in her voice.

Stathis shrugs.

"Fantastic," she mutters, wrapping her robe tightly around herself.

"Don't like the dark?" Rafael asks, bumping his shoulder against hers. "Stick with me. I'll protect you from the things that go bump in the night." He shoots me a look. "No offense."

I snort out a laugh.

"I'm perfectly capable of protecting myself, thank you." Mariana sniffs and speeds up, preferring to walk with Stathis rather than Rafael.

Rafael, irrepressible, grins, his hands on his hips as he watches her walk away.

"She likes me," he says, to no one in particular. "I can tell."

"I wouldn't hold your breath," I say, though I can't help the smile that I feel echoing on my own lips.

Aris is just silent, glaring at the back of his brother's head.

We walk a long time, and the rows of shops and columns in the rock give way to smaller buildings—homes, I realize, families gathering for their evening meals, lantern light illuminating children as they run between houses, calling out to friends. It isn't all that busy in the street, but each spacious home is occupied.

We are taken to a side tunnel that is more like the dorms at the School of the Silver Flame, and Stathis tells us they are the guest quarters. He shows me to the first one. It is a simple square room, but clean, and food and drink have been left for us. There is even a small room to bathe in the back, with warm water cunningly piped in from some subterranean source. Mariana seems to be in a hurry to get to her own room, eager to wash away the grime of the trip, and urges the group along. Stathis wishes us a pleasant night with a wink.

Aris follows me into the small room, closing the door behind him with a finality that makes my heart skip a beat.

We are alone, just the two of us, for the first time in weeks. Suddenly it is very hard to breathe. I become acutely aware of the coldness of the stone wall as I back up, my breath quickening as he fixes me with his predator's eyes.

In two strides, he is across the room. I think he is going to grab me, kiss me, but his brow furrows, and his hands do not touch me.

"Wren, what's wrong?" he asks, tilting his head to the side.

There is a breath of space between us, nothing more.

"N-nothing," I stammer, keeping my palms flat against the stone.

"You're glowing like a damn firefly," he says, though there is laughter in his voice.

I blink, tearing my gaze from his, and note the jade-green glow of my magic flaring from my skin, filling the room with soft light. I look toward the bed—the one, rather small bed—and back at him.

He catches the motion and laughs. "Oh, princess."

He holds his arms open, and I fly into them, like a moth to a flame, burying my head against his chest, hiding the stupid heat on my face. I feel the rumble of his laughter, like the purr of a cat, against my chest, and the rapid fluttering of my heart eases. I crack open an eye and see the green glow dim, then vanish.

Aris takes my chin lightly in his fingers, tilting my head so that I am looking up at him again. In the faint lantern light, I am sure that the embarrassment on my cheeks is still showing.

But he is smiling, and gods, it's like the glow of the sun.

"Are you scared of me? To be alone with me?" he asks.

I swallow but don't answer. Am I scared? I'm not sure.

He strokes the side of my face with one hand, his calluses like sun-warmed stone against my skin. I can feel myself trembling, like a nervous horse.

"I was willing to wait two years to be your Shield," he says, and he kisses me lightly. "I can wait a little while to be your lover."

"A little while?" I ask. I mean it to come out lightly, like I'm teasing, but it comes out quiet, unsteady.

He kisses me again, this time with more heat. When he withdraws, it is only a fraction of an inch. "A little while," he repeats, the heat of his breath whispering across my lips. "Patience has never been my strongest attribute. But I can learn."

Relief washes through me. Tension in my shoulders I didn't realize I was holding relaxes, and I let out a shaky breath. He catches me up in his arms and then lays me deliberately on the bed. He settles himself around me and kisses me again, lightly, teasingly, pulling me close against the heat of his chest.

"You should never be scared of me," he says, his tone serious as he draws a blanket over us. "Promise me."

"I promise," I whisper.

"You are mine," he says, kissing me again, his arms around me. "Mine to protect, mine to care for."

"You are mine," I echo, one finger tracing the scar on his shoulder. He is mine, and has been from the first time I saw him.

He rumbles an agreement, holding me close as I fall instantly asleep.

CHAPTER 15
ARIS

I have never in my life wanted someone like I want Wren.

I count my breaths, letting them out slowly. Like a tiger, I can be patient. I can lie still, waiting for the opportune moment.

Fine, fuck that. Wanting and waiting is the worst. My internal tiger is an idiot.

I roll over and stare at the stone ceiling, unable to sleep. Spyridon's words ring in my ears. *Is this the bitch who got our father killed?* Despite the insult to my Mage that had me wanting to rip his fucking head from his shoulders, the last bit is what I am really struggling with. Nestor is dead, then. I'm not sure how I feel about that. Sure, the man was an asshole and kidnapped my Mage, and put a manacle on me that could have left me permanently crippled. There was little doubt that death would be the punishment demanded by the Court of Shields. And I harbor no love for the man.

Still, he was my sire. I spent my childhood wanting to live up to his high expectations, had glowed under his sparse praise. Everything I know of fighting started with him. I was given a small sword —a knife, really—on my first birthday, to the chagrin of my mother, gods rest her soul, and immediately cut myself. I didn't cry, apparently, merely watched in fascination as my skin healed, and then swung the blade at him. Nestor always puffed up with pride when he told that story, like he'd known I was a gifted Shield from the start, never shying from pain, never backing down. Being a Shield, and preserving his own legacy, was all that mattered to him. That and his damned horses.

After my mother died, and then his Mage retired, he had seemed ... different. Lost. He spent his days training warhorses for other Shields rather than raising his children. My two sisters were raised almost entirely by our old housekeeper, Lena. My youngest sister, apparently, grew particularly wild. She'll be close to eighteen now, almost old enough to join the Shields at the school, though I doubt she'll want to.

Wren sighs in her sleep, eyes rolling under her lids, like she is having another nightmare. She has one almost every night now, the same one, some dark man on a horse causing her pain. I don't know if this is some sort of memory from when Nestor kidnapped her and killed her horse, Obsidian—like guilt manifesting itself in her dreams. Wren sighs again, rolls back over, and curls into a ball like she is in pain. How she hasn't choked herself sleeping with that long damned braid is a mystery to me.

Whatever was in the past, *this* is where I am needed now. I pull Wren to me, rubbing her back, stroking her hair, until the tremors pass, and she relaxes again. I nestle my face into her hair, breathing in the sweet scent of it, holding her small body against mine.

I will not fail her.

Wren is humming as she brushes out her hair, having spent an inordinately long time in the bath this morning. If she remembers her nightmare, she doesn't say anything. She is just tying off the end of her braid when a loud knock sounds at the door. We gather our packs and join the rest of our group.

Everyone looks rested—and thank the gods, they smell better too. Stathis blanched when Caelus tried to bring that damned putrid claw into the mine, and Rafael was only too happy to reduce it to ash.

It had kept us safe, though.

Nireus is a grizzled, serious Earth Mage who I haven't met before. His Shield, Petros, is a giant bear of a man, literally. Neither of them says much in the way of small talk. They just confirm our destination and start walking.

It gets harder to tell what time of day it is after we leave the main cavern and the green glass dome. We weave through rows of dwellings before reaching a copper-domed structure that actually exits the mountain, letting midmorning light stream into the caves.

Inside is a statue some twenty feet tall of Cephus, the god of earth. He is shaped from a block of white marble veined with gold, with a scythe in one hand and a hammer in the other. At his feet glitter hundreds of green crystals, and they throw the morning sunlight up at the god in shafts of dazzling green. His statue takes up the entire domed room, which is ringed with columns, like a temple. A few Earth Mages speak quietly in one corner, eyeing us, before departing and letting us admire the space.

"One of the great wonders of our world," Caelus says, reverence in his tone. "I never thought to see it myself. How magnificent."

"You should see the Temple of Ignatius in Estana once the king's done restoring it," Rafael says, feigning disinterest. "An eternal fire, burning without fuel. Stained glass in a thousand shades."

Caelus ignores him and reverently touches his fingers to his lips before touching the gems at the feet of the god of earth.

Wren walks around the statue, admiring it. "A hammer and a scythe?" she asks Caelus.

He nods. "A reminder that the god of earth controls not just rock but growing things. The Smith and the Farmer. Remarkable."

"Yes, too bad you've claimed a Water Mage," Mariana reminds

him, tossing her hair over her shoulder. "Can we get going, please? I'd like to reach the Temple of Caladrius before I'm old and gray."

"Afraid your charms are only skin-deep, then?" Rafael asks, cocking an eyebrow.

Mariana glares at him. "Hasn't kept you from admiring them," she shoots back.

He shrugs in agreement, chuckling.

She rolls her eyes at him. "Look, just stay away from me. Fire and water do not mix," she says, stalking off.

Nireus and Petros, our guides, are waiting for us at the entrance to a large tunnel.

"I'm all right with it getting a little steamy," Rafael calls after her.

Wren laughs, shaking her head.

"She wants me," Rafael says, grinning.

Wren claps him on the shoulder as she passes.

He starts whistling something bawdy—I think it's the ballad of "The Princess and the Troll."

Why Rafael has chosen to pursue Mariana, I have no idea. Sure, she's beautiful, and powerful too, which, to be honest, definitely turned my head when I first met her. But she's about as warm and passionate as an iceberg.

The tunnel is connected to several mining shafts. Caelus asks about them as we pass—predominantly iron, Stathis's specialty, out here, though there are also large deposits of quartz in green and purple. The green quartz Prasinos mostly saves for itself; the amethyst they funnel to the western port towns, where the island traders go crazy for it.

It is a boring day. The tunnel is large enough for us to walk two wide, and our guides keep up a good pace. The tunnel goes up and down, through a few larger mining chambers, where we pass Earth Mages by the dozen. It intersects a few times with other tunnels—how Nireus has a clue where we are going, I have no idea. We carry our own light in the form of spelled lanterns, and after a few hours, we don't pass anyone else. It is just us, in the dark, and the occasional creature. A few curious moles find Wren, even though they are blind. They are drawn to her, just like animals above ground, and she benevolently pats each of them as we pass.

I still don't like it. By midday, I feel sure that I'd rather take the chance on the outside of the mountains than have to do this again.

Wren slips her small hand into mine, giving it a squeeze. I turn to say something to her, and catch sight of Dimitra, just behind us, glaring.

Shit. I had the chance to tell Wren about everything last night, and I didn't take it. I might be fearless in battle, but in front of Wren, I am a damned coward. The way she looked at me last night, though, with fear, that had been bad enough. If she looks at me with anger and explodes—again, I think, remembering how she reacted after the manacle debacle—especially underneath a million tons of stone, we could be in big trouble.

"Three days," Wren reminds me. "Just three days."

I keep hold of her hand.

"Rafael is teaching me how to control my breathing, which can help control my magic," she says.

I let her talk. I am not afraid of closed spaces. I just don't like them, and I'm fucking on edge wondering when Dimitra or Mariana is going to start talking about our past. No amount of deep breathing or meditating is going to change that.

Something rumbles in the distance, and the pebbles at our feet clatter.

"What was that?" Mariana asks, grabbing Caelus's arm.

"Troll, maybe," Nireus says, nonchalant. "Or a cave-in. Hard to tell when it's that far off. Could be someone redirecting one of the older tunnels. Those new Mages from that school, they think they're so smart with their talk of epithermal veins and hydraulic fracturing. Bah!" He raises his hand and strikes the wall of our tunnel. "They have no respect for the structural integrity of a place, just go chasing down deposits, turning the mountain into a damn honeycomb. No wonder folks keep getting injured from collapsing tunnels."

"Injured?" Mariana says, the pitch of her voice rising.

Caelus keeps her arm linked through his and whispers softly to her, like he's soothing a panicking animal.

Nireus shrugs. "Injured, maimed, losing a leg or an eye. Don't worry. No one's died down here in weeks."

"Comforting," Rafael says, eyeing the walls.

But no further rumblings come. It is just us, the sounds of our breathing and scuffling feet, and the blackness.

We stop that night at a waypoint, a sort of campground in a large natural cave that is a glorious change from the confining tunnel system. There is a small pool of water and a flattened area between stalagmites the size of large trees, where people have obviously stayed many times before. Small bits of discarded equipment are left here, and Mariana spends a few moments neatening the space before she deems it suitable for her to sleep in.

The rumbling returns, just a few seconds long, every hour or so. The water is so still in the pool that the tremors cause cascades of ripples. The lantern light flickers off some sparkling deposits in the rocks, which I guess is kind of pretty. Wren is exhausted, though, and doesn't seem to notice any of it—she tries to act tough, but she is still recovering from the beating she took from that damned flying beast.

"I won't break," Wren says, catching me looking at her as she stumbles toward the campsite. "Just … a little tired."

I get her settled by the pool, and I'm pretty sure she is asleep within a moment of closing her eyes.

There is another wave of rumbling, more intense. It shakes the stalactites overhead and threatens to bring them down on us like a massive jaw closing. Wren doesn't stir.

"Aftershocks, probably," Nireus says in a bored tone, when he catches Mariana's wide-eyed stare. "Some of the Fire Mages have been trying a new way to break open the stones, some kind of detonation. It can be pretty destructive."

"Aftershocks," Mariana repeats, calming. She sits by the pool, tucking her feet and knees under her robe.

"Or trolls," Rafael says, tilting his head with a roguish smile.

Mariana whispers, and a stream of water from the pool douses the Fire Mage. He wipes wet hair back from his eyes, grinning.

"Still," Nireus says, eyeing the tunnel we came from. "Might be best if we keep quiet tonight, just in case."

CHAPTER 16

WREN

The winged man is waiting for me again.

This time, something seems different. He seems ... muted, though still dazzling by mortal standards, his skin too flawless, his face too perfect. This time also, the color of his hair and wings has changed—both black now, tipped about half-way with silver. And when he looks toward me, my skin does not burn. When he speaks, my ears do not bleed.

"I've been waiting a long time for you, Verena."

Aris shakes me awake. He'd better be grateful that we're underground, or I would set a hundred bees on him. Or scorpions, or stinging ants. Maybe all of them. I can't have been asleep more than a moment, I feel so exhausted still, but it seems I was out cold for the entire night—or what I have to assume was night, as it is hard to tell down here. I try to look into my center, my core, at the dark orb that Ismini taught me to see—it is there, but quiescent. Daytime, then.

We gather our things and start off again, bracing ourselves for another long day of walking.

The rumblings continue all day. We are like fleas on some poor dog's back, and he is trying to shake us off. No creatures keep me company today. Nireus encourages us to stay quiet, which has all of us—Mariana especially—on edge.

"Have you ever seen a mountain troll?" I ask Aris.

His lips tighten. "Once. That was enough."

"What are they like?" I ask.

We round a bend in the tunnel, into another natural cave, this one rougher, perhaps an older mining location. Tunnels branch out in a dozen directions, water dripping down stalactites to form little rivulets across the floor, perhaps in remnants of sluicing channels. Boulders larger than horses are scattered across the dark cavern. Nireus and Petros stop, and we nearly run into them.

One of the boulders moves.

It grows, up and up, unfolding—not a boulder at all.

"For the record," Caelus says, drawing his swords with a ringing of steel, "*that* is a mountain troll. Or rather"—he looks at two other suspicious lumps in the dark—"*those* are mountain trolls."

Aris has his swords out in a blink. I draw my knife, which feels pitifully inadequate, but I brandish it all the same. Maybe I'll start insisting we travel at night so that when shit like this happens, I won't be powerless.

"Take my shield," Aris says, reading my mind. He unhooks the round wooden shield from his back and hands it to me. I nearly drop it—it is heavier than it looks. He takes a moment to put his helm on, the steel fangs of the tiger's mouth forming the front and sides. It is a work of art, with magic woven into the metal. I can't say whether it will completely deflect the power of a troll's club, but it sure as all the hells has to help.

The two other boulders are standing too, grunting in the darkness, shadows of impossible size.

"Put out the lanterns," Mariana hisses.

Nireus shakes his head. "Doesn't matter. They can see in the dark. It would just put us at a disadvantage."

"Then let's light it up," Rafael says. Between his hands forms a growing ball, glowing like a miniature sun—and then he flings it high into the air, where it stays, illuminating everything in stark, blinding light. The light does seem to startle the trolls a little, but only for a second.

There are three of them, ten feet tall with short curved horns and longer tusks protruding from their lower jaws. Their skin is a pale, mottled gray, like they rarely see sunlight. They move like men, wield massive stone hammers like men. Around their waists they wear scraps of tattered fabric.

And around their necks, macabre necklaces of human skulls.

Some still have hair attached.

Bile rises in my throat, coating the back of my tongue—gods, I *cannot* vomit right now. I swallow hard, hefting Aris's shield in front of me. Aris whirls the swords in his hands, crouched and ready for a fight. Dimitra, Petros, and Caelus stand at his side, a wall of bristling steel.

The trolls ignore them.

They come for me.

CHAPTER 17
ARIS

It is an ambush. They've been lying in wait, and though their small brains register our presence slowly, once they lay eyes on Wren, they begin moving with the unstoppable force of an avalanche.

"Any words of advice on how to stop these things?" Mariana says, an orb of water coalescing in her hands.

"They're tougher than they look," Nireus says. "Just be careful where you aim your blasts. You don't want to cause a cave-in or risk running out of energy by going too hard, too fast."

"Helpful," Mariana mutters, but she steps in front of Wren too. I make sure Wren has the cave wall at her back, that there is no way for the trolls to get to her without going through us first.

"I suppose a strategic retreat is out of the question," Dimitra says.

"It is if you want to get to the temple before next month. This is the only way through," Nireus says.

"Fantastic," I say.

Three trolls. Three, against four Shields and three Mages. Hardly seems a fair fight.

But perhaps I underestimate them.

The first is upon us in an instant. It charges like a raging bull into our midst, trying to push through us with brute force, and swings its hammer like a scythe meant to mow us down. Petros catches the tip of it and goes flying across the room. I roll away from the blow, slashing at the tendons behind its knees as it passes. The thing bellows, shaking the walls around us—

Then it sinks, its massive feet vanishing into what had been solid rock a moment before.

"*Down*," Nireus commands, and the thing continues to sink—up to its bleeding knees, then its waist—before Nireus drops his arm, breathing heavily. He has reached his limit.

So much for showing restraint. Still, the troll is trapped. Dimitra throws a knife into its eye, none of us wanting to get within arm's reach of it, and it slumps over, a mound of putrid gray flesh.

It takes a moment for me to realize that the other two trolls are not following this first one, this diversion.

No. They are fixated on Wren, who has broken through our ranks and is crouching at crumpled Petros's side across the room, one hand on the gash on his forehead, the other clutching my shield to her chest.

"Wren!" I roar, racing toward her—but the trolls have her cornered, blocked off from me. I can see the panic in her eyes, and my heart thunders. *Not again. Not again.*

She is defenseless. Rafael shoots a blast of fire past me, singeing the hairs on my arm. It flares against the broad back of the nearest troll, which slows but does not stop, bending its head in a howl of pain—leaving its neck unprotected. The smell of charred flesh stings my nostrils as I leap and bury my first gladius to the hilt in its spine, severing the connection between its head and body.

It drops, its weight shaking the room. Debris rains down, but I don't stop. I can't. There is still another troll between me and Wren, and all she has is her knife and the shield. Petros appears to be unconscious.

Wren doesn't stand a chance.

But there are tunnels behind her, the entrances perhaps small enough to keep the troll from immediately following—buying time for us to bring it down.

I do not hesitate. I race past the troll, grab Wren around the waist, and barrel into the nearest opening, crashing onto my side and skidding along the floor of it for several feet. I can feel the fabric and skin tearing away down my arm, my elbow throbbing from the impact.

I leap to my feet, pushing Wren behind me. I am now down to a single sword but ready to eviscerate the troll if it comes a step closer.

Turns out, I was right. The troll is too big to enter the passage, and it bellows as it swings its hammer, trying to reach us, to no avail.

By now, Dimitra and Caelus have caught up, and the troll becomes further enraged as they harry it, drawing blood from a dozen wounds. Wren clutches my arm—I cannot move to help them, not when it means leaving her undefended.

A jet of water rises up from the channels, covering the troll's face, forcing itself into the troll's nose, its open mouth, down its throat. It is a gruesome sight, drowning the thing on dry land. I catch a glimpse of Mariana, her face twisted in concentration as she keeps forcing the water farther.

The troll stumbles, slamming into the entrance of our tunnel, and its hammer takes out a rotten post on the side farthest from us.

A post that was apparently keeping the roof of our tunnel from collapsing.

I force Wren farther back into the tunnel as rock and dust fall—not enough to completely block out the light but enough to make it a pain in the ass to climb over to get out. I can see the troll's massive back shudder and go still as it dies.

Wren lets out a breath but does not release my arm.

The ground rumbles again, and I turn, pushing Wren behind me, bracing myself for whatever is coming at us through the dark. I can't see anything, can't hear anything but the rumbling of the stone. I ready myself for an attack.

And then the floor falls out beneath us.

CHAPTER 18
WREN

I am falling, held so tightly in Aris's embrace that I can scarcely breathe. I can feel his back slam against a surface below the tunnel we were in, hear the breath leave his chest in a rush—and then we are skidding, down, down, down a steep incline that is smooth and slick with moisture, before we tumble into water as black as death.

I can't see. I can't hear anything except the water, and my own thrashing. I can scarcely tell which way is up, only that my pack is still on my back, weighing me down, pulling me under, but I don't dare let it go. I flail—I am a good swimmer, but the complete blackness is disorienting.

My hand smashes against a rock, a wall of some sort, and I grab it, feeling my fingernails rip with the effort. I hang there, panting. Should I call out for Aris? What if there are more trolls there in the dark? Can they see me, hear me?

A strong hand grabs mine, and I scream as I am hauled unceremoniously out of the water. Calloused fingers against my mouth shush me before being replaced by lips, desperate and aching. I can taste blood on his mouth, but I don't care—I cling to Aris with every ounce of strength I have left, the shock making me shake with quiet tears.

"How did you find me?" I whisper, my fingers finding his face in the dark. He is damp—from water or blood, I can't tell, though I suspect it is the latter.

"Shield magic. I will always find you," he says, kissing me again.

I struggle with the straps on my pack and search blindly inside, and a moment later, I have the spelled candle I've brought all the way from the School of the Silver Flame burning before us. Never have I been so glad for magic.

We seem to be in some kind of pit, like where runoff from the sluicing channels gathers before the water disappears under the far wall. It seems to be a natural cave, and there are a few side tunnels, at least one of which appears to have markings from miners on the walls. There is no way we can go back the way we came—we must have tumbled hundreds of feet down, the floor of our tunnel giving way into the ceiling of another. Thoughts jumble through my head. Should we stay put and wait for rescue? Or move on and hope that one of these tunnels connects with one of the major thoroughfares? I am sore, bruised, and soaked, but nothing seems broken. I set down my pack and wring out my shirt and robe as best I can. I suspect that my robe has a lot to do with the minor nature of my injuries. I'll have to remember to write a thank-you to Ismini and Panos for that.

Aris is not so lucky. He is breathing heavily and sits down, his back against the wall of our pit, one leg stretched before him, his sword and helm at his side. The heavy fabric of his pants is torn below the knee, the flesh beneath gaping, exposing muscle and a glimpse of white bone.

"I've had worse," he chuckles with a grimace. "Just give me a few minutes."

Before my eyes, the bleeding stops, and the flesh begins to knit together, until it is nothing more than a puckered red scar and blood-soaked fabric. I check him over—his side has taken the worst of the blows, and his clothing there is in tatters. He must have broken a few ribs, as he winces when he tries to move. I essentially landed on him, I decide, when we fell through. My protector, until the end.

That decides it. We are going to stay put, at least until Aris is well again.

I dig out some soggy rations from my pack and fill a cup with water from the pool. It tastes a little metallic but otherwise seems all right. I bring both to Aris and sit at his side.

"What now?" I ask.

He swallows a sip of the water, already breathing a little easier. The scrape down the side of his face, along his jaw, is shrinking, shrinking, until it is gone.

I take it back. *Now* I've never been so grateful for magic.

"Let's rest a few hours, until nightfall," he says. "Nireus might be able to get to us, but his depth isn't as great as Rafael's or Mariana's —he'll need to rest first. And by then, your powers will be awake as well."

"All right," I say, shifting closer to him.

He raises an arm and drapes it across my shoulders, and I lean into him, glad of his presence, his strength, his closeness. Even soaked as we both are, he is warm. His lips brush the top of my head.

"Do you think the trolls will find us here?" I ask. The words leave my mouth in a whisper, but in the absolute silence of the pit, they still seem loud.

Aris's arm tightens around me. "*Noli metuere nec timere*," he says. "Fear not, nor dread. We will face whatever comes our way, as always."

"So what do we do? Do you need to sleep? I can wake you if anything happens," I say.

His chest rumbles with a laugh. "Oh, I can think of a few more pleasant ways to spend the time," he says, leaning his head back against the wall, one finger trailing down my arm.

For a moment, I watch the way the candlelight flickers on his face, now the handsome profile I am used to again. The water droplets weave through his thick black hair, now grown nearly to his shoulders. This arrogant, incredible man has saved my life twice in the past hour alone. So what *is* it that is holding me back?

"Yes," I say, before I have a chance to doubt myself.

"Yes?" he asks, confused, fixing that sky-blue gaze on me.

"Yes," I repeat, and before my courage gives out, I reach out and put a hand on his chest.

He catches it in his, his thumb tracing circles, before bringing it to his mouth and placing a kiss on my palm.

I can't say anything else – but I don't need to. Heat floods me despite the chill of my damp clothes, rushing to my cheeks.

"Now? Here?" he asks, his lips pulled to one side in what could almost be called a smirk—almost. The look in his eyes is heated, like the blue heart of a flame.

I lick my lips, trying to coax some moisture back into my suddenly dry mouth, and his gaze follows.

"I've almost died at least three times on this stupid journey already, and so have you," I say, parting the fabric of his shirt. I run my hand against the hard planes of his chest, feeling the strong beat of his heart. "So when we get out of here ... yes. I want...," I trail off, unable to finish the thought.

"Are you sure?" he asks. He isn't moving anymore, scarcely breathing.

"Yes."

"No fear?"

"No fear," I say. To prove my point, I lean up and kiss him. I have no idea what to do, to show him what I want, no idea what I am doing—only that I want it, and need it. Want him. Aris. My Aris. I am tired of being afraid—of the gods, of monsters, of everything. I will not be afraid of Aris, of the good things in my life, too.

His hands graze the backs of my arms, lightly, before pulling me into his lap. He kisses me thoroughly, banishing any concern I may have had for his injuries slowing him down.

"Thank all the gods," he says roughly.

CHAPTER 19
ARIS

"You know, you purr when you're happy," she says, resting her head against my chest.

"So I've been told," I say, tightening my arm around her. Her black robe lies wrapped around us, a cocoon of warmth. I never want to leave it. I don't care if anyone ever finds us. I just want to stay here, like this, forever.

Trolls, cave-ins, claustrophobia and all, I decide I rather like these tunnels. Her bare skin is warm and soft against mine—and I wouldn't trade places with a king right now. We told ourselves we needed to get out of our wet clothes to let them dry properly—a pleasant lie. Then, with nothing else to do, we let our hands drift over each other's body, exploring, teasing. The candlelight cast its slight golden glow on her skin, glancing over curves and hollows. I ran a finger down her arm, marveling at her softness, so smooth— and left a trail of goose bumps in my wake. Gods, she is magnificent. I might not worship the gods, but I would worship her if she let me.

I want to have her, right here in this cave. Badly. I want to banish everything from her thoughts—the trials she's already been through, the nightmares, the monsters—and replace them all with thoughts of me, of us.

And the waiting, the tease—well, it's not something I have very much experience with, and it's a kind of delicious agony. She can clearly see the effect she is having on me—one heated glance with those jade eyes, and I was harder than the damned rock we lay on. Her pupils grew wide in the dark, wider still as her gaze drifted down, redness flooding her cheeks. My innocent little Wren.

Mine.

She lies against me now, one hand chastely against my chest. I drew the robe over us as we rested, once she'd checked my wounds and assured herself that I would live. I don't mind her fussing—it means her hands are on me, touching my skin, warm fingertips practically burning as they inspect scars that are already fading.

"What are you thinking about?" she asks.

I shift, trying to keep the silk of her robe off my hips. The feel of it against my skin makes me want to explode.

"I'm thinking I want to go back to that room in Prasinos with you and not come out for a week," I say, catching her up in another kiss.

She laughs against my lips. "A month," she says, sighing, running her hand over my chest, one finger tracing the scar of the wound she stitched up so long ago. "Do you ... do you think, after we get to the temple, that we'll find some answers? That we can go back, to Prasinos or wherever, just go where we want to go?"

"I think some of your destiny has been decided for you," I say, shifting a bit—the rock is biting into my spine, which has mostly healed, but it is still uncomfortable. "The rest, whatever it is you want to do, we'll do."

She considers this for a moment. She opens her mouth to speak, but another sound hits our ears.

"Oi, lovebirds! Is that you?" Rafael's voice echoes down into the pit.

Wren jumps, cheeks flaming, and scrambles for her clothes.

"Took you long enough," I yell back.

A bark of laughter drifts down to us.

"Hey, hey, Nireus! I found them!"

Nireus and Wren alternate making a series of stone handholds and steps in the stone. We have to stop a few times for both of them to gather their strength. Wren is a little slower at it than Nireus, but I am proud to see that her handholds are just as strong. It takes us a few hours to get out of the pit, and then we decide to walk a few more hours rather than wait at the site where the trolls were waiting. I retrieve my sword from the carcass of the mountain troll and clean the blood off in one of the small rivulets before drying it and returning it to its rightful place.

It is night now, and Wren keeps jade fire circling her hands as we walk, just in case. The Shields keep their weapons drawn too. Petros seems to be all right, though even with his enhanced healing, he has quite a goose egg on the side of his skull. He drifts a bit to the left as we walk but otherwise seems his normal taciturn self.

Eventually, the Mages have to rest, and the Shields all decide to stay up and keep watch. These tunnels aren't safe.

"I'm starting to wish we'd let you bring that claw with us," Dimitra tells Caelus.

The four of us sit at attention, each facing a different direction, for the night's watch.

Caelus gives a rueful smile. "Me too."

We wake the Mages after a few hours, before dawn. Wren needs more rest, but I don't want to wait any longer. She can sleep once we get to the temple. I doubt anything will come for her in the home of the god of night, not even mountain trolls, or whatever stupid beast is supposedly lurking there.

"We shouldn't run into any more trouble for the rest of the way," Petros says. He still moves a little stiffly, like he is taking a little longer to heal than Shields usually do. It must have been one hard blow to his skull to take such energy from him.

"*Amat victoria curam*," Caelus says.

Mariana huffs. "What?" she asks.

"It means we still need to be careful," Caelus says, unruffled.

She crosses her arms and keeps walking.

"What, they didn't teach you that phrase at the school?" Nireus says.

"I had more important things to do than learn the dead language of forgotten gods," she says. Caelus really doesn't like that – his hands clench at his sides, but otherwise he doesn't react.

"What, like learning how to drown people?" Rafael asks, uncharacteristically serious.

Mariana stops. "What?"

"I know for a fact the way you took care of that troll is not something they teach at the school," Rafael says lightly. He walks past her, fixing her with his stare.

He's right. That kind of offensive magic isn't usually taught at the School of the Silver Flame. There are some Water Mages in the army, but most of them work with the navy, helping the ships and whatnot. Most of the Water Mages in the army are healers, though I've worked with a few who had some true combat skills. None of them, though, were as intimate as what Mariana did. Throwing ice spears is one thing—forcing water into someone's lungs as you watch them drown is another.

"There's a lot you don't know about me," she says, staring Rafael down.

His smirk returns. "Oh, but I'd love to," he says. "What other secrets are you hiding?"

Mariana blanches.

"That move of yours ended up collapsing the tunnel," Dimitra adds, bringing up the rear of the party.

"And, what, you think I did that on purpose?" Mariana says, her voice going higher.

"You could have killed Wren, maybe killed them both," Dimitra says, pushing past.

"And ... you think *I* would do that?" she asks.

Rafael shrugs, but he is still, waiting for her response.

She throws up her hands. "You think I'm that petty? That, what, Aris slept with me to get me to agree to his claim and then broke my heart, so now I'm out to get them both?" she shrieks.

Beside me, Wren goes deathly still.

"I should be *grateful* to Wren for taking Aris before I made such a mistake. Who was I to think that he would remain true to *me* when his history so obviously proved he would not?"

Shit. Shit, shit, shit, shit.

"Or perhaps Dimitra let Wren get carried away by that flying hell beast for the same reason. Did no one think of that?" she continues, her voice rising.

"We should keep the volume down," Nireus says, glancing back down the tunnel.

Wren's green light gutters out.

Dimitra pauses to look over her shoulder, locking eyes with me. *You know me,* she seems to say. *I may hate Wren, but I love my honor more.* She does not refute the claim. She does not need to.

Wren seems less convinced. She swallows hard, keeping her gaze focused on the ceiling, and will not meet my eyes.

"Well, this is awkward," Rafael says.

Wren snorts, disentangling her hand from mine.

"Has everyone in this party slept with Aris, then?" she asks.

The words feel like cold steel plunging into my guts. Honestly, given the choice, I'd take the cold steel any day.

"I haven't," Rafael offers.

Wren glares at him, and he shrugs.

"Wren," I start. Gods, I should have told her. I had so, so many chances, and I didn't. But I won't apologize for what I did in my past. Maybe I should have told her earlier, yes, but I don't feel ashamed of having enjoyed my time with Mariana and Dimitra.

Wren raises a hand, not looking at me. "For the love of the gods, can we please just get out of here?"

Nireus leads the way, only too happy to distance himself from the drama. Wren is close behind.

The tunnel trembles as she walks.

"Fuck," I say under my breath.

CHAPTER 20
WREN

Gods, I am such an idiot.

We walk all day, mostly in silence. I can't even look at Aris. Sure, I knew there had been women before me—many, if I am being honest with myself. And I've told myself that I still want him.

But *Mariana*? I thought Mariana's antagonism toward me was due to Aris claiming me in the arena when the rumor had been he was going to claim her. So he'd been sleeping with her to get what he wanted from her? Using his charm to persuade her that he was the best choice at the games? Lying, manipulative bastard.

Gods, I am starting to wish that he *had* claimed her after all. Or anyone else, really.

And Dimitra? I should have seen that coming. I've seen the way they look at each other, their ease together. She is strong and proud and certain of her place in this world—everything I am not. Why wouldn't he want to be with her? She understands him, because she's just like him.

"Night Mage, I do not wish to interrupt what are surely very important and weighty thoughts," Petros says, coming up beside me.

I glare at him and am pleased to see him flinch.

95

"But … until the sun rises, at least, your magic is shaking the tunnels badly enough to risk another cave-in."

"Then you'd best stay away from me," I growl, looking over my shoulder at the rest of the group. Only Aris meets my stare. No remorse, no regret—he looks at me like this is *my* fault, that I should have seen this coming. And once he's slept with me, once he's gotten what he wants, he'll probably brush me off just as easily as he did the both of them. Arrogant, competitive *asshole*. The ground underneath me rumbles.

I walk the rest of the way in silence. I can feel the moment when the sun breaks through the horizon, feel my magic grow dormant. Petros breathes an audible sigh of relief when the green glow flickers and dies from my hands. We continue on through the smooth gray passages for the rest of the day, not reaching the town of Aeturnus until nearly dusk.

We emerge about midway up a mountainside, overlooking Aeturnus. It is a small town, nestled in a valley between massive snowcapped peaks. Evergreen forests dot the landscape. The homes and buildings are made of neatly fitted stones and massive logs laid on their sides. The buildings huddle together around a small town square and a single road. Smoke curls up from chimneys. It is a calming, cozy scene.

At my feet, the snow begins to melt as waves of heat roll off me, reminding me that my temper has not cooled, not in the slightest.

"Send word to the temple guardian that you will be ready to see him in the morning," Nireus instructs us. "The inn over there will give you lodging for the evening."

And with that, Nireus and Petros turn to go.

"You're not coming with us?" Mariana asks.

They shake their heads.

"We prefer the quiet of the mountain to the noise of town," Petros says carefully.

Nireus gives a nod, and they slip back into the blackness of the tunnel without leaving a trace.

"They probably just wanted to get away from you, troll bait," Mariana says.

I raise my chin, like her words don't affect me, like none of this affects me, and walk away.

I head down the mountain. Even in the falling night, I can see the Temple of Caladrius on the mountain opposite us, across the valley. It is made of black stone, possibly obsidian, with columns larger than trees and an angled portico that must span a space larger than half of my hometown. A winding stairway leads up from the town to the ledge on which the temple sits. The temple looks like it is carved back into the mountain, like it extends beyond what I can see.

"Where are you going?" Aris asks, coming after me. He moves easily, like he's still full of energy.

Damn Shield magic. I'm exhausted. All I want is a bed to fall into, and he looks like he's ready to go out and run ten miles.

"To the temple," I say. I don't need to explain myself to him. If he doesn't trust me, fine. I can make my own way—though the idea makes something clench inside my chest.

"What about the inn?" Mariana asks, clutching her blue robe tightly around her. Her breath makes little white puffs in the cold mountain air.

"As far as I'm concerned, you've all done your duty by bringing me this far," I say, pointedly looking at them one by one. "I'll continue alone."

"Like all the hells you will," Aris says, standing at my side. "You can be mad at me all you want, princess, but I am your Shield. Where you go, I go."

"That won't be necessary," I say, the words catching in my throat, which has suddenly gone dry. "I'm sure Dimitra or Mariana would be happy to keep you company. And then you can go claim yourself a 'real' Mage."

His eyes glitter, his lips tightened to a thin line. I am getting to him.

Good.

"Stay the night at the inn," he says. "The path to the temple is too dangerous at night, and you're exhausted. You'll just get yourself killed."

"I am the Night Mage," I throw back at him. "I can light the path."

"I will throw you over my shoulder if I have to," Aris says, crossing his arms. The fabric on one arm is in tatters, revealing fading scars from our fall. The wolf tooth he wears around his neck catches the light for a moment. Gods, I was so infatuated with him in the tunnels that I missed what was staring me right in the face. I bet Mariana and Dimitra are laughing at me.

"You can try," I say, crossing my arms too.

"Why go now?" he says, trying a different tactic, though I can see he is still eyeing me, looking for an opening to make good on his threat.

The cold is making my eyes sting, the tears practically freezing in place. I swallow hard. "I just don't want to be near you right now," I say, softer than I meant to. Thank the gods that the rest of our party has gone on ahead, and they are at least pretending not to eavesdrop.

Aris runs a hand through his hair. "I'm still your Shield, Wren," he says. "Let me take care of you. You need to get some rest. You can yell at me later."

"I will," I promise. I turn from him, heading instead toward the inn, but I don't miss the slight smile on his lips.

"I have no doubt," he says, following.

I am just too tired to fight.

He makes sure we are given a room with two beds. There is an adjacent bathing chamber—with hot water from some underground source, like in Prasinos, a luxury I could certainly get used to—and we are brought food and wine.

"I'll get you some water," Aris says, moving for the bottle.

"No need," I say, grabbing it from the table. I go to the bathing room and shut the door on him.

I sink to the floor and take a long pull from the bottle. The wine is acidic and burns my throat, but it makes a warm place in my belly when all that I've felt today is cold and numb.

But I can't cry. I made the decision to be with Aris—gods, I practically begged him to sleep with me back there in the cave. I knew what he was, what he is. The only bright spot in all of this is that I haven't actually gone through with it. I try to see things from his point of view—so what happens between a man and a woman is just, what, a transaction? A brief moment of pleasure to be enjoyed and then discarded?

I think back to our last fight, when Ismini offered me guidance. Gods, I wish she were here. I could use one of her hugs, and one of her scones. "Whatever is going on between you and Aris, never doubt that your protection and well-being are his only concern," she said. I am pretty sure that still holds true. That, and maybe adding "Night Mage" to his list of sexual conquests.

I take my time bathing and washing my hair, then put on some loose pants and a shirt from my pack. I towel my hair dry, braid it—doing all the little things I can while waiting for the wine to give me the courage to go back into the other room. That's why people drink this stuff, right? For the courage to do the things they can't do sober?

Eventually, my head is buzzing, and my steps are becoming unsteady, but still I feel no braver, so I gather my strength, take a deep breath, and head back into the other room.

But it's not Aris waiting there for me.

It's Rafael.

It looks like he's had a bath too. His long golden hair is brushed back, and even though he's wearing what appear to be very comfortable pajamas, he still has his red robe on. He pats a spot on the bed next to him.

"Let's talk," he says.

I raise an eyebrow but make my way over to him, swaying only a little from the wine.

"Let me see that," he says, taking the bottle gently from my hand. He sniffs it and gives it a small sip, then nods his head thoughtfully.

"You're going to feel terrible in the morning if you keep drinking this," he says, handing it back.

"Where's Aris?" I ask, sitting next to Rafael. I take another pull from the bottle.

"Out for a run. I told him I'd watch you while he was gone."

"I don't need a sitter," I say, making a wry face. "It's nighttime. I'm not powerless, and I'm not a child."

"I know," Rafael says, unruffled. "But you are important to him, and he doesn't want to take any risks with your safety."

I look down at my fingers, clutching the glass bottle tightly. "Not important enough for him to trust me," I mumble. It sounds stupid when I say it out loud—the words of a naive little girl whose heart is aching.

Rafael tips his head in agreement. "I've known Aris a long time," he says after a moment. His gaze turns distant. "You can't blame him for his past. I can tell you now, none of the other women can hold a candle to you. Not even Dimitra. He's never looked at anyone the way he looks at you."

I squirm, not meeting Rafael's eyes. I focus on the fire instead, watching the flames dance. "And how is that?" I ask. I don't know what kind of answer I'm hoping for. Apprehension twists in my gut —but that might just be the cheap wine.

"Like a man in love," Rafael says, without a trace of mockery.

My heart stutters, and the wine bottle drops from my fingers, landing with a thud on the floor. Fortunately, it remains upright, and only a splash escapes before I recover myself and pick it up. I scuff the spot of wine on the wooden floorboard with my toe, watching it stain.

"Aris doesn't love me," I say quietly.

"Well, he's certainly upset with you at the moment," Rafael says, stealing the wine back.

"Upset with *me*?" I squeak indignantly, forgetting my dark thoughts for a moment. "He's the one who kept his ... his ... womanizing a secret."

"Because he was ashamed," Rafael says, taking a drink. "And you threw your claim, the only bond that Aris holds sacred, right back at him. Telling him to claim a new Mage? That was like slapping him in the face, or worse. Like castrating him, maybe."

I wince. Yes, I did say that.

"When a Shield claims a Mage, that bond is for life," Rafael reminds me.

Heat flushes up my neck in an uncomfortable wave of embarrassment and guilt.

"I didn't mean to—I mean, I didn't realize ..." I mutter, trying to put my wine-addled thoughts together. I was so mad at him that I just lashed out, going right for his jugular.

"He didn't tell you about Dimitra and Mariana, because he didn't want to lose you. And when you fell from that lion creature's grasp? I've never seen the man so scared. He nearly ripped Caelus's head off when he was trying to bandage you up."

"Why can't he choose another Mage? Caelus did," I say, though I realize that I actually have no actual knowledge about Caelus's past.

"Caelus is a rare exception," Rafael says, handing me back the bottle. "Aris craves that bond, that stability. Think about it. His father was a demanding asshole, and his mother died when he was young. His siblings are also pretty much all assholes. His last Mage, his best friend, died in his arms. Underneath those chiseled muscles and that sex-fiend veneer is a man who desperately wants connection—and you dismissed the bond that is most important to him in the entire world. The man would die for you, Wren—and you rejected him." There is an earnestness on his face that I don't usually see—Rafael is the one I can count on for levity.

"Careful, Raf." I swallow wine that's suddenly sour in my mouth, trying to process everything he's just said. "It sounds like you might be a little in love with him too."

Rafael grins but doesn't deny it. Instead, he looks at me slyly, and the corner of his mouth pulls up in a smile. "Too?" he says.

I pick up the pillow behind me and smack him with it. "If you say anything to him, I swear I will have rats crawling into your bedroll for a *month*."

"Mercy, Night Mage," he says, laughing and putting up a hand to defend himself. "And never fear—Aris isn't my type."

"Oh?" I say, thinking about the way he's been chasing Mariana. She is as warm and inviting as frostbite.

Rafael is quiet for a moment, eyeing me, trying to decide if he wants to keep talking.

He does.

"I'd be lying if I said I hadn't thought about it," he says, stealing the wine bottle back. He takes a deep drink, not meeting my eyes. "But you keep my secrets, and I'll keep yours."

"Deal," I say, giving him a tired smile. I find that my anger has ebbed, leaving behind only exhaustion.

I reach over and squeeze Rafael's hand. He nods, squeezing back, like we've just made a silent pact.

He's given me a lot to think about. Sure, Aris should have told me about Mariana and Dimitra being his lovers, but he didn't want me to reject him, like I did. Rafael has known Aris since they were at the School of the Silver Flame together—if anyone knows what is going on in my Shield's thick skull, it is Rafael.

"So, you know any good drinking songs?" I ask, desperate to change the subject. Guilt squirms in my chest. I heard Rafael whistling a number of times as we rode, and his tunes were always cheery. I could use some cheer right now.

"A few," Rafael admits. "Don't tell Aris, but the man can't carry a tune to save his life, or remember lyrics. That man will never spout poetry to get you into his bed, that's for sure."

I wince.

Rafael gives me a sidelong glance, takes a long pull from the wine, and clears his throat. "Gods. We might need another bottle at this rate," he says. He stands, shaking out his long limbs, and begins.

. . .

Said the Mage, "Never fear,
For it's time you all hear
Of the day I killed trolls in a mine.
And I know they are dead,
For I cut off each head
And ended the night with some wine."

"That's ... horrible, actually," I say, giggles bursting from my mouth before I can help it, though his voice takes on a smooth, rather beautiful baritone when he sings.

Rafael takes a deep—and unsteady—bow and steals back the bottle.

"Not my finest work, I'll admit," Rafael says, grinning.

"You have a lovely voice," I say. "Do you write all your own songs?"

"Some," he admits, looking down at his long fingers. "Not much of a musician, though. Tried to get Dimitra to learn the lyre once. It was a disaster."

"I hope you find someone to sing with someday," I say. *And I hope it's not Mariana.* I keep that to myself, though.

"All in good time," he says, stretching his legs out before him.

I twist my hands in my robe. I'm not really sure how to broach the subject, so I decide to just go for it. Maybe the wine is starting to give me some courage after all.

"Do I, um ... do I need to worry, about Dimitra?" I ask. I am certain that Aris is over Mariana, but Dimitra was his friend first, and still is.

"Their relationship is ... complicated," Rafael admits. "But you will never encounter anyone more honorable than Dimitra. She has sworn to protect you, and she will, even if it costs her everything."

We sit in companionable silence for a bit, lost in our own thoughts, passing the bottle back and forth. I don't like what Rafael said about Dimitra, and I turn his words over and over in my mind until the repetition—and the wine—has me feeling dizzy.

Eventually, Aris comes back, his hair slick with sweat despite the cold. He looks at the two of us suspiciously.

"Everything all right?" he asks.

"It will be," Rafael says. He takes a final drink and gives me the bottle back, though it is now empty. "Good night, Wren."

"Good night," I say, and I give him a smile. He feels like the closest thing I've had to a friend in a long time, and I silently swear to take his secret to the grave.

He leaves, and Aris locks the door.

Without a word, I lie back in the bed and pull the covers up to my chin. My mind is spinning from the wine, and my chest aches. I close my eyes tightly, not wanting the moisture starting to build in them to leak out.

Aris wordlessly gathers his things and goes to bathe. When he emerges, wearing loose pants for sleeping and toweling his hair, our eyes meet. For a moment he freezes, droplets of water on his muscular chest glittering like molten gold in the firelight.

He averts his eyes, and moves to the chair by the fire. I keep waiting for him to say something—anything. To deny what Mariana and Dimitra said. To apologize. He does neither, and I feel something crack and shrivel inside my chest. *Coward.* To him, what happens between and man and a woman is just … what, a brief moment of pleasure? Or *is* there actually more to Aris, a true desire for connection?

Aris is sitting by the fire, staring into it, like he is looking for answers there as he warms his feet, like maybe he does feel badly about the situation and just doesn't know how to express that. I don't imagine that apologizing is something that Aris has done very often in his lifetime. And I want to believe that I am different—that *we* are different, together.

"Did … did you have a good run?" I ask, my voice cracking the silence.

Aris turns to me, raising an eyebrow. The firelight dances over his muscled chest, caresses the scar on his left shoulder. The scar he sustained trying to save his last Mage—and I know he'd do the same for me. I swallow hard and look away.

"Yes," he says after a moment, looking back at the fire. "How about you? Did you and Rafael have a good time?"

"We did," I say, hating how forced our conversation sounds, like we are strangers to each other now.

"Did you put him up to it?" I ask. I wrap my arms around my knees.

"Why? Did he say something nice about me?" he asks, his voice heavy with doubt.

He's not looking at me. I wish he would. The room feels colder when he looks away from me.

"He said there was more to you than meets the eye," I say carefully.

Aris lets out a long breath and runs a hand through his hair absently. "I don't know about that, princess. I'm quite a lot to look at."

His tone is harsh, self-deprecating despite the words. He doesn't speak with his usual arrogance. It might be the most vulnerable he's sounded, and that snaps the ice inside me. Before I can think better of it—I blame it on the wine and Rafael's influence—I pat the place beside me on the bed.

"I'm going to sleep. Are you coming?" I ask.

He looks at me then, incredulous, the fire dancing in his blue eyes.

"You want me to?" he asks.

And I do—gods damn it all, but I do. Not only have I gotten used to his touch, his warmth, his strength at night, but I need it. Crave it. The bed feels too large and too lonely without him in it.

"Yes," I say. Then I hold up a finger in warning. "To sleep. That's it."

He gets up, moving cautiously, like he's afraid I am going to change my mind. He settles his weight on the mattress beside me and curls around me, pulling me close when I do not pull away. He lets out a long sigh into my hair, and I can feel tension leaving him.

"I'm still mad at you," I say. I am not quite ready to forgive him, especially when he hasn't said a single thing in his own defense yet.

This elicits a snort of laughter. "I know," he says.

We lie there in silence for a while, and despite the anger and the fear and all the other emotions from the tunnels that have been raging under my skin for the past three days, I start to relax too. Despite it all, he is my friend, my protector, my Shield. I am not sure if I want to be his lover, but I am sure of the rest. I will never be alone, never want for a partner. Maybe that will be enough.

"Did you sleep with Mariana?" I ask. I need to hear him say it.

His breathing stops.

"Yes," he says after a moment. "Once."

"And Dimitra?"

"Off and on," he says.

He is very still behind me, and I am glad I don't have to look at him.

"Wren, they are my past. You are my future," he says. "You are mine, as I am yours."

I give up and roll over to look up at him, putting a hand on his face. In the firelight, his eyes glow like stars, and he is almost painfully beautiful to look at.

He turns, kissing my palm. "I've claimed you, Wren, and you have claimed me. There is no stronger bond, no bond more important, not to me."

"The only bond that means something to you is that of a Shield, then?" I ask, not sure if I want the answer.

"It's the only one I know," he says. He leans up on his elbow. "I am no saint, Wren. I've never said otherwise. But you have all of me now, the Shield ... and the man—if you want me."

The choice is mine. He's giving me that power. It's a dizzying thought, and for a moment, I can't say anything at all.

"I don't know how else to show you," he says, and he pushes a curl back from my face. "Over time, maybe."

"Maybe," I say, rolling back over, though I draw his arm around me. His body is warm, comforting, and it fits with mine like we were made for each other. With his steady heartbeat at my back, his strength around me, my head stops buzzing from the guilt and thinking about tomorrow and the wine and Aris's past and finally, finally, rests.

CHAPTER 21

LEO

M*y Wren,*

I gather by now you've gone through the tunnels, so I'm directing my next message to Aeturnus and the Temple of Caladrius. I myself am on my way to Roallac. It seems their coast is having some trouble with pirates from the Isles, and they wish to discuss having our navy assist them. Anything that leads to peace with Roallac in place of the years of petty feuds between us is welcome.

I hope you find the information you seek. We're renovating the other temples in Estana, and I hope to uncover some further manuscripts or relics that may help us learn more about your purpose, for I do not doubt now you were brought into my life for a reason.

Yours,
Leo

CHAPTER 22
ARIS

Wren has another nightmare. This time, she is thrashing, like it is something she wants to escape. Green light begins to flicker around her head, like an eerie halo. I wake her up before she can incinerate the bed. Again.

I wasn't sleeping anyway. I kept thinking about this story that Lena, our old housekeeper, used to tell us, about the first King and Queen of Ocron, about how the Book of Gold imbued them *both* with the power to lead, for the land under their rule to prosper—not just the king. Adriana loved that story. We must have heard it a thousand times. The meaning she always took from it was that the gods believed women to be as strong as men, and that's why they made no distinction in gifting the Ocronian royalty, or even Mages and Shields. Though Shields tend to be men, Mages are more often women, thus keeping the balance. And King Mathaios and Queen Yanna's first child was a girl, a princess. Though they later had many sons, Princess Emilia was the one who inherited the Book of Gold's gift. When Emilia was made queen, she erected a golden statue to her parents, which still stands in Estana's city center.

Thinking about it now, though, I realize that the important thing about that story isn't that men and women are equally worthy in the eyes of the gods. It's that they are worthy *together*. Mages and Shields are meant to be paired, to strengthen each other, to defend each other. King Mathaios and Queen Yanna were gifted together. The land became stronger because of their unity. I didn't pay all that much attention to my history lessons—other than the battles—but I do recall that Ocron flourished under their rule like it never had before. Fields yielded three times their usual crops. Animals—and people—gave birth to more offspring than had ever been recorded. It was an era of prosperity that has continued to this day.

I imagine what Wren and I could achieve together.

It might be enough to make a tiger change his stripes after all.

If, in fact, she decides she ever wants to talk to me again, to be touched by me again. And *gods*, do I want her to. Before we left Estana, she'd trembled under my touch, her eyes wild with want, with *need*—even then she hadn't let me do much more than tease her, caress her. The tortured anticipation of seeing her *shatter*, of finally breaking through her reservations, having her trust me enough to give herself to me completely? The thought alone is enough to disrupt what little sleep I did get.

It's early, but neither of us can go back to sleep. She won't look at me, at least not more than silent, furtive glances. I want to touch her, hold her, reassure her, but honestly, she might set *me* on fire. I have no idea what Rafael said to her, and she won't tell me. She's trying to work through everything, and I need to give her space. So instead, we head out so I can do a little exercise in the courtyard.

The inn is well kept, the log walls well insulated against the mountain cold. Still, there is a chill bite to the air in the hall.

Which is probably the reason Rafael has a blanket draped around his naked body.

"Oh, um, you're up early," he says, easing the door shut to another room—but not before we catch a glimpse of Mariana sitting up in her bed, long white hair loose and tousled, a smirk on her lips.

"Couldn't sleep," Wren says, crossing her arms and assessing him with a small smile. "You?"

"Uh, same," he says, clutching the blanket a little tighter around his waist. He runs a hand through his messy hair to flatten it, the thick, waxy scars on his hands a pale contrast to his tanned skin. His face is flushed, and he shoots me a sheepish look. I don't honestly care if he's sleeping with Mariana. She used sex to try to manipulate me into claiming her at the games – I almost feel like warning Rafael, but he's an adult, and can make his own stupid decisions.

"So, Dimitra and Caelus are outside, exercising," Rafael offers, to change the subject. "I'm just going to go, um, get dressed." He points across the hall to another room.

"We were just on our way out," Wren says, still fighting a grin as we continue down the hall.

I'm pleased to see her smile at something, though I'd rather she were smiling at me. Gods, I am a selfish bastard. I even want all of her smiles to be for me alone.

The inn has a space out front where the snow has been cleared, and Caelus and Dimitra are going through a series of calisthenics when we approach. I join them for a while, and it feels good to stretch, get blood moving to my chilled muscles. The gray skies overhead start to release a dusting of snow, but not enough to stick to the ground. I glare at the soft flakes, these harbingers of cold feet. Walking in slush all day is going to stretch my already thin control on myself to a breaking point. My boots don't hold a waterproofing spell the way Mage robes do—I'll have to ask Mariana to redo it, and right now I'd sooner cut off my own balls than talk to her.

Cold, wet feet it is, then.

I focus on my exercise, let the familiarity of the movements, the burn in my muscles, the bite of the crisp air in my lungs fill me. In moments like this, I am like a weapon being honed, and weapons do not dwell on the past. A sword that was wielded by another person or two is still a good sword, as long as it stays sharp. A sword isn't defined by its past. Swords don't dwell on feelings. They exist in the moment, having been made for one thing and one thing only.

And my "sword" is screaming at me to be "wielded". A *lot*. Thank the gods for the cold, I guess, that keeps my blood circulating to the muscles of my arms and legs, to my chest and back, and away from more sensitive parts. I push harder, purposely avoid any sparring, anything that might bring me into contact with Dimitra. I hope Wren notices. *See? I can behave.*

Wren just flips through one of Caelus's books, either oblivious or ignoring me, neither of which I can tolerate. I shed my shirt, sweating despite the cold, and further increase the speed and intensity of my workout, finally earning a smirk when I catch her watching me over the top of her book. Which is good, because honestly, I was starting to get worried.

Just after dawn, Rafael and Mariana join us. Mariana struggles to keep a grin off her face; Rafael doesn't bother trying.

"So, are we ready to go, then?" Wren asks, closing her book.

The walk through the town is mostly quiet. People are just beginning to stir. Snow dusts the roofs and swirls gently in the air, though the stone paths are swept clear. It's a nice town, actually, clean, well cared for. If it weren't so damned hard to get to, I imagine it would be quite a nice spot.

The base of the mountain where the temple sits is farther away than it looked yesterday, and it takes us nearly two hours to reach. This is followed by a climb up several hundred steps cut into the rock face. It is no great struggle for the Shields and Rafael, but Mariana and Wren become winded, and we need to stop a few times on the way, though Wren fights to conceal it. Her face is red from the snow and exertion, and I fight the urge to pull her robe up, tuck her braid into the hood, and pull it tighter around her neck. Everyone else is focusing on breathing, and not talking. Which isn't great, because then my mind starts having conversations with itself, and even in my mind, I sound like an asshole.

Stefan and I had been brothers in all but blood before I claimed him in my first games—the claim strengthened that bond, strength-ened us. Before I claimed Wren, I had barely known her. Is the connection I feel to her—the need to be near her, to make sure she is protected—the bond between a Mage and her Shield? I never thought about kissing Stefan, that's for sure.

We keep climbing, and the way gets a bit steeper, which is good, because I can focus on making sure everyone stays safe and not daydream about the way my little firefly would feel underneath me, the way she'd look, totally bared to me—all smooth curves and glowing eyes and gold skin flushed pink.

This time *I* stumble, which I haven't done since I was a toddler, and nearly fall down a thousand steps. *Fuck.* I try to focus on the stone at my feet, the burn in my muscles, the bite of the cold, and—eventually—I regain a little composure.

At one stop, Wren sits on a rock ledge to catch her breath, looking out over the valley. Other than the town below us, there is nothing but rocky, snowcapped mountains and patches of pine as far as we can see.

"Seems like such a strange place to build a temple for the god of night," she says, standing and readjusting her pack. "Why not some-place more accessible? Or in Estana?"

"There is a temple for the god of night there as well," Caelus says. "It's smaller, though quite impressive. But here, the boundary between the realm of the god of night and our world is thin. Here, the first priests were able to hear him and discover his divine will."

Wren gapes at him.

Caelus catches her gaze and shrugs. "The other temples are much the same—based in places where the will of the gods is made clearer."

I've never been to the Temple of Rigrasil myself. I wonder briefly what it would be like, to be in the presence of the god of day. Would he be proud of me, his creation? I imagine he would.

We finally reach the top of the stairway. The temple itself is massive and has been carved from some kind of shiny black stone that looks nothing like the gray mountain around it. The columns are so vast that I doubt the six of us with linked hands would be able to reach around one. The portico is unadorned. We are dwarfed in the entryway, none of us speaking, none of us venturing farther in. It is like entering the mouth of some great black beast, at a threshold we are unsure of crossing.

A man steps from the shadows, tall and broad-shouldered, a massive hammer leaning back against one shoulder. His black clothes and bearded face are smudged with stone dust. He looks more like a stonemason than any priest I've ever seen. A smile lights his face, and he gives a deep bow to Wren.

"Welcome to the Temple of Caladrius, Night Mage."

CHAPTER 23
WREN

The temple is darkness itself, but the polished black stone of the exterior is already warming beneath the sun's rays. I expected it to feel cold from the snow, but it's not. It feels inviting. The man who came out to greet us seems friendly, too. That might be because this is the first time someone has used the phrase "Night Mage" in the past few days without it sounding like a curse.

"You must be Tekton," I say, feeling the apprehension in my chest loosen. "Leo ... King Leonidas wrote quite highly of you."

The man beams, shifting a hammer on his shoulder that looks like it weighs a ton. He is quite tall, and broad, like he's spent a lifetime working hard, not as a temple priest.

"You look like a Shield," Dimitra says, assessing him, and I'm surprised to realize that I've been thinking the same thing.

His smile falters, but only for a moment. "You have a good eye," he says, extending his hand to her.

Once we are all introduced, he continues. "My parents are both Shields, Cassius and Umbrenia Varro."

The Shields nod like they recognize the names.

"But you are not?" I ask. "I thought children of Shields were Shields, like children of Mages were Mages."

He shrugs. "The god of day did not see fit to bestow that particular gift on me."

Dimitra mutters a single word, "*Forsaken*," laced with scorn, so softly I'm not sure that I heard her correctly.

Tekton clearly does, though. Whatever it means, it makes him flinch.

"So you've dedicated yourself instead to the god of night?" Rafael says, cocking an eyebrow. He smoothly steps in front of Dimitra, and Tekton relaxes, easing back into the role of our host.

I shoot a look at Aris, who shakes his head, just a little. I'll ask him about it later, then.

"You're a sharp one," Tekton says. He has an easy, open manner —welcoming, even. "Come. You must be eager to see the temple and get settled."

The massive entrance gives no indication as to the true size of the place. The temple extends deep into the mountain, carved into the rock itself and adorned with black stone and flickering spelled lanterns.

"What is this stone?" Caelus asks, running a hand over a column.

"Obsidian," Tekton says.

I walk beside him and have to crane my neck to look up at him. He has dark hair that curls around his ears, and a short dark beard. His eyes glitter like the obsidian stone around us. He looks like a Shield, with the same aura of strength that the others project. I suppose he must feel ashamed of not having the Shield's gifts, though, and I regret my earlier comment.

"I'm ... sorry, if we offended you earlier," I say as we walk. I almost say "if *I* offended you," but I think whatever Dimitra said may have offended him more.

He looks a little startled. "*You* could never offend me, Night Mage. This temple is your home, and by extension, I am your humble servant while you grace us with your presence." He shoots a glance over his shoulder, but Rafael remains firmly between him and Dimitra.

"Servant?" I say with a wry smile, bringing Tekton's attention back. That sounds horrible, for both of us.

He shrugs. "Servant, stonemason, historian, cook, whatever the temple needs."

"But not priest?" I ask.

He shakes his head. "None here, not for very many years. I keep the temple in order for the god of night, but he has never deigned to reveal himself to me."

"You said 'us' earlier," I say as we continue down a straight passage. So far, I haven't seen anyone else in this massive place. Our footsteps echo down the hallway.

Tekton nods. "You'll meet Delphine soon," he says, glancing around like he might catch sight of her. "She's a little shy around new people. But it's just us two."

"What about the monster?" Rafael asks. I'd told them about the monster Leo mentioned in his letters.

Tekton lets out a bark of a laugh and lifts an eyebrow. "Monster?" he asks.

"There's a rumor about a monster here, and that's why people stay away."

Tekton strokes his beard for a moment. "Not unless you count the rats I found in the cellar last month. Delphine shrieked when she saw them. I went near deaf there for a day," he says with a sheepish grin. "A monster guardian makes for a good story, though. Keeps the young ones from coming around here, getting lost in the halls or making a general nuisance of themselves. They used to dare each other to sneak around here at night. Caught a pair of them a year or two back, carving their marks on the wall with a knife as proof of their 'bravery.'"

"What did you do to them?" Rafael asks.

Tekton flushes. "I may have ... threatened to bring the divine force of the god of night down to smite them where they stood. Haven't seen anyone else since."

Rafael chuckles. "Sounds like *you* are the monster in the stories, then."

Tekton gives him a smile, but it doesn't reach his eyes.

The passage opens into a wide space with a towering black statue in the middle—a man with folded, feathered wings astride a great black horse. An opening high in the mountain lends a ray of light to the cavernous room, which glints off the statue, making it seem like it might come to life at any moment. A sinking feeling starts in my gut.

I know this man. I have seen him in my dreams a dozen times.

"Night Mage, may I present to you Lord Caladrius, the god of night."

The room goes dark.

Before me stands not a statue but the winged man from my dreams himself, this time standing beside the horse, one hand stroking his mane. The horse lifts his head and trots across the space to me, whickering, and nudges me with his head. He is a massive creature, a warhorse like the ones the Shields sometimes ride, with feathering on his legs. He is pure black, with not a single white hair on him.

And I know him. I recognize this dream horse immediately.

"Obsidian," I say, stroking his nose. It is impossible. He died, cut down by the traitorous Nestor. "How can this be?"

"I sent him to watch over you, of course," the man says, his voice like rolling thunder, though not unpleasant, and this time it does not hurt my ears. It is impossible—and yet the horse knows me too, prancing around me like a show pony in delight, tossing his mane and sniffing me all over.

"He did get quite attached to you," the man says.

I turn from Obsidian to look at the man—and this time, my eyes do not burn.

He must be at least seven feet tall, with feathered wings folded over his back like an owl's. In my dreams, they were white or sometimes black tipped with silver—now they are solid black, as dark as his hair, as dark as his eyes. His skin is the white of polished marble, his features so perfect he looks like he was carved by a master sculptor.

"Caladrius," I whisper.

He moves around me, pacing, looking me over, like he is assessing me.

"Verena," he says. At last satisfied, he stops to face me, his arms folded. "Welcome home."

"Wren? Wren!" a voice calls, as if from very far away.

I am pulled from the darkness, like waking from a dream.

I blink and find myself on the floor of the cavern, Aris cradling my head. Tekton looks alarmed and then breathes out a sigh of relief when I turn to look at him.

"What happened?" Aris asks.

I sit up, rubbing my head, which is starting to throb, and try to ignore the pallor of Aris's face.

"I saw him," I say, looking at the statue. "Caladrius. And the horse—it's Obsidian, Aris. He sent Obsidian to watch over me."

I'm crying, and I don't know why. Hot tears are rolling down my face. Gods, I've missed Obsidian. The fact that he's still alive—well, sort of—makes me happy. So why am I crying? Is it some leftover magic from Caladrius? I mean, I'll take tears over burst eardrums and burnt skin. I bury my face for a moment in Aris's shirt, not wanting to make eye contact with anyone, and I'm able to pull myself together after a moment.

Aris glances at the statue, his jaw tightening.

"Who in all the hells is Obsidian?" Rafael asks, hands on hips.

"My horse—well, *his* horse, I guess," I say, looking back at the statue. "He joined me at the school and kept me safe as we traveled. A guardian, sent by Caladrius."

Tekton fetches a glass of cool water from somewhere, and I down it, suddenly parched. Now all of Obsidian's quirks make sense—his protectiveness, the way he responded to me, more intelligent than any horse I'd ever known. At the time, I attributed it to my growing magic and affinity for animals. I've never considered that he might be something more.

"Does this kind of thing happen often here? These visions? I've been seeing him in my dreams too," I say.

"Not in the past several hundred years, Night Mage," Tekton says. His brow is furrowed.

"Can you stand?" Aris asks. There is a gentleness to his actions, a worry that he would not otherwise give voice to. I scared him, I realize. I must have had some kind of fit and just dropped in front of him.

"I'm fine," I reassure him. But when I go to stand, my knees buckle, and all the strength seems gone from my legs.

"Come. I've prepared your rooms. Let's get you settled so you can recover," Tekton says.

Aris scoops me up in his arms—a little humiliating, though not unenjoyable—and carries me down one of the dozen side passages that radiate out from this central space.

"This place is more rabbit warren than temple," Mariana remarks, and she is right. Though it is carved into the mountain, it might have rivaled the size of Estana's palace. She raises an eyebrow at me resting in Aris's arms but doesn't comment. I can feel my face heating. I wonder if he ever carried her this way. From the look on her face, I'd guess not, and that makes me a little smug despite everything.

"There used to be nearly fifty priests here," Tekton says, opening a pair of wooden doors with black adornments. "Now there are just two caretakers."

The first room we enter is maybe twenty feet across, with a pair of frosted windows dominating the far wall. They have peaked arches and a foil pattern in dark metal tracery flowing across them. It might lead out to a ledge or patio—it's hard to tell—but Aris moves directly through the first room, past a fireplace and some overstuffed chairs, and into the next room.

The bedroom is similar in size and shape to the sitting room, with the same arched windows letting in filtered light. The room is dominated by a large four-poster bed hung with fine dark curtains, and dark linens have been made up neatly. I sigh as Aris settles me down—it is so comfortable that in my exhausted state, I feel like I might never want to get up.

"I've made up rooms down the hall for the rest of your party," Tekton says politely. "If you'll follow me, I'll show you the way."

"Get some rest," Aris says, getting up.

My hand flies to his arm, and he stills. He looks down at me, a question in his eyes.

"Stay," I whisper.

He nods and settles himself on the bed beside me so that I can rest my head against his chest, his arm draped around me. I begin to drift off to sleep almost immediately as the others file out.

Dimitra's eyes glitter in the darkness as she looks back at me before she disappears out the door, as silent as a wraith.

CHAPTER 24
ARIS

When Wren used her magic—really used it, like when she fought Saroya or made the magic tornado back at the school—she lost consciousness for days. This time is different. The fit, or vision, or whatever, seems to have left her exhausted, but only the usual kind of tired. She sleeps easily now, stirring a little to move closer to me, one small hand draped across my stomach.

Patience. I will be patient. She's beginning to trust me again. Sort of. At least, it seems like her unconscious wants to.

This place is huge, far larger than I anticipated. It is like a city, or at least a town. I was expecting some dusty priests, maybe some cryptic historians, with thick glasses and bent backs from reading too much and moving too little.

Tekton peeks in on us in about an hour, politely knocking at the door. He is also the complete opposite of what I was expecting. To be a Shield without an animal shift or healing or enhanced strength? Gods, I'd never be able to live with myself.

"How is she?" he asks, gaze softening as he looks at Wren sleeping.

"Fine," I say, tightening my arm around her a little.

"When she's awake, just keep coming down this corridor. It'll end at the dining hall. Fortunately, Delphine's a better cook than I," he says, pointing to his right.

I nod, not wanting to disturb Wren further.

He takes the hint and leaves.

The room is nice. Dark, simple, neat. Nicer than anything at the School of the Silver Flame by far, though not as opulent as Estana.

Wren rests another hour before stirring, her face flushed from sleep. She rubs her eyes, sitting up.

"Was I out long?" she asks, blinking.

"Not long," I say.

She sits and rocks back on her heels, watching me, like she wants to say more. She bites her lip instead.

"Hungry?" I ask, tearing my gaze away from her mouth back to her eyes.

She nods, tucking her hair back behind her ear. "Famished."

The dining hall is a large rectangular space with two long tables clearly meant to hold all the temple's priests at once, flanked on either side by large stone fireplaces. Caelus, Dimitra, Rafael, and Mariana are seated at the far end of one table, steaming mugs before them, looking at a book and a piece of parchment. Tekton is poring over another book, wearing rounded spectacles perched low on his nose. He jumps when he sees us, immediately seating Wren and offering us fresh bread and a barley and vegetable stew.

"Thank you," Wren says, looking up at him gratefully.

Tekton beams. "I know firsthand how strict the Shield diet is," he says with a rueful smile. "Here." He hands me a mug of ash water, scented with clove and other spices, almost like a tea. It isn't bad.

"I, uh, hope you don't mind that we got started," Tekton says, gesturing to the books and papers.

"Feeling better, Night Mage?" Rafael asks.

Wren nods, sipping her own, ash-free drink.

"Did the god of night have any insight to offer?" Caelus asks.

She considers, then shakes her head. "It's like ... I've been seeing him, in my dreams, for a while," she says, staring down at her cup. "At first it was actually painful. When he spoke, I could feel my ears rupture and bleed. When he looked at me, my skin burned. I could feel it in my dreams as if I were awake, but when I woke up, I was fine, no marks or anything on me."

Shit.

She takes a breath and continues. "It's like he had to tone himself down somehow, so that he could communicate with me, and it took him some time to figure it out. And here—I didn't even have to be asleep. The vision was the same, only he ... well, he welcomed me home."

Tekton is watching her carefully, as still as a statue himself.

"I don't suppose he said anything about how to get the monsters to stop chasing you?" Mariana asks. "Or get a better handle on your powers so you don't burn us all up?"

"Monsters?" Tekton asks, sighing wearily. "There are no monsters here, I told you."

"Not here, everywhere," Caelus explains. "Her magic seems to be calling creatures to her. At first it was just animals—birds, horses. Then trolls. A kraken destroyed her home. More trolls. Then a giant flying creature I've never heard of before, like a massive lion with bat wings."

"And then *more* trolls, mountain trolls this time," Mariana offers.

Tekton narrows his eyes.

"What is it?" Wren asks.

"The, um, flying creature—did it have a scorpion's tail? Big claws?"

"Likes to drop people from high places?" Wren says, crossing her arms. "That's the one. What is it?"

"A manticore," he says, removing his glasses and pushing back from the table. "Come on. Let's go to the library."

"What's a manticore?" I ask, getting up.

"I've got some pictures in the library, in the older books," Tekton says, striding from the dining hall.

We follow in a rush.

We have just taken another turn down a lantern-lit hall when something moves in the darkness. My swords are drawn in the same breath, my body between it and Wren.

A gasp comes from the shadows.

"Easy, friend," Tekton says, placing a hand on my wrist. "That's just Delphine."

"Who is Delphine?" I ask, still not getting a good view.

"I am," a girl says, stepping from the darkness. She is twelve or thirteen, maybe, a few years younger than my youngest sister. She has brown hair pulled back in a dirty ponytail, pale skin, and dark eyes like Tekton's. She wears a short brown shift despite the cold, and no shoes. She goes to Tekton's side, clings to him, staring at us all with wide eyes. She's about at the age when Shields really start to fill out and gain muscle—right now though, she's all gangly limbs.

I sheathe my swords, the sound unnaturally loud in the silent hall.

Delphine glances between us, unblinking.

"You're pretty," she says, looking at Mariana.

Mariana raises an eyebrow. "I am *gorgeous*, actually. And this is your ... what, daughter?" Mariana looks to Tekton.

He ruffles the girl's hair affectionately. "Niece. When my sister and her Mage—her husband—were killed in a skirmish with the Black Water Witches, the care of Delphine fell to me."

Delphine tugs Tekton's sleeve, and when he bends down, she whispers something urgently into his ear. He nods gravely as he listens, then straightens. She scampers off, disappearing once more.

"She's ... shy," Tekton says, rubbing the back of his neck.

"She's not a Shield either?" Dimitra asks, looking the way the girl vanished. There is still derision in her tone, but also, maybe, pity.

"No," Tekton says slowly. "Curse of the family, I'm afraid. Come on, the library is this way."

"Saroya said magic was fading," Wren says to me, waiting until

Tekton is probably out of earshot. "Is that what she meant? Magical families having nonmagical children? Fewer gifted each year?"

"Yes," I say. "And no new lines have appeared in ages."

"But all your siblings are Shields," she says as we walk.

I puff out my chest with a little pride. "Yes. Our lineage is strong. We can trace it all the way back to the First Shield himself."

The place is a labyrinth. I am sure that Wren, with her poor sense of direction, would find herself turned around here in no time.

"Earlier Dimitra said something, when Tekton said he was a Shield without powers."

I nod. It's a slur, the worst thing you can call anyone, in my mind, which is saying something. I keep our pace slow, letting the others get ahead of us a little way, and drop my voice.

"Forsaken. It means someone—like Tekton and Delphine—who should have been born gifted. Their god abandoned them, found them lacking in some regard. It's kind of like calling him a bastard, like you doubt his lineage is what he claims it to be."

Wren stares down the hall. "That's horrible," she says, glaring at the back of Dimitra's head. "It's not like it's his fault."

"The forsaken might outnumber the gifted someday, if magic continues to fade," I say.

Wren nods. "We'll figure this out," she says, shifting her gaze back to Tekton, who stands at a large door, ushering us inside. "We have to."

This passage ends at the library, a small room where bookshelves line the walls. A large round table dominates the center, and a stone fireplace lights the space with a warm glow. There are silver candelabra of spelled candles too, with plenty of light to read by.

Tekton moves to one of the shelves, where the books are thick with dust, their leather covers cracked with age. He puts his glasses back on and runs a finger down the spines before pulling out a large tome. He blows a plume of dust from it and lays it on the table.

"I haven't gone through this one in ages. Hang on," he says, flipping through. It seems to be some sort of book about the gods, divided into sections for each.

He stops when he reaches the section for Helene, goddess of wind. Her image is drawn on the page, eerily beautiful, though the paper is thin and frail. Yellow hair flows around her to her ankles, a crystalline crown sitting atop her head. She is as beautiful as the statue of Caladrius, maybe even more so—but fierce. She is no sweet summer breeze—she is the winter tempest and the summer hurricane.

And behind her in the distance—a pair of manticores.

"What does that mean?" Wren asks, tracing one with her finger. She looks up at Tekton, whose brow is still furrowed.

"I'm not sure. No one's seen them in centuries," he says. He sits in the chair by Wren and flips through the pages rapidly, looking for something. He quickly finds it. "Here it is. Manticores are the messengers of the goddess of wind, sent to dispatch those who displease her."

Wren frowns. "So ... the goddess of wind is sending these things after me? It's not my own magic attracting them or something?" she asks.

"I doubt the goddess of wind has control over mountain trolls, or krakens," Mariana says.

I hate to admit it, but she does have a point.

"No," Tekton agrees, flipping through some more pages. "Mountain trolls fall under the realm of Cephus, the god of earth. And the kraken is the pet of Aenon, the god of water," he says, pointing in turn to the images in the book.

Rafael lets out a low whistle. "So ... the elemental gods are out to get Wren? Why?"

"Their own magic is fading," Caelus says softly. "Wren represents a new era. The god of night is now in play. We will have to hope that the rules of their game may be revealed in time."

"And I am his lackey," Wren says, crossing her arms.

I snort. I don't like games. Strategy was always my least favorite lesson—which meant I spent twice as much time on it as I did anything else.

"I don't know a lot about the gods, or whatever games they may be playing," I say.

"Shocking," Mariana says.

I glare at her. Her lips form a thin line, but she holds her tongue.

"But I do know that a phalanx of soldiers is stronger than any one man—or god," I say, resting a hand on Wren's shoulder. "Whatever comes our way, we will withstand it. Together."

She gives me a weary smile, lacing her fingers through mine.

"So, now what?" Dimitra asks.

"Well, Wren should be safe here," Tekton says, closing the book. "The power of the god of night surrounds this place. Not even the god of day himself could touch her here."

"So I'm safe as long as I never leave this temple?" she asks, frowning.

"Maybe that's what he meant by 'welcome home,'" Rafael offers.

"So, what, we're done now? Wren stays here. We all go home. And that's it?" Mariana asks.

"I can't just stay here forever," Wren says. Then she shoots a guilty look at Tekton. "No offense."

"None taken," he says lightly. "I think the bigger questions are *why* was Wren put into play, and why now?"

The room is quiet for a minute, save for the crackling of the fire. Everyone finds a seat at the table, desperate for something to do, for the motion to distract them for a moment.

"What about the Book of Silver?" Wren asks.

"What?" Tekton asks, turning to Wren.

"The Book of Silver. Panos said you had a translation of it. Is there something in there that could be helpful?"

"I'm afraid we have only a partial duplicate," he says, pulling a well-worn, thin leather volume from another shelf. This one has been read recently—no dust.

"I'd still like to read it, if that's all right with you," she says, reaching for it.

For a moment, Tekton clutches the book to his chest before surrendering it.

"Of course, Night Mage. But—do please be careful. I'm rather attached to it—that's the original copy, by the first temple guardian, Thanassis Sarkides, himself, written nearly three hundred years ago."

"I'll be careful," Wren assures him, opening it. "Um, what language is this?" she asks, wide-eyed.

Tekton smiles sheepishly. "The language of the gods," he says. "I can help you read it, but it's slow work. And I've got a dictionary around here somewhere to help with the harder words. No one's actually spoken it since my great-grandfather's time."

"I do," Caelus offers.

"What?" Tekton asks.

"I speak it," Caelus says. "The gods were an important part of my life growing up, and remain so to this day. Their language was one of my primary studies. *Ea alis volat propriis.*"

Tekton beams. "A Shield and a scholar! Come, let us work on this together—Night Mage, we can have the first part translated for you before the day is through," he says, fetching paper and a quill from a shelf.

"All right," Wren says. She squeezes my hand before releasing it. "But, Caelus, what did you say? Just now?"

He grins, canines catching the firelight. "She flies with her own wings."

CHAPTER 25

LEO

My Wren,

I am thrilled to hear you have made it safely to Aeturnus, and that the temple is proving to be helpful. We are most disturbed by the theory that the elemental gods may be trying to reach you in our realm. Panos assures me that the gods cannot cross into our realm directly, not without the power of the Three Books, which were created using the combination of all their magics a millennium ago. Alas, those tomes have been lost.

I must tell you a great secret. Ocron believes that the ruling family— my family—is in possession of the Book of Gold, the book that initially gave my family the power to rule, for the land to flourish under our care, the book that says we were chosen by the gods themselves.

In reality, that book has been missing for some time. There is a book of solid gold in our treasury, locked away, but it is a fake, a copy. It doesn't even have anything written in it. I hope that you will not think less of me for this deception—I am not in possession of the book, but it must still be in existence, or Ocron as we know it would crumble. Over the past few gener-

ations, the actual book has become less important as the gods have faded from our collective minds.

It becomes obvious to me now that we have made a grave error in not seeking it out sooner.

For now, stay at the temple—though it pains me to write this. We are working to determine the whereabouts of the Book of Bronze and the Book of Silver, and my spies are being dispatched with strict orders to seek out the Book of Gold in its hiding place.

I will not rest until I can send you good news.

Yours,
   Leo

CHAPTER 26
WREN

While Tekton and Caelus work on translating what they can, I am left free to look about the rest of the library.

"Are all of these in the language of the gods?" I ask, opening the fifth book in a row in that long-dead language. I'm starting to get frustrated.

Tekton gives me a sheepish smile. "Mostly, Night Mage. I would be happy to teach you sometime, so that you can read through whatever you like. This library is yours, after all."

"Focus on the translation," Aris says gruffly.

Tekton's eyes return to the book, a faint red hue just visible around his beard.

"How long are we planning on being here, then?" Mariana asks. Her arms are crossed, and she still sits at the table.

"Let's see what we find in the texts," Caelus says, not raising his eyes from the book. His hand is already writing furiously across a blank page.

"Why? Tiring of me already?" Rafael asks, nudging Mariana's shoulder with his.

She snorts, but a small smile cracks her stony face.

132

"Well, I'm no use here," I say, rubbing my dust-covered palms on my robe. "Let's go back to the foyer, with the statue."

"You'll just pass out again," Dimitra says.

I'd almost forgotten she was there. She's so quiet, lurking in the corner there. Like a ghost.

"Maybe," I say, looking at her, raising my chin. "But who better to ask about the god of night's plans than the god of night himself?"

"Have you been able to summon him intentionally before?" Dimitra asks.

"No," I admit. "But what have I got to lose by trying?"

"Men have been driven mad trying to communicate with the gods. Women too," Mariana says, looking me over.

I roll my eyes.

"And we wouldn't want that. Besides, I hope Aris doesn't mind carrying you around all the time. He's a Shield, not a porter."

"He's my partner," I say.

The word catches Aris off guard, and I can't tell if he's pleased by it or not.

"And what are *you* planning on doing with your time, then, besides watching your Shield do all the work?" I ask, deflecting.

Mariana smirks, eyeing Rafael up and down. He looks startled, but not displeased.

I throw my hands up and stalk out of the room.

"Partner?" Aris asks once we're alone in the hall. He's close to me, too close—I can feel his heat and smell his leather-and-sunshine scent, even over the dusty stone that surrounds us.

"What would you prefer I'd said?" I ask.

He growls, stuffing his hands into his pockets. "It's just ... impersonal," he grumbles, but he doesn't say anything more.

We come to a crossroads, and though I head left, Aris heads right.

"Statue room is this way," he says, nodding his head in that direction.

Right. Got it.

But as I turn, my eye catches on a sliver of white etched into the dark stone.

Four scratches in a row, each about six inches long, along the wall by the corner, like something scraped it. I put a hand to them—the gouges are deep in the rock.

"What is that?" I ask.

Aris looks over my shoulder, suddenly just a hair's breadth behind me, which isn't at all distracting.

"Tool marks? Like a pitchfork?" I guess, though why Tekton would have a pitchfork this deep in a mountain was beyond me. "Or from those kids sneaking in?"

"No," Aris says, touching the marks as well. "These are claw marks."

"Gods," I say, trying to focus on the marks and definitely not on the very solid chest that is currently touching my back. "A Shield?"

"There's no animal I know of that large," he says, spreading his fingers over the marks. From thumb to pinkie, he only reaches two of the lines.

I swallow hard, a shiver running through me. "I'm sure all kinds of magic were used here, when the temple was built," I say, my mind scrambling for an explanation. "Maybe it's like a builder's mark."

Aris touches a mark in the middle, at its deepest point, and white powder comes off on his fingertip. He rubs his fingers together, like he's testing it.

"No," he says again. "This is new."

"So there's a monster in these halls after all?" I say, my heart rate picking up.

Is Tekton lying to us? What *did* happen to all the other staff in the temple? I start imagining a creature prowling these halls, preying on unsuspecting victims, and suppress a shudder.

"Come on," Aris says.

He goes to put an arm around my shoulders, to guide me back down the tunnel on the right, but I flinch from his touch reflexively.

He closes his eyes a moment, letting out a breath. His hands clench, then relax.

"Come on," he says again, stepping aside so I can pass him.

We go the rest of the way in silence.

The cavern with the statue is as intimidating as it was before—even more so now that I know I can reach Caladrius himself here. Maybe.

I stand before the statue for a while, but nothing happens. I walk around it, admiring it from all angles, waiting for that tingle down my spine that precedes my magic flaring up—but nothing. I even try sitting in front of it, closing my eyes, and finding my center like Ismini taught me.

"The god of night must not like being summoned," I say, half-joking. The floor is cold, and my back aches.

Aris leans against the far wall, watching me. "You'll figure it out," he says.

I sigh and stand up, my spine cracking.

A loud boom echoes down one of the side halls, and I jump. Aris is there immediately, between me and that entrance. A crash, like a landslide—and then, silence.

Tekton comes running into the cavern, his glasses in one hand, followed closely by Rafael. They skid to a stop when they see us.

"Oh, thank Caladrius," Tekton says. "Those are the older parts of the temple—unstable, as you can tell. We've been digging up all kinds of artifacts down there—Delphine and I." He looks down the side hall, then nods to Rafael, and they jog down it, out of sight.

Tekton returns a few minutes later, gray dust in his dark hair.

"I hate to impose, Night Mage, but may I borrow your Shield for a moment? There's a section down there that has caved in, and I need some help moving the stone."

Aris looks at me.

"Go on," I say, sitting back down, looking up at the statue of Caladrius. "I couldn't be anywhere safer than here in front of the god of night."

"Five minutes," Aris growls, heading after Tekton.

The man nods, and they take off.

I continue to meditate. My nose itches. Then I squirm, trying to settle myself on the cold stone. It's no use, though. I can't concentrate. I sigh and lie back on the floor. The light overhead dims suddenly, like somewhere high up something has flown over the aperture of the cavern, momentarily darkening it. I wonder if there are birds here, or mice. It would be nice to see some friendly faces.

"Hard at work, I see," Mariana says.

I lean up on my elbows, looking at her and Dimitra coming down the hall.

"No luck, then, Night Mage?" Dimitra asks, in a slightly less frosty tone. Slightly.

"Not yet," I admit. "What are you two up to?"

"Snow's let up. We're headed into town for supplies. Plus this place gives me the creeps," Mariana says, shivering dramatically. "I'd kill for some decent red wine. And I'm on my last moonberry."

"Last what?" I ask.

Mariana laughs in disbelief. "Moonberry. You take one a month to prevent pregnancy and your cycle. Gods, girl, what rock have you been living under?"

I feel heat in my cheeks and mumble something incoherent. I look at Dimitra—her gaze has darkened to something almost feral.

"Are you *trying* to get pregnant?" she asks pointedly.

"What I do is none of your business," I fire back.

She glares at me. "Do not burden Aris with an unwanted child because of your own foolishness," she spits.

I am too stunned by her words to move, much less speak.

"What do you envision?" Dimitra continues, prowling closer. "The two of you living together happily in a little home somewhere, a litter of baby abominations playing at your feet? He is a wild thing, untamable, as I am. Do not delude yourself otherwise."

Her words hit me like a slap, and indignant rage joins the embarrassment on my face. Mariana is as surprised by Dimitra's vehemence as I am, but she gives the Shield an approving look. I clench my teeth to keep from shouting at her and my hands are trembling with my surge of emotion. Her words have cut me deeply—where do I see myself after this quest? Will I continue to work with Aris, never putting down roots anywhere? The idea is tempting – but a home would just give the gods another target. I'm not sure what I want for myself–marriage? A family? – all I'm sure of is that I need Aris to be in my life.

But none of that is Dimitra's business.

Dimitra storms out of the cavern in a rush, Mariana close on her heels.

I stare after them a long time, grateful that the sun is still up—as mad as I am, I might have brought the whole mountain down on her head.

"What's going on?" Aris says, jogging back into the cavern.

I shake my head, smiling up at him. When he offers a hand to help me up, this time I take it. He pulls me to my feet, and suddenly we're there, our hands clasped between us, just a breath apart. He bends like he's going to kiss me—but Dimitra's words echo in my ears, and I take a step back.

"No luck," I mumble, wiping my suddenly sweaty hands on my pants. "Get the cave-in sorted out?"

"Helped Tekton move the worst of it. Want to head back to the library and see how Caelus is faring on the translation?" he asks.

I nod, rubbing my arms.

Caelus hasn't made much progress without Tekton, but he's working hard, his brow furrowed as he painstakingly copies out the words. So far, it's a lot of nothing.

Here is the word of the Book of Silver, copied from the original source by Thanassis Sarkides, first guardian of the Temple of Caladrius, the god of night, the bringer of dreams, the lord of the dark, the controller of tides, the master of the stars, the ...

. . .

It goes on in the same sort of tedium for another few lines.

"I'll let you know when I get to something worthwhile," Caelus says. "I'll stay up all night if I have to."

We sit with him for a while, until I begin to nod off in the chair.

"Go to bed, Night Mage. Perhaps Lord Caladrius will visit you in your dreams," Caelus says.

He makes a good point. Also, I am tired all the way down to my toenails. That little nap I took earlier has barely taken the edge off the exhaustion from traveling, and traveling, and traveling.

I yawn and get up. We run into Rafael and Tekton on the way to our room, both of them now covered in dust, though Rafael's robe remains immaculate.

"I'm telling you, let's just blow it up and call it a day," Rafael says, and Tekton laughs, shaking his head. Whatever mess they've been working on, they seem to have bonded. Rafael shakes his head, and dust flies from his golden mane like snow.

When we get to our room, Aris watches me carefully, his eyes glowing in the candlelight. There is a question there—so many questions. Suddenly it's hard to breathe. I am briefly reminded of the ball in Estana, when Leo walked me back to my rooms, a similar question in his eyes.

Leo never made me feel humiliated, the way Aris has. He never made me feel betrayed either, or foolish.

But neither did he make me feel like heat and lightning and *magic* the way Aris does.

"I'm going to sleep," I say clearly, so that there's no room for misinterpretation.

Aris nods, running a hand through his hair. There's a flicker across his face.

Is that disappointment, or am I imagining it?

"I'm going to help Tekton move a few more things in that hall that collapsed. I'll check in on you in a bit."

"All right," I say.

We're staring at each other awkwardly, uncertain how to say goodbye. Do we hug? Do we kiss? Do we shake hands?

He nods again after a moment, almost like a mockery of a bow. "All right, then," he says. "Good night, princess."

I stand alone in the room for a long time, listening to his footsteps fading away down the corridor. The words sting, and I feel unsettled.

It takes me a long time to fall asleep, despite feeling exhausted. Once I put my head down on my pillow, the quiet thoughts that have been waiting all day suddenly all begin to roar at me like a thousand peals of thunder. I toss and turn, finally burying my head under the pillows. I know I can't block out the sound of my own thoughts this way, but it seems to help all the same.

I wake a bit later to the sound of the door opening. I think it's Aris coming to check up on me, and my pulse begins to race, but am I excited or anxious or something else entirely? The door closes again though, a breath later. When I sit up, I see a small cloth bag next to the spelled candle on my bedside table, a folded note beside it. I open the bag to see a handful of small round things inside, looking like dried blueberries. The writing on the note is unfamiliar, written in a tight, neat script.

One every month. <u>Do not forget.</u>

CHAPTER 27

ARIS

Tekton is stronger than he looks. For a non-Shield, I'm impressed. We work late into the night clearing out the rubble of the collapsed passage. I gather that this sort of thing is a regular occurrence—a sign, perhaps, that the hold Caladrius has on this place is weakening, which is an interesting thought. Would Wren be as safe here as Tekton has boasted? Still, the exercise clears my head, which is much needed. Wren's got it buzzing so much I can barely think straight. Every time I get a moment of clarity, I'll remember the feel of her lips, the smoothness of her skin, the sighs from her mouth—and then, fuck, I'm buzzing again and throwing rocks around like a lunatic, trying to find peace in the work.

The other thing I like about Tekton is that he doesn't talk much. I guess he's used to being alone, and I don't like small talk, so we get on well enough. He was chatty enough with Rafael, who has been absent for a while now, probably off with Mariana in a dark corner somewhere. Tekton seems like he wants to talk a few times—but then always closely his mouth again. Delphine comes by at some point, her bare feet nearly silent on the stone. She is a pale ghost and doesn't speak. Honestly, it's creepy. She watches us for a bit and then drifts away, becoming one with the shadows as she leaves.

"Sometimes I wish she had a sibling," Tekton says, staring after her. "I'm afraid I'm not good enough company for her."

"Siblings are overrated," I say, heaving another stone out of the way. It clatters down the small mountain of rubble we've moved.

A light sound down the hall pricks my ears, bare feet against stone—if I were in tiger form, my ears would be swiveling and my tail thrashing. Delphine made no noise as she passed, and I know my traveling companions well enough to recognize their footfalls by now. The steps pause, and there's a faint scuff as one foot hesitates, a tell I know well. *Shit, and double shit.* I let out a long breath. "I have five, and they all hate me."

"Not all of us, dear brother," a light voice says. "I merely loathe you."

And then from the shadows emerges my youngest sister. Stark naked.

"What brings you here, Adriana?" I ask, wiping some of the dust off my face.

Tekton seems startled, which is fair—I mean, there is a strange, naked woman right in front of him. I wonder if, living here alone as he does, he's ever even seen a naked woman before. He shrugs off his shirt, revealing a frame well used to hard labor, and hands it to her. My gaze snags on a series of scars across his ribs, parallel lines widely spaced. Like claw marks.

Adriana takes his shirt between two delicate fingertips, and she eyes Tekton with a predator's gaze. I recognize that look, and I don't like seeing it on her. She's only, what, eighteen? Seventeen? I mean, I guess that's older than I was when I first ... *Shit.*

To make it all worse, Tekton is turning red. Adriana arches an eyebrow after her analysis of him, then puts on his shirt. Slowly. It only comes halfway down her thighs.

"I never could sneak up on you," she says, glancing at me. "It's good to see at least that much hasn't changed."

I cross my arms, waiting for her to answer me. She rolls her eyes, another family trait.

"I bring a message, of course, brother dear. Why else would I be here?" she says, whirling a scroll of paper around one palm.

"You're working as the king's messenger?" I ask, incredulous.

Adriana is a hawk shifter—the only bird in our family, except for our mother. Still, I expected her to enroll at the school this year, like the rest of us.

"You'd know that if you spent any time with your family." She snorts. "Or what's left of it, anyway. Myron's Mage is pregnant with his child. Did you know? You're going to be an uncle."

Myron, my second-oldest brother, is only slightly less of an asshole than Spyridon.

"Congratulations, I guess," I say. I try to remember the name of his Mage and fail. I think she is a Fire Mage. Gianna, maybe. "Why aren't you at the school?"

"Why don't you have a real Mage?" she counters, hands on hips. "I have to say, it *is* nice not being the only black sheep in the family anymore."

"You must be famished after your trip," Tekton says, having recovered the use of his tongue. "May I offer you something?"

"That would be wonderful," Adriana purrs, and she links her arm through his, batting her eyes up at him. If possible, the man turns a deeper shade of red, and he clears his throat. She winks at me and walks barefoot with Tekton down the hall, with all the poise of a queen.

It's going to be a long damned night.

In the dining hall, Tekton brings out ash water and stew. Adriana perches on a chair, and we catch up on the past few years. She used to be my favorite sibling—and I guess she still is, though that isn't saying much. She's harder than I remember, and there's a leanness to her now. The child is grown up. She looks the most like our mother, with lighter skin and brown hair, and the same blue eyes that I inherited. The harsh look, though, is all Nestor. She might be beautiful otherwise.

"Don't worry. I won't be here long. Just until your 'Night Mage' gives me a letter to bring back to the king." She looks at me to see if she can get a reaction from me. She runs a long finger around the rim of her cup. "They write each other quite a lot, it seems."

"The fate of the country is at stake. Of course they write often."

Adriana raises an eyebrow, taking another sip of her drink. She leans back, exposing an expansive length of thigh. Tekton mumbles something about checking to make sure Delphine is asleep and leaves.

"So, what are you really doing all the way out here in the frozen west, brother?" she asks, venom on the last word.

"On a quest with my Mage," I respond. I lean back, putting my boots on the table, my hands behind my head, every limb relaxed, showing her exactly how little I care about her jabs.

"So she calls the shots, then," Adriana says, a look of approval on her face. "I like her already."

"She's the Night Mage. There's nobody like her in the entire world," I say.

She smirks, lacing her fingers together on the table. I've given her an opening, revealing how much pride I have in my Mage. If we'd been fighting with swords, I'd be dead.

"Oh, you have got it *bad*," she says, crowing. "Tell me, is it true she had to wear two manacles to keep herself under control?"

"Keeping Wren held back is not a good idea." I examine a torn edge of a nail, then worry it smooth between my teeth.

"I heard she set a pack of wolves on Darius Hall," she says, leaning forward. "And that she made a tornado of green light at the school, so strong no one could stop her."

"Aris stopped me," Wren says, coming out of the hallway.

It must be dawn, or close enough. Inside this damn mountain, it's hard to say. Wren looks a little more rested—the dark circles under her eyes a little less dark. She's redone her hair, and her cheeks are still a little flushed from sleep. I want to kiss those pink spots, get them to flare into the bright color they go when she's flustered. Instead, I worry that damn nail down, though my eyes don't leave hers.

"It's a sad day when my brother is the levelheaded one," Adriana says. She doesn't get up, just looks Wren over and then looks back at me. "*That* is the Night Mage?"

"It is. And you are …?" Wren asks coolly, coming to sit at my side on the bench. She looks Adriana over, taking in her lack of pants with a snort.

"Adriana. Aris's sister. I've heard so many delicious things about you, Night Mage." She clasps her hands together on the table in front of her, as eager for gossip as always.

"I've never heard anything about you at all," Wren says. She gives me a pointed look.

I shrug. "Not much to tell," I say. "She's working as a messenger for Leo."

"And she's not wearing any pants because …?" Wren asks.

"Well I couldn't shift my fancy ball gowns with me when I flew here," Adriana retorts. "Does nudity bother you, then? How *ever* do you get on with my dear brother?"

"The letter, now, before I toss you off the damn mountain," I say.

Adriana huffs. "Here you go." She hands the scroll off to Wren.

She tears it open, and I try to ignore the fact that those damn pink spots on her cheeks flush crimson.

"She's just here to take your reply back," I say. "Let's not keep her waiting long."

"Oh, no, take your time," Adriana says. "We have *so* much catching up to do."

Wren scans the letter.

"How are things in Estana?" I ask, trying not to worry too much about the contents of the letter.

Adriana shrugs. "Boring. The tournament was fun, though. They only let full Shields compete, which was a shame. I really think Rea could have given Zale a run for his money."

Rea is between me and Adriana in age. I've always thought of her as a female version of Nestor. She is a lioness shifter, too, just like he was a lion. I haven't seen her in ages. She was always a bit of a bully. You'd think, being the only two girls in a family of boys, that Adriana and Rea would have bonded, but you'd be wrong. Rea always felt she had something to prove and had no qualms about knocking down anyone in her way—most often Adriana. Adriana, from the day she was born, just didn't give a fuck.

"Who's Rea?" Wren asks distractedly.

"My other sister," I answer quickly, before she gets any ideas about me keeping other women in my life a secret from her.

Wren nods, folding the letter. "Tekton has some paper in the library," she says absently, and she heads for the far hallway.

We meet Delphine on the way, who looks at Adriana in awe. Adriana takes in the waif the same way she'd look at a stray dog on the street—vague interest, and a little pity.

"Is it true that you're a hawk Shield?" Delphine says.

Adriana preens at the attention. "It is," she says.

"And you can fly wherever you want?" Delphine asks, looking down at her bare toes, not missing the fact that Adriana's feet are also bare.

"Wherever I want," Adriana confirms.

Delphine lets out a long sigh. "That must be nice," she says, and she drifts past us dejectedly.

"Her family are Shields. She and Tekton were born without gifts, though," I whisper to Adriana as we leave. "Try not to rub it in."

"Forsaken? Oh, that's so sad!" Adriana says, looking over her shoulder at the girl, now sitting on a bench, staring at her feet. I think Adriana might feel genuine pity for her, and I realize that I do too. She's like a clipped bird. Adriana actually puts a hand over her mouth, like she's worried Delphine might hear her.

"And she's trapped here?"

"Her parents died," Wren explains, walking quickly. "Tekton is her uncle, and he's the temple's guardian, so she's here."

"Shame," Adriana says, twirling a piece of her hair. "You know, he's kind of cute, for an ungifted."

The sooner we get her out of here, the better.

CHAPTER 28
LEO

My Wren,

We're on our way to Roallac. I'm reminded of the fact that while the gods gifted my family with the Book of Gold, they did not bestow the same divine prestige on the rulers of Roallac. Though it has never been my desire, it is a long-held belief of some in Ocron that the Book of Gold means that Ocron should rule over not just our country but the world. I do not know why the gods neglected our neighbors so—I must regret the invasion of your homeland in Aclines; it was necessary to gain the port access—but I certainly have no wish to rule over Roallac. I am much more fond of the people and the rolling plains of my own country. Roallac is a country of snakes, and I'm afraid I mean that both literally and figuratively.

I think I must write to you often, to stave off the boredom of the road.

It's either that or try to talk to Zale. The man is as loquacious as a rock. Or Lady Orothea, who I believe is still trying to get her claws into me. She's used her family's home near the Roallac border as an excuse to accompany us. Gods help me.

Thinking of you is an infinitely nicer pastime.

Yours,
    Leo

CHAPTER 29

WREN

First the run-in with Dimitra and Mariana, now Aris's sister—
the bullies at the School of the Silver Flame look lame by
comparison. I fantasize briefly about how things might have been
different if I'd stayed—if Saroya hadn't kicked me out, that is. How it
would have been if I'd just had something like water magic. I could
have stayed in Spit, and my lighthouse ... At the thought of my ruined
home, my eyes start to prickle, so I walk faster and try my best to
think of nothing at all except how not to get lost.

In the library, I'm greeted by crows of triumph from Caelus and
Tekton. Neither appears to have slept. While Caelus's Shield magic
gives him the ability to go for days without sleep, Tekton has no such
talent—his eyes are red-rimmed, though there is an infectious smile
on his face.

"I see you've managed to find another shirt since I saw you last,"
Adriana says, slinking in behind me. She takes a seat at the table,
crossing her legs, the hem of her ... shirt riding up indecently. Wasn't
Tekton wearing that shirt yesterday?

I look at Aris, but he just shakes his head wearily.

"And we've made excellent progress," Caelus says, spreading a sheaf of papers out in front of him, looking for one in particular.

Mariana, Dimitra, and Rafael trail in shortly. Caelus finds what he was looking for, seizes it, and holds it high, bringing the room's attention from Adriana's enviably long legs back to more important matters.

"Not only do we know *what* the books do—we know *where* to find the Book of Silver," he says, slamming the paper back down on the table.

It's a map, I see. I walk around the table to get a better look.

"What the books *do*?" Aris asks. "They're books."

"Magic books," Caelus corrects him. "They give whoever is in possession of them the ability to communicate directly with the gods, whichever one they wish. Like how Wren and the god of night can talk in visions and dreams. They can ask for guidance, or for miracles, maybe. That's why the Book of Silver and the Book of Bronze were hidden—no mortal should have that kind of power."

"But King Leonidas has the Book of Gold," Aris says.

I wince. I haven't told him what Leo told me in one of his recent letters—actually, I haven't let Aris read any of them. He might misinterpret Leo's playful banter.

"His family has long been able to withstand the temptation to abuse the book," Tekton says. "That's why they stayed in power. No fool would dare go up against a family with the gods on its side."

"You've been a guardian here how long, and you're just figuring this out?" Mariana asks.

Tekton turns red. "I've been busy," he mumbles. "It's a lot of work, keeping up the temple alone."

"No one's blaming you," I say, putting a hand on his shoulder and shooting Mariana a glare. She flips her hair back over her shoulder. "It hasn't really mattered before. But you said you also know *where* the Book of Silver is?"

"It had to be hidden someplace where no one would be able to get to it," Tekton says, looking down at the map.

I see the wide expanse of Ocron. My old home, Spit, is in the far southeast corner, barely more than a single wiggle of land. To the northeast, the larger mass of Roallac, with the wetlands on its southern point. To the east, the Isles.

After that, my knowledge of geography fades. But it turns out there's more to the west of Ocron.

A lot more.

A massive archipelago arches like a jagged crescent moon, the open side facing Ocron. North of it, another landmass, slightly smaller than Roallac, left mostly blank. Caelus stabs it with a finger.

"Why is it blank?" Dimitra asks, hovering over my shoulder.

I fight the urge to drive my elbow into her gut.

"It's not blank," Caelus says, grinning. "It's ice. And mountains. But mostly ice."

"Ice?" I repeat. "What, the whole thing?"

"The whole thing," he says.

I've never seen him so excited. It's kind of strange, actually.

"Why ice?" Aris asks.

"Why *this* ice?" Dimitra adds.

"It's impossible to reach, except during the summer. In the summer, this land never sees a night sky. The sun stays up for months at a time, melting the ice just enough to uncover the resting place of the book."

"So why has no one gotten it before now?"

"The vault has to be opened by use of the magic of the six gods," Caelus continues. "All six. Wren is the only one in the history of the world to have the power of the god of night—Wren can open that vault. She has the power of the night—the fire of the stars, the earth of the moon, the water of the tides, and wind of the turning of the world. Plus she has the healing of Lord Rigrasil."

The room falls silent as the gravity of his words soaks in. I can open it. I can get the book—and with it? I can talk to the gods, maybe even the elemental ones. I can find out what Caladrius is after. I can ask the other gods to stop sending their messengers after me and getting innocent people killed.

A log on the fire crackles and splits, the sound so suddenly loud that I flinch.

"I, um, hate to point out the obvious here," Rafael says. Everyone turns, even Adriana, to look at him. He's standing by the fire, his gaze unfixed as he thinks. "But if the ice only melts under the summer sun, when there's no night for months on end, then how is Wren supposed to access her magic to open the thing?"

He's right. My magic only works at night, and—conveniently—there will *be* no night.

Shit. Whoever hid this thing *really* thought it through.

"Wait, why does Wren's magic only work at night, when Shield magic works all the time?" Adriana asks. "Since it's a gift from the god of day, shouldn't it only work during the day?"

I shake my head. I have no idea.

"Maybe Rigrasil is just stronger," Aris says with a grin.

I jab an elbow into his side. He jostles me back.

"So what, we find the place during the summer then camp out until it gets dark again? How long would that take?" Rafael asks.

"I am not 'camping out' on the side of some gods-damned mountain waiting for Wren's magic to decide to cooperate," Mariana huffs.

"The light of the god of day often reflects into the night—maybe Wren's magic will work even if the sun hasn't set," Caelus says.

"I'm getting a headache," Mariana says. "Why don't we just go in the winter, then, and melt the snow in the way? It's just frozen water. Between Rafael and me, I bet we could take it down."

"I'm sorry. Did I hear you correctly?" I ask. "You're offering to help me?"

"For the good of the country, of course," she says. But a smile sneaks across her face anyway, and I feel a glimmer of hope. I'd assumed that Mariana – and the rest of our party – would return to Estana now that we'd reached the temple.

"Not even an army of Water Mages could take down that much ice," Caelus says. "And you don't even know where to start looking—the location is only revealed in the summer. Plus, in the winter, with the storms, you'd be lucky to even find it, not to mention find a ship that would take you there."

"We could try," Rafael offers.

Mariana beams at him.

"Let's just ... think for a second," Tekton says, leaning back. He strokes his beard with one hand. "Wren, do you want to write all that down and send it to the king? Maybe his academics know something about this."

"Leo would definitely want to know about this. Panos too," I say, taking the proffered paper and quill.

"May I have some too?" Mariana asks, uncharacteristically polite. "My family lives up near the Roallac border. If Wren is sending a letter to the king there, can you carry one for me as well?"

Adriana shrugs. "Sure."

Aris's eyes narrow at Mariana, but he doesn't say anything, just stands there with his arms crossed, looking broody and too damned handsome.

"I need some tea," Tekton says, standing—and a little wobbly. "Maybe let's break for a while, clear our heads, come back to it in a bit."

"Is breakfast involved?" Rafael says.

Tekton grins. "Of course."

By nightfall, no one has come up with any brilliant ideas. Aris, Dimitra, and Caelus have gone off to work in the collapsed tunnel, helping Tekton shift some of the debris. Adriana has flown away. I stay in the library, flipping through the books that are actually in a language I can read. There's a lot of history about the place. It seems a lot of people kept hoping for the god of night to bestow his powers the way that the other gods had given theirs—people flocked to his temple, enlarging the warrens, donating priceless artifacts in an attempt to get his attention. They all failed. The god of night was waiting for me, it seems, though it still isn't clear why. My mysterious benefactor has not made an appearance since that vision here.

Tekton startles me by appearing at the door to the library. It's late, and he's coated in dust like he was the first time I saw him. He's grinning widely, his hands to either side of the doorway.

"Are you busy, Night Mage?" he asks, unable to keep the excitement from his voice.

"No epiphanies so far, I'm afraid. Why?" I ask, closing a book.

He beams. "Come with me. There's something you need to see."

I trail after him, pestering him with questions, but I get no response other than a mysterious promise that whatever he's about to show me will be worth the wait. He takes me back to the central cavern with Caladrius's statue, then down another corridor. This one ends in a large room with a spiraling staircase. Tekton's brought a lantern, and its light reflects off the polished black stone. We go up. And up. And up. I'm starting to get short of breath, despite a lifetime of climbing stairs back at my lighthouse, though that was only three flights—we've gone up what feel like dozens.

Finally we come to a door.

"We call this part of the temple the Mountain's Edge," he says proudly, and he opens it.

We're standing on a granite balcony with a balustrade of delicate stone spindles as high as my chest, so perfect they must be the work of a very talented Earth Mage. We're high up on the side of the mountain, and the air is crisp and cold and clear. I wrap my black robe tighter around me, grateful for whatever spell Panos and Ismini put on it to keep it so cozy. It might look like silk, but it feels like a big wool blanket right now. Tekton seems unfazed by the cold, or maybe he's just used to it. He ushers me out farther onto the balcony. The little valley that Aeturnus is snuggled in seems to be the only relatively inhabitable space around for miles, with a little trickling river to its far side. I can see for miles across snowcapped mountains.

And above us—swirling rivers of jade-green light float across the starlit sky, mixed with streamers of red, blue, yellow, white, and emerald. It's the most breathtaking thing I've ever seen. Something in me awakens, the orb of black magic at my core sparking in recognition. *This* is the god of night's true magic—the Sacred Wind. Ribbons of color twist and flow, casting their flickering light across the landscape. And I'm surprised to see it isn't just green—in the way that my magic isn't just the magic of the god of night but that of the elemental gods too. A flash of red, a streak of blue. All mixed together, like painting with light.

"It's not usually so clear," Tekton says, leaning on the railing beside me. "Lord Caladrius is welcoming you home, indeed." A light breeze ruffles his hair, and he inhales deeply, savoring the night air. He's so at home here it makes me miss my lighthouse even more.

I let green light flicker around my fingers, holding it aloft—the shade is an exact match. We watch the lights dance in silence for a long time, until even with the robe, my nose and ears are burning with cold.

Up here the words of Caladrius echo in my mind: *Welcome home.* And it does feel like home. I'm up high in a tower, like my lighthouse. There's nothing and no one, except Tekton and the sleepy town far below us. The night sky unfurls before me, the stars brighter than I've ever seen them before. I close my eyes, and I can almost smell the salt of the ocean on the cold breeze, almost hear the sound of waves on rock. My chest aches. I never thought I would miss the lighthouse so much—and it's gone now, completely destroyed by the god of water's kraken.

"I grew up in a lighthouse," I tell Tekton. He's resting his forearms on the stone railing. He waits patiently for me to continue. "It … well, it almost makes me feel at home up here. So thank you."

Tekton is quiet a long time, the green light casting shadows across his face.

"You were the guardian and caretaker of your lighthouse, the way I am the guardian and caretaker of the temple," he says.

I nod to confirm.

"We are more alike than I would have thought, Night Mage," he says.

"Call me Wren," I say.

He nods, keeping his gaze fixed on the green lights.

We stand like this for a long time, in comfortable silence, until the night grows late. I'm more at peace now than I can remember being in a long, long time.

A cloud passes over the face of the moon, momentarily blocking the light. Something occurs to me then, a thought so outlandish that it must have been inspired by Caladrius himself.

I've figured out how to get to the Book of Silver.

I grin, hope filling me from my toes all the way up to my frozen ears. I open my mouth to tell Tekton, but before I can—

A roar echoes up the stairs behind us, shaking the very mountain with its rage.

CHAPTER 30
ARIS

Honestly, clearing out the collapsed tunnel is a good distraction. There is another exit from the temple here, and we can cart the boulders and other debris out there and basically dump them off the edge of the cliff. We repair what we can and chuck the rest.

I think this corridor must have been some sort of storage. We come across a room full of musty old black cloaks, spare carts, ropes, all kinds of things. Another room is full of dried food—beans mostly —enough to supply the temple for ages, if they didn't mind eating like Shields.

It's around midnight when something glitters on the ground, catching my eye. I've just hefted yet another boulder into the cart. Caelus and Dimitra are working in a nearby room, checking to make sure nothing has been spoiled or needs to be replaced, though there's no sign of the rats Tekton mentioned. I pick up my lantern from its perch on a bit of rubble behind me and bend to look at the object. Despite this being a temple for a god, there has been nothing of worth here, no jewels or precious metals or art besides the single statue. Either Caladrius is not an ostentatious god, or what things of value this place did have, they have been sold off over time as interest in the god of night has waned.

The glittering object is about the size of my palm, glossy black with glints of blood red. I turn it over—it is roughly diamond-shaped, and so thin at the edges that it is almost translucent. Perhaps it is a sliver of obsidian, or a shard from a stained-glass window, though I actually haven't seen any of those around. I am amazed that this hasn't been broken by the frequent cave-ins that this part of the temple seems to experience.

That's when it hits me. It isn't a rock or a gem or a piece of glass.

It is a scale.

A really, *really* big one.

And judging by how little wear there is on the edges, and the lack of dust on the surface, it isn't that old.

A shiver goes through me, something like fear clawing up my spine. I turn the scale over in my hand, tracing the paper-thin edges, visions of massive serpents and monstrous reptiles dancing before my eyes. What if we aren't as safe in the temple as we thought?

What if the story of the monster lurking here in the temple is true?

Wren.

She's in the library. Caelus and Dimitra are with me. Rafael and Mariana are likely occupied with each other. That leaves only Tekton, who slipped out to "check on his niece" a few hours ago and, I realize now, never returned.

Fuck.

Is Tekton a Shield after all? Has he been playing us all along, ingratiating himself with us, for some wicked purpose? Is he an agent of some other god, luring us into a false sense of security so that we let our guard down around Wren?

I am faster as a tiger, so I shift immediately, the scale clattering to the ground. I race out of the chamber. Dimitra calls after me, but there's no time to stop and explain.

I careen into the cavern with the statue of Caladrius, my claws gouging lines into the stone as I turn, and then down another corridor to the dining hall, and then the library.

The library is empty, Wren's book lying closed neatly on the table. Has Tekton lured her out of here somehow? It's night, which means her power is at its fullest. She wouldn't go down without a fight—but I don't hear the sounds of a struggle, or screams. Surely in this maze of rock, that kind of sound would travel.

Calm down, I tell myself, but all the while my mind is alive with echoes of Stefan, my first Mage, and the death that I caused. *Not again, not again, not again.*

Maybe she was just tired and went to bed. I reach for the bond we share, the magical chime I can hear that ties me to her presence. It's a distant silver bell, as always, and I am somewhat reassured that she can't be that far off.

But it's not coming from the direction of our bedroom.

I race through the halls, my paws eating up the distance, my ears swiveling to catch the slightest sound of Wren, my nose flaring – but I catch neither sound nor scent of her.

I finally reach a wide room with a spiraling staircase that disappears out of view, spelled torches casting light over the space. I can feel the pull of the claim, the bond between a Shield and their Mage, in that direction. Wren went up those stairs, which means I should too.

But the way up the stairs is blocked.

In my way is a wall of black scales, and a tail ten feet long slithers across the floor with a dry sound like a snake. The creature has been looking up the stairs, like it wants to go up them too. It turns a wedge-shaped head toward me, yellow eyes scored with vertical pupils that narrow when they fix on me, bared fangs bigger than my hand gleaming white in the darkness. Smoke curls from its nostrils.

A dragon.

A gods-damned *dragon* is between me and my Mage. No one has seen a dragon in ages, maybe millennia—so what the actual *fuck* is it doing here? A dragon could be the agent of the god of fire, I realize.

So much for Wren being "untouchable" here. So much for her darling god of night's protection.

I roar my challenge. The dragon must be six feet at the shoulder, with feathered black wings folded along its back. It shrinks back toward the staircase, like it could climb them and escape—or climb them and get to Wren.

So Tekton is a dragon Shield? Is that even fucking possible? And I admit, I might be a tiny bit jealous. The exits from this room are too small for a dragon to have come in here, though—he must have shifted once he got here, after imprisoning Wren at the top of those stairs, like a princess in children's stories. My tail swishes as I prowl, teeth bared. Tekton might be a whole lot bigger than me right now, but I've got years of fighting experience on my side. He must realize this, too – he's practically cowering, the tip of his tail shaking against the floor.

Plus, Dimitra and Caelus have finally caught up. A tiger, a leopard, and a wolf against this beast? I'm starting to like my odds and ready myself in a crouch, my Shield magic flaring through me, filling me with strength.

And then Tekton is running down the staircase. Wren is close on his heels, one hand clapped over her mouth in astonishment. Tekton's eyes are so wide I can see the whites all the way around.

Tekton.

It takes a second to register. The dragon is not Tekton.

"No!" he yells, still running. He leaps down the last steps and lands between me and the dragon, putting a hand on the thing's chest. "Stop! Don't hurt her!"

What in the *hells*?

And then the dragon shifts. Black scales give way to pale, dirty legs.

And it's Delphine.

Tekton shrugs off his thick coat and gives it to the girl, covering her small frame all the way to the floor. He puts an arm around her shoulders and sighs. He pinches the bridge of his nose, like his head hurts, like he's trying to think of some lie to tell us to keep us from ... well, something. Locking them up, fighting them, tossing them off the mountain—though I guess in Delphine's case that last one wouldn't do much good. A *dragon* Shield. *Gods.*

The rest of us, though, have not shifted back. Caelus's hackles are raised, and Dimitra's lips remain pulled back in a snarl.

Tekton and Delphine have got a lot of explaining to do.

Wren comes to me, putting one hand on my back. Green light crackles in her other palm, reflecting in the unblinking glare she's giving them.

"I didn't want you all to find out like this," Tekton says, rubbing the back of his neck.

"You didn't want us to find out at all," Wren says accusingly.

He winces but doesn't deny it. "Can we just—it's late. She usually comes here and gets some flying practice at night but ... can I put her to bed, and then meet you in the library? I'll explain everything, I swear."

A growl rumbles in my throat. Tekton droops a little, but his arm stays protectively around Delphine. Shy, barefoot little Delphine. A dragon Shield. Lord Rigrasil certainly has a strange sense of humor. Either that, or magic has become way more twisted than we realized.

"Just ... bring some tea," Wren says wearily, her fingers stroking the ruffled fur on my neck. The green light in her palm gutters and goes out. "I have a feeling it's going to be a long night."

We follow Tekton and Delphine out of the room and through the corridors. Wren and I stop by our room so I can get dressed. Wren, as usual, keeps her back turned toward me when I shift. If she'd still rather look at the blank wall than at my naked form, well ... it's almost enough to injure my considerable pride. Almost.

By the time we get to the library, the rest are there, even Rafael and Mariana, though Mariana's long hair is mussed, and Rafael is only wearing one sock.

A moment later Tekton enters with a kettle and a stack of cups. He sets the kettle on a swinging arm over the fire, fidgeting with it for a long minute.

Six sets of eyes stare at him silently, waiting for answers.

"I'm sorry I didn't tell you," he starts to say.

"More like you're sorry we found out," Mariana says, crossing her arms.

"Let him say his piece," Dimitra scolds her.

Mariana scowls but stays quiet.

"What I told you about us is mostly true. I was born without a Shield's magic, though the rest of my family is gifted. Delphine, though … well, my sister thought she was ungifted too, that there was some sort of curse on the family, or that magic was fading from our bloodline, as we'd heard it was from some others. The day we found out my sister and her husband had died was the first time Delphine shifted."

Tekton takes the whistling kettle off the fire and pours us each a mug, letting the activity ease his nerves for a moment. He drops a spoonful of ash from a small bowl into the Shields' mugs, ever the considerate host.

"She burned down our house, that first time," Tekton says after a moment, now settling himself into one of the chairs at the table. "The second time, she accidentally killed one of the neighbors, who had dropped by to offer his condolences. After that, I knew I had to get her out of there, at least until she had some control over her shifting and fire-breathing. It's another reason this job was so appealing—it was as remote as I could get."

"Why didn't you bring her east, let her train with other Shields?" Caelus asks.

Tekton straightens. "What better place for her than with family?" he says. "She's not old enough for your school, not for a few more years. I wanted her to have time to grow into her abilities first."

"So Delphine is the temple monster?" Rafael asks.

Tekton nods. "I'm afraid so. We mostly practice her flying at night, when she's less likely to be spotted."

"Has there ever been a dragon Shield before?" Wren asks.

I shake my head. "Never. We're always predators, usually mammals, and some birds, like Adriana. I've heard of a crocodile Shield once before, and I've heard that the navy has a shark Shield, but that's it."

"So where did Delphine come from?" Wren asks.

"A good question for the god of night," Caelus says.

"If only we had the damned Book of Silver," Mariana says with a sigh. "Or if only Wren could get enough control to access her visions herself."

Wren flushes but doesn't retort. I move to grasp her hand in mine, to reassure her—she gives me a brief squeeze before letting go.

"Well, we can't get the book," Rafael says, "so maybe we should focus more on helping Wren with her magic, see if we can trigger another vision."

"That's ... maybe not true," Wren says.

Six heads swivel to stare at her.

"What?" Mariana says.

"I've figured out how to get the book," she says.

In that moment, I swear none of us dares so much as blink. Even Mariana is on the edge of her seat.

"Well?" Mariana asks, breathless.

"An eclipse," Wren says.

Tekton's mug clatters to the table, a few drops spilling. The sound makes Rafael jump.

But damn it all, she's right.

Night during the day. Wren would be able to access her powers, and then we could get into the vault with the Book of Silver, together.

"*Dies tenebrosa sicut nox,*" Caelus says in awe. "A day as dark as night."

"Let's say you're right," Rafael says, steepling his hands on the table. "Eclipses are rare, but that aside, should we even get the book? I mean, I trust you, Wren, but should any one person have access to that kind of power?"

"Leo does. It hasn't corrupted him so far, or his family," I say.

Wren shoots me a look but doesn't say anything.

"So why the fuck did we come all the way out here when we could have just used the Book of Gold?" Dimitra asks.

"We didn't know we *could* use it," Rafael reminds her.

"So we go back to Estana and get it," Dimitra says, crossing her arms.

"Back through the tunnels—where there are bound to be more trolls—and across the entire continent? Are we just supposed to hope another manticore doesn't get us?" Mariana huffs. "No, thank you. We've come this far. And no one's seen the Book of Silver in a hundred years. Where's your sense of adventure? Don't you want to be the one who finds it?"

Rafael frowns but doesn't contradict her.

"People are dying," Wren says quietly. "The troll attacks. The kraken at Spit. The manticore on the Western Road. I don't ... I can't let this continue."

"So then we need an eclipse," I say. "Tekton, do you know anything about them? Have a book or something that could help?"

"No. We go back," Dimitra says, lifting her chin. She stares me down, like she used to when I was a recruit.

"We lose nothing by learning a little more before we make a decision," Caelus says tactfully.

I turn from Dimitra.

"Well," Tekton says, rubbing his chin. "I know someone who can help."

CHAPTER 31
LEO

My Wren,

That is grave news indeed. Access to the Book of Silver would be the most remarkable thing to happen in our generation—aside from yourself, of course. But please be careful—a lot of very dangerous people would kill to get their hands on it.

I am sending word to Commander Markos about your young Shield friend. Though she seems unusual, I have no doubt he will do his best to help her. Please let Tekton know that he has my personal assurance that she will be safe and well cared for, should she wish to come east. If not, Panos is already curating a stack of books that they should find helpful. I'll send them by horse as soon as I can.

I have arrived at Roallac. The queen has been quite gracious, and we were treated to a show from her Water Mages which was most impressive. I am optimistic that a friendship may develop between our countries at last.

Stay safe, little bird.

. . .

Yours,
    Leo

CHAPTER 32

WREN

"What if the next eclipse is in a thousand years?" Aris asks when we get back to our room.

I frown. I'd been worrying about that too.

I start folding clothes and stuffing them back into my pack, just to give my hands something to do. We haven't exactly decided when we're going to leave to meet Tekton's acquaintance, but I want to be ready to go when we do. He and Caelus still want to smooth out a few more details before we leave. How many more people have to die while the gods toy with me? What if I were to let them have me, then, and be done with it? Would the mutilations, the destruction, all stop?

"I have to believe that I was given this gift for a reason," I say, snapping the pack shut and fiddling with the buckle. I will not give in. I do not give up. That has never been my nature, and I'm sure as all the hells not going to start now. "What's the point of being the Night Mage if I can't get to the book?"

"Why don't we just use the Book of Gold to talk to Caladrius? Make our way back to Estana? That seems a whole hells of a lot easier. I'm sure Leo would let you borrow it, if you ask him nicely."

I glare at Aris, and he smirks. He seems to think that I have some sort of crush on Leo still, that I have some power over him.

"You're agreeing with Dimitra?" I ask, raising an eyebrow.

Aris throws his hands up. "She has a point is all I'm saying," he says. "I don't want to put you in any more danger than we already have. At least in that direction, I know the risks. But if you feel that this is the way we should go, then we'll go. I'm with you, to the end."

I'm so distracted by this train of thought that I don't realize Aris has moved, like a predator cornering its prey, until he strikes—pinning me between his arms against the wall, the way he did ages ago at Leo's party.

And just like before, my stomach flutters like a nervous bird, making my breath catch—and he knows it.

He turns the full force of those sky-blue eyes on me, leaning in to whisper softly in my ear. "And what if the next eclipse is a long, long time from now? What should we do in the meantime, do you think?"

"I don't know," I say, my ability to form rational thoughts suddenly vanishing.

He leans down, slowly, giving me plenty of time to pull away if I want to—but I don't. He kisses me softly, teasing me, leaning his hard body against mine until I melt, my hands sliding around his neck and into his soft black hair. I haven't kissed him since the tunnels, and *gods*, how I've missed it. Everything about him feels warm and solid and unyielding, and for a moment, I believe all the gods could throw their very worst at us, and nothing would come of it. They'd break against him like waves against rock.

"Have you forgiven me yet?" he asks, nuzzling the place where my neck and shoulder meet.

"No," I whisper, though there's no venom in it, no conviction. I'm worried he'll be upset, but his eyes sparkle, like he can hear the doubt in my voice.

"Pity," he says, kissing me again, and when he pulls away, my traitorous body follows before I can stop it. "How can I change your mind?"

"I don't know," I admit.

He pulls back, watching me for a moment. "I am yours," he says simply.

My insides melt. He sounds like he means it, or at least he believes he does.

"I just … I don't know how to do this. Us," I fumble, waving a hand between us.

He catches it, and I can tell he feels the shaking in my fingers. He links his own with mine, holding my hand softly against his chest. Something is running through his mind, and I desperately want to know what it is.

"What is it?" I get up the courage to ask.

"I don't know how to do this either," he says, with a half smile.

His confession breaks the tension a little, and I let him pull me into him, let him wrap his arms around me, rest his chin against the top of my head. It feels so good there, being held, being warm and safe, hearing the soft, slow beat of his heart. To be with Aris—not just sleeping with him but truly *with* him. To want *him*, not his body —or at least, not just that. To learn the great depth of his emotions under that arrogant mask he wears—his rage, his loyalty, his passion. To want to *know* him. To want to call him mine, not just my Shield. I've always been alone, but in a way—despite his bevy of lovers—so has he. We are in uncharted seas.

After a moment, I feel Aris clear his throat.

"Nestor gave my mother a ring. It meant little to him, an empty promise, something he could use to bind her to him. There was no loyalty there—not on his part, anyway. That tradition means little, from what I've seen."

A ring. Gods. Aris *is* serious. I'm glad my face is still buried against his chest, because I'm sure my face is as dark red as a Tamdosan rose.

"It means something to me," I mumble, the words leaving my lips before I think. My father wore his until the day he died, a promise to the woman he would always love. In accordance with

Aclinese tradition, I threw it into the sea after he died. I cried parting with it, but I knew my mother's ring was out there too, somewhere, and I took solace in knowing that at least in some way, they'd always be together.

Aris pulls back, and his eyes search mine for a long moment. He bends and gives me another kiss, soft and sweet. I want to capture this moment, when we seem like the only two people in the world, like our little frail beginning is more important than gods and metal books and man-eating beasts. When he makes me feel like I am the only one for him in the entire crazy world.

He cups my cheek for a moment, then steps back, running a hand through the hair I've mussed, tying it back. He lets out a long breath, hands on hips, assessing the room. I'm left feeling flustered and confused all over, my skin tight and tingling and overly warm. He turns and goes to pack his own things, keeping his eyes trained on his task, not meeting mine.

"Come on. Let's go chase the moon, princess."

"Do your swords have names?" Delphine asks.

Aris snorts. "They are swords, not pets."

"All the great heroes name their swords. Odall the First Shield named his," she counters. She's seated at the base of the statue of Caladrius. Her dirty bare feet swing back and forth as she talks. "God's Light and Sun Fury."

"What would you name them?" I ask.

She frowns, considering. "I'd have to think about it," she says, with a gravitas that belies her age.

I guess when you only have Tekton to talk to, you don't get to be a silly little girl much. As much as I'm coming to like Tekton, I'm seeing myself in Delphine's situation, a girl in a tower, without much companionship. A girl alone. She doesn't even have animal friends to keep her company. She studies her bare toes for a moment, frowning in concentration.

"Such an important decision should not be made lightly," she ultimately decides.

Aris nods gravely.

"Oh! Here, I made you something," she says. "So you don't forget me." She pulls out a cleverly knotted bit of leather and gestures for Aris to give her his wrist. He does so, with one eyebrow raised, as she loops it around and secures it. He raises it, inspecting the bracelet with a satisfied nod.

"It's well made," he says. She beams at the compliment, swinging her legs, and *gods* for a moment I have to smother a giggle at her unashamed awe at him.

We're waiting in the cavern with Caladrius's statue for the others. Delphine seems much more friendly since we discovered her secret, and I'm happy to think about anything for a moment besides Aris and *rings*, for goodness' sake.

"Can't I come with you?" Delphine pleads, pouting her lower lip. "I haven't been *anywhere*."

"Commander Markos will be a good mentor," Aris says, with more patience than I've probably ever seen from him. He's sitting at the base of the statue, next to her, talking to her like an equal—and I guess she is. She's a Shield, like he is, even if she's a bit unconventional. It'll be a brotherhood for her. I can only hope the Shields will accept her better than the Mages at the school accepted me. With Saroya gone, she may have a chance.

And if the Shields turn on her, I'll help Aris tear the school apart.

"Tekton will bring you to the school when it's time. I will visit you there," Aris continues.

"Promise?" she asks, gazing up at him.

He nods gravely. "I promise. *Juncti nitimur.* Together we strive. It's an old Shield saying."

"What if they don't like me? What if I'm too different?" Delphine asks, and something inside my chest cracks.

Gods. This child is a miracle, but she's still a child, with a child's fears.

Aris doesn't belittle her concern.

"They might not like you," he admits.

Delphine looks crestfallen, and I'm afraid he might make her cry. I move to sit on her other side. I don't touch her, don't put an arm around her or anything, but she appreciates the closeness and leans into me a little. I give Aris a reproachful look over Delphine's head. Was it so very long ago that I was at the school, in the same position?

Aris clears his throat. "Let me tell you something," he starts.

She sniffles and looks up at him, her dark eyes red-rimmed.

"Shields are competitive by nature," he says. "If they don't like you, it's because they know you're stronger than they are."

"Really?" she asks. "A freak like me? I've never even had any real training."

"You are not a freak," I say firmly.

"You are the first dragon Shield in the history of the world," Aris reminds her. "And a friend of me and the Night Mage. You'll receive personal training from the Shield Commander himself. In a few years, Mages will be falling all over themselves to be paired with you at the games. So who cares if a few stupid Shields don't like you? We like you just fine, and so will your future Mage."

I'm not prepared for Delphine's reaction. She lets out a strangled sound, throws her arms around Aris's neck, and holds him tightly. He hesitates for a moment before hugging her in return, patting her back as she struggles to contain her emotions.

"*Vires, honos, fides,*" he tells her. "Strength, honor, faith. Have faith, little dragon."

Aris meets my gaze over her messy hair again. Watching them together brings a pang to my chest, and I remember Dimitra's words from the other day: *What do you envision? The two of you living together happily in a little home somewhere, a litter of baby abominations playing at your feet? He is a wild thing.* I have to look away and busy myself with tying and retying the straps on my pack.

"All ready, then?" Tekton says, striding into the space and breaking me out of my dark thoughts. His small pack looks a little ridiculous on his massive frame.

I shake my head, trying to get focused on the task at hand. We stayed up far too late planning this trip. Tekton will take us as far as the tunnel's first junction. From there, he promises a straight shot to Basti, which is a small town on the coast, and the home of the astronomer.

Dimitra, Rafael, Mariana, and Caelus aren't far behind. Caelus has his nose in a book—Tekton has lent him a few, and I am glad of Caelus's enhanced strength, because that bag of his must weigh a ton now. He's even added a second satchel that hangs across his chest.

Tekton hugs Delphine farewell, and she promises to behave for the day or so before he returns.

"No shifting," she swears solemnly.

It's strange how attached I already feel to the temple. The morning sun shines on the polished obsidian of the columns, already warming them. I have felt peaceful here, knowing I was sheltered from whatever the elemental gods were throwing at us, but I can't stay here forever, caged. Not when innocent people are dying. Not when answers are out there, somewhere. My stomach tightens as we start down the steps, my skin growing chillier the farther we go.

We walk through the town and back up the other side of the valley to a tunnel near the one we entered Aeturnus from. Once there, it is a few hours' hike up, down, and around as the tunnel rambles along. This one doesn't seem to be punctuated by any mines, like the others. It's just made for travel through the mountains. We move quietly, none of us happy about being back underground. We don't even stop for meals. Tekton just doles out bread and cheese and a waterskin, and we keep going. I wonder if we'll encounter any more of Cephus's mountain trolls on this trek. The tunnel seems too small for them, which does give me some small amount of comfort. Aris is even more on edge, but I think that has more to do with the enclosed space than the risk of attack. I keep close to him, and I think it helps both of us.

By nightfall—though time is hard to judge, and I'm forced to rely on whether or not I can feel my magic awaken—we make camp at the first junction. Down the left tunnel, Tekton promises we'll reach Basti in two or three days. These passageways are narrow—barely wide enough for two people across—but the junction is a relatively open space, and we are able to camp relatively comfortably. Gods, I already miss the bed back in the temple. I thought I'd grown accustomed to sleeping on the ground during our travels, but here there aren't even mice or snakes or groundhogs to keep me company. No soft grasses to lay my blankets over. Just cold, unforgiving stone.

Rafael casts a spelled fire in the middle, warding off the worst of the chill and giving us plenty of light that needs no fuel. I nestle down in my bedroll, trying to get comfortable—and watch Aris and Dimitra talk quietly by the fire.

ARIS

After our last surprise in these gods-forsaken tunnels, I'm not taking any chances. Rafael's got this space well lit, and the Shields stay up, watching and listening.

Wren falls asleep almost instantly, but she isn't peaceful. She's tossing and turning, and I start to wonder if she's having another nightmare, one of those ones where Caladrius appears. When she spoke about his visits—the pain he inflicts when he talks or even looks at her—I'd never felt so helpless, and I hated it. He's not something I can protect her from. It is my single duty as her Shield, and I fail. I cannot protect her from this immortal asshole. The feeling of impotence is overwhelming. I wonder if Caelus would know something, anything about how to help her, but I don't ask. To do so would be to give voice to my fears, and I'd rather keep those to myself.

Otherwise, it's a quiet night. Dimitra and I swap stories about old missions, like the time the four of us—Dimitra, Rafael, me, and Stefan—were dispatched to help some Water Mages put out a wildfire.

"It took Rafael's singed eyebrows a year to grow back." She grins. "He was mortified."

"Was not," he grumbles from his bedroll, eyes closed.

Dimitra chuckles. "He was," she whispers to me, leaning closer. For a moment, the firelight brushes her skin with gold, and her eyes shine up at me.

I look away. She clears her throat, sitting up. Caelus returns from a brief patrol down one of the tunnels, having found nothing of interest. He pulls a book out of his pack, one that I haven't seen him read before. Emblazoned on the green cloth cover is a golden dragon.

"What's that?" I ask.

Caelus doesn't look up from the book. "Tekton gave it to me," he says. "Apparently, dragons are the messenger of Lord Ignatius. Strange, don't you think, that a Shield would develop that particular shifting ability?"

"I suppose the god of fire and the god of day have always been closely linked," Dimitra says. "The sun is made of fire, is it not?"

"It is," Caelus says, flipping a page. "Centuries ago this author compiled information on dragons. It's not much, but did you know that when Delphine is fully grown, her scales will be tougher than any armor? After the last dragon was killed by Saint Theramenes, scales from its back were taken and used to make a suit of armor for the Ocronian king."

"I remember that story," I say, thinking back to the tales our housekeeper would tell when she bribed all of us into bed at night. "I thought it was just a myth."

"It's real," Caelus says, turning a page. "Or it was."

I think back to the scale I found while clearing the tunnel. It seemed so delicate, like glass. I wonder aloud if Delphine is vulnerable now, and how long it will be until her scales harden.

"I'm not sure," Caelus answers, flipping over another page. "I'll let you know if I find anything. I do know that her throat and stomach will be the only places steel can penetrate once she reaches maturity. She'll be the toughest of us all, by far."

I like that idea. I think maybe I'll write to Delphine and tell her that. She needs some self-confidence, and that's something I have loads of experience with. Having an impenetrable hide, plus her fire-breathing? The gods themselves will tremble before her. I twist the leather strap on my wrist, thinking.

The rest of the night is uneventful. I ask Caelus if I can borrow his book when he's done. He gives me a strange look—just because I don't often read doesn't mean I can't—but he agrees.

When I ask Wren about her dreams in the morning, she shakes her head. One of her curls has sprung loose from her braid and threatens to fall across her face. I brush it back, tucking it behind her ear.

"No visions," she says.

She is probably lying—I just don't know why. Either she didn't learn anything of use, or she doesn't want me worrying over her. She gives me a peck on the cheek, turning pink at taking such a liberty, before turning and rolling up her bedroll.

She's so different from other women I know. More guarded, more reserved, more serious, though she does have a wicked sense of humor at times. At first I thought her immune to my charms—which is, of course, absurd. Then I thought her indifferent, which I may have taken as a challenge. I know she feels something for me, even if she won't admit it to herself. Something beyond the claim of a Mage and a Shield. Something beyond bedmates. If it takes years, I will crack that exterior shell again. I have to—she is mine, as I am hers.

"You awake?" Dimitra says, punching my shoulder as she passes. She's still pissed that we're not going back to Estana.

I snort and pick up my pack, settling my shield over it and hoisting the whole thing.

The damned trip takes us two more days. Camping in the tunnel is even more claustrophobic than the junction, but we don't have a choice. The Mages can't keep up with us, and they need rest, even if only for a few hours. Every distant noise, every falling pebble, every real or imagined tremor has me reaching for my swords.

Finally, on the evening of the third day after entering the tunnels, we emerge.

Wren shouts, then claps a hand over her mouth. Tears run down her cheeks, and before I realize what I'm doing, I have my arm around her shoulders.

Basti lies down the hillside from us—for that's what we've emerged on, the foothills, with the peaks of the Dragon's Spine range rising behind us like a beast ready to pounce. It's a sprawling town made of brick and wood, covered here and there with thick vines that look like they're trying to choke the life out of the place. Smoke and the smell of fish reach us even here, carried on a cool breeze. Hells, I'll take the stench over the stale air of the tunnels any day.

But Wren's looking beyond the town, at the sea, rolling out before us like a blue blanket all the way to the horizon. There are small chunks of ice in the water here, crowding the harbor mouth, and snow still dusts the houses, though spring is far underway elsewhere on the continent. But Wren's gaze is fixed on the sea, eyes wide, her breath coming in irregular gasps. The sun has just set, and the water ripples with reflections of the pink and gold clouds.

"Homesick?" Rafael asks as he passes, eager to get to the town.

Wren sniffles, then nods, straightening her shoulders and shrugging off my arm. She heads down after Rafael, wiping her face. It's strange to me that she still tries to hide her tears—she didn't care when I was a tiger, before she knew that was just my shifted form. I was her confidant then. But Aris Valorius is not a Shield easily defeated—I will win her confidence back again.

But for now, all I can think of is how badly Basti stinks. I take it back, I'd almost rather be back in the tunnels. The smells here would have overwhelmed my tiger senses—even as a man, I have to breathe through my mouth to keep the odor from making me retch. Mariana holds the sleeve of her robe over her nose—I wonder if a spell in the cloth obscures the smells, which would be pretty damn useful if any of our Mages knew the proper way to replicate that. I'd put one of Rafael's dirty socks over my nose if it was spelled and meant I didn't have to breathe Basti's stink.

We make our way into the town and, after a few moments, find a man who can point us in the direction of the astronomer. It seems he's well known due to his eccentricities. He's in a thin stone tower on the far hill, away from the town a mile or so.

"Says the town lights mess with his delicate instruments." The man snorts, going about his business.

Wren wants to head there immediately. The symmetry of this man's situation and her own is not lost on me—an eccentric in a tower, known by all but somehow still an outsider. I think that Tekton and Delphine and the temple reminded her of her own lighthouse in a good way, of beauty and family and belonging. I wonder if this particular trip will remind her of her lighthouse in another way —how the people of Spit feared her, how she even worried at one point they would physically force her out. Her mother hadn't been from Spit, and so to the miscreants on that rocky peninsula, Wren was an outsider too.

Gods, I'm sounding as philosophical as Caelus now. I need to punch something, to get my blood pumping to my muscles instead of my brain.

"He's an astronomer. He'll be awake all night anyway," Wren argues.

Mariana crosses her arms. She does *not* agree with this plan. The sun has set, and the town looks even less friendly by the minute.

"Can we *please* have a night where we don't have to sleep on rocks first?" Mariana says. "And a bath?"

"The sooner we get answers, the sooner you'll be rid of me," Wren retorts.

Mariana purses her lips, considering.

"I don't like the look of this town," Dimitra says. She's got a knife in each palm, ready for trouble. It's a rough place, and we're already attracting attention.

"Come on," I say, siding with Wren. "Let's just get this over with."

Mariana rolls her eyes and lets out an exasperated sigh, but she follows.

We skirt the town, heading north toward the tower. It takes us about an hour, since the terrain gets rougher the farther we go. Wren is quiet as we take the overgrown path up through the trees. I'm not sure what I hope this astronomer can tell us—I guess that we don't have to wait too long before an eclipse. If we do, we might have to change our plans, go after the Book of Gold or Bronze after all. Caelus has been writing to a friend in Estana, who is quietly trying to track down the Book of Bronze. The librarians in the east are nearly a cult, it seems—fanatical about all books, but especially the divine ones. If anyone is going to know how to find them, it'll be a librarian.

The tower is a tall, shaky-looking thing. The top resembles a lighthouse, with walls of glass and a conical roof, and some strange-looking metal device on a small balcony. It is far larger and more complex than any telescope I've seen before.

There's no light in the tower. Rafael lights the way with a glowing globe—probably just showing off for Mariana—and Wren keeps a steady green glow going around her palms. We're surrounded by dense pine forest—just the kind of place bandits would love. Dimitra does not sheathe her knives, and even Caelus seems on edge, his top lip curled back just a bit, exposing his canines.

Any bandits, even by the score, would be no real contest for three Shields and three Mages.

Dimitra pounds on the door, the force of her fist rattling the rotting wood in the doorframe.

Again.

And again.

No one is answering.

"Maybe he's not home," Mariana says. "Can we go now?"

"Oh, I bet he is. Watch this," Rafael says, winking at her.

He whispers something and pushes his hands upward over his head. A shaft of light as bright as the sun shoots up, illuminating the top of the tower like daylight.

"What in all the *hells* are you doing?" a voice screeches. A figure with long white hair leans over the balcony, squinting down at us. "You're messing up my readings!"

"Oi, astronomer!" Rafael calls. "Can we talk?"

The figure mumbles and disappears. An eternity later, the door before us opens.

He's younger than I would have thought, not yet forty, though his hair is so blond it seems white, like an old man's. He's tall and lean, almost bony. He keeps his gaze fixed on a point on the ground a few feet in front of us, not meeting our eyes.

"What do you want?" he asks. He does not come out but keeps the door between us.

"We want to ask you about an eclipse," Wren says, pushing to the front of our little group.

He looks up briefly, registering her black robe. "Night Mage," he says, returning his gaze to the ground. "Very well. But make it fast."

I'm surprised he knows what she is, black robe or not. Has word of the Night Mage reached even this eccentric hermit? We're not exactly being discreet, but I did hope we wouldn't be attracting too much attention in a town like Basti.

We enter the tower and go up a short flight of stairs to what must serve as a kitchen or dining area—but given the piles of books and papers and bread crusts and apple cores, he doesn't have guests often.

"An eclipse," the hermit mutters, shuffling about the room. He's wearing clothes that were probably black or dark brown once. They're tattered now, as are the old shoes on his feet. I catch a glimpse of mismatched socks.

"Yes," Wren says, crossing her arms. He's not what she expected, clearly. "A complete solar eclipse. When is the next one?"

"Well, that depends," he says, still pacing, wringing his hands.

We wait.

"On what?" Mariana says.

He jumps. "On where you are," he says. "Here, or there, it's different, you see."

"Oh, this was a waste of time," Dimitra mutters. "He's mad."

The astronomer starts sorting through some papers on a table, ignoring ones that flutter to the floor like fall leaves. They're all covered with minute scrawl, page after page of it, front and back, from edge to edge. Words and formulas and detailed drawings— though of what, I have no idea.

"If you are here," he says, still shuffling papers, "you'll be waiting a long time yet. Another three hundred twelve years, six months, and three days."

"Three hundred years?" Wren says, drooping.

"Three hundred twelve," he corrects her. "Six months, and three days."

Wren looks up at me, her brow furrowed. I want to reassure her —if the timing of his eclipse is problematic, then either we don't have the correct information, or this isn't the path she's meant to take. I don't find it disheartening, but the anguish in her jade-colored eyes hits me as hard as a physical blow. She wants an answer, *needs* to understand her roll in all this.

"And if we are not *here*?" Rafael asks after a moment, breaking the deafening silence. Clever Rafael.

"Well, then where are you?" the astronomer asks. He's stopped and is looking at the floor near Rafael's shoes.

"North. In the Abelon Wastes," Rafael says.

The man shrugs. "There you have not long, not long at all," he says, seizing a piece of paper. He squints at it, his mouth moving as he reads.

"How long?" Mariana prompts, crossing her arms.

"Twenty-five days, twenty hours," he says, still looking at the paper.

Wren turns toward me, eyes widening. Twenty-six days, more or less. We could have answers. This mess could be over. Less than a month.

"How long would it take to get there by boat?" Dimitra asks.

"Oh, that depends. It depends," he says. "With fair winds? Not long, not long at all."

Mariana sighs, flipping her elaborate braid over her shoulder. "With a Water Mage like me on board, it won't be a problem," she says.

"Are you done?" the astronomer asks. "The Joquirax meteor won't come this way for another thousand and one years. I must see it. I must."

"Do you have a chart, for this eclipse?" Caelus asks.

The man winces and, without looking, nabs a single piece of paper from a tottering stack.

"Here," he says, thrusting it at Caelus. "Now get out. Just take it."

We're ushered out of the tower, and he slams the door behind us. I can hear his footsteps pounding up the stairs inside as he rushes back to whatever he's been doing.

"Twenty-six days," Wren says as we head back toward town. "Do we believe him?"

"Seems all right," Caelus says. "Raf, a little light, please."

Caelus reads as we walk. There is a small map with a circle drawn on it, and a path running across in an arc—I'm assuming the predicted path of the eclipse, but I don't really get it. Star charts and maps I get. This is another level entirely, but Caelus seems certain that the strange man was right, or at least he was consistent with whatever this piece of paper is telling him.

"So, now what?" Mariana asks. "Please don't tell me we're camping out here tonight. It's late. My feet have blisters. And I'm starving."

"We're all tired," Dimitra says—and she's right. The Shields haven't slept in three days, and that's pushing it, even for us.

"So we find an inn, and then tomorrow—a ship," Wren says,

striding down the hill. She seems invigorated—justified, I guess, like Caladrius gave her powers for exactly this reason, a little less than a month from now.

We find an inn close to the outskirts of town that smells a little less putrid than the rest of the area. There's no bath available. The only room available is one with several bunks in it, though at least our group is the only one occupying it. I take the first watch—uneventful—and once I wake Caelus a few hours later and crawl in beside Wren, I'm asleep within seconds.

CHAPTER 34
WREN

I wake up deliciously warm, Aris's strong arm wrapped around my middle, holding me to him. I savor the contact, listening to his quiet, steady breathing. I lie quietly for a few minutes, enjoying it. I never realized, while sleeping alone, how wonderful it could feel.

I open my eyes to find Dimitra glaring at me from a bunk opposite. My face heats, and I untangle myself and get up, smoothing my hair back. She goes on tying her boots and gathering her numerous knives like she wasn't just watching me—watching us.

Whatever Aris thinks, she's not over him.

She runs her fingers through her cloud of black hair, tying it back. By now, Aris is stirring. He stretches like a cat himself, arching his back and yawning hugely. Mariana, Rafael, and Caelus are nowhere to be found.

The three of us head downstairs to an open dining hall. It's simple, with rustic wooden tables and benches, but clean. We sit by the others and are brought tea and food. A pair of cats find me and twine about my feet as I eat, meowing for attention. I pick up the smaller one, a ginger cat, and pet him while the others finish. The big calico decides to sit on my boots and wash her paws daintily.

"We're going to be cutting it close," Caelus says, spreading a map on the table, anchoring the curling ends with our mugs. "This time of year, they say the weather is unpredictable. We may have trouble finding a ship to take us to the wastelands."

Mariana tosses her silky hair back with a shrug. "A Water Mage is never refused passage," she says. "I'll renew their ship's water-proofing spells. That alone should more than cover the trip."

"How often do those spells get renewed?" Caelus asks.

"About once a year," she says, her fingers drumming on the table. "Of course, the stronger the Mage, the better the spell. Mine will last at least five."

A guarantee that their ship won't sink while the spell holds? I imagine every ship in the port will be eager to have Mariana on board.

"Show off," Dimitra mutters.

Mariana raises an eyebrow—and then, of all things, giggles. This alarms me. When did those two become friends? And have they perhaps bonded in their mutual hatred of me?

Gods, I think sleep deprivation might be making me paranoid. *Fantastic.*

"All right. So Mariana and I will go to the docks and secure passage," Caelus says, rolling up the map. "The rest of you should stock up on supplies."

"Supplies?" Rafael asks.

"We're going to the frozen north," Dimitra reminds him. "Not even your fire power will be enough to keep you from freezing your balls off."

He shrugs. "Point taken."

"You should split up," Mariana says, eyeing us. "And leave your robes and weapons behind. I don't like the look of this place, and you're too conspicuous with them."

"What about you?" Rafael asks, crossing his arms.

"It's a port town, and I'm a Water Mage trying to book passage. I fit in. You do not. Fires are not a good thing to have on a ship."

Ismini's last words to me float in my vision, as if I were reading them, the ink suspended in the air: *Don't ever take off your robe!* And I don't want to.

Still, Mariana has a point. I'm the only one on the continent with a black robe. If anyone were looking for me, I wouldn't be hard to spot with it on. Hells, even the weird astronomer-hermit knew who I was, immediately, with my spelled silk garment. Not even the orange cat fur will stick to my spelled robe—it just rolls right off, like water off a duck's back. It's easy to tell it's no normal piece of clothing.

"Well, like all the hells am I leaving my swords behind," Aris says, crossing his arms.

Mariana rolls her eyes. "Honestly, take some of your little knives or whatever if you're worried you won't be able to handle a few street thugs without them."

Aris glowers at her.

"And hurry up," Mariana says, standing. "There's a bathhouse just north of here, and I want a chance to go before we set sail."

"Bathhouse?" Caelus asks, blinking.

"Water Mage," Mariana reminds him, pointing to herself. "I can sniff out a bathhouse a hundred miles away."

Caelus rolls his eyes.

"Sure, good idea," Rafael says, grinning, his mind clearly on getting Mariana undressed. "Errands and supplies. Let's go."

The morning is still young when we head into town, and I feel naked without my robe. It's strange how attached to it I've become. I feel exposed, and I don't like it.

The town is a maze of narrow streets and crowded buildings. The roads are packed dirt, and how Aris is able to find anything here is beyond me. We go down what seems to be a main street, crowded with shop windows, and down a side alley to another wider street.

This one appears to be more street vendors than shops, with faded awnings overhead to protect the merchants from the elements. We pass an old woman frying up some small fish, and then a family selling nets. Though Aris isn't wearing his shield or swords, the growing crowd parts before him. He towers a head or so over most here. So much for being inconspicuous.

We find an older couple selling coats and all kinds of cold-weather gear. Aris makes me try some of the items on, making sure they'll be snug. His hands linger on the lapels of the coat as he fastens the buttons—my own fingers, wedged into wool-lined gloves, are much too clumsy. The pad of his thumb brushes against my lips for a second, his blue eyes finding mine, the morning sun behind him making him glow. Gods, he is so beautiful. The breath catches in my throat for a moment—but then he turns and begins to haggle with the vendors. I work on disentangling myself from the gear, which already has me sweating, and my heart is beating much too rapidly—and by the time I'm done, Aris is handing over a few gold coins to the couple. They thank him profusely and rush to bundle our purchases for us.

The clothes are bulky, but I insist on carrying at least one bundle, despite the smirk I get from Aris. It's not heavy, but it is huge and unwieldy, and I have trouble seeing around it. He makes it look easy, carrying one under each arm. We take our time in the market. For a moment, it's nice to just pretend we're normal people out shopping. Aris eyes some daggers on display, though none are up to his standards, and I let my hands trail across a row of silken gowns as fine as those worn in the halls of Estana's palace. My fingers stop on one in shades of purple, with lace at the cuffs. A sudden daydream overtakes me, in which I'm just a girl, and Aris is just a boy, and I'm wearing this beautiful dress, and ...

"You don't need the dress," Aris murmurs, lips close to my ear.

I startle at the sound. "No? Too impractical for the frigid north?" I say, my throat gone dry.

"Fancy clothes are for people who don't have a body like yours."

"So no fancy clothes then," I repeat, cheeks flaming. I don't deny that my body does strange things when Aris says things like that, like *he* finds *me* attractive. Strange, tingly, aching things.

"I'd prefer no clothes at all."

His breath is a warm tingle on the side of my neck, a tingle that is rapidly spreading throughout my body.

"You'd like that, wouldn't you?" I say, breathless, looking back at him.

He grins wickedly, a flash of white teeth against his tanned face, still so close to my ear that his words feel like a caress themselves. "Oh, I would."

We continue, my heart rate refusing to return to normal. I run into him when he stops abruptly, near a jeweler's stand.

"Ah, beautiful jewels for a beautiful lady?" a slim man calls. His teeth are bright in his weathered face, a thin mustache draping down to his chin. He sweeps a hand over his wares—sparkling purple and green amethysts, which must be from Prasinos.

Aris puts down his bundles to inspect the stand. There are geodes larger than the largest bird's egg, cracked open to reveal their sparkling secrets. There are crystal obelisks and carved figures of the gods. On the side, there are trays and trays of jewelry, and it is to these that Aris turns. In a moment, he settles on a green pendant hung on a silver chain.

"The perfect color to match your lady's eyes!" the man croons.

Aris turns to me, something unreadable in his eyes. "Turn around," he says.

What in all the hells? Aris doesn't give gifts. I distinctly remember hearing him say he never needed to resort to it before, unlike some people—specifically, Leo, after gifting me an obscenely large bouquet of Tamdosan roses.

But I turn, pulling my braid over my shoulder. He settles the chain around me, the pendant resting on my chest. He stoops to fasten it, his breath hot on the back of my neck. I lift the necklace to inspect it—it *is* beautiful. I've never owned anything so fine.

Hells, I'll bet no one in Spit has ever owned anything as fine as this jewel.

"Keep your eyes down," he whispers, fingers smoothing the chain. "We're being followed. Two men, near the end of the row, at the fishmonger's."

He plants a soft kiss on the side of my neck. If he's trying to make the people in the market believe that he's just a lover buying his lady a present, well, he has *me* halfway convinced. I lift the pendant slightly, like I'm admiring the faceted green stone, but I shift my eyes past it until I see the two men Aris mentioned. They're large, possibly Shields themselves, and not particularly subtle. One of them has a wicked scar on his face—and they're both looking straight at us.

I turn, faking a smile.

"It's stunning," I say, my hands moving to unclasp the necklace.

Aris catches them, bringing them to his mouth for a kiss. For a split second only, his eyes leave mine, glancing over my shoulder.

"It's yours," he says. "But you look tired. Why don't you head back to the inn? I'll meet you there in a moment."

There is no sparkle in his eyes as he says this, just a silent command. *Go,* he says. *I'll be right behind you.*

I beam at him like I imagine a lover would and pick up my bundle. On second thought –to keep up our ruse – I turn, standing on tip-toe, and touch my lips to his. A lady must thank her suitor for his gift, after all.

Aris is stunned, his lips half-parted. He opens his mouth to say something, but nothing comes out. I put my hand on his cheek, his tan skin sun-warmed against my palm.

"Hurry," I say, my face heating. His eyes narrow, a wicked smirk curving his lips.

"Go," he says, his voice low. It's practically a purr.

I turn reluctantly and make my way down the street toward the inn. Or at least, in the direction I hope our inn is. The necklace is warm against my skin. Aris didn't actually have to buy it, I think, feeling a little giddy.

Well, it's not a ring, but it's a start.

Gods, girl, get a grip on yourself. You're being stalked. *And it's not just the elemental gods out to get you.*

I bet any number of people would want access to the Night Mage. Hells, I was nearly kidnapped in Estana once, by the Aclinese governors, who wanted to use me to pressure the king to ease up on their taxation. Do these men want to kidnap me too, demand some sort of ransom? I imagine Leo would pay it, whatever they demanded.

And if they want something worse? Maybe to remove me entirely from this twisted game the gods seem to be playing?

I pretend to stumble, dropping my bundle, which gives me an excuse to turn and look behind me again as I pick it up.

The men *are* following me. They're not even doing a good job at being discreet, and they're much closer now.

Aris is nowhere to be seen.

I swallow, pick up the clothing, and keep walking, fear starting to make my heart—and feet—speed up. I don't see Aris, but he's there. I know he's there. He wouldn't abandon me.

So where the hells *is* he?

I take a turn, and I see the inn at the end of the road. Relief floods through me.

And then a strong shoulder jostles mine, and I'm pushed left into a small alleyway.

"Hey!" I shout, whirling.

My heart drops as I realize it's one of the men who have been following me. He's huge, dwarfing the small alleyway. There's no way I can sneak past him, so I have two choices: I can stand my ground, or I can turn and run. I have no doubt he'd be able to catch me before I could reach the far side of the alley, so my decision is made for me.

Calm down, Wren. You don't know that they know you're the Night Mage. Maybe they just think to rob you. Aris was spending money in the market; they're probably just thieves.

I stand up tall. Like all the hells am I handing over the green pendant.

"May I help you?" I ask, channeling as much of Mariana's practiced disdain as I can. The man is taller and broader than Aris, and older too. Likely more experienced. His nose has definitely been broken a few times, and his cheek is bisected by a nasty scar.

I clutch the bundle of winter clothes in front of me, getting a good grip on the twine securing it. It won't cause any damage, but it should slow him down a little if I decide that fleeing is a better option.

"There's a pretty bounty on your pretty head," he says with a grin, revealing teeth that are a little too sharp to be natural.

Shit.

Where is Aris?

I take a step back, adjusting my grip on the bundle. A second shadow enters the alley—the other man, as big as the first, pale-skinned with dark stubble on his scalp and face. If they're both before me, then this means, I hope, that there's no one behind me. I didn't get a great look at the alleyway before I was shoved into it, and I don't want to risk looking back now.

"Don't try screaming for help," the first one says, drawing a gladius.

Shit. So he *is* a Shield. Stronger and faster than I'll ever be. I scramble to remember Aris's training. *Fight to escape. Fight to buy time. You'll never beat a Shield.*

"Everyone in Basti is going to want to catch you. We're just lucky we found you first."

"So I'm just supposed to, what, come quietly with you?" I say, planting my feet firmly. It may be midday, and I may not have magic, but I'm not powerless.

"That would be the idea," he says. "Come now, where is your escort? Run off at the first sign of trouble?"

This man is a Shield, so he must know that Aris is mine. Which means he also knows that Aris would never abandon me. He'll want to get out of here with me before Aris shows.

So I need to buy time. I decide to fight back in the way I know best.

"What do I need him for? *I'm* the one you should be worried about," I say, trying to imitate Aris's smirk. I stand tall, one hand on my hip, assessing them. "Awfully brave to come after me with just the pair of you. Whoever hired you clearly has no regard for your well-being." I sigh, like I'm bored with the whole thing. "Ugh, and amateurs too," I say, looking each man in the eye.

The one in the back, the pale one, glances at his partner every few seconds and adjusts his grip on his sword once, twice.

Good. He's uncertain now.

"We know you have no power in the day," Broken-Nose says.

Pale-Man glances to him again.

"Do you?" I say, and I attempt to arch one of my eyebrows. Whenever Aris does it, I can practically feel his amusement, his arrogance. I don't think I'm having the same effect, but I try all the same.

"Don't worry. I'll be sure to send your remains back to the Great Hall of Shields," I say, hoping to prey on their Shield training.

Pale-Man winces, but Broken-Nose grits his teeth.

"*Vires, honos, fides.* Which part does 'abducting Mages' fall under, I wonder?"

"Shut *up*," Broken-Nose growls. His hand tightens on his gladius.

I hesitate, not wanting to provoke him *too* much, but decide to keep talking. I need to give Aris time to get here, to find me. *Can* he even find me in this alley? I'm not clear on how accurate his tracking skills are, using the claim to find me—when I was kidnapped, he said he could hear me, like a bell, ringing. *Please, gods, let him hear me now.*

"I might let you live, if you leave now," I say. I meet their eyes, staring them down. "The last Shield who attempted to harm me was Nestor Valorius—oh, you've heard of him? Good. He was five times the Shield you two could ever be. And now he's dead."

I inwardly cringe at speaking of Nestor like that—so flippant about his death—but I need these men to believe I am capable of such a thing. They don't need to know that it was the law of the Shields that demanded—and took—his life.

"Unless you want your pretty tongue cut out, *shut up* and come on," Broken-Nose says, extending his other hand, like he wants me to take it. His thick fingers curl though, ready to make a fist if I refuse.

I eye it with all the disdain I can muster. Wherever Aris is, I hope he hurries.

My time is up.

I bounce forward quickly on the balls of my feet, like I'm going to lunge at them—and I'm rewarded with a flinch from Broken-Nose.

Then I chuck the bundle of clothing at him, pivot, and run.

I hear a shout of surprise as they stumble back, and for a moment, I allow myself a delusion of victory. I pump my legs as fast as they'll go, my boots striking the stone in a cadence that almost matches the pounding of my heart. The alley isn't long, but there's no debris I can hide behind, no doors, and no barrels or boxes I can heave at my pursuers. I see a stack of broken chairs, though, and race toward them, intent on grabbing them—to use as a weapon if I can, or an obstacle otherwise.

But then I'm yanked off my feet, my braid now firmly wrapped in the hand of the pointy-toothed Broken-Nose. My scalp throbs, and my spine is jarred when I land on the cobblestones, sending shocks of pain through my back.

"Guess we're doing this the hard way, then," he says, leering down at me.

From my vantage point, looking up at him, I can see the sky above, clear and clean, in such a contrast to this dirty little alley.

And then, finally, I see Aris—jumping from the roof like a wrathful god.

CHAPTER 35

ARIS

The idiot leans back as he sees Wren's eyes shift to me. My dagger is tight in my fist as I leap, and his hand is severed at the wrist before my feet touch the ground. He roars as blood spurts over the brick walls, his dismembered hand lying before him.

Wren scrambles to her feet, and I push her behind me.

"Took you long enough," she says, panting. She is unhurt—though I'll take more than just this bastard's hand for daring to touch her.

"I had something to take care of," I say, not taking my eyes off the men in front of me. Where there are Shields, there are Mages. I found one Water Mage trailing the Shields. He was easy enough to overcome—one smack of his head against the cobblestones, and he was out. I do not envy him the headache he'll have when he wakes. Considering neither of these bastards has gone gray, he didn't hit the ground quite hard enough. I hadn't taken the time to stop and check, needing to get to Wren. Her fear ran through our bond, the silver chime of our claim ringing frantically.

The Shield in front of me has stopped bleeding, the stump of his wrist already clotting, the tissue starting to close. The other Shield has removed his shirt and has it pressed against the wound. For the moment, they ignore us. The hand will not regrow, but neither will such a wound kill a Shield. Hells, I've seen a Shield lose an entire arm in battle once. He just picked up a sword in his remaining hand and kept fighting.

The other Shield—now satisfied that his partner isn't going to bleed out—steps around One-Hand. He wields a gladius and takes up the fallen sword as well, whirling them both as he comes toward us. "I'll have your balls for a necklace, pretty boy," he growls.

"Run!" I shout at Wren. "Go back to the inn. Get the others."

"I can't leave you to fight them alone," she says.

"You can, and you will!" I roar back. "I can't worry about you and fight them off at the same time." I can't risk her getting hurt. She's helpless during the daytime. And fuck it all if she's not standing by my side anyway, a piece of wooden debris in her hands, wielding it like a club.

The one-handed Shield has recovered, and to his credit, he is stumbling to his feet, his face a mask of rage. He draws a wicked-looking knife from his belt with his other hand and tries to force his way past the other man to get to me first.

"*Go!*" I shout.

I hear Wren take a deep breath behind me, and then the clatter of her shoes against the cobblestones as she runs.

Gods, I haven't had a decent fight in ages. I briefly wish I had my swords, but as Markos always says, it's a poor Shield who blames his weapons for a lost battle. *I* am all the weapon I need.

"Drop the knife, Shield," a voice barks out behind me. I turn, my back to the wall, and risk a glance down the alley.

The other Mage, another Water Mage, has Wren by the throat, a bubble of water over her mouth and nose, suffocating her. He's not much taller than she is, a lean, feral-looking man. He doesn't wear the blue robe of a Water Mage, so clearly these assholes aren't School of the Silver Flame alumni. They've had similar training, though, and the Shields use our weapons.

Wren struggles mightily against the hand at her throat, but the magic is too strong. Her face is red with effort, her legs thrashing out at the Mage, but his fingers only tighten around her neck, forcing water down into her lungs.

Seconds tick by. A bead of sweat runs into my eye. *Not again.*

"Choose, Shield," he says. "Drop your knife, or watch your Mage drown."

Wren's panicked eyes catch mine, and I want to tear the whole damn alleyway apart, brick by brick.

I pivot, throwing the knife. The Mage moves with impossible speed, and the blade just glances off his cheek, drawing a thin red line. *What the fuck?*

Wren's eyes roll back, and she drops. The weight of her body is too much for the Mage to hold up with one hand, and her knees smack the cobblestones.

"*WREN!*" I bellow. Rage lances through my chest, as hot and real as a spear, and I fall to my knees too, waiting to feel the inevitable collapse of our bond, the collapse of my consciousness as I go gray.

But my Mage isn't done.

The fall is a ruse. The water orb still covers the lower part of her face, but her hand fumbles blindly at the top of her boot.

Draws the knife I gave her.

And plunges it into the leg of the Mage.

He howls, falling, and the water mask around Wren's face drops.

She gasps, dropping back against the wall, taking ragged gulps of air. I am at her side instantly, easing her down into a sitting position, my other hand checking her neck for injury. I can feel my Shield magic raging through me like never before. Wren grabs my hand, nodding to me, still unable to speak. Her eyes shift behind me, and I stand, ready to tear these fuckers limb from fucking limb. The Water Mage is screaming, trying to hold pressure on his leg. Looks like she got an artery—I feel a rush of pride. Bright blood wells between the Mage's fingers, staining the puddles of water at our feet.

I turn my focus to the Shields and crook my finger at them, a feral grin on my face. *Come on, assholes.*

A bark and a growl sound behind me, and then a giant wolf with yellow eyes is leaping over the injured Water Mage and landing at my feet, baring gleaming fangs at the Shields.

"About time," I mutter.

Caelus snarls at the Shields and jumps for the nearest one, catching a mouthful of fabric and tearing it as he goes.

The Shields draw their weapons, egging Caelus on with insults.

Mariana is down the alley next, racing toward the Mage.

I check Wren again, who waves me off.

"I'm fine," she assures me, coughing weakly, spitting out more water.

"Help Caelus," Mariana commands as she rushes to us. "I've got this one."

Water coalesces from the humid air, forming whips that lash into place around the Mage's wrists and ankles. They heave him from the ground and slam him against the wall. Blood continues to stream from his leg, dripping off his boot. The water that Mariana throws freezes in an instant, leaving him bound off the ground, arms and legs splayed in manacles of ice.

Wren calls to me and tosses me her knife. It's a clumsy throw, but I manage to grab the hilt. Without halting my momentum, I turn and heave it into the face of the Shield facing Caelus, the one who still has two hands.

He ducks to the side, the knife just missing him.

The one-handed Shield is not so lucky. The knife catches him in the throat. He must have been this Water Mage's claimed Shield, because the Mage lets out another roar of agony as the Shield dies, and it echoes along the alley like a roll of thunder.

"Don't you want to know what I did to *your* Mage?" I taunt the remaining Shield.

He's torn between wanting to check on his partner, wanting to attack us, and wanting to run. I'm guessing the ugly one-handed Shield was the leader. This guy doesn't seem able to make a decision about what to do next. He glances at my hands, which are now empty.

I may be out of weapons, but a Shield is never defenseless. Claws begin to extend from my hands where once there were nails. Usually the shift is the work of a moment, but it can be slowed down, with practice. It's a nice way to make your prey squirm.

And squirm he does.

In fact, the man flat-out bolts, his decision made. Caelus is hot on his heels, howling.

"Coward," I say, and I spit in the Shield's direction. My claws retract.

I turn and find Wren crumpled against the wall, one hand on her chest. She's soaked, and her hair is disheveled, stray curls going every which way. Otherwise, she seems unhurt.

"I'm fine," Wren says again, though she clutches at my sleeve. She turns her attention back to the Water Mage.

Gods. All I want to do is scoop her up and get her the hells out of here, but I also want revenge. A lot of bloody, bloody revenge.

"Who *are* you?" I roar at the Mage.

Mariana still has him pinned to the wall. His face is contorted with pain, but his skin has lost its flush of life. He pushes himself weakly against my hand at his throat, not really putting any effort into it.

He's gone gray. Between that and his blood loss, well ... I don't have a lot of time left to get the excruciating revenge I want.

"He won't say anything," Mariana says with a huff.

When a Shield and a Mage bond, they both become stronger. But when one of them dies, the other usually withers. It's a risk that generally keeps the weak out of the school and the games, which is fine with me.

This Mage will never regain his former power. Some never even talk again, or eat, or even breathe. They just stop. Mages can reach this state even just by overextending themselves.

Like Head Mage Saroya did, after Wren pushed her too far.

Like I nearly did when my first Mage, Stefan, died—until Wren pulled me back.

Mariana grabs one of his hands and rips the sleeve back to expose a faded tattoo on his inner wrist, of a serpent biting its own tail, forming a circle.

"Black Water," she mutters with disgust, pushing the tattoo away from her. "He wouldn't tell you anything even if he weren't gray. They're all fanatics. They'd rather die than reveal anything."

"The bitch speaks true," he hisses, like it takes all his energy to get those words out. "And we will not be the last to come after your Night Mage. You can be sure of that."

I grant him the mercy of a quick death and snap his neck. Mariana loosens her ice manacles, and he falls to the ground in a bloody heap, eyes already glassy.

I kneel by Wren's side. She flinches at my touch.

"You killed them," she says, looking up at me, her jade eyes wide, unblinking. Afraid – of these men, or of me?

"They would have kidnapped you, or worse," I remind her, raising an eyebrow. Besides, I only killed two of them. Caelus will probably get the credit for the other pair. And I'd do it again, a thousand times over.

"Come on," I say, hoisting her to her feet.

She's unsteady, trembling, shaken. In shock.

"I've secured the ship. We leave on the next tide, about three hours after sunset," Mariana says, wiping her palms on her robe.

Wren stumbles as she tries to walk, leaning heavily on the wall. Her breath is still coming in gasps.

I gather Wren into my arms, picking her up. She squeaks a little in protest, but not much.

"Remind me never to insult your knife skills ever again," I say.

The humor works, breaking her shock a little, or at least cracking it. She gives me a small smile.

"Don't worry. I will," she says. She wraps her arms around my neck, leaning into me as we head back toward the inn, and I swear I will pray to Rigrasil a thousand prayers tonight for keeping her safe today under his watchful eye.

CHAPTER 36
LEO

M^{y Wren,}

That is grave news about the eclipse. Do you mean to go after the Book of Silver, then? Do you think the god of night will reveal his true purpose to you? That the elemental gods will call off their bestial henchmen? And in the Abelon Wastes, of all places? I'll admit, it is a perfect hiding spot.

Roallac has been rather pleasant. The queen and I continue to have productive talks of opening trade routes and ending the traditional embargoes. I won't bore you with the politics, but I am quite excited that the long-standing animosity between our nations may be at an end. Did you know that she grew up without her parents too? Her mother died in childbirth. Her father's identity remains a matter of much debate, as her mother never married. Queen Evanthia has never married either, though it seems she is looking to remedy that fact.

Travel swiftly back to me, little bird, and stay safe.

. . .

Yours,
    Leo

CHAPTER 37
WREN

I turn Leo's letter over in my hands. I've read and reread it a dozen times, but the words just slip from my mind, like raindrops rolling off my black robe, leaving no impression. The Shield who delivered the letter is another hawk Shield, a tall, lean boy who barely waited for my scribbled reply before shifting again and leaving. The king himself had requested him to return quickly, he told us, puffing his skinny chest out a bit. And the boy didn't want to miss the events at Roallac—which is quite the entertaining place, apparently, despite its reputation. It seems Queen Evanthia really is trying to make a good impression—but it is hard for me to focus on that, or anything, right now.

I've seen death before, seen Aris kill for me before—but only monsters, never men, though I suppose often they were one and the same. Something inside me shifts. It is one thing to know that Aris *can* kill; it is another thing entirely to see him do it, and with so little effort or regret.

The look in the Mage's eyes haunts me. He was looking at me, his dark eyes narrowed with hate—right before Aris twisted his neck so savagely I could hear the bones snapping, like thunder. Every time a log in the fire cracks and pops, I find myself twitching as it echoes the sound of that man's death.

"How do you know they were Black Water?" Dimitra asks.

Mariana smooths the hair back from her face. "The tattoo. My family lives near the Roallac border," she reminds Dimitra. "My parents. My grandmother. My sisters. You can't be a Water Mage in that part of the country and *not* be aware of them. They have forever been trying to infiltrate the north of Ocron."

"What did they want with Wren, then?" Rafael asks.

They turn toward me, but I have no answers to give.

"Do you think they know we're going after the Book of Silver?" Rafael continues.

"How would they?" Mariana asks. "No one except the six of us—and Tekton and Delphine—know that."

I squirm. "And Leo," I mutter.

Dimitra whirls on me. "You mean to tell me you've been writing to the king about our mission, sending those letters to him *while he's in the heart of Roallac?* Did it never occur to your feeble mind that they might be intercepted?"

"What did you think I was writing about?" I snort. "And I assumed your Shield messengers would be capable of protecting my letters," I spit back, furious. "Or do you have so little faith in your fellows?"

"Let me see that," Dimitra says, snatching Leo's letter from my hands.

I jump up, hands clenched—but Aris is faster, and he grabs Dimitra's wrist in a flash. Their eyes meet, something unreadable passing between them, and then she opens her fingers, the paper falling from them. Aris catches it and reads it aloud.

I bury my face in my hands. Everyone is staring at me, and I can't bear to look any of them in the eyes. Was this my fault? Is the blood of those dead men on my hands?

"So the entire world could know our mission by now," Mariana says, crossing her arms. "Well done, Night Mage."

"It was a mistake," Aris says, not looking at me. "And we don't know that her letters were intercepted."

"How else would they know?" Mariana throws back. "Unless someone else *here* is betraying us."

"We cannot turn on each other now," Caelus says softly. "No more accusations. The ship leaves in a few hours, and we must be aboard. There is no guarantee that we will find another captain willing to take us, not even with Mariana's gifts."

"We should go back," Dimitra says. "If the Black Water Witches know we're going to Abelon, then we should return to Estana instead. We can still use the Book of Gold."

I squirm again. "Leo doesn't have it," I say.

The room goes silent.

"*What?*" Dimitra demands. Her face is contorted with rage.

She moves like she's going to come to strike me, but Aris is between us in an instant. He glares down at her, his expression now the fearsome mask of a Shield. I understand why his opponents must shake in fear. I'm sure if I weren't already sitting, my knees would give out, and even still I have to take a deep breath. He will—and has—killed for me. Dimitra realizes this at the same time I do. Her scowl changes, falls away, and for a moment I see the woman instead of the Shield. She looks stunned. Betrayed.

I swallow and try to explain myself again. "Leo doesn't have the Book of Gold. It's been missing for ages. He's trying to track it down."

Dimitra is shaking with repressed anger. She raises a finger at me. "From now on, any letters you get from the king, we *all* get to read them. Understand?"

I cross my arms. "You don't tell me what to do. If you don't like it, you can leave."

Dimitra throws up her hands, muttering a string of curses. "Aris, talk some sense into your Mage," she says, her voice barely controlled.

Aris turns back toward me and takes a deep breath before speaking. "Wren," he says, his voice level. "Is there anything else you want to tell us?"

I shake my head.

Rafael crosses his hands behind his head and lets out a low whistle. "Well, I guess we don't have a choice, then," he says. "To Abelon we go."

Mariana tosses her head, her white-blond hair sliding over her shoulder. "Agreed. But we still have time for a bath. I'll go get my things." She walks out of the dining hall, Rafael close on her heels.

I'm a little surprised that Mariana doesn't have more venom for me. I guess the Book of Silver is enough of a temptation for her. She's made no secret of the fact that she wants to be the one to find it.

Dimitra is still glaring at me—or more accurately, at the green pendant around my neck. I grab it self-consciously—it is a very obvious outward sign of Aris's feelings for me, and she does not approve, especially since she thinks I'm hiding information from them. It isn't that I don't trust them with that information—I don't think it is something Leo wants me sharing. If the public knew he didn't have the Book of Gold, it would severely undermine his rule.

"What are *you* staring at?" Dimitra snaps at me.

I narrow my eyes. *Someone I hope will spontaneously combust.*

"Nothing," I say.

"Are you all right, then, Wren? From the attack?" Caelus asks.

My hand moves from the pendant to my neck, which is likely already bruising from the Black Water Mage's grasp. My tailbone throbs, and I think my knees are skinned from where I fell. There are dark patches of stiff, dried blood on my pants. I'm not feeling great about taking a look at what's underneath.

"Fine," I utter, trying not to think about the Mage's glassy eyes after he died. "I'm fine. Just ... tired of being useless during the day."

"You weren't useless," Aris says, and he settles a hand on my shoulder. "You kept a level head and distracted him long enough to save yourself. You would make a good Shield."

A good Shield? A good killer, like him? I realize he's trying to pay me a compliment, but it feels hollow. I give him a small smile—which does little to convince him, I think—and push back from the table.

"I need to get my robe," I say—and I vow never to take it off again, no matter what. I can't help but think that the Black Water Mage's tricks would not have had any effect on me if I'd had it on. Hells, I'll even bathe with it from now on.

"And I think," Aris says, wiping a smudge of dirt off his face and examining the residue on his fingers, "that we should see that bathhouse now."

"Of course. Lucia!" the innkeeper yells, from where he was definitely eavesdropping, and his wife scurries up. She gives Caelus directions, with assurance that we'll be pleased with the place. "This time of day, you'll have the run of the place. They're free for public use, though not used often enough, in my opinion," she says gruffly. I think back to the first time we saw—and *smelled*–Basti, and I have to agree.

I've never been to a bathhouse before, unless I count the weird bathing pools at the School of the Silver Flame. If I have to bathe in the same room as Dimitra and Mariana ... well, I'd sooner just stay sweaty and dirty.

"I couldn't help overhearing your conversation," the innkeeper says, making a show of cleaning a mug, feigning disinterest.

Aris grunts.

Rafael and Mariana return with their things, Rafael's hair mussed where it wasn't a few moments ago.

"Quite a stir going on in Roallac these days," the innkeeper goes on, and he spits on the floor, like just the name of the country leaves a bad taste in his mouth.

"What have you heard?" Caelus asks. Mariana pouts at the delay.

"Well, you know how sailors talk," he says. He leans on the bar top, beefy arms crossed in front of him. "The waters around Roallac haven't been right for weeks now, maybe more. Tides running against themselves, keeping any ship from entering their harbors."

"That would take a lot of water magic," Rafael says skeptically, though I can tell the comment has piqued his interest.

"Aye," the innkeeper agrees. "Why are they keeping outsiders on the outside, then? What do they have there that they don't want no one seeing?" He raises his eyebrows, like he's thrilled with the idea of a conspiracy.

A prickle goes down my neck—Leo. *Leo* is there. If what the innkeeper is saying is true, and ships can't get in, then can any get out? I shoot a glance at Aris, who shrugs. The messenger Shield didn't mention this. Does Leo even know?

"Sailors also talk about krakens and mermaids. It doesn't make them real," Mariana says, tossing her hair.

"Krakens *are* real," I remind her, thinking of my lighthouse.

Mariana shrugs. "Says you. Come on, Rafael. Let's go."

"You know, there are private baths," Aris murmurs in my ear.

I jump at the sound—I didn't realize he was so close. My ear burns where his breath touched it, and any thoughts about water magic and tides and ships and golden books vanish from my mind.

I wonder for a moment if he means to reassure me, that I won't have to share a bath with Dimitra and Mariana, but when I look up, there's a fire in his eyes, and a thrill runs through me that has nothing to do with the onset of evening and my magic returning to me.

Private. Meaning just *us*.

I manage to nod and stand up. My legs protest at the movement, but I get up. A bath does sound good. Getting the mud and whatever else off ... well, I try to think about that and not about Aris, naked and dripping wet. I don't succeed.

Mariana is already out the door, dragging Rafael by the hand.

The bathhouse is, fortunately, only an easy five-minute walk south of the inn, set back into the hills a bit. It is an unassuming building, which initially sets Mariana pouting again, but once inside the weathered stone walls, we are greeted with a long pool a few feet deep, full of gently flowing green water that lends the air a pleasant tang of metal and minerals. The water flows in from hot springs, I imagine, and the air is pleasantly warm and humid.

"Come on," Mariana says, grabbing Rafael. She drags him along past the columns around the long rectangular pool, down through a doorway, and into some corridor. Her laughter echoes in the stone room.

I can only imagine what it looks like when it is full of people— gods, do people really bathe together like this, all in one place?

"I'm going to the frigidarium, and then the caldarium," Caelus says, with as much enthusiasm as I've ever seen him show.

"What's that?" I ask. The words are foreign to me.

"Cold water," Aris says with a shiver. "Then hot steam. Some Shields swear by it for muscle recovery."

"They do," Caelus says with a wolfish grin, and he heads off, actually whistling one of Rafael's tunes as he goes.

Dimitra snorts. She carefully avoids making eye contact with either me or Aris.

"I'll meet you back at the inn," she mumbles, and she heads off down a different hall.

"Come on," Aris says. He takes my hand and tugs me after him. My feet feel a little stuck to the ground, but I follow.

"Did you bring that salve?" he asks.

I blink, surprised. Of course I brought it. The innkeeper's wife took one look at the marks on my neck and then shoved the little tub into my hands, refusing payment or thanks. She then gave Aris a wicked look, like she suspected he was behind the marks. They had an epic stare-down until she finally threw up her hands and relented.

"If that man touches another hair on your head, miss, I'll have those hands chopped off. Just you see if I don't!" she promised.

Aris rolled his eyes, but I think part of him was charmed by her ferocity.

We head through a door and explore a short stone corridor with rooms to either side, labeled by temperature—cold, warm, and hot. As the innkeeper's wife said, we essentially have the run of the place, and other than the soft burbling of water, there is no other sound. Someone must have been here and prepared the place, though, lighting lanterns and candles throughout, making it cozy and inviting.

Aris opens a door and steps through. He leaves it open behind him, and for a moment, I stand in the doorway, half in and half out. I bite my lip as I consider what exactly I am doing here—going into this bath, with this man. Excitement and apprehension twist in my gut, and I feel a little nauseated and a little like I could take flight.

Aris stops when he doesn't hear me behind him. It's a beautiful little room, truly—tiled and well stocked with soaps and fluffy towels, with steaming cloudy green water that looks terribly inviting. Candles are set in little reflective alcoves around the room, and it smells amazing too, all mineral and herbal and soapy. He waits, but I do not enter. My feet are stone, though my heart is racing.

Aris waits a moment longer, his hand extended to me, then turns and comes back to the doorway.

"You take this one. I'll be across the hall if you need me," he says. My tongue is stuck to the roof of my mouth, which is suddenly parched.

There's no anger in his voice though, no resentment, no disappointment. And before I can stop him, he's stepped across the hall, into a similar chamber on the other side. He closes the door behind himself without turning back around.

I consider this for a moment. I set down my bag, get out the little tub of salve that smells of mint and lemon. I twist the cap on and off absently, pondering. Should I go after him? Should I just bathe here?

This man trusts me. Wants *me*. And on those rare nights I don't dream of Caladrius, it is Aris's eyes—and body—that haunt me. There are times I think I will actually *burn* if I don't touch him, if I don't feel his skin against mine.

And now—he's waiting for me.

So what am I waiting for?

I take a deep breath and step across the hall.

I hear a splash as I open the door. He pauses, a bar of soap in one hand, one eyebrow raised. His hair is already slicked back, water sluicing along his square jaw, glittering on his eyelashes.

Wearing only the leather bracelet Delphine gave him.

"Wren?" he says. It's a question, I think.

"I need help with the salve," I blurt out lamely, holding out the ointment. I realize that my hand is shaking a little—and that it's green. I'm glowing again, lighting up the dim room like a star.

But gods, I can't even process that, because I can't take my eyes off Aris. He's submerged almost to his chest, sitting on some kind of ledge. The water whirls lazily around him, and when I realize that the water is clouded with soap and minerals—therefore offering some minor amount of modesty—the green light flares brighter, throwing into relief each chiseled muscle, each ragged scar. Somehow the scars do not detract from his beauty at all—they are a mark of what he has survived. Without them, I wouldn't even believe he could be mortal. Gods, he takes my breath away.

We stare at each other for a moment, while I'm still glowing and holding out the damned salve.

Aris turns to place his soap on the side of the bath, then holds out his hand to me. "Come here, then, firefly," he says, and one side of his mouth tilts up in a grin.

He doesn't move toward me, though—which means that to hand the salve to him, I'll have to walk *into the room*, across the tiled floor. I'll have to make that decision to go to him. He looks so relaxed— he's always been comfortable in his body, comfortable with touch and affection, whereas I'm skittish as a mouse.

I shuffle into the room, and the door swings closed silently behind me. I walk toward him as calmly and steadily as I can, trying desperately to breathe normally, though I feel a little faint. It's probably from the steam and the mineral fumes.

I glow brighter.

I hand the salve over. For a moment, our fingers touch, wrapped around the little jar. My breath catches in my throat.

And then Aris's hand is reaching not for the salve but for my wrist—and he yanks me off my feet, clothing and all, into the bath.

I come up spluttering a second later, blinded by water and by wet curls flopping all over my face, and probably looking like a half-drowned cat—and just as mad.

"*What* in the name of the *gods*, Aris!" I yell, wiping the hair back from my face. "What is wrong with you?"

He has a damn smug look on his face, and he's trying hard not to laugh. I glare at him, but he offers no apology. I throw the salve at him, hitting him in the chest, and make my way to the edge of the pool. There is indeed a ledge there, and I climb onto it and heave myself out. Water streams down my clothing, pooling on the floor and running back into the tub. My braid hangs heavy down my back.

"You are a pain in the ass. You know that?" I bark, wringing out my braid. I cannot believe the kind of thoughts that were running through my head just moments ago, making my heart squeeze and head dizzy. Now all I feel is indignation and rage. Maybe I should turn his damn bath into a frigidarium for him, freeze him in it like Mariana froze the water in that alleyway. *Gods!*

Aris just crosses his arms over his chest, one corner of his mouth pulling up in a smirk. "Calm down. You have dry clothes to change into. And you're not nervous anymore," he says.

I stop, my braid still dripping in my hands. My normal, brown hands. That aren't glowing.

And damn it all, but he's right. A choked sound escapes me, followed by laughter. In a moment, I am laughing so hard that I'm crying, the salt of my tears joining the water still streaming down my face. And gods, it feels so good to just let it out.

I'm still giggling and trying to catch my breath when I look back at Aris. He's still grinning, the arrogant ass, and still sitting in the pool.

"Come in, Wren," he says, and his voice is so smooth, so reassuring. "I don't bite. I just don't like it when you're scared of me."

"I'm not scared of you," I tell him.

He raises an eyebrow. "You've only glowed a few times, Wren—once when your life was at risk, and whenever you are alone with me. I don't like it," he says, then frowns. "Is it because of those men earlier?"

I look at the floor, study the water pooling at my feet, dripping across the blue tiles. It's not about the men. True, the effortless nature with which Aris killed them made my blood run cold, made me view him a little differently.

But what is going on now has my blood aflame. I look up, meeting his steady gaze.

"Close your eyes," I tell him.

He smirks again but obeys. He even puts his hands over his eyes, to assure me that he's not peeking. His hands that killed men today. Hands that I've had wicked dreams about. My stomach flutters.

I consider what I'm about to do—and overthink it, probably. I mean, this isn't any different from what we did in the cave, right?

I get out of my wet clothes. They hit the tiles with a soggy plop, and I hurry into the water, sitting low on the ledge so the water reaches nearly to my chin.

"All right," I say.

Aris lowers his hands. And I swear, in the candlelight of the room, that his sky-colored eyes glow with their own brilliance.

I swallow thickly.

He raises the salve in one hand, gesturing toward my neck. "Can I help you with that?"

Gods. Can a naked, dripping-wet Aris rub his hands all over me? *Yes. Yes, please.*

I nod, speechless. I turn my back toward him, pulling my braid over one shoulder. I busy myself with undoing the tie at the end as he approaches, to give my shaking hands something to do.

I unravel the braid as Aris opens the salve. He uses one hand to gather my loose wet hair out of the way, then carefully applies the medicine. His touch is gentle, the salve cool and soothing, but I still can't repress a shudder when he touches me. His hand stills.

"Does it hurt?" he asks. He's so close I can feel the heat radiating off him even over the warmth of the water. His mouth is right next to my ear, his breath brushing my skin.

I manage to shake my head, and he continues. He makes his way around my neck, slowly, carefully, not touching me anywhere except my neck, though my skin prickles with his closeness. The scent of mint and lemon combines with the mineral water in a heady steam. I continue to work on my hair, and then Aris has to move around me to reach the front of my neck. His pupils are huge, nearly swallowing the sapphire of his eyes, but he keeps them firmly on my neck, dedicated to the task at hand.

"Thank you," I murmur.

He glances up for a second only. "It is the first and paramount duty of a Shield to care for their Mage," he says, in a flat voice that makes me wonder if this is some sort of Shield law, some rule he's been drilled in since he was a child.

"You are a good Shield, Aris," I say.

His eyes shut, his unfairly long black lashes fluttering. He takes a deep breath. And it's true—despite everything, despite the ease with which he dispatched the men who attacked me, it's true. He is a good Shield. A great one. As Ismini said, my protection and well-being are his primary concern.

"I am," he agrees.

I chuckle, and his eyes open, dark and huge in the dim light. "And I am yours. Your Shield," he says.

Something turns over in my chest. Mine. It's almost worth braving the wrath of all the gods to hear him say that.

His fingers lower to rest on the dip between my collarbones. "But I could be so much more, if you would let me. If you wanted me to be."

The breath catches in my throat. He continues, fingers trailing down my breastbone.

I don't stop him.

"I scared you today," he says. It's not a question.

I hesitate for a moment, then nod. "Yes." The word escapes me, as soft as a whisper. I can see his lips thin for a moment, pressed together. He doesn't like that answer at all.

"Death is a part of living, for a Shield," he murmurs. He seems lost in his thoughts, his gaze a little unfocused. His fingers reach my stomach, dancing slowly underwater, down toward my navel. The water keeps me from seeing his hand fully, but I can feel it, every scorching fingertip. "I suppose that is what makes me want to seize life to the fullest. I don't want to waste a single opportunity, a single chance to feel *alive*."

"I see," I say, considering exactly what kind of "opportunity" he means. "And is this how you seduce your women, then, Aris? Dunk them fully clothed into water? How many fancy ball gowns you must have ruined over the years." I mean for it to sound flippant, teasing, but I'm afraid it comes out accusatory. I am no good at playing coy. I have no experience in such things.

He grins, though, a predatory look, taking it as a challenge. "I don't have to seduce you, princess," he says, moving closer.

Instinctively I turn my face up to his, waiting for his kiss. Instead, he dips, merely pressing his forehead to mine, his nose against mine, and I can't help the small whine of disappointment that escapes me. His breath mingles with mine. His chest moves with mine. We are one heart in two bodies.

"You already can't keep your eyes off me."

"Arrogant ass—" I start to say, but I am cut off by him—finally—making good on that kiss.

His lips are strong, confident, just like the rest of him. A thrill runs through me, and I can think of nothing else in the entire world except this moment. His hands trail over my collarbones, my shoulders, run down my arms, pulling me closer to him—and I shudder and break the kiss, overwhelmed and caught up in his spell at the same time.

"All right," he says, pressing his forehead to mine again, stroking the side of my face with the back of his fingers, as he might soothe a frightened horse. "All right. I'm just … glad that you're all right. You scared me earlier."

"*I* scared *you*?" I say. The water swirls around the top of my breasts, the smooth brown skin just visible. Aris is doing an admirable job of trying not to look. "I thought nothing scared you."

"The thought of losing you does."

He cups my face with his hands, giving me another lingering kiss. I feel it from my lips all the way down to my toes, curling now against the tiles of the bath floor.

"Now wash up. If we stay in here much longer, I'm not going to be able to control myself."

The James is an impressive ship. Over a hundred feet long with three masts at least fifty feet tall, it sits at the end of a long dock. A dozen or so men and women are loading cargo in crates and barrels, and it seems they are nearly done.

Mariana strides up the gangplank to the ship with an air of confidence like she owns it. Her long blond hair flies out like a silky banner behind her—I wonder if it's Rafael's magic that dried her hair so quickly. My own damp braid is still leaking water droplets down my robe—they run right off, due to the spells it has, but I am envious. I wonder if I could get him to teach me that trick. Aris's hair is still damp too—leaving little damp spots where the curling ends reach his shoulders. He catches me looking and gives me one of his signature smirks. Basti might be a dangerous, dirty little town, but their bathhouse has clearly done us all some good. Even Caelus looks positively perky.

I lived next to the sea most of my life, saw countless ships like *The James* sail past my lighthouse, helped keep them from wrecking on the shoals—but never have I actually set foot on anything so large. My father had a small rowboat that we sometimes took out on those rare days when the sea was calm, when we gathered mussels and fished for squid in the secret deep spots of the Spit. That rowboat was so small that I was able to trail my fingers over the side, dipping them in the sea as he rowed.

The James is a different beast altogether. It is with a mix of anxiety and anticipation that I follow Mariana aboard, my robe pulled tight around me. No matter what she says, I am not taking it off again.

"This is it, then?" a voice calls. A lean, tanned woman with giant gold hoops in her ears and an eyepatch over her left eye strides down the stairs from the quarterdeck, hands on hips. A thinly rolled cigar trails smoke between her fingers, and a black cloth bandanna keeps cropped brown hair back from her face. Aris openly admires the long, curved blade belted at her trim waist, and the handles of more knives are visible above the tops of her tall boots, in the small of her back, and at her shoulder. She seems young to be a part of this crew—and a woman besides. Aclinese ships tended to have all-male crews, something about women aboard being bad luck or something. I think I like this ship already.

Mariana and Caelus step forward to greet her.

"This is it," Mariana confirms.

The crew seem glad to have Mariana on board—Rafael they are less thrilled about. A Fire Mage aboard a wooden ship has the potential to be a serious problem. Rafael, though, just grins at them, crossing his arms, letting a flame dance across the tips of his fingers. The light casts his handsome features in an eerie glow. I smack his arm to get him to quit, but he doesn't douse the light, or seem the least bit apologetic about antagonizing the crew.

"Right. I'll take you on to meet the captain, then," the woman says, ignoring Rafael and taking a puff of her cigar. She lets the smoke blow softly from her mouth in a ring. She looks our group over, eyeing Aris appreciatively, and beckons us to follow with a nod of her head.

I briefly consider whether I can get away with some sort of petty spell, since the sun is setting—flaring up the fire in her cigar, perhaps, or dousing her in seawater—but I restrain myself and loop my arm assertively through Aris's instead. He cocks an eyebrow at the possessive touch but has the good sense not to comment.

As we cross the main deck, there's a commotion over the port side, the side that's facing out to the sea. The crewmen rush to the rail, lean over, and point with excitement. I exchange a glance with Aris, who shrugs.

A moment later, a massive tiger shark nearly twenty feet long is shooting up from the water, its skin a striped bronze, by far the biggest shark I've ever seen. Shouts go up from us, and whoops from the crew.

For a moment, the shark pauses in the air, like it's enjoying the crew's admiration—before it crashes to the deck in a splash of water, soaking us all.

I wipe the water from my face and realize that I'm staring not at a shark but at a man. A Shield. Nearly seven feet tall, red-haired and - bearded with freckled, tanned skin.

Nude.

Heat rises to my cheeks. He is enjoying making a spectacle and comes over to us, wrapping a muscled arm around our companion and planting a loud kiss on her cheek. She elbows him affectionately. Scars wrap around his middle, big jagged ones like from the jaws of a shark.

"Leave off, Stig," the woman says. "If you're done fishing, go finish loading the cargo. You're late."

He gives me a wink and then lets out a low whistle as he looks over Dimitra. She is not amused and gives him a rude hand gesture.

"Aye, aye, Stella." He whistles cheerily as he walks away from us, not bothering to put on any clothes.

"Ignore Stiggur," our companion—Stella—says to us. "Captain allows him leniency because he's good protection for the ship. Too much leniency, if you ask me." However, there's a smile on her face as she looks over at him.

"They didn't ask you," a husky voice says. Emerging onto the main deck is a woman who is Stella's mirror image, except for the eye patch and cigar. Her twin.

"Cap'n," Stella says, touching her brow. "All crew accounted for. This here's the Water Mage." She nods toward Mariana.

"Right," the captain says. She's got the same short brown hair and gold earrings as Stella but wears a wide tricorn hat on her head, a fluffy gold feather falling from one side. A long gold brocade vest is corseted under her breasts, pushing them up. It's tied tight to accent her slim figure—and to display the two curved swords at her sides. "Captain Loren Seagraves," she says, extending a hand to Mariana, like she's the only one here.

Mariana preens. "Mariana Alagona, Water Mage of Ocron," she says.

The women size each other up.

"What's a fancy group like you want in Abelon?" Captain Seagraves asks, hands on hips.

Stella takes another slow puff of her cigar. The smoke stinks, even over the smell of rotting fish and salt in the air.

"King Leonidas hopes to establish a trade route," Mariana says, rolling her eyes, like she's bored with the whole thing. "I'm just here to ensure smooth passage across the Broken Sea."

The captain nods, still ignoring the rest of us.

"Well, let's get on with it, then," she says. "Stel, get them settled in the officer's quarters."

"Then where will I sleep?" Stella pouts.

"With me, love," Stig says—still naked—wrapping his arms around Stella's waist from behind.

"Not if you want to keep all your parts intact," she says, and she digs her elbow sharply into his gut.

It doesn't seem to bother him much, as his grin just widens.

I look back at the captain to see that she's staring at me with sharp, hawkish brown eyes, unblinking. Something about her gaze makes me nervous, and I have a flash, like a vision, of how I must look to her. A small girl in a black robe, playing at being a Mage. No one special, not beautiful like Mariana or confident like Dimitra. Not worthy of the company I keep. I have to remind myself that I am not that girl from Spit anymore, that I am *the* Night Mage, and a friend of the king. I straighten my spine.

Captain Seagraves looks me over, turns, and disappears up the stairs to the quarterdeck.

CHAPTER 38
ARIS

I hate boats.

I like water, of course. Tigers are natural swimmers. Even as a man, I enjoy water—particularly baths.

But there's something about being on a boat—the rocking motion, maybe, or the idea that I don't have immediate control of my surroundings, those are the things I hate. Add in the cramped bunks we're stuck in—too small for two people—and it's no small wonder that I'm awake all night. Not to mention I can't keep Wren out of my mind. The way the water in the bath swirled around her breasts—I ache just thinking about it.

"It's a ship, not a boat," Loren says, breaking my wandering thoughts, and I'm able to put Wren's curves out of my mind—and let my blood flow back to my brain—for a moment. Sort of.

Loren has taken the night's watch at the helm, steering us due north. As a Shield, I can go several days without sleeping. I wish I could just sleep this journey away, but the claustrophobic quarters have me on edge. Dimitra and Caelus, too—they're on the forecastle, sparring in the dark. The lantern light flickers off their blades, and some of the crew have stopped to watch.

"How long until we reach the Wastes?" I ask.

She shrugs, the rows of gold hoops in her ears flashing in the faint lantern light. "This time of year, a few days. A week, tops," she says, minutely adjusting the wheel.

She calls out a command to a man in the rigging, invisible in the dark, and the sails billow out like a pregnant woman's belly.

"Won't be a comfortable trip," she continues, eyeing me. "Rough seas. You'll be grateful to have your Water Mage on board."

"Fantastic," I mutter.

Loren cuts a fine shape, all long and lean and fierce. She knows it. And I like it here well enough, standing at the stern of the ship with her, watching the clouds sail by overhead. The waves are large but not harsh, like rolling black hills. I could almost pretend to be back on the wide grassy plains of Ocron, if not for the pitching of the ship and the smell of salt and fish.

We talk a bit, trading stories. She and the eponymous James, her lover, captained this ship together for a few years. Mostly they ran between the archipelago and coastal continental towns, like Basti—that is, until James had an accident, falling to his death from the rigging. Since then she's been on her own, though she changed the name of the ship. I mention that I thought ships were always considered feminine, and she snorts a laugh.

"You would think that, wouldn't you?"

After a while, the next shift comes on, and Loren is relieved.

"Heading in for a nightcap," she says, looking me over. "Want one?"

I like Loren. She's direct, knows her own mind. In another time …

I shake my head, looking instead over at Caelus and Dimitra. "Not tonight."

She shrugs and leaves.

I wait until I hear the door below close before heading up to where my fellow Shields are training. The pitching of the ship makes it harder to focus, and I lose myself in the work, going through forms and exercises with Dimitra and Caelus. Wren comes up an hour or so before dawn to meditate or practice; she sits cross-legged at the stern of the ship, eyes closed. The ship's cat, Guppy, struts around her for a bit, rubbing his face on her elbows, trailing his tail around her back, until she gives up and settles him in her lap. He is content to sit there and nap—and I am insanely jealous of the creature. I roll my shoulders, trying to get my focus back on the stretches Caelus and I are doing. It almost works too.

"Mind if I join?" Stig says, sauntering up. "Haven't been around so many Shields since I was back at the school."

"You went to the school?" Dimitra asks, looking him over like he's a slug or something to be crushed beneath her boot.

"Aye, pretty lady, that I did," he says, giving her a wink.

She snorts, whirling her daggers in either hand.

"Year between Myron and Lukas—brothers of yours, I'd wager," he says, eyeing me.

I shrug. "Sometimes."

"Why didn't you claim a Mage?" Dimitra asks.

Stig grins, glad of her attention. "Because I ain't crazy," he says. "Besides, I don't need a claim to boost my strength. I threw Myron right across the arena once. Can't say he was much of a challenge."

Myron won the games the year he graduated. Regardless, the man is a seven-foot wall of muscle, and the only aquatic Shield I've ever met. I'd be a fool to underestimate him—but I'm really, *really* itching for a fight with someone besides Dimitra and Caelus.

"Myron never was decent in a fight," I say, which is completely a lie. Myron broke my nose half a dozen times before he turned ten, and gave me more beatings than I can count. He always was a bastard, cruel to me from the day I was born. He liked to pick on our sisters too, until I taught Rea to kick him in the balls when he tried.

"That so?" Stig says, eyeing my swords. "Why don't you show me what *you're* made of then, kitty cat?"

"Kitty cat?" I say, raising an eyebrow. *Oh, this is going to be fun.*

He shrugs, grinning, showing off a lot of bright white teeth that are just a little too pointed. Dimitra tosses him a gladius. He snatches it from the air with practiced ease, gives it a swing, and gives Dimitra another wink—which she ignores.

"Ain't all of Valorius's brats cats?" he asks. "That old man of yours was an asshole. Hard to forget too, the way he'd go on about the 'strength in his bloodline' and all that shit."

"On that account, we can agree," I say.

We start to circle, prowling around the deck. A tiger against a tiger shark. Maybe Stig and I have more in common than I realized.

Caelus and Dimitra have backed off and are leaning on the rail. Caelus wipes the sweat from his face, and the crew pause their chores to watch. I sheathe my gladiuses and drop one onto the deck by Dimitra, wielding the other. No point eviscerating the man if I can help it. I can feel my magic burning in my veins, my muscles coiling, ready to pounce. I can feel my canines growing longer and more pointed as we prowl, sizing each other up. The sun beats down on us, though the air is cool and crisp. Even Wren has stopped her meditating to watch, the cat curled up in her lap.

The deck tilts, and Stig leaps, swinging Dimitra's gladius down like a hammer. He's not holding back—good.

I whirl to the side, my sheathed sword smacking, hard, against his back as he passes.

He laughs, arched backward against the blow.

"You're quick," he says, turning around, ready again. "Either that, or I'm getting slow."

"And old, my love," Stella yells from the rigging, though he can't be far over thirty.

Stig raises a hand carelessly, acknowledging the comment but brushing it off.

We go again, and this time he's more careful. He circles like a shark, eager for blood in the water. He uses his size—and the deck's swaying—to his advantage, raining blows down on me that could cause some serious damage. As it is, he is splintering the wood of the deck instead. Stella remarks that she'll make him repair it later, but he doesn't seem to hear. He's absorbed in the fight, focused on me. His red hair becomes dark with sweat, his swings more erratic.

"Come on, Aris—the crew won't get back to work until you finish this," Stella yells.

Stig definitely hears that one and lets out a string of curses. He's good—strong, fast. But he's no match for me. With the next pass, I swipe at the backs of his knees, making him fall. I yank back on his hair, my sheath at his neck.

"Yield," he says hoarsely. He's breathing hard but grinning like a fool.

Dimitra's sword clatters to the deck, and she retrieves it with a smirk. I let go of the shark Shield and give him a hand back up.

"Your brother would have pulled some dirty trick to beat me," he says, throwing an arm around my shoulder. "Perhaps there is some strength left in your bloodline after all. Now, come, let's eat, and you can tell me about what's been happening at the school since I left."

We're headed to the ladder when Stella leaps from the rigging, landing lightly in front of us. She puts a hand on Stig's chest to stop him.

"Not yet," she says, nodding at the deck behind us. "You fix this mess; then you eat. Or the captain will have your hide for a new pair of boots. And *yours* for a fur hat." She glares at me. She's grinning, though. She enjoyed the show.

I seek out Wren, finding her still watching, petting Guppy. She rolls her eyes at me, but I can tell she's pleased.

Stella whistles, and another deckhand tosses up a tool belt and a sharkskin sander. She hands them to us.

"Go on," she says to me. "See if you look as pretty sanding the deck as you do when you're prancing around it."

"You tell me," I say, grinning.

Stig huffs. "Come on, then, before my woman decides she likes you more than me," he growls, pushing me away.

We spend the day working side by side. Stig speaks his mind easily, and in another life—one without boats—I think we could have been friends. It doesn't take long to repair the deck, but then he takes a turn at the helm, and we talk for hours about swords and fighting and the Shields we know. It almost feels *normal*, in a situation that is anything but normal. At nightfall, he brings me an ale, and we drink in comfortable quiet until Stella comes and drags him off, one hand already down his pants.

Wren is up in the rigging with two of the crew, hanging little green lights along the ropes to light their way. It is a small bit of magic, but they cheer like it is something spectacular. She grins and looks down at me. She points up and tilts her head—up toward the crow's nest. With the way *The James* is swaying, like all the hells do I want to go up there.

But then she gives me a smirk, a heated look that I so rarely see from her, and I leap to the rigging without another thought. She laughs and starts climbing, racing away from me, but if there's one thing Wren needs to learn, it's that you never run from a predator. My tiger instincts kick in, and I scramble up the ropes and seize her ankle just as she reaches the crow's nest. She gasps, and I haul myself up, grabbing her around the waist and throwing her over my shoulder. Her head is pointed down over my back, and she swears at the height, grabbing at my shoulders.

"Don't you *dare* drop me!" she squeals. I let out an indignant sort of huff, as if I could let anything happen to her, and grab the rail of the crow's nest and haul us over. It's a small space—a little larger than the half barrel it looks like, with the mast in the middle, but it does give us a hint of privacy, and I fold myself into the space to be with her.

Before I can let her down completely, she's laughing and kissing me, her arms thrown around my neck without hesitation. *Gods!* If there were a little more room up here ... As it is, I have to settle with her straddling my hips, her body flush with mine. Her mouth is soft and needy against mine, her tongue teasing mine with quick little movements, her body quickening against mine in ways that she does not understand, hot against me in a kind of tantalizing agony. I feel drunk, or drugged, wanting more with each taste I get. I reach for the ties of her shirt—and she freezes, a breath leaving her quickly, her eyes as wide as a frightened deer's.

I move my hand to her neck instead, sweeping her cloud of hair back, and plant kisses there until she relaxes against me again. I move my hands to her hips, holding her there against mine, kissing her until I lose track of time and the stars overhead spin. I let her smooth hands explore what they will.

"Tell me if you want me to stop," she breathes.

I'm sure she's trying to offer me the same reassurance I've given her, but I stop that thought with another kiss, catching her lower lip between my teeth, just a little, before letting go.

"Never," I growl.

She smiles, ducking her flushed cheeks, curling up against me, one hand playing with the green pendant around her neck.

"We'll have to go back down eventually," she says, raising her eyes to mine.

I tighten my arm around her. "Eventually," I agree. "But not yet."

I hold her until the moon rises, until she begins to drift to sleep in my arms. I help her down the rigging and back into the bunk in our quarters. She falls asleep immediately, a smile on her lips. I hope it's me that she's dreaming about.

If I were to have one perfect dream for the rest of my life—one that didn't involve us being naked, at least—this night would be it. Suspended high up in the sky, we could pretend for a little while that nothing else existed—no magic, no monsters, no guilt.

Until the crash of dawn comes—and with it, something out of a nightmare.

CHAPTER 39
WREN

Guppy realizes the danger a moment before I do. His orange fur suddenly stands on end. His claws extend—drawing a drop of blood from my thighs—and he takes off, racing down the deck to disappear. I was trying to meditate again, though I am tired from staying up too late with Aris last night. And I'd do it again—those stolen moments, the look on his face, not one of frustration, as I'd expected, but one of wonder. Almost worship. I'm still daydreaming about the feel of his lips on mine, the skin of my neck prickling with the memory of his kisses, as Guppy yowls and disappears into the hold.

The sea is quiet and gray with just a glimmer of gold sunshine on the surface—a beautiful morning. The boat jostles slightly, like maybe we've hit something. We're so far from land, I can't imagine what it could be. Wreckage from another ship, perhaps? I scramble to my feet just as another *thump* sounds from the side near me, and when I lean over the railing I see a disturbance in the dark water, a heaving and shuddering, like water about to boil.

And then a giant fleshy appendage erupts from the water like a waterspout, fifty feet long and five feet thick, and swipes across the bow of the ship like an arm clearing off a messy table—headed right for where my Shield is stretching with Stig near the bow. Not even Aris has time to react.

Aris is slammed against the railing, his back arched over backward at an unnatural angle, then flipped over the edge, disappearing from sight.

"*ARIS!*" I scream, already down the ladder and on the main deck. The sailors are yelling, but I can barely hear them over the frothing of the ocean. More tentacles emerge from either side of *The James*, wrapping over the deck in a deadly embrace. My way is blocked, so I stab my knife into one of the tentacles and use it as a handhold to pull myself up and over the mountain of writhing flesh, barely able to hold on. It's like trying to wrestle a moving tree trunk. I'm dragged across the deck as the tentacle flails.

I have to get to Aris. What if he's injured? What if ...? I can't bear to think any more. I just move. I am floundering, up and over one tentacle, under another, as the creature adjusts its grip. The crew scramble for weapons and hack at the thing with swords and knives. The wood groans under the strain, the railing splintering. I can see Caelus and Dimitra on the forecastle, their swords out, and the tip of one severed tentacle thrashes at their feet, oily blue blood making their footing slick.

And still I do not see Aris. Has he fallen overboard? Is he trapped underneath the ship, or the creature? I think of the way his back bent over the rail, and my head spins. That kind of blow could kill a man, or leave him useless below the waist. And if he is trapped under the ship, without air ... Such an injury to a man like Aris, if he even survived it ...

I push the horrible thoughts from my head. *Aris is all right. He has to be. I just have to get to him.*

The suckers on the tentacle before me are bigger than plates, their edges rippling as they seek purchase. I hear Captain Seagraves behind me, shouting orders. Everything is in chaos. I smell salt and fish and then suddenly char—Rafael is sending carefully aimed fireballs at the thing. It thrashes in response, knocking another sailor overboard.

I briefly register Stig roaring like a hurricane, a wild grin on his bearded face. He dives over the side of the deck, shifting as he goes. I catch just a glimpse of his tail before I lose sight of him.

I am almost at the ladder. I can make it. My fingers reach for the wood, scrabbling for a hold—then a tentacle slams against me and pushes me against the forecastle deck, pinning me with slimy, putrid strength. I am being squished, my ribs screaming as they fight to expand and bring a breath into my burning lungs.

What a stupid way to die. I hope that if anyone ever writes my life story, they embellish this part a bit. The only reason I can draw breath at all is that I'm squeezed in next to the ladder, which bears the brunt of the beast's weight. It's creaking, though, the far rail already splintering ... I squeeze my eyes tight.

And then the pressure eases. The tentacle lifts and then falls away, severed. It flaps briefly at my feet, coating the deck with its blue blood, before its weight and the pitching of the ship carry it over the side.

And standing behind it is Aris.

He is coated with the thing's blood, his face the stern visage of a Shield, his magically-enhanced muscles rippling and ready to fight. His gladiuses drip with blue, his clothes with salt water. One side of his face is swollen, and a cut on his shoulder is already closing.

I have been in the presence of a god and did not tremble. Aris, though? He is vengeance incarnate.

And never have I been more glad to see him.

In a blink, he sheathes a sword and closes the space between us to put a hand on my shoulder.

"Are you hurt?" he asks, looking me over, like he's ready to take on the whole world for me. I tremble under his grip, not from fear, but from relief. If Aris is with me, everything will be all right.

The ship pitches suddenly, and he falls against me, bracing

himself against the wood at my back. I grab him and am able to keep upright.

The ship groans, filling the air with splintering sounds as we are lifted from the water before suddenly plunging back down again. A wave surges across the deck, sweeping sailors from their feet.

Aris pins me with his blue eyes, and for a heartbeat, I can't see anything else. Gods, I thought I'd lost him. The thought alone nearly killed me. I need to tell him …

Then the ship groans again, the morning sun blinding me as I look over Aris's shoulder, and I blink myself back to my senses. I shake my head, putting a hand on his chest to reassure him.

"I'm fine," I say. There will be time later for words.

He accepts this and turns back to the beast strangling the main deck.

A mantle has emerged from the sea, twenty feet long at least, with a wild alien eye several feet across roaming the ship, looking for something.

Looking, I fear, for me. Gods, have I doomed everyone on this ship to die here, ripped apart in the middle of the Broken Sea? The thought makes me dizzy. It cannot be a coincidence that this thing is attacking at daybreak, when I am powerless.

Mariana is on the quarterdeck, sending blasts of icy spears toward the exposed eye. Her robe and hair fly about her, but she keeps her footing as the ship bucks, fearsome concentration on her face.

One icy spear hits, and the creature roars in rage. The mantle disappears beneath the churning water, only to then turn, and the star-shaped underside of the beast emerges, a beak large enough to split a horse in two clacking loudly. It latches on to the side of the ship and rips a gaping hole as easily as teeth tear into bread.

Aris looks upward, where the tentacles are wrapping around the ship's masts. The foremast shatters, splinters of wood flying across the deck. One hits a sailor in the arm, and he drops, screaming. White bone sticks out of the mangled limb, and another sailor rushes to use his belt as a tourniquet. The injured man keeps screaming, audible even over the crack of the wood as the beast tears the ship apart. We are doomed. This thing will kill us, and it's my fault. Aris must have a similar thought.

"Wait here," Aris tells me, and he races for the mainmast, sheathing his other sword as he goes.

Like all the hells I will wait. It might be daytime; I may not have my magic—but I still have my knife.

I clench the blade between my teeth and haul myself up the splintering ladder to the forecastle. From here, I can see Stig in the water, harrying the giant monster—a kraken, I realize at last.

The beast of Aenon himself.

Stig has taken a chunk out of the mantle and is chomping at the base of the two long feeding tentacles. I see a row of suckers latch on to him, and his tail lashes, whipping the sea into foam. Then I lose sight of him as he's dragged down.

Aris has reached the mainmast and is climbing, the way hampered by fallen rigging and flapping sails. He nearly falls, saved only by his fingertips grasping the splintering wood. He heaves himself up with a single hand and gets to his feet.

I wonder if there is another creature in all the seas that can stand against this thing. I wonder if *we* will last against it, or if my story ends here, with all of us drowned or torn apart by this monster, this pet of the gods.

My ears are filled with the sound of shattering wood and clacking jaws and screams from the sailors and the pounding of blood in my head—and then, of all things, my ears are filled with song.

The air around me shivers with it, the song rising from the water all around in urgent, high-pitched waves.

A great black body emerges from the deep, breaching as its narrow jaw tears a tentacle from the base of the kraken. The mantle lifts and dips again as yet another whale—another black beast, forty feet long—grabs another arm, shearing it off. The kraken roars. Its remaining tentacles release their stranglehold on the ship and instead latch on to the whale, its suckers ripping into flesh, scrambling to keep the whale's jaws away.

Briefly the mantle emerges from the water, its remaining eye rolling and wild.

And from the mainmast, leaping with all the strength and speed he possesses, comes Aris. He dives like a sea hawk, with swords instead of talons, outstretched, roaring like a beast himself.

He buries the swords in the kraken's remaining eye.

The creature stills and sinks into the waves, pulling the two whales—and Aris—with it.

CHAPTER 40
ARIS

The water is *fucking* cold.

My blades sink into the beast's eye with sickening ease before reaching what I hope is its brain or heart or *something* important, and the thing shudders and falls still. The sea around us is foamy with oily slicks of blue blood and loud with wailing sailors. The groaning of the strangled ship, at least, has ceased.

But while I was briefly buoyed up on the mantle, it is now being pulled under by the strength of two giant whales, eager to make off with their meal. The seawater closes over my head before I can get a decent breath, and the force of their retreat to the depths pulls me along with them.

Also, the kraken has a fucking tentacle wrapped around my waist. The suckers are still pressed tight against me, and I can feel my skin tearing as I'm dragged along, red blood mixing with the blue. I'm whipped through the water as the whales turn, and it's all I can do to keep my grip on my gladiuses. I'll be damned to all the hells before I let that fucker take my gladiuses with it. I may not have named them, like Odall, but I'd sooner let it take an arm.

Besides, without them, I don't have much of a chance of getting free of this thing.

The blades went in easy but seem stuck in some sort of bony plating. The sea is turbulent now around me—I can't see anything in the chaos, so I have to rely on touch and the strength of my grip. I wiggle my swords back and forth, back and forth, for what seems like an eternity—until finally one breaks loose.

My breath is quickly running out, but the other sword is loosening too, and with one more heave, it unsheathes itself from the creature's carcass. I plunge both of them into the muscular band around me. The tentacle squeezes harder, some kind of macabre reflex, and despite myself, I release a stream of precious air, the bubbles glittering like priceless jewels as they float away.

I wrench my blades free and stab again, and again, blindly, trying to pry the muscles away from my chest. The grip of the tentacle at last begins to weaken, but so does my grip on consciousness.

I stab again, desperation starting to give way to panic.

But the kraken's grip releases, and I swear I can hear my ribs breaking as I push free. With one furious kick against its rubbery mantle, I am free.

Below me, the beast is rent in two by the whales, which disappear into the murky depths.

I look up—the ship is silhouetted above me, and it's moving away. A few thoughts penetrate past my pressing need for air – I'm sinking. And the ship is leaving.

A rush of anger overcomes me. This is *not* how Aris the White Tiger dies. Not without seeing Wren through her quest. Not without Wren ...

I kick with all the strength I can summon. I sweep my hands before me. My lungs are burning, fighting to inhale, even if it's just to breathe in the water around me. My chest aches with more than a lack of air, warning me that my injuries are severe. My eyes burn with the attempt to look through the salt, so all I can make out is the vague lightness above me, the approximate direction my air bubbles are taking. The sea around me is cold, and the steel isn't helping my buoyancy.

When I finally break the surface and inhale a breath of gods-blessed air, my limbs are screaming with the effort in a way I've never felt before, not even when I wore a manacle. I wipe the water from my face and take a few more deep breaths, sheathing my swords. The swell of a wave lifts me, and I spy *The James*—shrinking into the distance, leaving me injured and treading water.

Fuck that.

The ship is listing badly, and with damaged masts, it can't possibly make good time. I might have a chance at catching it if ...

But I cough, spitting out a clot of blood. *Shit.* I wince, struggling to keep treading water. I try to swim, but my left side feels like it's caving in. The waves lift me and crash over my head, and forget swimming—soon it's all I can do to keep air in my lungs instead of water.

And I'm not alone, I realize, as my legs are bumped by something swimming past me. Blood in the water tends to attract things—big, sharp-toothed things.

A fin breaks the surface, attached to the body of a shark at least twenty feet long and wider than a horse. If it thinks I'll be an easy target, that will be a fatal mistake. I grab the knife at my belt, ready for whatever else the god of water—who is rapidly becoming my least favorite god—is throwing our way.

The shark circles me, and I spin with it, treading water, and wait for it to make the first strike, ignoring the pain in my side. Like with the kraken, I decide I should go for the eyes. I follow it, turning, waiting for an opportunity and trying to keep my head above the waves.

But the shark just continues to circle me, flicking its tail impatiently in a rather unsharklike manner, flashing its striped flank at me.

That's when it finally dawns on my scrambled brain.

Stig.

The fucking shark Shield.

A bitter laugh escapes me just as a wave splashes more salt water into my mouth. I spit it out—staining the water red—and reach out to grab the shark's dorsal fin, the skin like sandpaper against my chest as he begins to swim. He is a massive, powerful beast, and he tows me back to *The James* in a few minutes. I swallow more than my fair share of salt water along the way, and my stomach roils in protest.

Dimitra is at the rail, one hand shading her eyes, and points and shouts when she sees us. A rope is tossed overboard, and even with my Shield strength, I am barely able to climb it from the sea, barely able to fight the pull of the current as *The James* attempts to make way. I am spent. When I get to the top, I turn and vomit out the seawater and close my eyes for a second as the world spins around me.

Caelus and Dimitra grab me and haul me unceremoniously over the rail—and then I'm tackled by Wren, her black robe enveloping us both, her warm arms around my neck and her face buried in my shoulder. I push her wild hair back from my face and struggle to get an arm around Wren as she shakes, crying. Gods, she seems to be holding on to me tighter than the kraken did. My chest screams with pain, but I hold her back just as tightly. I squeeze my eyes tightly for a moment, grateful to be back at her side.

"You *fucking* idiot," Dimitra says, shaking her head, but there's a smirk on her face.

"Are you all right, brother?" Caelus asks, squatting at my side.

I take a deep breath, glad to be back on the ship, even if it is in sorry shape. Stig hauls himself up and plants his feet firmly on the deck, laughing in a way that has me questioning his sanity a little. He is then tackled by Stella, who nearly knocks his naked ass back overboard. He meets my eye—I don't have the breath to thank him, but I nod in silent thanks, and he gives me a nod back.

I struggle to my feet, Wren and Caelus helping me. I shrug Caelus off once I have my footing but keep my arm around Wren. I am never letting her go.

The main deck is a mess. Blue blood is smeared with red, coloring nearly the entire deck. Most of the railing is splintered, along with a good bit of the forecastle. The foremast is gone. Rigging, sails, and pulleys hang at all angles from mangled yards. We are listing badly to the starboard.

Mariana is repeatedly kicking a bit of severed tentacle, like she could vent all her anger on that single bit of flesh. Her robe is flapping wildly around her, blue blood streaked across her face and chest. I've never seen her in such disarray.

Rafael doesn't seem to notice. He strides across the deck to her before lifting her in his arms and planting an open kiss on her mouth. She immediately wraps her legs around his waist, coaxing a tired whistle from some of the crew. Without another glance, Rafael carries her below deck, ducking through the door, not once moving his lips from hers.

A tired laugh escapes me, followed by a grunt as I realize that I must have broken several ribs. Gods, even *breathing* hurts now that the blaze of battle is wearing off.

"We should get you below too," Wren says. I raise an eyebrow, and she flushes, slapping one hand gently on my chest. "You need rest."

"I know what I need." I lean down to nuzzle the side of her neck and plant a kiss on the soft skin there. I can feel her breath catch in her chest. Broken ribs and who knows what else, Wren is still all I can think of. And this time, she doesn't push me away.

I bend double to relieve a sudden pang in my back. Gods, did I rupture my spine or something? *Can* you rupture your spine? I groan, catching my breath, and catch sight of a pair of fine black boots stomping to a halt before me, streaked with blue and red blood.

I straighten, and see Loren standing before me, hands on hips. Her fine white shirt cuffs are rolled up, her hands wiped clean but her clothing stained and ripped from the fight. Her eyes are blazing, her lips pressed into a thin line.

"Someone had better start explaining what the *fuck* just happened here," she says, her voice shaking with fury. One hand is resting on the hilt of her sword, and I cannot, I just *cannot* summon the strength to fight her right now.

"What happened is that we saved your fucking boat," Dimitra says between clenched teeth.

"*Ship*," Loren snarls, rounding on us, so angry that her words come out in an uneven rush. "I have been sailing my entire life! I have never seen—not even heard—of anything like that before. And now not only do I have the gods-damned Night Mage aboard my ship, but a hell beast nearly tears it in two! And if you think those two events are unrelated, you're even dumber than you look."

The crew have stopped their work and are openly staring at us.

"Perhaps we should take this to your quarters, Captain," Caelus says, all dignity and calm. He glances meaningfully at the crew. We don't want them to know all that Wren is, all that she is capable of— although, honestly, at this point I could care less about what anyone thinks.

Loren glares briefly at Caelus before returning her gaze to me and Wren. After a moment, her hand releases its hold on her sword hilt, and she turns, beckoning with one finger for us to follow.

CHAPTER 41
WREN

The four of us—Aris, me, Caelus, and Dimitra—follow the captain through the door, which is barely still hanging by a single hinge, to her quarters. The cabin is large, considering we're on a ship, spanning the entire width of the hull. The back is a wall of windows, though two are broken and one is missing entirely. In the middle is a desk, strewn with maps and a compass. A small shelf holds books and scrolls, perhaps once neatly stacked but now they are all scattered across the floor. The captain sighs as she looks at them, running a hand over her face, smearing speckles of blood. A wide bed, covers pulled up, sits in one corner. This is a woman who values order, tidiness.

And what a mess we've managed to make.

Captain Seagraves stalks to her desk. She takes a moment to roll the maps, setting them down neatly, and puts the compass in a drawer. She pulls out a crystal decanter from that drawer after a moment's consideration and pours several drinks' worth of an amber liquid into a goblet. She takes a long draw without offering any. She sits, laying a knife in front of her, to be in easy reach should she feel the need to use it.

"Talk," she says, glaring at us.

Talk. Aris is barely staying upright. I want him to sit, but of course, he won't. He's at least starting to breathe a little easier, though. There's a trickle of dried blood at the corner of his mouth, and I want to wipe it away, but Dimitra is glaring at me, so I turn instead to the captain. Being here, with Aris, feels a lot like being in Head Mage Saroya's office. We exchange glances, not really sure where to begin.

"Well?" Captain Seagraves barks. "Are you really on a mission to establish trade in the Abelon Wastes?"

"No," Caelus admits, diplomatic to the core. "We are not. We are sorry for deceiving you."

"*Dec-deceiving* me?" she stammers. Her face is pale with rage. She stands, bracing her hands on the desk. "My ship is too damaged to sail. We are *days* from the nearest port. Two of my crew are dead, and Samuel will lose an arm!"

She sits back down heavily, taking another long swig of her drink. "Should've known your offer was too good to be true," she says.

"You lot are lucky that I demanded payment up front," she adds, gesturing toward us with her cup. She puts her feet up on her desk, leaning back. "If we make it to Abelon, you can thank your Water Mage. Without her, we'd be at the bottom of the Broken Sea by now."

"We *are* on a mission sanctioned by King Leonidas," Caelus says carefully.

Beside him, Dimitra locks her hands behind her back, feet apart, the model of a soldier at ease. Aris still has an arm around my shoulders, but he is leaning on me less.

"We are taking the Night Mage," he says, gesturing toward me, "to the Wastes. It was revealed to her in a vision that Lord Caladrius himself wants her to make the journey."

Captain Seagraves splutters a bit in her drink, then wipes the back of her hand across her mouth.

"So you're all a bunch of crazy zealots, then?" she asks with a harsh laugh.

"Hardly," Dimitra says.

"You're telling me," Captain Seagraves says, pointing at me with her goblet, "that *this* girl summoned a kraken to attack my ship?"

"Lord Aenon summoned it," I say quickly.

Her eyebrows rise.

"We think. The elemental gods seem to have a ... grudge against Lord Caladrius for creating me, for giving me his magic. A kraken tore my home apart too." A pang pierces my chest as I think of my beloved lighthouse.

"And you didn't think to tell me this before we sailed?" she asks, her voice dangerously calm.

"We ... had hoped it wouldn't be necessary," Caelus says.

I swallow hard. This woman is not blinking. She is weighing her options, and I'm sure at least one of them involves throwing us all overboard.

"And the whales?" she asks after a minute. "Let me guess—you prayed to Caladrius, and he decided to send them to save you?"

"Something like that," I mutter.

Captain Seagraves inhales sharply.

"I ... am good with animals. They like me. Protect me, generally," I mumble. I squirm a little under her direct gaze.

Guppy chooses this moment to start rubbing against my boots, meowing for me to pick him up. Poor thing. He's got a streak of drying blue blood down one side, but otherwise, he seems all right. I'd bend to pet him, but I think Captain Seagraves might just stab me if I make any sudden movements.

She puts down her goblet and leans back, closing her eyes. "Do you *realize* how insane this all sounds?" she says softly.

"We will make sure that you are compensated for your losses," Caelus offers.

For a long moment, she doesn't say anything. Then she lets out a long breath. I wonder briefly if she considers just throwing us all overboard.

"If we make it to Abelon, I will expect to be *well* compensated," she says. "And the families of the dead as well."

"I swear it," Caelus says.

I'm not sure exactly when he assumed the role of speaker for our group, but I'm glad he has. Aris is shades paler than his usual golden tan, and I fear Dimitra would sooner stab this woman than attempt diplomacy. I'm the *last* person she wants to talk to right now, so Caelus, the scholar-Shield, is the only chance we have here.

"Very well," Captain Seagraves says, standing from her chair. I'm impressed that she's as stable as she is, considering the amount of liquor she just downed. "Let's see if we can salvage this ship."

"Captain, may I request that you don't ... let word get out about the Night Mage and our quest?" Caelus asks as we turn to leave.

She chokes back a laugh. "Who would I tell? And who'd believe it, anyway?"

We make it back to the deck, where the crew are scurrying to make repairs. Stig's finally found some clothes and is hauling buckets of seawater up to wash the gore from the deck. A stack of tentacles is pushed to one side, a great stinking heap.

"Why keep those?" Dimitra asks.

Captain Seagraves shrugs. "Squid is good eating," she says, striding past us. "Oi, Stella! That yard is going to come down on your head, you daft wench!"

At the thought of *eating* the kraken, my stomach clenches, and bile coats the back of my throat.

"Let's get to it, then," Dimitra says, rolling her shoulders. She goes to the mainmast and begins work on the rigging.

"You need rest," I tell Aris, who is headed for a jumble of sail and wood from the fallen yards of the mizzenmast.

He looks back at me, a smirk on his handsome face. For a moment, I forget about Mariana and Dimitra, I forget about my anger—hells, I forget how to breathe. All I can see is the sparkling blue of his eyes, the curve of his lips. Gods, I was so worried about him. If anything ever happened to Aris, I wouldn't go gray—I'd go green, a jade-colored star hells-bent on vengeance. I'd go to the immortal realm and face Aenon himself.

But I can't bring myself to say anything. Aris gives me a wink after a moment, rolling his shoulders like he's just finished a workout.

"I've never felt stronger," he says.

CHAPTER 42
ARIS

So that was a lie.

I hurt in a thousand places. I'm sure I cracked a few ribs—
one may have punctured my lung—and my right shoulder is definitely dislocated. I get Caelus's attention and nod toward my shoulder. He understands at a glance—Shields are used to this sort of
thing—and wordlessly rolls it back into place.

Fuck. That hurts.

And yet, once the brief lightning flash of pain is gone, it is already
settling back into place. I can feel the tissues re-forming. I've never
really prayed to Rigrasil before this trip, but lately it's been a daily
occurrence.

"Let's get to it, then," I echo, rolling my shoulder, and Caelus
joins me in moving some of the mess from the mizzenmast.

It takes all day. One of Loren's crew stays in the crow's nest,
scanning for more trouble, but thank all the gods—except Aenon,
fuck him—he finds none. Rafael and Mariana rejoin us in a bit. We
repair what we can, replace what we can. The foremast is gone, but a
few of the sails on the mainmast and the mizzenmast function just
fine.

After her brief respite, Mariana is back in the thick of it. She stands by the wheel on the quarterdeck, her hands outstretched. *The James* zips along at speed, the sails hardly doing anything. Wave after wave pushes us along, obeying Mariana's command.

She might be a pain in the ass, but she *is* incredibly strong.

By evening, though, even Mariana's reserves are spent. Rafael brings her below to rest, and Wren takes her turn.

Jade-colored light coalesces around her hands as Wren urges the ship onward, the ship's cat curled at her feet. It's a little jerky at first until she gets the hang of it, and we're all thoroughly soaked by rogue waves, but after a while she has us going as smoothly as Mariana had. Rafael's got all the lanterns lit with his spelled, heatless flames, and we blaze onward through the water like a shooting star. Pride swells in my chest—Mariana might be strong, but *my* Mage is the strongest.

"So why didn't we do this from the beginning?" Stig asks, dumping a pile of torn rope at my feet.

"Thought it would attract attention," I say, accepting a mug of barley soup from him. It's tasteless, but it'll do. I need the energy.

"Aye," he agrees.

Stig looks up at Wren. The wind is blowing her robe back like wings, the green lighting her face up in an eerie glow. Her mouth is set in a firm line, her hands outstretched. There's a tremor in her fingers, but she doesn't stop.

Gods, I am so fucking proud of her. And also very glad I didn't die today.

The air has changed from the cool promise of spring back into winter's chill. This far north, Mariana and Wren have to curb their magic. Loren's afraid they'll steer us right into an iceberg, and at their initial speeds, we'd be splintered in an instant. The girls are grateful for the reprieve. Mariana and Wren have never really gotten along—which, I suppose, is largely my fault—but they seem to have come to a sort of mutual understanding. Without their efforts, we would all likely have drowned at sea. The crew realize this, too, which is probably the only reason they haven't tossed us all over the side.

Wren is exhausted. I bring her whatever food I think she might find appetizing—on a ship, that's not much—but she's too tired to even eat. After a few bites, she falls asleep sitting up, and I have to tuck her into her bunk. I come back when Mariana needs a break, and she's still sound asleep. It takes me several minutes to wake her up, and it pains me to see how worn she is, the way the bones in her hands and her ribs are starting to jut out as the magic drains her strength, making her lose weight rapidly. Magic takes a toll at the best of times. Using it for days on end ... well, I worry we are getting dangerously close to burning her out.

With Mariana and Wren taking shifts pushing *The James* along, we make excellent time and limp into dock at Abelon City in just three more days. Abelon City is coated in ice. The port, too, has a crust of ice, and *The James* crunches through it with a sound like glass shattering. Rafael stands at the bow, ready to melt whatever the ship can't handle, but he's not needed. Whatever spells Mariana has placed on the ship are holding firm, and the ship finally glides to a halt at the dock.

I've never been to Abelon City before. From the rail, I can make out the wall, extending into the harbor with a gap just wide enough for a few ships. The wall is as tall as the one at the School of the Silver Flame, though not as thick. The pier and dock take up about half of the waterfront; the rest, a series of warehouses and storefronts.

We leave *The James* with little ado from Loren and her crew. Caelus and I carry our packs. Rafael tends to Mariana, who is white with exhaustion. Wren is able to keep upright, I'm pretty sure just through sheer stubbornness. Her legs do wobble when she steps onto the dock, and she stumbles into me for a moment before she regains her footing.

They need rest. We're directed to the Broken Tusk tavern and inn, a long building not far from the pier. The road is packed dirt, and the patches of ice make the footing tricky. Eventually, Wren loops her arm through mine for stability, any pride long gone. We pass no one, even though it is only midafternoon. The air is chill, and snow dusts the simple log buildings. Still, the weather is not bad enough to drive everyone indoors. I've heard the people of Abelon are a suspicious people, but it's a little eerie not seeing a soul as we go. Not even a rat or a pigeon. We trudge along, any gladness we had at being back on dry land quickly giving way to exhaustion.

Beyond the wall, I had glimpsed a vast pine forest to the west of the town. To the north are a series of farms. I'd mentioned to Loren that I thought farms in the frigid wasteland here were strange—how could anything grow here, even with earth magic? She replied with a wicked smirk—the farms aren't meant for growing crops.

They are for raising mammoths.

Up here in the Wastes, mammoths are used for transport and travel much the way that horses are used in Ocron. The beasts don't do well in Ocron—we've been trying to breed them for the army for generations without success. Not even our best healer Mages can keep them alive for more than a few weeks—but up here, apparently, they thrive.. They don't know if it is some dietary staple they get here or what—all I know is that as a boy, I dreamed of riding a great mammoth bull into battle, his tusks tipped with steel, my Mage at my side, the bards telling our stories at every inn and tavern across the continent. Even now, I am very much looking forward to seeing one face-to-face.

We get to the inn, and over the door there is a tusk instead of a sign, though the meaning is clear. The tusk must be thirteen or fourteen feet long, a great ivory curve cracked and stained with age—and the tip is broken off. The beast that grew this must have been massive, even by mammoth standards.

The walls of the inn are formed by sturdy logs joined by white mortar. It's significantly warmer than outside, even if it is as strangely devoid of people. The innkeeper's wife bustles out to meet us. She is a matronly woman, and once she gets a glimpse of the state of Mariana and Wren, she tsks and ushers us up some stairs.

"Supper will be ready in an hour," she says, briskly ushering us into the rooms.

The rooms are private, though there are only a few. Rafael and Mariana enter one without delay.

"I need a drink," Dimitra says, grabbing my arm as I pass. "Join me." She turns her golden eyes on me, the invitation plain.

I shrug her off. My priority is Wren.

"Some other time, maybe," I tell her.

Caelus and Dimitra pick one with bunk beds, and I guide Wren into the third. Honestly, I'm not even sure she registers the space at all. Her eyes have a distant, hollow look that I don't like.

It's a sparse room, with barely room for more than a bed, but it is clean, with a small fireplace and stacks of blankets. If Wren has any trepidation about sharing a bed with me, she's too tired to care. By the time I get the fire stoked and turn back, her boots are off, and she's curled up under a thickly padded quilt, eyes closed.

Gods. Not *once* in those last three days did my Mage complain. True, Mariana stepped up, but she made a big spectacle of it each time, making sure everyone knew it was *her* waterproofing spell that had saved their ass. Which, all right, was true. But when Mariana was too tired to go on, Wren stepped up without a word, burning like a quiet green flame all through the nights.

I slide off my boots and my outer layers and get in beside her, wriggling about in the blankets until I'm comfortable and we're both covered. Wren sighs and curls up until her back is arched just right against my chest. I drop a kiss just below her ear and fall asleep in the next breath.

CHAPTER 43

WREN

I think I could have slept for days if Aris had let me. Instead, he insists on waking me at dawn. I'm glad he waited until the sun was up—I am so tired and grumpy that I might have set him on fire to get him to leave me alone. I grumble all the while I add layer upon layer to my clothing—the fireplace has done little to warm the room, and it is going to be colder outside than I've ever experienced before. I stuff the gloves in a pocket and shrug my arms into the big coat, keeping my black cloak to put on top. I'm pretty sure I look like a big, round black ball, or maybe a well-fed bear ready for hibernation. I turn to get Aris's help with the overlapping clasps, still fighting to keep my eyelids open—and my mind goes completely and utterly blank.

Aris is pulling on a pair of snug, dark leather pants, giving me a momentary glimpse of his sculpted backside. He must hear the air escaping my lips, because he looks back at me over his bare shoulder, smirking when he catches my eye. I can't even blink. Heat rushes to my face, and I can't blame it on the layers I'm wearing. The room is suddenly sweltering.

"Enjoying the view, then, princess?" he chuckles, reaching for the rest of his clothing. I swallow; my tongue feels thick and stupid. The muscles of his back are so well-formed, a living work of art. My fingers ache to run down the groove of his spine, to feel the soft warmth of his skin. I clear my throat.

"Just wondering why you get to wear … that," I say, gesturing again at the pants which do nothing, *nothing*, to conceal *anything* about his form, "when I am bundled up in so many layers that I can barely move."

Aris shrugs on a shirt and prowls over to me, a predator's glint in his sky-blue eyes.

"I'd be happy to get you a similar pair," he says, arching an eyebrow. "I'd thoroughly enjoy it, actually." I feel a sweat start to break out on my forehead.

"No, that's not...I mean," I stutter, and he chuckles, running his eyes over me from top to bottom, like he's envisioning it. *Me*, wearing something that form-fitted, that revealing? I might as well be naked! I narrow my eyes at him, furious at the pleasure he's taking from teasing me. "You wish," I manage to spit out.

"Oh, for so, so many things," he says. The air between us practically crackles, like a storm before the lightning strikes. His eyes flick down to my lips, which are still parted and tingling despite the venomous words that want to spew from them. He lifts a hand, running it down my forearm. Even through the layers, I feel a familiar flame ignite beneath my skin.

"I'm your Shield. Your protection. I need to be mobile. You just need to keep warm. The leather is a practical choice."

"Practical. Right," I say, still feeling slightly dazed, which is probably due to sleep deprivation and near-starvation and definitely not the proximity to Aris. When he looks at me like that though, it's like staring into the sun.

He grabs my coat lapels, yanking me from my stupor and planting a heated, desperate kiss on my lips.

"You make a cute little black puffball, though," he says, his lips still touching mine. "But are you sure I can't change your mind about the leather?"

I smack his arm, and he relents with a laugh. He's in a better mood this morning, and I can feel my own lightening in response.

We head down and sit in the inn's common room, where he rewards my cooperation with another kiss, and makes sure I have enough food for a small army. Mariana and Rafael are already there, though they're prone to sleeping in—well, not sleeping really, but getting out of bed late—but I guess Mariana is as famished as I am. She's working on her second bowl of oatmeal, two apple cores already sitting in her empty bowl. She has lost weight these past few days too, and she didn't have much to lose. Her face is drawn, but there's a light in her eyes, an alertness that's been missing lately. I'm sure I look just as rough. I certainly feel like it. My skin feels thin, fragile. I've never used so much magic for such a long time, and I'd be perfectly happy if I never, ever had to again.

Aris and the other Shields go out to the courtyard to stretch and work their muscles. I watch him through the window, admiring him as always. It's cold, and his face soon gets a wonderful red flush. Vapor rises from his head and curls like smoke from his mouth. He and Dimitra are talking easily as they work, and he laughs at something she says.

Gods. What am I going to do about him? I have to get over his past. But am I going to be jealous of every woman he so much as speaks to, forever? Am I going to be continually looking over my shoulder? Or should I just see if we can resume our relationship, and take him at his word until he gives me a reason otherwise?

By the time they're done, Mariana and I have consumed enough for six men, and I'm feeling stronger by the minute. Magic takes an enormous toll, and lately I've been too tired to even eat after finishing a shift on *The James.*

I'm surprised to see Captain Seagraves, Stella, and Stig walk into the courtyard. I guess they'll need to stay here too, while the ship gets repaired. Captain Seagraves talks to Aris for a moment before continuing into town, clasping hands with him before she leaves, her crew trailing behind her.

"You're quiet," Rafael says, looking at me. "Feeling all right this morning?"

"Fine," I say.

"What did that roll ever do to you?" Rafael asks, nodding at the crumbs falling from my fingers. I've torn it into shreds.

I smooth my hands on my pants. "It's nothing," I mumble.

"Leather pants, Aris, really?" Mariana says, following my gaze and rolling her eyes.

"They're better for mobility," I mumble, reaching for my mug and using it to hide the color on my cheeks.

I'm saved from further interrogation by the Shields. They are served ash water and massive bowls of oatmeal, and they tuck in while Rafael unrolls a map.

"So, I bought this in town while the girls were eating breakfast," he says, smoothing the parchment across the table. "It's got more detail than the one at the temple, but not much."

The map shows the rough wedge of land that is Abelon. We're in the only town on the island here—the rest is ice, and then mile after mile of mountains. Some of it, mostly in the south, is forested in pine.

"How large are the mountains?" Dimitra asks.

"Pretty big," Rafael says, tracing the ones just north of the town. "These are the foothills. They're not that bad. We can hire some mammoths to take us through them pretty quickly. Since the weather is warming, the glaciers won't be entirely frozen anymore, and we'll have to be careful here."

"Where is the door?" I ask.

Rafael frowns and scratches the back of his neck. "So, the thing is, no one's actually *seen* it before—we're just going by Tekton's translation from the book," he says.

Mariana huffs. "So we've based this entire expedition on the chance that some priest three hundred years ago correctly transcribed the single copy of the Book of Silver available in the world, and the astronomical guesswork of a mad hermit?" She crosses her arms. "Perfect."

"That's not entirely true," Caelus says. He pulls out the map that the astronomer gave him. He lays it out next to Rafael's map. There are curved lines bisecting Caelus's map, but that means nothing to me. He traces one of the lines for a moment, his mouth tight.

"*Vires, honos, fides*," Caelus chants softly. "*Fides*. Have faith."

Aris rolls his eyes.

Caelus looks at Rafael's map again. He asks the innkeeper for a quill—and then he carefully sketches the curved lines onto Rafael's map.

"It's like looking for a needle in a haystack," Dimitra mutters.

"Nope. That's a lot easier. You just burn the hay," Rafael says with a wink, watching Caelus.

"Now, I'm making a few assumptions here," Caelus says, still sketching. His yellow eyes are narrowed, and he's almost talking to himself.

"Such as?" Mariana prompts. She's leaning over the map now, her eyes sparkling. For all she feigns disinterest in our quest—or as much as she views accompanying me as a chore—the lure of the mystical book has piqued her interest. What a tale it would be if we actually found it, monsters and gods aside.

"Well, the location should be as far north as possible, to take advantage of the fact that the summer will have continuous daylight, and thus leave Wren's power at its weakest," he says, gesturing to the northern part of the island.

"Also, the path of the eclipse will need to achieve totality in order for Wren's power to activate, which narrows the location to ... here," he says, drawing a rough circle.

Aris is leaning back in his chair, arms crossed, and he raises an eyebrow at Caelus's map.

"How much land does that leave us to search?" he asks.

Caelus frowns. "A few square miles," he says. Then he looks up, meeting my gaze. "And only a few days to do it."

"So we split up," Rafael says, rubbing his hands together. "Mages on mammoths. Shields will shift and cover more ground that way. We'll signal somehow if we find it."

"Over my dead body are we splitting up," Aris growls. "We'll have to find another way."

"Such as?" Dimitra asks.

They lock eyes, a wordless conversation between them. The tension between them grows, and I twist my hands in the cloth of my pants to keep from shouting at them.

"I'm not leaving Wren," he says, annunciating the words carefully.

Dimitra's predatory gold eyes flick to mine, then down to the green pendant around my neck. Heat climbs my neck, but I don't look away.

"I'll scout ahead. I'm a wolf—this terrain won't slow me down," Caelus offers.

Mariana crosses her arms, apparently miffed that her Shield doesn't show her the same amount of protectiveness that Aris shows me.

"Ice is just frozen water," she explains, like we're all children. "I can skate across snow faster than you can run."

"You're telling me you can walk on water?" Rafael asks, his eyebrows almost reaching his hairline. She looks back at him over her shoulder and shrugs.

"Rigrasil's *balls*, but it's cold here!"

The words jar Aris, and he blinks, his gaze lifting over Dimitra's shoulder.

There, standing in the open door—as naked as the day she was born—is Adriana, twirling a rolled letter in one hand, her pale body turning pink from the elements. She attracts a fair bit of attention, the few patrons in the inn openly ogling her, which I suppose was her intent. She's more similar to Aris than I think either of them wants to admit.

A smile lifts one side of Aris's mouth.

"I think I have an idea," he says.

"So let me get this straight," Adriana says. She leans back in the chair, the front two legs precariously leaving the floor. The innkeeper's wife, bless her, found a tunic, leggings, and boots for her. Even in plain, simple clothing that is several times too large for her, Adriana is stunning.

"You want me to come with you on a quest into the frozen wastes to find a magic door that may or may not exist, behind which may or may not be the mystical Book of Silver, which will let Wren communicate directly with the god of night and the rest?"

"During the height of the eclipse—don't forget that part," Rafael throws in. Mariana sighs.

"Right," Adriana says, nodding slowly. "Well, you're all a bunch of lunatics, aren't you?"

"This was a great idea, Aris," Dimitra says. "Let's tell your baby sister all about our plans so she can go blabbing off to everyone on the continent on her way home."

"Oh, no, I'm coming," Adriana says, slamming her chair back onto the floor. "Are you kidding? Even a wild-goose chase through the mountains is better than being the courier for the king's love letters."

The room goes silent. My cheeks flame with embarrassment.

"They're not ... I mean ..." I start to say. I look at Aris. Gods, I haven't done anything wrong! Why am I embarrassed that Leo's been writing to me so we can both keep abreast of the plans? He's the king of the continent!

Aris holds up a hand. "The point is," he says tersely, pointing at the circle Caelus drew, "we have very little time. We need Adriana's sight. She'll be able to cover more ground than us."

"True," Adriana purrs. "I am quite fast."

"So it's settled," Caelus says. "I'll arrange for some mammoths and a guide. I want us moving as soon as possible."

"If it's mammoths you want ..." the innkeeper calls from the bar in the back of the room. Gods, I forgot we weren't alone here. How much has he overheard? And does it matter? By the time he can get word to anyone outside Abelon, I hope to be long gone from here. "I've a buddy that'll take care of you. He'll be your guide too, anywhere on this frozen hell you want to go, for the right price."

"Well, what are we waiting for? Let's get this over with," Mariana says.

CHAPTER 44

LEO

M*y Wren,*

Things are becoming a little more heated in Roallac. What was supposed to be two weeks' stay has now extended into a month. Queen Evanthia continues to draw out negotiations—to what end, I can't say. Dare I assume that it is to keep me at her court for longer? But why? If she is hoping that a prolonged visit will mean an alliance of a different sort between our countries, I'm afraid I must disappoint her, as my heart belongs to another.

An interesting thing happened yesterday. The queen and I were taking tea on one of the terraces, as we've been wont to do almost daily during my stay. She brought up the Book of Gold, quite slyly, asking if she might see it when she comes to Estana—not that I've extended any such invitation. I deferred the idea and changed the subject, complimenting her instead on the shrewdness of her negotiations as we continue to work on our treaty. She did not seem happy to drop the issue.

It seems, little bird, that we are not the only ones seeking the books. I

will take your advice on the use of certain key words in our correspondence, though I hope to never need them. Not even my spymaster shall know of the code, and I have burned your last letter, as per your instructions.
   Stay safe.

Yours,
   Leo

CHAPTER 45
ARIS

I've seen a lot of epic shit since I claimed Wren.

Mammoths, though, have got to be in the top three.

About ten feet tall at the shoulder, they are covered in long, dense dark fur. They have big, flapping ears, and a hump on their shoulders. Their long, flexible trunks are flanked by a pair of tusks. One of the creatures, the bull, has one tusk that is at least fifteen feet long and as big around as a tree, a giant, sweeping ivory curve. The other is broken off short. The females in his harem have shorter tusks, but they are still impressive. I bet they could knock over a building with those tusks. Shame the army never successfully implemented them. I could have realized my boyhood dream.

And Wren, of course, is petting them like they are kittens. I am more afraid of her getting trampled as they vie for her attention than I am of her getting gored. She giggles as they crowd her.

"Oh, you are magnificent. Yes, you are," she says, stroking the side of one of the females. Another mammoth lifts her braid with her trunk, giving it a little tug, like a toddler trying to get her attention.

"Well, that's different," Brodie says.

Brodie is the shepherd, though that seems an inadequate term.

His "flock" is a small herd of mammoths. There are eight of them, ranging from the massive bull to one "small" young one, who is only about six feet at the shoulder.

Brodie scratches behind one ear, and I'm suddenly concerned he has fleas. His hair hangs in greasy strands that were probably reddish at one point. He hasn't shaved in this decade, and his hat and clothing seem to be a patchwork of different animal skins. His mammoths, in contrast, appear well tended to and well groomed.

"Animals like Wren," I say.

Brodie shrugs. He's less concerned about his herd trampling Wren than he is about making sure he gets paid, half in advance.

Caelus goes over the map again with him. Brodie waves one hand dismissively.

"Sure," he says. "We'll get you to the Mirrored Pass. Should take six, maybe seven days." He scratches again. I move back a step. "Summer's nearly in. We should be making good time."

"How many days do we have until the eclipse?" Dimitra asks Caelus again, like we haven't all been asking him that every hour for the past week.

"Ten," he says grimly. Not much of a margin for error.

"We'll be there with time to spare," Adriana crows. Confidence, it seems, is a family trait. Or arrogance, depending on who you ask. She's bundled in so many layers that she can barely walk, and her face and head are wrapped in at least three scarves. Only her eyes are visible, icy chips of blue.

Loading up the mammoths is an arduous task. Each one has to be fitted with a special saddle the size and heft of a large chair, which then has to be buckled around their massive girth with a series of straps as wide as my waist. Brodie checks and then double-checks each, in a slow, methodical manner that has Mariana tapping her foot, impatient to get on.

"Last thing you want is to be sliding off a poorly placed saddle," he chides her.

It takes agonizing hours, but eventually we set off from Abelon

City. Wren and I mount up on one, and I reach around her for the reins. Brodie assures me that the female we're on will follow his bull without question, but I hold the reins all the same.

Dimitra refuses to get onto the last one with Caelus.

"I'll walk," she says.

Brodie looks at her like she's stupid. "We're to cover near thirty miles today, maybe more tomorrow. I doubt even a strong girl like yourself can keep up in these snowdrifts," he says. "Get up."

She gives him a feral grin and shifts.

Brodie apparently is unfamiliar with the shifting abilities of a Shield—as are his beasts. The lead bull that Brodie will be riding threatens to rear up and trumpets out a challenge that echoes into the cold air.

"What in all the hells!" Brodie bellows, looking back at Dimitra in her feline form.

She is a glorious leopard, sleek and strong, with black rosettes all over her deep golden coat. Her tail swishes, freeing itself from the remainder of her clothes, and she takes off at a run, headed north. I itch to go with her—it would feel good to have the ice crackling under my paws, feel the muscles of my tiger form bunch and stretch as we race across this wasteland.

Wren inhales sharply as the mammoth dances under us, her trunk flailing as she shakes her head, and I am recalled to the situation at hand.

Brodie grabs the bridle of his bull, calming the beast with a few quiet words. He tosses Dimitra's clothing and weapons up to Caelus and mounts the bull by scrabbling up the harness, not using a mounting post like we did. He grumbles a bit as he settles himself in front of our packs.

"Let's get on with it, then," he says, and he shakes the reins with a cry. "*Heeyah!*"

The bull tosses his trunk again and sets out at a trot, following Dimitra's paw prints north.

There is nothing up here. Once we leave the town, we pass a few small copses of trees, but otherwise, nothing. It's a vast, rolling, frozen wasteland. The air is a little above freezing, but only a little. This means that the glaciers we cross are made all the more treacherous, the ice breaking without warning. The mammoths are mostly good at picking safe paths, but once, Mariana and Rafael's mammoth goes down to her knees in frigid water, before trumpeting and scrambling back, nearly dislodging her passengers. Mariana grabs the saddle, and Rafael grabs Mariana, so they do fine. Still, I am relieved when we get to the far side of that particular glacier.

"I liked the mountains at Aeturnus better," Wren grumbles, patting the shoulder of the beast we're riding. She's nicknamed her Tawny, as she's a little lighter in color than the others. Sure. Why not?

Still, she has a point.

"They're called the Wastes for a reason," I say. I let my hand stray from her hip to the curve of her belly, eager to distract her.

She smacks it away. "Hands to yourself, Shield," she chides, but there's laughter in her voice.

Good.

"You like Aeturnus?" I say. I bend to place a kiss on the side of her neck. This time, she doesn't swat me.

"Mmm," she says. She leans back into me, just a little. "I liked the temple. It reminded me of home, of my lighthouse."

"We'll go back, when this is done," I say, my lips still grazing her skin.

"I've written to Tekton and Delphine," she says. "I'm going to ask Adriana to carry it, when we're done here. Just an update on our progress."

Tawny slips a bit, and Wren grabs at my arm to keep from sliding off. I maybe flex my muscles under my coat. She turns and shoots me a knowing grin.

"Show off," she mutters, but her eyes stray to my lips. "That had better be your sword hilt pressing against my back, Shield."

It is not.

And I swear if I can't keep my mind off how Wren looked in the bath at Basti and how good she feels pressed against my groin, I'm going to go mad. It's not like I can steal away and give myself a little relief out here – there's little cover to provide privacy, and I don't like an audience.

Madness it is, then.

I bend to kiss her—before a shout from Rafael gets my attention. He's waving at Dimitra, still in leopard form, as his mammoth tosses her head in warning. Dimitra seems to have had no trouble on the terrain, her great paws leaving bounding prints in the snow as she passes. She waits for us by a small grove of ancient firs as the sun starts to set, her tail swishing impatiently. At her feet are two plump geese. Not only has she staked out a campsite—she's caught dinner. Wren gives a disappointed pout at my distraction.

I squeeze Wren's hip as I jump off Tawny's back. Wren doesn't hesitate to slide down into my arms. I bend to kiss her one more time for good measure, and she lets me. Ever since the ship, she's been less shy, more accepting of my touch. I run the tip of my tongue against the seam of her lips, and she opens with a gasp that nearly finishes me. She doesn't pull away until she hears Rafael's cough behind us, and then she stumbles off, muttering something about starting a fire, her face flushed all the way up to her ears. I choke back a laugh, shrugging when Rafael gives me arched look, and go help her set up the camp.

CHAPTER 46
WREN

All right, I haven't entirely decided to forgive Aris for his past … philandering transgressions. But something inside me shifted after the kraken, something that was desperate to tell him how I felt. And he's been patient, to my surprise. He hasn't been shy about giving affection, not even in front of Dimitra and Mariana, like he's proving something to them and me. I'm not overly comfortable with attention in public, usually—but I find I don't exactly mind it anymore either, even if Dimitra looks ready to tear my heart out, glaring at me with her golden eyes from the shadows of the trees. In fact, I feel almost smug.

"I'll take the reins there," Brodie says, and he takes Tawny and the other mammoths a short distance away. He lets them drink glacial water from a small stream and then ties them each to a tree. It's a laughable setup—one toss of their heads, and the trees would be uprooted easily.

"I do hope they don't run off in the night," Mariana says, narrowing her eyes at Brodie.

He shows off broken teeth in a snaggled grin. "No chance of that, miss. Been training 'em like this since they was born. Sometimes," he says with a wink, touching his temple with a finger. "Sometimes all that's holding you back is in your mind."

I think about this for a while as Rafael and I gather fallen branches for a fire. Brodie might be a stinky fellow, but he cares for his herd, and there's a wisdom in his words that surprises me.

We clear a patch of frozen ground and lay out our wood. The sun is setting, as much as it will do this far north anyway, and any warmth that was in the air is rapidly fading.

"Your turn, Night Mage," Rafael says, gesturing toward the wood. He looks annoyingly warm in just his regular clothes and red robe—I guess that's one advantage of being a Fire Mage. They never have to worry about getting cold.

Brodie has other ways of coping—he pulls a dented flask from some pocket of his garments and takes a long swig.

"Remember, focus on your core first," Rafael coaches. He comes to stand beside me, and his presence is comforting. "Picture the flame in your core—then push it out. I have to use words, but you do it however you want."

I close my eyes, taking a deep breath. I hear movement behind me, a soft padding of feet and rustle of cloth. Dimitra must have shifted and is getting dressed. She's been quieter than usual lately—I thought nothing could disturb Dimitra's calm focus, but she has seemed distracted since we landed in Abelon. I hope that the run today was good for her, cleared her head. I know Aris wanted to go too—but he wanted to stay with me more.

And then I wonder if *that* is what has Dimitra so wound up. Since the morning I woke up to find her glaring at me, she's been colder than usual, not offering to help me with my knife skills or even talking to anyone.

I try to focus on seeing the ball of darkness inside me, but I keep getting distracted by the sounds. The plop of some snow falling from a tree. The soft snorting and trumpeting of the mammoths. The far-off crack of ice.

"You kind of wonder when we're going to see a minion of the god of fire," Rafael says. I hear him shift a little. "We've seen the kraken, the manticore, the trolls. I'm feeling a bit left out."

I can't help the smile that curves my mouth. I'd be surprised if he's managed to think of anything at all besides Mariana lately. He has fallen for her hard.

"Let's spar tonight," Dimitra says. There's a change in her tone, a softness that I only hear when she's talking to Aris.

I hear a grunt, Aris dropping some more branches behind me before moving off. I try not to think about those damn leather pants. I feel rather than see Dimitra come up behind me, likely eager to get warm now that she's without her fur coat.

"Concentrate," Rafael urges. "Breathe. Let your breath become the flame."

I let out a shaky breath.

"He'll come back to me, you know," a voice hisses in my other ear. "He always comes back to me."

My eyes snap open, and as they do, a great blast of light erupts from me and incinerates the pile of wood before us in an instant blast, momentarily blinding me. I can feel waves of heat rolling from me, lifting the hair from my neck and the robe from my back in a hot, dry wind.

Behind me, the hissing voice has become a scream, a shriek— Dimitra is aflame, fire engulfing her, crisping her hair like it is dried grass, melting the skin from her hands as she fights to put it out.

Rafael has the fire under control in a heartbeat, maybe even sooner—but the damage has been done. The left side of Dimitra's face is blistered and peeling, her cloud of dark hair melted to her scalp. She groans as she tries to peel a piece of her coat back from her hand, but the skin on the back of her hand lifts off, exposing white tendon.

I turn and vomit, emptying the bilious contents of my stomach into the remnants of what was to have been our fire. The liquid spits and steams as it contacts the ash, the putrid smell of both making me feel light-headed.

Gods. What have I done?

"Are you all right?" Aris asks, one hand on my back.

I wipe my mouth and stand, nodding with more confidence than I feel.

"Is *she* all right?" Dimitra says. Her voice is harsh, thick with pain. She doubles over, the left side of her face blackened and distorted. My stomach clenches again.

"Gods. I am so sorry – what can I … how can I help?" I ask, my hands shaking like leaves in a storm. How could I have lost control so badly? Has all my time working on control with Rafael over this trip been for nothing? Dimitra looks like something from a nightmare, her panting breaths wheezing through her burned lungs.

She spits at me, the only act of defiance she can manage before groaning again. Rafael settles her down on the ground, rubbing her back soothingly. Caelus comes over with his pack and starts immediately applying a salve to Dimitra's hands.

"Keep moving them. We don't want the damage to set in," he says.

"You'll be fine by morning, Mitra," Aris chides, unconcerned.

I swear in that moment that if Dimitra's hands weren't blistered, sloughing messes right now, she'd be heaving her daggers right into his pretty face.

And then I realize—Aris is right. Yes, I lost control—but also, Dimitra is a Shield. She'll heal by morning, likely without so much as a scar. I didn't mean to cause her pain—in fact, I feel terrible about it, and I'm certain her screams will haunt me for a long, long time— but a part of me has to wonder. Is my power off-balance because we are so far north, with the sun still visible so late in the day? Or, a small, dark part of me wonders …

Did she provoke me on purpose?

We gather more wood, and this time Rafael lights it. Brodie, not surprisingly, has decided he'd rather camp over by the mammoths than with us.

"I'll be warm enough on my own," he says, eyeing me, before taking another swig of his drink and wandering off.

By the time we've got the geese dressed and cooked, Dimitra's face is already less swollen, the clawing of her hands more relaxed. Her breathing is easier, less stilted by pain.

Guilt still gnaws at my stomach, though, and I have to fight it to get down a few bites of food. Dimitra's in no shape to spar after the meal—in fact, she's downright morose, sitting far back from the rest of us, her golden eyes flickering in the firelight as she watches me, unblinking.

"Maybe we all turn in early tonight. Been a long few days," Rafael says.

Caelus nods, getting up and stretching. "I'll take the watch tonight," he says to Aris. "Get some rest."

That night, I think the only thing that's keeping Dimitra from twisting a knife in my back is that fact that Aris is curled up tight against it.

The next morning a messenger hawk arrives, making his way with tired wings as we break camp. Dimitra is nearly healed, as far as I can tell, though the hair on the left side of her scalp is only stubble. The right side, I'm astonished to see, has regrown to nearly its previous length. Shield magic is incredible. She looks like she's had a pretty rough night – her eyes are bloodshot, and her face is haggard from pain. My stomach twists when she catches me staring, and I look away.

The hawk nearly flops onto the ground when he lands, a scroll tied to one leg. His beak is open, and he is panting from exertion.

"Hey, Daniil. What's the rush?" Adriana says, stroking the bird's back.

A blink and a gust of wind, and the bird is now a man. He's rangy and pale-skinned, sweat dripping from his dark, cropped hair. He rests on his hands and knees, trying desperately to control his breathing. Caelus hands him a mug of water, which he gulps down. Adriana brings him a blanket and drapes it over his shoulders. He can't be much older than she is—and he's not just in a rush; he's scared. Panicked. He hands me the scroll with trembling hands and wide eyes, still breathing too hard to speak.

This one is not on the fine, wheat-colored paper that Leo usually uses. This paper is the color of bleached bone, a green ribbon tied around it. The seal is different too—black wax, with the image of a snake eating its tail.

CHAPTER 47
QUEEN EVANTHIA

*T*o the Night Mage,

Word has reached me of your quest to obtain the Book of Silver. Your friend Leonidas is quite the talker when the proper leverage is applied.

I shall be blunt. I have your king. In exchange for his return, I demand the Book of Silver and the Book of Gold. Fetch them both for me, and I will release him.

The rest of his party have already found their demise in the Roallac snake pits.

Do not let him share their fate.

You have until the winter solstice. At that time, I shall assume you are no longer interested in preserving the life of your king, and I will execute him.

And then, I will come for Ocron.

. . .

Evanthia Trifera
  Queen of Roallac
  High Priestess of the Black Water Witches

CHAPTER 48
ARIS

Wren's hands are shaking, and her face has gone pale.

"What?" I ask.

She hands over the paper.

"Of all the fucked up … What is she thinking?" I shout. I crumple the paper in my hand, ready to heave it into the flames, but Wren stops me.

"No," she says, and she nods toward the rest of our party. "They all need to read it."

"What does this mean, 'leverage'?" Mariana asks, one hand covering her mouth.

"Torture, usually," Rafael says, reading over her shoulder.

"Oh, gods," Mariana says. She turns and buries her face in Rafael's chest.

Adriana reads it last, seated next to the hawk Shield Daniil.

"Grave news, my friend," she says, sitting cross-legged on the frozen ground.

He nods, swallowing the second mug of ash water Caelus has handed him.

"It came out of nowhere," he says, his youthful voice cracking a little. "She threw a party for us, announcing to everyone how glad she was that our countries would soon be allies. Gods, we had no idea!" He slams his fists against the ground. His head droops for a second.

"How *did* you get away?" Dimitra asks. Her arms are crossed, her eyes glittering. She does not trust this messenger.

A growl starts in my throat, and Daniil looks up, surprised, his eyes wide, darting between us.

"Oh, fuck off, guys," Adriana says. "Can't you see he's exhausted?"

Daniil swallows hard. "I don't know," he says, dropping his gaze. "I should have died with the rest of them. The number of Water Mages who just … they just appeared out of nowhere! Coming out of the swamp like ghosts! The queen needed a Shield messenger, and I was the only one with King Leonidas that day. She wanted to make sure that her message would get to you, carried by someone you would trust. I should have died with the rest of them!" He drops his head, and we pretend not to see the tears dripping down his face.

Fuck.

"Fly home, to Estana," Adriana tells Daniil gently, rubbing his back. "Warn them about what is coming."

The Shield shifts and flaps tiredly but manages to get airborne after a moment, winging his way southeast.

"So what do we do?" Rafael asks, still holding one arm around Mariana.

"We should have kept him, interrogated him," Dimitra says, spinning a knife in either hand.

"He's not the enemy!" Adriana barks, hands clenched. "He's been through enough!"

"Has he?" Dimitra says, whirling on her. "Our friends have been *killed.*"

"Wren, do you know who was with Leo?" I ask her. My voice is quiet, but everyone turns and looks at her.

She looks down. "No," she whispers. "Zale and Rubita won some kind of tournament. They went with him, as the king's champions. I don't know if … if Ismini and Aleka …" She can't even finish the thought.

I grab her, holding her tightly against me. She's shaking, and I can feel her hot tears through my shirt. She grabs the fabric tightly, burying her face in my shoulder.

"What about Markos?" Dimitra asks. "Was Commander Markos with them?"

"I don't know," Wren says into my chest. "Leo didn't mention anyone else by name."

Everyone grows quiet for a long moment, wondering who of our colleagues, our friends, might have gone with Leo on this trip. Markos could very well have gone—and sure, I didn't like Zale, but I barely knew the guy. Rubita was a fine Fire Mage, one I'd almost claimed myself.

Were any of my siblings there? Something that could be fear threatens to grab ahold of my chest—but the White Tiger does not feel fear (at least, not when my Mage isn't concerned). Spyridon, I reason, is at Prasinos. Rea is at the school, and Adriana is with me. That leaves just Myron and Lukas. *Fuck.* I might not be close with my siblings, but they are the only family I've got. I don't want anything to happen to them.

And if something has?

I swear to Rigrasil I'll have the snake bitch's head before this is done.

"Mage Ismini is an academic, and Shield Aleka is the captain of Estana's guard. They would not have left the city," Caelus offers, his calm voice intruding on my murderous thoughts.

Wren nods, releasing my shirt. "Right. So we get the Book of Silver," she says, her mouth a firm line. "And then, well, maybe Caladrius can help us."

"Maybe," Dimitra scoffs. "That still leaves us without the Book of Gold. And if King Leonidas dies—after the queen died without giving him children—his succession is at risk. The power of the book has always passed to a direct descendant—Ocron may lose the power of the book entirely. Not to mention the Mages aren't as strong as they were."

"With a new Head Mage and magic fading, I'm not sure that there are enough Mages to launch an assault against Roallac," Rafael adds flatly. "The best of us were in the king's entourage, and they're already dead."

"So we get the Book of Silver and send word to Head Mage Iraklis, and let *him* find the Book of Gold, and we take both to Roallac," Mariana says.

"So Evanthia is the head of the Black Water cult," I muse, looking at Mariana.

She shrugs. "There have always been rumors that someone powerful was in charge," she says. "They had to be under someone's protection. But they're so secretive, not even King Leonidas's spymaster knew for sure."

"They're not a secret anymore," Rafael mutters. "What does Evanthia want the books for, anyway? Why does she need both? Wouldn't one do?"

"Let us read your letters, then," Dimitra snaps, holding her hand out to Wren. "I want to read them for myself. All of them. See what you missed."

"No," she says defiantly, her cheeks flaring red. She shoots me a look that is decidedly guilty.

"Why not?" I ask her.

Her lips tighten, and she won't answer me.

"Wren, why not?" I ask again, quietly. What is there in those letters that she doesn't want us to see? Doesn't want *me* to see?

This whole time she's been upset with me for having slept with Mariana and Dimitra—before I was with her—has she been writing explicit letters to Leo, and he to her? I guess there could be other secrets in the letters, I tell myself—maybe something about her magic, or her dreams.

What a fucking fool I've been. Of course she'd rather be with Leo.

Why be with me, relegated to a life on the road, when she could be a queen herself? And wear nice clothing, like that gold gown Leo gave her, instead of the same thing every day? To sleep in a feather bed instead of the cold, hard ground? I wonder, too, if she feels *safe* with him, like *I* can't protect her. After all, our entourage *was* his idea. And Wren had agreed. I feel like all the air has been sucked out of my chest.

"What secrets are you keeping?" Mariana says, eyes flashing. She goes to Wren's pack and starts pulling things out. Books, clothes, her spelled candle, and a small brown pouch all are overturned onto the ground.

"They're not there," Wren says, snatching her things back. Her cheeks flame red. "I burned them all. After you mentioned that my letters could fall into the wrong hands reaching Leo, I realized his could too. I didn't want there to be any evidence left for searching hands."

"Hands like mine?" I ask, crossing my arms.

Wren rolls her eyes. "This isn't about you," she snaps.

"Lovers' quarrels aside, there could have been information in there about the queen and her intentions," Rafael says, as diplomatically as he can.

"There wasn't," Wren says, shaking her head. She plops onto a rock, putting the fire between us. "He was hopeful, actually, that his visit was going well, that they were going to come to some sort of alliance. I know there was talk of the Water Mages in Roallac going to the school to learn from Ocronian Mages."

"He was inviting the Black Water Witches into Ocron?" Dimitra says, incredulous.

"Not all of their Water Mages are Black Water Witches," Mariana snaps. "My family has been living under that particular cloud of prejudice for some generations now, as have all Water Mages from northern Ocron. They're an unofficial group who give water magic a bad name."

"Well, they're 'official' now. Do you know anything about them that might help us?" Rafael asks, looking down at her with a tenderness that has me wanting to burn my eyeballs. Together they seem the golden pair—her long white-blond hair, his groomed golden mane that puts my own to shame. I want Wren to trust me the way they trust each other, to look at me the way Mariana looks at Rafael. Despite everything, jealousy stabs low in my gut, as real and painful as any knife. "Do you know anything about the strength of her forces?"

"They're strong," Mariana says, biting her lip. "Honestly? I don't think Ocron would stand a chance. Our best bet is to get those books and hand them over, like the queen says."

"We can only guess where the Book of Silver is, and we don't know where to start on the Book of Gold!" Dimitra yells.

"Then we should get moving, shouldn't we?" Mariana shouts back.

"All right, then," Adriana says, standing up and dusting off her pants. "I've had enough of your bickering. I'll scout ahead, meet up with you at camp tonight, or I'll return sooner if I find anything."

In a blink, she shifts and takes to the sky.

My little sister is a pain in the ass, but she is a brilliant flier. I envy her ability to just get up and fly away from this situation, fly away from Wren.

"I'll go get Tawny," Wren says, eager to get away as well.

Brodie obviously knows something is up with us, and has been keeping his distance, though he's gotten the mammoths ready for travel.

I remove my coat and boots. "I'll walk."

I was right, racing through the Wastes as a tiger is exactly what I needed to clear my mind. Dimitra runs beside me, a blur of black and gold. Our paws eat up the miles, and when I glance over my shoulder, I can barely make out the forms of the mammoths behind us—can barely see Wren.

I really should wait for them, but the mammoths get nervous around us in our shifted forms, and there's nothing and no one around for miles. Wren doesn't need my protection. Or so I tell myself.

The exercise keeps thoughts and emotions from overwhelming me.

And then there's Leo. How the fuck are we going to find both books before the snake bitch decides she's had enough and tosses him into her viper pit? And do I really care? *Gods*, of course I do. I'm just jealous of anyone that Wren thinks about, especially if those thoughts are ... stimulating.

We find a likely campsite about another fifty miles north, with a glacier-fed stream beside some more pine trees. They're so huge that the ground underneath is littered with pine needles and is actually fairly sheltered. Dimitra and I catch our dinner from the stream, enjoying the fresh fish. We often used to hunt in such a manner. Barley and ash water is good for a man, but this? This is primal, delicious, feeding the shifted side of myself, giving in to its wants and needs.

Being a tiger is much simpler than being a man. Am I a shifter or true animal? Which face is my real one? It is hard to know at times.

I consider making Wren catch her own dinner but in the end decide I'm not a total asshole, and that the others will be hungry too. We stack up a few more salmon on the bank and wait for the mammoths to arrive.

I want to talk to Dimitra. I consider shifting back, but it's pretty damn cold, and my clothes are still a few miles south, in my pack. Shields spend a lot of time naked, but I'm not eager to shift back in this weather without my clothes nearby, and preferably a roaring fire.

Still, the thought of Dimitra and me, naked together beneath these pines, letting out some of this pent-up frustration ...

I stay a gods-damned tiger until the mammoths arrive.

That night is my turn to keep watch. Wren tries to talk to me a few times, but I don't want to.

"Let's just get this book, and we can figure the rest out later," I say.

She bites her lip, and her eyes glisten. In the crisp evening air, her skin is tinged deliciously pink, and I want nothing more than to grab her and kiss her until she knows *exactly* who she belongs to, to tear that coat from her shoulders and claim every inch of her curves, from the smooth brown swell of her breasts and down ...

"Get some rest," I tell her instead, and clear my throat. "More long days ahead of us."

She nods wordlessly and sets up her bedroll by the fire. Tonight, at least, she can't make the flames at all—I guess even though it's technically "nighttime," since the sun is still up, Wren's powers aren't active. I don't know that I'll ever get used to the strange nights here, the way the sun never really sets. It's at best a twilight, all night long. It's damn eerie.

Dimitra, I notice, stays far back from the fire. She might be healed, her hair even regrown, but she is not eager to experience that pain again. I've been burned once before—honestly, the worst pain I've ever been in. Worse than getting stabbed or shot with an arrow or gnawed on by a Fremulon wolf. I shouldn't have been so flippant with her last night about her pain.

It turns out to be a long, boring night—just me, the wind in the pines, and the stars overhead, their pale glow unable to compete with the light of the sun. I spend a lot of time pacing, daring so much as an insect to enter our campsite undetected.

I wonder if Caladrius is looking down on me and laughing.

CHAPTER 49
WREN

I dream of Caladrius again. I was starting to wonder if I ever would, but he's before me, without Obsidian this time. Tonight his hair and wings are black, tipped with silver. His appearance mirrors the moon's phases, I realize. Tonight, just as before, he is breathtakingly beautiful. When the moon is full, I imagine he is so brilliant he's impossible to look at.

We're in some kind of open space, and it's cold, deathly cold. It's dark too, and windy, and there's some kind of illumination from a source I can't make out. It feels like we're on the top of a mountain in the middle of night, though I know I must still be sleeping under the pine trees.

"You need to hurry," he says, his voice like rolling thunder. His hair falls around his perfect face like a silken veil, long and straight. "The time is approaching."

"Where is the vault?" I ask, clenching my hands against the pain of his voice. My ears aren't bleeding, but that doesn't mean the conversation between a god and a mortal is comfortable. Still, he's confirmed that we are at least in the right place, at the right time, and that gives me courage. "Tell me."

"So formidable you are," he says, and a smile curves his wicked lips. "Giving commands to a god."

I swallow. *Formidable* is one word for it. *Stupid* might be another.

"It's why I picked you, Wren. Out of the multitudes. You are the one with the strength to see this through."

"See what?" I ask, exasperated. "Just tell me where to go, and I'll go!" Leo's life may depend on it.

"Keep going," he says. His wings flex a little as he paces around me, so long that the silvery tips brush the ground. He pivots on his heel, turning his back on me, like he's going to leave.

"Wait!" I cry. "Why does Evanthia want two books? What can she do with two that she can't do with one?"

He looks back over his shoulder and arches an eyebrow, amused. "She already has the Book of Bronze in her possession."

"What?" I ask, the word like a whisper from my lips. I hadn't even thought of where that book was supposed to be—a dreadful lapse, I now see. The Book of Bronze in the hands of that snake woman. *Gods.*

Caladrius continues to speak to me over his shoulder, like I'm not even worth his full attention. Me, his own creation.

Arrogant ass.

"She wants all three, little Night Mage. She and Aenon."

The scene begins to fade, and Caladrius with it, until all I can see besides mist and shadow is the perfection of his face, in profile, turning from me.

"Keep going."

I wake, and I'm back under the pines. The sky is not dark. This far north, the sun never entirely sets. It dips but doesn't set. As a result, I haven't been able to truly access my magic in days, not since that flare with Dimitra. And that felt wrong, like my magic was out of control. I don't dare try it again.

A glimmer of the Sacred Wind sparkles through the sky above, an echo of the brilliance I saw in Aeturnus. It fades soon, along with the pain in my head of Caladrius's visit.

I'm cold, too—no Aris to warm my side tonight, no friendly rabbits or groundhogs burrowed in beside me either. Rafael and Mariana are sleeping under the same bedroll, and I don't see any of the Shields. For the first time in a while, I feel truly alone.

I wiggle out of my bedroll and step to the smoldering coals. I add in a few branches, and as the sun rises, I have a cheerful fire going. The heat thaws my cold fingers and toes, but it does little to warm my heart.

Dimitra and Aris come strolling back into camp. They've been sparring, judging by the sweat on their faces and the way Dimitra twirls her daggers in her palms. Aris is rolling out his left shoulder, laughing at something Dimitra has said—and then he catches my eye and stops in his tracks.

"Another dream?" he asks. He scoops some snow into a tin mug and sets it by the fire to melt.

"Yes," I say. I avert my eyes, and though I busy myself with arranging bits of wood by the fire, I can feel his gaze on me.

"Anything *relevant* this time?" Dimitra asks with a snort of laughter. She's in a better mood, and I can feel my own blacken in response.

"Only if you think that Evanthia having the Book of Bronze already is relevant," I snap. "And that she and Aenon are planning something when they have all three books."

"Wait, what?" Rafael asks, waking up and rubbing his eyes. "Who has the Book of Bronze?"

"Roallac," Dimitra spits.

"So ... Evanthia can talk to Aenon? Be a magical conduit for him, the way Wren is?" Rafael asks.

I whirl on him. "What did you say?"

"Magical conduit? It's a theory Caelus and I have been tossing around. The gods can't cross into our realm, but maybe their magic can. Wouldn't that be something? With the full power of Caladrius behind you, not even Aenon would stand a chance."

"It's just a theory," Caelus says, dropping down from a perch in one of the pines.

Gods, I didn't even notice him up there. I rub the back of my neck.

"The books open not just a way to communicate but a way for power to be transferred from a willing god to a willing subject. There are some references to it in the books Tekton gave me, but they're all secondhand accounts."

"I don't remember agreeing to any kind of transfer," I mutter.

Caelus shrugs.

"But what does Evanthia need all three for, then?" Rafael asks.

"He didn't say," I answer.

"Well, that's a big help," Mariana says, yawning and stretching as she sits up. She looks perfectly poised, even just waking, not even a hair out of place.

"He seemed worried, though," I say. "He kept repeating, 'Keep going.' Like he wants to make sure Evanthia can't get all three."

"But you're the only one who can access that vault, right?" Rafael adds. "So why don't we just leave the damn book where it is? Problem solved."

"Because then Evanthia will kill King Leonidas," Dimitra says, crossing her arms. "Which will likely destroy Ocron as we know it. There's no heir, no one for the Book of Gold to work through."

"Not to mention, if we have the Book of Silver, we may have our own weapon," Mariana adds. "If she's already got the Book of Bronze, she's going to be much too powerful for anyone to stop. We need to keep going."

"It is the will of Lord Caladrius that we retrieve this book," Caelus says, his voice measured. "I will see it through."

As we pack up, Adriana flies back to us. She shifts as she lands, timing it perfectly, landing on her feet effortlessly. I toss her a blanket, which she accepts with a graceful shiver. Her eyes glitter with energy, and she waits until we're all crowding around her, giving her all our attention, to hear her news.

"I think I found something," she says.

What Adriana found turns out to be the work of a single day and night's flying, but several days' worth of travel by foot, even by mammoth foot. We trudge up and down mountain paths. Mariana and Rafael take turns melting ice or hardening it to make passage possible, and we make decent time, but far slower than over the relatively gentle rolling hills in the south. The mountains become bigger and more jagged the farther we go, like the land itself is trying to keep us from reaching our destination. Dimitra leads, her leopard form at ease among the rocks and glaciers. Aris alternates running with her and riding with me, though he keeps his hands to himself. Somehow I feel colder when he's there than when he's gone.

I miss my tiger.

It's a beautiful landscape, even if it is harsh and barren. There is less prey here—no more geese and hardly any fish. No wonder they call it the Wastes. There's not even much interesting to look at, which means my mind has plenty of time to run wild. What exactly are they doing to Leo over in Roallac? Is he really being tortured? My heart breaks at the thought of my warm, kind friend—who only ever wanted to do what was best for his country—being at the mercy of some crazy snake queen. Tears prickle my eyes more than once, and I'm afraid they might freeze on my eyelashes. I have to force myself to think of something else, anything else. I start reciting Ismini's lessons in my head—though I can't use my magic here, I figure it's a way to practice at least, like stretching a muscle.

After five days, we reach the base of a mountain that Brodie calls Ignis Peak.

"There," Adriana says.

She's riding with me today. Aris and Dimitra are somewhere in their shifted forms, scouting head. Adriana points a slim white finger over my shoulder to a point high on the mountain, which towers over us, shadowing the landscape. It's a jagged beast, raw as the edges of a saw blade and dusted with snow.

And there, on a ledge far, far above us, is a glimmer of black, right where we thought it would be, right where Adriana found it.

The door to the vault—made of polished obsidian.

We have to leave the mammoths and continue on foot. Brodie promises to wait at the bottom of the mountain for us.

"I've been in these mountains longer than you lot have been alive," he says, scratching his chin through his beard. "And I ain't never seen no black door in the stone before."

"We'll be back in a few days," Caelus says calmly, putting on his pack.

"So you say," Brodie says.

I give Tawny a scratch behind her floppy ear. She runs her trunk over my braid, giving it a light tug. I don't like leaving her any more than she does, but the terrain would be impossible for her. I give her another scratch behind her ear and promise I'll see her soon.

The path isn't easy for us either. The rock is sharp, and honestly, there *is* no path. Dimitra forges ahead, back in her Shield form. She must be part mountain goat by the way she springs about. I'm used to stairs and hard work, but this mountain has me panting for breath after less than an hour.

We push on all day, too winded to hold conversation, which is fine. Aris doesn't seem to want to talk to me anyway. He does stay by my side, and once, when I slip, he catches my elbow, keeping me from slicing open an arm or a leg on some razor-sharp rocks.

Later, he said. We can talk about it later. Gods, I wish he'd let me talk know. I try to focus on the task at hand—scaling Ignis Peak, getting to the door, preparing for whatever might be behind it.

"If you don't want to do this with me, I'll understand," I tell Aris quietly, once the others have moved on a little. "You don't have to come with me."

I feel like I'm giving him an out here, a peace offering.

He looks at me like I just stabbed him in the back.

"Over my dead body," he growls. "I am your Shield, Night Mage. Whatever else happens, never doubt that. Where you go, I go, until the end."

I am surprised by the tears that jump to my eyes. My Shield. Not my lover, not my friend. My Shield. It seems a cruel echo of earlier, when I called him my partner. Now I understand just how much a comment like that can sting.

"I didn't let you read the letters because I was worried you'd overreact," I spit out. I didn't mean to say it, but damn it all, it's been eating away at me for days now.

"I don't like to share," he says bluntly. "I won't share you with him. I want all of you, Wren. All, or nothing. I claimed you, as you claimed me."

I can't think of anything to say. Leo is my friend, my supporter, my king. I realize, in a sudden flash of clarity, what Aris must have known all along—that Leo chose our traveling companions, and that he must have known Aris had slept with Mariana and Dimitra. He chose them specifically to expose Aris's nature to me, to drive a wedge between us—to show me that he, steadfast Leo, is the better choice.

I haven't decided if I'm pissed about that or slightly impressed. I want to believe Aris when he says he is mine. And I need to show him that I do trust him, that I want him. Just when things between us seem to be on the mend, one of us fucks it up again.

They say you can't make a tiger change his stripes, but maybe Aris can change his, and maybe I can change mine, if we claim each other—claim everything, the good and the bad, the past and the present. And our future.

CHAPTER 50
ARIS

The final climb up Ignis Peak is—physically—one of the hardest things I've ever done. The way is steep, nearly vertical at times. We've been sticking to the valleys and known paths for the most part, letting the mammoths do the hard work. We have two days to make the climb, and honestly, I'm not sure we are going to make it. I sent Adriana back to Tekton, and then on to Estana, to tell them what we are doing. She pouted a little, but she went. I think she was excited to see Tekton again—which I don't really want to dwell on too much.

Dimitra goes first, Caelus second—scouting the way, finding the safest routes. Then the Mages. I bring up the rear, ready to catch anyone who tumbles. It is slow, arduous going. Mariana is the weakest, physically, but her water magic does give her some help—when the way looks impassable, she carves stairs out of blocks of ice. She's using a lot of energy, so we try to spare her as much as we can. Who knows when we'll find ourselves in need of her magic, what might lurk behind that vault door?

Honestly, I'm hoping it's the Book of Silver just waiting us inside, without traps or monstrous guardians or anything.

Knowing our luck, it won't be that simple, so I mentally prepare myself for everything I can think of—trolls, manticores. Probably no kraken here, at least. The ice itself could pose a problem, but between the six of us, we'll figure it out.

The first night—though "night" is relative, I guess, as it's almost fully light this far north in the relatively warm summer months—is miserable. We have to stop to let the Mages rest. We find a ledge with a shallow indentation that is almost a cave, with room enough for us to huddle together. Mariana erects an ice wall, extending from floor to ceiling across the opening with a small vent along the top, essentially sealing us—and our warmth—in.

Wren's face is red with the cold. When she takes her hands from her gloves to warm them, I can see them shaking from fatigue. Rafael has created a small ring of glowing rocks, imbued with his power and exuding as much heat as a roaring bonfire. We have to be careful of his magic too—if he overextends, if he goes gray, we could be in a lot of trouble, especially since Wren's power is nearly nonexistent here.

The "cave" is crowded. We can lie side by side, but that doesn't leave much walking room. I pick my way over to Wren after she eats and lie down beside her. She looks at me, the question clear on her face, but she's too tired to even give it voice.

"I'm going to shift," I tell her, rearranging her bedroll under us and pulling my own over the top. "You need warmth."

At this, she does let out a snort of a laugh. "I thought you were going to try 'we're warmer naked together under one blanket than each in our own,' or something," she says, but even her voice sounds tired.

"Well? How about it?" Rafael asks Mariana, one eyebrow raised.

She laughs, leaning into him, enjoying the heat from the glowing rocks, and probably from him as well. She whispers something to him, and he puts an arm around her, drawing her closer. I look away.

"My fur coat will keep both of us warm," I say, removing my

boots. They'll come off when I shift, anyway. "And besides, I don't like having cold feet."

"I know," Wren says, settling under the blankets, her lids heavy.

I get in beside her. "But if that doesn't work," I whisper, my lips touching her ear, "I'll be happy to try the other way."

She chuckles at that and relaxes a bit. I shift—thank the *gods* for giving me a thick hide—and I'm instantly feeling warmer. I stretch out, and Wren untangles my shed clothes and covers me with the rest of the blanket. She snuggles in next to me and lets out a sigh of contentment, burying her face in my furry chest. The redness in her skin softens. The harsh lines of tension on her face ease.

"I do like your leather pants, you know," she says into my fur, like she's admitting some dark secret. I can't say anything, so I just let out a rolling *whuff* of acknowledgement. She nestles in closer, a smile on her chapped lips—and she's asleep in the next breath.

When I wake, it takes me a second to remember where we are. Sometime in the night, I shifted back. It happens. Wren is still asleep, her head pillowed on my chest, the blankets pulled up nearly to her ears. She's still got a thick knitted hat tightly pulled over her head. She is breathing slowly, her warm breath whispering across my skin, making blood flow to all kinds of uncomfortable places.

Gods. I don't care if Leo wants her—he can't have her, no one else can, not as long as I have breath left in my body. I let her sleep, wishing I could somehow transfer some of my own strength into her small body. I'd carry her up this fucking mountain if she'd let me.

"You're purring," she says.

I look down and realize she's awake, and staring up at me with her jade-colored eyes.

"Am I?" I ask, arching an eyebrow.

"Yes," she says, but she's smiling too, and she burrows back under the blankets, putting one tentative hand on my stomach. She traces the lines of my muscles there, her fingertips dancing over scars, circling, teasing lower and lower, her roughened fingertips grazing the trail of hair below my navel.

I roll over, trapping her underneath me, between our blankets, cradling her pink cheeks in my hands. I let her feel *exactly* what she does to me, easing my hips down on hers. Her eyes widen before drifting into a hazy, heated look, her mouth forming a little *O*.

"Don't start what you're not ready to finish, princess," I say, my voice sounding thick and gravelly, which I blame on the cold air. I kiss her chapped lips before she can protest, losing myself momentarily in the feel of her body beneath mine. *Gods!* I wish we were anywhere else but this frozen hellhole. We have to get moving, but all I want to do is stay under these blankets.

Wren beams up at me, one small hand on the side of my face, her eyes bright, and I swear it's like I can read her mind. We still want each other, whatever else has happened—so, honestly, fuck all the rest. Her cheeks are wind-burned, her hair wild. Neither of us has bathed in days.

She's the most beautiful thing I've ever seen.

Wren is mine, and I am hers.

We make it to the top of this gods-forsaken place with a few hours to spare. We eat a little and rest, keeping anxious eyes on the sky. The sun is a pale gold disk overhead, offering little warmth.

"How much longer?" Mariana asks, for the tenth time.

Caelus has the maps out, spread across his lap, and he looks between them and the sky every few moments. "Not long," he says, frowning.

"You said that an hour ago," Mariana huffs, going to stand by

Rafael. He puts an arm around her, and the snow that has settled on her coat turns to steam. She lets out a sigh.

Wren is pacing, her tracks making a little path through the packed snow and ice as she walks. Her breath comes in little clouds, and she, too, keeps an anxious eye on the sky. For the tenth time, she goes to the door, putting one gloved hand against it.

I've never seen a door like it. It's smooth obsidian, and the pale sunlight flashes across its dark surface. It's large, maybe twelve feet tall, and wide too. It probably weighs a ton, so it's a good thing that I'm here. It's going to take some serious muscle to wrench it open.

Inscribed on its surface are six circles arranged in a hexagon, their edges just touching. We saw the same image on one of Panos's scrolls, back in Estana. White and black at the top, then red, yellow, green, and blue. One for each god, made out of some kind of faceted stones set into the obsidian. There doesn't seem to be a handle anywhere, or a hinge.

We eat. We sit. We pace. We take a piss off the side of the mountain—or I do, anyway.

And we wait.

Dimitra stands at the edge, looking out across the Wastes, arms crossed. She's already honed her knives and swords, checked and rechecked their sheaths. Whatever is behind that door, she's ready for it, and not for the first time, I am glad she's with us.

"Now!" Caelus says, jumping up, startling us all into action. "Now, Wren!"

We look to the sky.

CHAPTER 51
WREN

I don't see anything.

And then—a flicker, at the edge of the sun. I squint, trying to make it out.

"Wren, now!" Caelus urges.

I tear my eyes from the spectacle above me and go to the door. We might only have a few minutes to do this, to open a door that has been closed for hundreds of years. I peer inward, to my core, to the sphere of darkness that stays there. It is quiescent, but as the air grows cold around me, as the day darkens, it comes to life, growing, like a dark fern unfurling.

I hear Caelus gasp behind me—and then Aris is at my side, one gloved hand in mine.

"Let's go, Night Mage," he says, squeezing my hand.

Together we step forward. I place my hand on the door.

The day continues to darken.

Dies tenebrosa sicut nox.

I reach for the tendrils of shadow at my core, bringing them forth, letting them flow through me to the obsidian door.

Nothing happens. It's like the door is made of ice, like the rest of the damned mountain—my magic just skitters across it, not finding purchase.

Aris lets out a breath.

"What are you waiting for?" Mariana asks, her voice harsh. "Open it!"

And still nothing happens. I try again, and again. Sweat collects on my brow despite the cold as precious seconds tick by. Aris shoves his shoulder against the stone slab, trying to force it open.

And still—*nothing*—happens.

Dimitra lets out a growl of frustration. Whatever hope I had is dashed, broken to pieces, and I feel nauseated. This should work! Caladrius told me to come here, to be *here* for the eclipse. It *has* to work! I look to Aris, unsure exactly of how to apologize for dragging him all the way up here for nothing—

A wind stirs his hair, lifting the black strands in a playful twirl. His eyes hold mine, widening slightly, as the air around us crackles with energy. My tendrils of night magic become visible, like ribbons of smoke whipping around us.

The wind grows stronger as the day becomes night, darker than *any* night we've seen up here in the frozen north. I dare to shoot a glance toward the sun—it is a black disk haloed in golden light. I've never seen anything like it, and I can feel all the hairs on my skin standing on end.

The wind blows harder, a gale now, a tornado of icy crystals and air. Aris grips my hand tightly, like he's worried I'm going to blow away. I raise my other hand off the door to shield my eyes—

And with a groan that makes the mountain shudder, the door swings inward.

Before us, a circular tunnel of blue ice with a slightly flattened floor extends before us and down, into darkness, smooth walls like glass reflecting the light a little.

"Inside!" Caelus urges.

We surge toward the opening, and I realize he's worried that the door will close on us with the end of the eclipse.

How we'll get back out, I have no idea.

At least the tunnel keeps the worst of the wind out. Rafael gets a lantern from his pack and lights it with just a spark of his magic. He wants to conserve his strength—we all do. The lantern is more than sufficient, though, lighting up the blue-tinged ice before us.

"Get behind me," Aris growls, and he draws his swords.

I can feel the eclipse ending more than I see it—inside we're already in the dark. The dark energy at my core grows silent again, pulsing, waiting.

Thank the gods that the door remains open. Caelus lets out a shaky breath.

"Let's get this over with," Aris says, rolling his shoulders to loosen them.

Dimitra draws up beside him, bristling with steel. They strip off their heavy winter coats, which will only hinder their mobility. Maybe Aris was right about wearing his damned leather pants, after all. In the freezing air, his body heat turns to vapor, the sweat freezing on the strands of his hair. He puts on his great tiger helm, protecting his neck and face. The metal—and his eyes—reflect the icy light of the tunnel. He is a fearsome sight. He double-checks the knot on the bracelet Delphine gave him, and my chest squeezes. I wish I was back at Aeturnus.

We make our way down the tunnel, the only sound that of our breathing and the crunching of our boots on the ice. Twice I slip, nearly taking out Aris as I slide down. We walk for several minutes, the tunnel of ice eventually transitioning to gray rock.

Ahead there is a bluish glow. As we approach it, the tunnel widens, and then we are in a cavern of immense size. Stalactites and icicles nearly as big as my lighthouse extend downward from the ceiling. Ice that grows in sparkling spikes from the floor punctures the snowdrifts like a strange forest.

The floor of the cavern is ice and snow, mounded in drifts and piled around an obsidian column in the center of the room. The light —sunlight, it must be, diffusing down through the icy dome overhead—glints off a book, untouched by the snow.

And the book glitters.

Silver.

"Thank all the gods," Caelus whispers, and he moves forward.

"Wait," Dimitra hisses, a hand on his arm. "Listen."

I don't dare to breathe. It is there—*right there!* All the nightmares, all this travel, all of it feels justified now that the Book of Silver is within our reach.

And then—

A sound like a whisper of wind, like an echo, sighs through the room.

"What is it?" Mariana asks. Her hands are outstretched, ready to call the frozen water around her to her command.

The snow around the column shifts, falling in miniature avalanches.

"Brother, I believe your god of fire is making his appearance at last," Caelus says, drawing his own blades. The sound rings through the cavern.

Rafael utters a word, and a flame appears in either hand, ready to be wielded. The light reflects in his brown eyes, which are steady.

A groan, a growl, and the snow continues to move, shaking the icy stalagmites on the ground—no, they are crystalline spikes, protruding from the scaly back of a beast that is rising up and up, of impossible size. A head larger than two horses, wedge-shaped and horrible, swings on a neck like a pearlescent tree trunk, scales glittering in the dim blue light.

It shakes its head, throwing off a hundred years of sleep. Tattered wings feathered in shades of white and blue lie folded across its back. A spear-like tail whips across the floor, evidence of the creature's displeasure.

I guess the legends are all true, then—for what better hoard exists in all the world than this book?

And this creature of fire, hidden away in a cavern of ice, will defend it to the last.

CHAPTER 52

ARIS

A gods-damned dragon.

"When this is over, you can add a dragon's tooth to your necklace," Dimitra says, a feral grin on her face.

"When this is over, you can make a dagger from one," I counter. My magic sings through my blood, my gift coming awake—the gift of battle, the gift of death.

"Are we sure this isn't a Shield, like Delphine?" Mariana asks.

As if in response, the creature roars, shaking the air around us. It must have been sleeping here for ages—hibernating for an eternity, waiting to be disturbed. And now that we've disturbed him, he is fucking angry.

"I'm sure," Caelus says, stepping in front of her.

"Fantastic," she mutters.

"Distract it as much as you can," I say, scanning the room. "Keep its focus away from us. We'll circle around back and see how it likes steel."

"What do I do?" Wren asks. She has her knife drawn, a grim look on her face.

I grab her and kiss her, hard.

"Get the book," I say, lifting a finger. "If you see an opening, take it."

She nods, her jade eyes wide but steady. She is the smallest of us, which should work to her advantage. She is strong and fierce and quick. She is ready. Dimitra and Caelus are having similar conversations with their own Mages. Mariana wears a look of concentration I've never seen on her before, not even when she was keeping *The James* afloat. She barely notices when Caelus leaves her side; she keeps her eyes on the dragon, and on the book.

The dragon roars its challenge again, showing its dagger-like teeth, massive clawed feet stomping against the snow. Its long body is wrapped around the column with the book, protecting its prize.

"Let's clear the path," I say, and I take off, Dimitra on my heels.

Caelus goes the other way, all of us circling the outside of the cavern, trying to get around behind the beast. The dragon swings its head this way and that, trying to keep its silver eyes on us. By splitting up, we divide its attention.

It doesn't like that.

Rafael shoots blasts of fire from his hands that explode when they hit the dragon's face, leaving scorch marks on its white scales, but doing little real damage. The dragon bellows, and a glow forms deep in its throat. Mariana flings her magic at a few of the icy stalactites, rattling them loose. They shower down around the dragon, bouncing harmlessly off its sides like rain off a window. Dragon hide, it seems, is as tough as Caelus said.

Good thing I'm tougher.

The dragon's tail whips across the floor again, and I leap over it, rolling when I hit the stone floor, my momentum never ceasing. I swipe at the tail of the beast, and my swords glance off the smooth scales, not even scratching them. Those scales might look like fancy jewels, but they're harder than rock.

Shit.

The dragon rears its neck back, a growling sound issuing from its throat. I feel the heat of its breath fill the air as it unleashes its fire against the Mages, a long, continuous blast of flame, the heat so intense that the ice and snow it contacts turn immediately to steam.

I risk a glance over my shoulder. Wren is picking her way across the cavern, moving from boulder to boulder, making herself as small as possible. If she can get to the book, the dragon *should* stop attacking since she can call on Ignatius to muzzle his beast. Theoretically.

The blast of dragon flame is directed at and deflected around Rafael and Mariana. Rafael's red robe flares behind him as he parts the fire, sending it instead behind them, where it melts the rock it contacts. Mariana cringes behind him, eyes closed as the flame roars past her.

The great silver eyes blink, their attention caught by movement on the other side of the cavern.

The dragon has seen Caelus making his way around the cave, trying to flank it. Still flaming, the head swivels, directing the flame away from the Mages.

Mariana reacts the second she realizes what's about to happen, flinging snow across the room to intercept the flame—

But she's too late.

Caelus manages to leap behind a small boulder, deflecting the direct blast of the fire around him. I hear his screams of rage and pain as the leather armor is burned off his back.

The dragon turns again, still flaming, melting rock wherever it touches, like now that it's ignited, it has to burn and burn and burn until it is spent. Caelus roars, the rock around him turning red and starting to crumble.

Overhead, the ceiling shakes.

I slam the pommels of my blades down against the ground, as loudly as I can. The sound cracks through the room like lightning.

It works.

The dragon turns toward me and Dimitra. Caelus is safe, panting behind the molten remnants of the boulder, but now we are trapped, like a pair of mice before a great cat. The dragon's claws skitter across the icy ground, scrambling for purchase, buying us a few precious seconds to react. I anticipate its movement, and with no cover present, no convenient boulders to duck behind, I have no other choice. His head swings our way in an inexorable arc.

I throw myself between Dimitra and the inferno without a second's hesitation.

I never thought it would all end like this. Still, if I have to die, let it be during an epic battle, one where my name will be remembered in songs and tales for generations.

My last thoughts, a desperate plea to Rigrasil—*I hope Wren survives this. I hope she doesn't go gray.*

CHAPTER 53
WREN

I crouch behind a boulder, holding the edges of my robe tight around me. I'm not sure what spells Ismini and Panos put into the black silk, but it's protected me from broken bones and cold. I can only hope that it offers some protection against dragon flame.

The dragon is an enormous, ancient beast, his ribs visible through the moth-eaten scales of his once-gleaming hide. I feel less rage toward him than I did toward the manticore, or the kraken. This is an animal defending his home—I wish desperately there were a way for me to communicate with him, to calm him as I have wounded creatures in the past. Surely he cannot be so different from them.

He's flaming, a great bonfire issuing from his toothy jaws in a continuous stream. I screech at him when he turns toward Caelus, but the sound of my voice is lost in the chaos.

Caelus's screams, though, I hear loud and clear. It is the worst sound I've ever heard in my life.

I leap up, deciding I have to do something, to try to talk to the dragon or at least distract him—just in time to see Aris and Dimitra decide the same.

Aris, my Aris, the mightiest Shield in a generation, sees his friend in danger and slams his swords against the ground, creating a sharp crack of sound.

The dragon whirls on him, still flaming. My heart stops—

Aris leaps between the dragon and Dimitra.

I wonder what it will feel like to go gray and die, for I have no desire to go on existing in a world where Aris doesn't.

CHAPTER 54
ARIS

Dimitra shoves me hard from behind, with both hands, sending me sprawling before her—

Under the belly of the flaming beast. I roll, looking back. For one agonizing moment, I see her eyes, golden, through the flames, searching for mine with her last breath, her hair billowing on the waves of heat about to engulf her.

And then she's gone, and all I hear is Rafael's howls of grief echoing through the chamber.

I bite my tongue, pushing through the agony, and keep moving, rolling as the dragon tries to stomp on me.

Above me is a moving wall of pearly scales. The beast continues to flame, and as it turns, my boots are singed by the fire, which melts leather and skin and sinew. I roar through the pain and adjust the grip on my swords. With every ounce of strength—every scrap of magic imbued in my veins by the god of day himself—I stab upward with both blades, under the breastbone of the dragon, thrusting until only the hilts of the gladiuses are visible.

The flame ceases, and the animal sways as hot blood runs down my arms. I roll to the side, a great claw raking my chest as I move, my blood mixing with the dragon's, hot and slick. The pain roars through me, leaving me blind to everything else as I scramble from underneath the dragon.

The beast falls to the ground in a cloud of steam and snow, and it does not move again. I stand, but at first my feet will not hold me. The flesh on them is seared white and red, and my heel bone is exposed on the right. I stumble, pain lancing up my legs. My shirt is dark with blood, stuck to my skin, rent by that great claw that nearly eviscerated me. My breathing is stilted for a minute until the wound begins to clot, to close. Burned skin begins to heal; blisters fade. Within moments, I can stand again, though my feet still throb with an intensity that nearly takes my breath away. I search for Wren among the chaos, but most of my visual field is blocked by the fucking dragon carcass. My ears are ringing—everything sounds distant, like I'm underwater.

I spit on the dragon and hoist myself up, steadying myself using its bulk as I make my way around the other side. I feel numbed, except for my feet. I don't want to turn. I don't want to see what has happened to Dimitra. She could have survived, maybe. We can survive burns, though I'm not sure about dragon fire. Until I turn and look, I can hold on to that thread of hope.

"Rafael! RAFAEL!" Mariana screams.

I hear the smack of her hand against his face once, twice—he is slumped near the cavern entrance, kneeling, his face emotionless.

But he is not gray. He doesn't speak; he doesn't move—but he is not gray. I've seen Mages go gray, the way Saroya did when Wren pushed her too far, the way the Water Mage in Basti did. Their skin changes color, the life leached out of them.

Rafael is not gray, but grieving. In shock. And Mariana won't let him go. She is distraught, kissing him, raking her hands through his hair, pleading with him, sobbing over him. She is trying desperately to save him, the way Wren saved me. With love, though Wren didn't know it at the time.

I glance back at the dragon. Dark blood stains the snow beneath it.

I force myself to raise my eyes. Where Dimitra stood, where she chose to make her last stand, there is nothing but ash and molten metal from her weapons, melted by a flame hotter than anything Mage-made. I don't move. For once, I can't.

"It is a good death," Caelus says, cautiously putting a hand on my shoulder. The skin on his back is a charred mess, but already the blackened flakes of skin peel off, revealing healed skin below. "An honorable death, saving the life of a friend in battle. She may go before Rigrasil now with her head held high."

Fuck that.

I want Dimitra *here*, not in some land-after, not earning her eternal reward for a life of service and hard labor, if that shit is even real.

But I don't shrug off his hand. And Caelus doesn't move.

My oldest friend—the one who knew me better than I knew myself, who gave her own life to save mine—is nothing but ash. There's not even anything to bury in the Shield vaults in Estana. There will be no tomb where people can come to grieve, to read her story embossed in bronze across her crypt. *Here lies Dimitra Gataki, a better Shield and friend than the rest of us could ever hope to be.*

And then a ringing fills the air, a chime, like the pull of my claim amplified a hundredfold. Caelus can hear it, though, and Mariana too. Even Rafael raises his unblinking eyes at the sound.

Before us all stands Wren, the Book of Silver in her hands.

Its terrible price, on mine.

CHAPTER 55
WREN

"Well done."

Caladrius's silken voice purrs in my ears. I can't see him—all around me is darkness, the walls of the cavern gone. I strain my ears, but I cannot hear Aris.

Rafael's wails, however, even more than Caelus's wounded cries, echo in my heart.

"Are you the god of the dead?" I demand.

Caladrius materializes before me, ebony hair and wings this time.

"Whatever gave you that idea?" he asks, looking at my hands.

I have the Book of Silver in them. His eyes are hungry for it, but he does not—or cannot—reach for it.

"Are you or are you not?" I demand. "You brought Obsidian back from the dead, didn't you? Bring her back! Bring back Dimitra!"

Tears are running down my cheeks—whatever hatred Dimitra harbored for me, she was also loyal, fierce, and a devoted friend. Aris's friend.

A great Shield. And to lose her and possibly Rafael too, for this book?

It damned well better be worth it.

A small voice inside me—the one that whispers, the one I'm not proud *of—says that Aris must have known that by putting himself between Dimitra and the dragon, he would die, that he would likely have doomed me as well, because of our claim.*

He had the choice between me and Dimitra—and he chose Dimitra.

I feel like someone has punched a hole straight through my chest. Dimitra. His best friend, his lover. And why wouldn't he? She's strong, confident, beautiful. She understands him as I never will. And he deserves that.

And so I plead with the god of night to return her to us, to him.

"That is not within my power," Caladrius says, cocking his head to the side. "Obsidian was never mortal to begin with. Do not trouble yourself. The woman died with honor."

I stare down at the book. Tears trickle from my nose and drip onto its sacred cover before running off the metal. I sniffle.

"And Rafael?" I ask, looking up at the god of night through my soggy lashes. "Will he live? Will he ... go gray?"

"I don't know," he says. His wings move up and down a little, in an exaggeration of a shrug. "I do not predict the future, little human."

"Then at least tell me, why did you want me to have this?" I ask. I am still clutching the Book of Silver. Briefly I consider leaving it in the vault, resealing the door. Then no one could ever get it. I'd find another way to save Leo. "I have to give it to Evanthia."

The darkness parts, and Caladrius is before me now, resplendent in his black robes, his wings trembling with rage. A snarl is on his perfect face, where before I've only ever seen a kind of benign patience.

"You will do no such thing, little Night Mage," he says.

The air around me shakes, as though with a thunderclap. I grasp the book tighter.

"She will kill Leo," I say, though this comes out softer than I wanted it to.

Caladrius arches an eyebrow. "And if you give the Book of Silver to the witch, she will kill thousands," he says. "Everyone you've ever loved will die at the hand of her witches and their familiars. Aris. Ismini. Tekton.

Delphine. They will erase Ocron as easily as waves erase footprints on the sand."

"I thought you couldn't predict the future," I say with another sniffle. "And why do you care?"

Could I do this? Trade Leo's life for the rest of those in Ocron? There would be no Ocron without him, anyway. Ocron is lost either way.

At least if I give her the book, we might be able to buy some time.

"The blessing of the Book of Gold will not end with your king, pet. I was there when the books were made. I can assure you, it will endure. But with the power of the three books, Aenon will walk the land of mortals, just as we did once before, ages ago. With the books, he can have the world to himself and keep the rest of us bound to the immortal realm. With the three books, he can alter magic."

"What does that mean?" I ask, feeling like a vise is squeezing my chest, like I'm having trouble breathing. Alter magic?

"My brother has not told me of all his plans," Caladrius says, and he ruffles his feathers a bit. He paces, circling me, dark mist obscuring the ground.

"But know this—each book can only be destroyed or altered in the presence of the other two. He could destroy the Book of Bronze, and thus kill every ungifted person in your world—the magic that sustains their lives, snuffed out as easily as a candle in a breeze. He could destroy the Book of Gold, and the ruling power of Ocron will wither, leaving the country a barren land of ash and bones."

Caladrius stops and pins me with his gaze, his eyes glimmering silver. The hair on the back of my neck stands on end.

"And if he were to tear pages from the Book of Silver, every Shield and every Mage, save those gifted by Aenon, would perish. He could wipe them out, one by one. Element by element. So you must collect the books, little Night Mage. You, and none other. Bring me to the mortal realm, and I will protect you. Bring me to the mortal realm, and your countrymen will live. I swear it."

I am pulled from the vision, and I gasp at the sensation, cold air flooding into my lungs.

I am still in the cavern, the corpse of the dragon before me. I look down—I still have the book, glinting softly in my hands, lighter than I would have guessed it to be. I try to open it, but the covers hold firm.

My head is pounding, and my mouth has gone dry.

All around me is chaos. Aris is slumped to his knees, covered in blood, gazing blankly at the pile of ash that was Dimitra. He is not moving. His feet are bare, burned skin flaking off the bottoms. I have to look away—my heart is shattering, my vision blurring.

Near the cavern's entrance, Mariana is holding Rafael to her, stroking his hair, mumbling things into his ear. He's dazed, his eyes unfocused—but he's not gray. A shaky breath escapes my lips.

"Night Mage?" Caelus asks, cautiously approaching me. "Are you all right? Did the god of night speak to you?"

"I ..." I start, but my throat seizes up.

I look back at Aris again—and he's looking at me now, but not getting up from his knees. The anguish on his face nearly breaks me. Dimitra—his lover, his friend—is gone. And she died to protect him. Part of me wants to go to him, to comfort him the way Mariana is comforting Rafael, but I don't. I'm stuck, still in shock over the revelations of Caladrius.

"Evanthia wants all three books so she can bring Aenon to the mortal realm," I blurt out.

Mariana stiffens. She kisses Rafael's cheek and then makes her way across the cavern to me, picking her way around melted boulders and fallen stalactites.

"With all three books, she can destroy magic," I continue. "She could kill all the ungifted, or end the magic that helps Ocron prosper. She could ..." Again my throat seizes up, and I have to swallow twice before I can continue. "She could tear pages from the Book of Silver, and anyone with magic other than water magic could be killed. All the Shields, all the Mages. Aenon could rule this realm, unchallenged."

"But … *why*?" Caelus asks, stroking his chin. "Why would Aenon do such a thing? Partner with a mortal queen, turn on his fellow gods?"

"I don't know," I admit. Suddenly I am bone-tired. "Caladrius wants me to get the three books, to bring *him* to this world," I tell him, since Caelus is the only one sort of paying attention to me. I'm still trying to sort out what I heard myself. "He promises to protect us."

"And you believe him?" Mariana says. The contempt is clear in her words. She gives a snort of laughter. "Typical. You naive girl. Did the god of night promise that the world would be unchanged, unharmed? No?" she says, seeing my head shake. "Only that you would live? You should have asked him if he planned on plunging our world into eternal night, to remake it to his own liking rather than maintaining balance." Her hands are clenched in fists at her sides. "Why the god of night chose *you*, I will never understand."

"Why don't *you* ask him, if you're so smart?" I say. I am done with her criticism, her attitude. If it were night, I would summon a whirlwind that would blow her away. I would put her in a prison of solid ice so that I'd never have to listen to her criticism again.

She looks at me and then the book, something unreadable on her face.

"What? Don't think you can handle talking to the god of night yourself? Then stop tormenting me!" I scream, holding the book out. I have had it with her venom, with the lot of them. I should never have involved any of them in this stupid, stupid quest.

Several things happen then, all at once.

A fist of ice slams into my chest, pushing me several feet back and knocking the air from me. I fall to my knees, clutching my sternum, trying to force breath into my stunned lungs.

Aris is instantly at my side, one hand on my back, having moved so fast across the cavern I could scarcely follow him. I am not badly hurt, but both my hands are clutching my chest, and I am panting hard.

Both my hands. My empty hands.

The book. I dropped the fucking book.

Mariana steps forward and picks it up, cradling it in her arms like it is a newborn baby. The look on her beautiful face is reverent, almost fanatical. She looks over her shoulder, back at Rafael. "I did warn you to stay away from me," she says, her voice strange and soft. "*Wall.*" She flings up her hand, and a wall of solid ice springs up from the ground, cutting her off from the rest of us. It nearly reaches the ceiling and is so thick that her form is distorted behind it.

"Mariana? What …?" Caelus says, his hands falling to his sides.

"My queen will be most pleased with this gift, Night Mage," Mariana says with a bark of harsh laughter. "Don't forget—you have until the winter solstice to bring her the Book of Gold, or your Leo will be killed. And my queen can make a man beg for weeks before she ends him."

"*You're* a Black Water Witch?" Caelus asks, falling to his knees, a look of complete horror on his face.

I think she nods—with her behind the ice wall, it's hard to tell.

Aris snarls, pushing himself up and running to the wall. He slams into it, but not even his prodigious strength can budge it.

"You fool!" he spits. "You're trapped behind that wall, with no way out except through me."

He draws his gladiuses and stabs them into the ice, to the hilt, but the ice does not crack. It must be several feet thick, too much for his blades to penetrate. He stabs again, and again, yanking the swords back and plunging them in again, chipping off bits of ice— but it's not enough.

Mariana laughs. She turns toward me. I can't find any words to say to her.

"Take care of Rafael and Caelus for me," she says. There's a wistfulness in her voice, where before there was only cruelty and ice.

She turns, a blue blur behind the ice wall.

"*Push*," she says to the cavern wall behind her.

The rocks scream as ice and snow rip through them, exploding outward with such force that stalactites fall from the ceiling, great icy spears, and Aris yanks me to the side to keep me from being crushed. I get up from the ground just in time to see Mariana disappear.

I push Aris off me. He doesn't notice. He roars, shifting, and slams into the ice wall again, this time with several hundred pounds of tiger strength. The damn wall is twenty feet long, a semicircle, and at least twice as tall.

The wall groans when Aris slams into it, but does not fall.

He roars again, the sound echoing in the chamber—and races across the room. He spins and runs back toward the wall, gaining momentum, then makes a leap at the wall, his claws scrabbling for purchase.

For a moment, they hold, and he tries to scale it.

But then he slips and falls ten feet to the snow below, his paws bloodied.

He shifts back, clutching his right hand—several fingernails have been ripped off. I flinch and bring him his clothes. He accepts them wordlessly, his face contorted with rage as he glares at the wall.

Caelus studies the wall for another moment, then shakes himself, like he's ridding himself of the momentary stupor Mariana's betrayal cast over him. He stabs a gladius into the wall, like Aris did, and then another.

"I tried that, brother. It's too thick," Aris pants, pulling his shirt on.

I realize then that he's missing boots—the skin of his lower legs and feet is red and oozing, the bottoms of his pants gone, the edges of the leather charred. I've never seen him so injured. He barely seems to notice.

Caelus shoots Aris a wry, wolfy grin, then grabs the swords and pulls himself up. He rips one from the wall, reaches as high as he can, and in an amazing feat of strength, pulls himself up. He uses the swords like alternating handholds, using nothing but the force of his upper body and the determination of his will to climb over the wall. Even with his Shield-gifted strength, it is slow going, but he doesn't falter. Such is the devotion of a Shield to their Mage.

Or, possibly, such is his rage.

I turn to Rafael, who still sits at the entrance to the cavern, not really watching anything, eyes not blinking.

"Raf? Can you melt this?" I ask him, waving my hand at the wall of ice. "We have to get after her! We have to get the book! *Rafael!*"

He doesn't respond.

While Caelus continues to climb, I make my way around the dragon, up to the Fire Mage. I put a hand on his shoulder. He doesn't move, doesn't acknowledge me. His golden hair hangs in front of his face, obscuring his eyes, but he makes no effort to push it away. He's breathing, but his gaze is distant, fixed, like his mind is somewhere else right now.

"We need you, Rafael," I say—a wish, a prayer.

A shudder goes through him, but otherwise, nothing. He's not gray—his golden skin is still golden—but Dimitra's death and Mariana's betrayal have hurt him in a way no blade ever could.

I hear a grunt and a thud as Caelus vaults over the top of the wall and slides down the other side. For a moment, he leaves through the opening in the cavern that Mariana left, and disappears.

He returns a few minutes later. He doesn't need to say anything—we all know immediately from the droop of his shoulders, visible even through the ice barrier.

She is gone.

CHAPTER 56
ARIS

We exit the cavern and go back out the obsidian door but can find no trace of Mariana anywhere. Caelus raises his head, sniffing at the air, like he would be able to smell her—but she's vanished. Knowing her water skills, she's probably *walked* right across the Broken Sea by the time we even make it down the damn mountain.

Brodie is quiet when we get down—just the four of us, and no book. He gets us back up on the mammoths without a word and kicks the bull into a quick trot that eats up the miles. Caelus and Rafael ride their own mounts—both silent, lost in their own personal grieving. For a while, I think Rafael might fall off his mount, but he never does. His hands are slack on the reins, his gaze still distant. If it weren't for the fact that the mammoths are herd animals, and his female is going to follow that bull anyway, who knows where he might have ended up?

I ride with Wren. I wrap one arm around her middle, holding her tightly against me, burying my face in the soft floral scent of her hair.

For once, she doesn't fight me. She lets me hold on to her, feel her softness and warmth and comfort, for as long as I need to. She doesn't talk, doesn't push. There is no more of her teasing, no furtive kisses, no banter. But she lets me hold her.

I don't cry. I can't. If I did, Dimitra would have laughed at me for being a sentimental fool. Only this thought bolsters me. I wonder if this is what it feels like to go gray—one part of you so vital, gone forever. I'm no poet, but my world is a grayer place without Dimitra in it.

We make camp only when we need to. The mammoths are hardy animals, and one night we actually just keep going, all through the night. Wren sleeps in my arms, swayed to sleep by Tawny's rolling gait.

The days of travel are a godsend, in a way. It gives us each time to process our losses. I stay awake for days. With the unending daylight, time begins to lose all meaning. We rest when we are tired; otherwise, we push through.

When Wren sleeps in my arms, her head heavy against my chest, sometimes I hold her a little tighter, in a way she doesn't let me when she's awake, like I could protect her from the world the way I couldn't protect Dimitra or Stefan. Like I can be her literal shield.

Why do I fail the important people in my life? I am Aris, the White Tiger. I am better than this. I do not dwell on failures. I do not let fear and doubt rule my mind. I was to be the strongest Shield in a generation—everyone told me so. My teachers, my peers, even Nestor. Now, instead of the bards writing songs about my epic deeds, they'll only note how I failed. I will not be remembered in the Great Hall of Shields, with my deeds inscribed in the texts, to be read and wondered at by generations to come. At best, my story will wither, Night Mage or not.

And I cannot get Dimitra's eyes out of my thoughts. She didn't even have time to scream—just one last look at me, those golden eyes burning into me as surely as dragon flame, before she was gone.

I must doze off at some point on the trip. Honestly, the whole thing is fuzzy. The only thing I remember is the feel of Wren's hair against my face, the warmth of her body in my arms.

And the rage burning in my chest.

As we dismount the mammoths for the final time at Brodie's farm, Adriana swoops out of the sky and lands next to a stack of mammoth-fur blankets. She wraps herself in one as she shifts.

"What happened?" she demands, switching from bare foot to bare foot on the icy ground. One look at our group, now down two members, and she knows something has gone horribly wrong. I look at her, my little sister, my closest kin—and I just don't have the words to tell her.

Her eyebrows shoot up.

"Aris. What happened?" she asks again.

"They were betrayed," Brodie summarizes, rolling a stalk of grass in his mouth. "Water Mage took the book for the Black Water queen and left. Your cat-shifting friend was killed by a dragon. The red one ain't handling it well." He nods toward Rafael.

Adriana purses her lips, shifting something underneath the furs.

"Well?" I ask. "Why aren't you back in Estana? Do you have another message for us?"

She frowns. "Not really."

We make it back to the Broken Tusk and find Loren and her crew waiting for us.

"A little bird told me you might be needing passage back to the continent," Loren says, handing me a mug of ale.

"That so?" I say, eyeing Adriana—but drinking deeply. To the hells with it. A drink is exactly what I need right now. Well, that and one other thing—but if I can't have Wren, then lukewarm watery ale will have to do.

"Ship's been put back together, better than new," Loren says, clinking her mug against mine.

The words barely register. I finish my ale and grab us both another round.

"So, what now?" Adriana asks, pulling up a chair. She's found clothes, thank Rigrasil, and sits with her feet folded under her.

"We get back to Ocron," Caelus says. He isn't drinking, but he is digging the tip of a dagger into the wood of the table. "I can find her. Betrayal or not, I'm still her Shield. I'll get to her before she gets to Roallac."

"We'll head to Estana," I tell her. "Me and Wren and Rafael. The Book of Gold might not be there, but we have to start somewhere."

My hand goes absently to my chest pocket, where I keep a tooth of the dragon—I think I'll turn it into a dagger, the way Dimitra would have. Gods, I miss her. I miss her like I'd miss a limb—with a throbbing ache, one that I fear will never go away. But we must go on. For some reason, everyone wants these damned books—and they'll have to go through me first.

Wren is quiet. She stares into the flames, turning her mug absently in her hands, not drinking from it. She hasn't shared her thoughts with me lately. I hope she's thinking about Caladrius, and whether the god of night is toying with us, and not thinking about Leo. I don't doubt Evanthia is keeping him alive—he is worth more to her alive than dead. This doesn't reassure Wren much. I think she is also jealous of Dimitra, like I shouldn't be grieving her loss. True, we were lovers, but we were friends longer.

Gods. I am tired down to my very bones.

We turn in early, preparing to catch the morning tide on *The James.* Wren isn't in the room. I don't remember seeing her slip out, but then, I've had a few drinks, and honestly, I wasn't thinking all that clearly before them. I take off my swords and drop them onto the bed, followed by my shield. Outside, a storm has picked up, and I'm glad we're not on that damned boat yet. Rain pelts the roof in a constant torrent, and the wind is making the shutters slam against the windows. I go to secure them, leaning out to grab one before it breaks off—and a flash of green lightning illuminates the town and the docks. *The James* is rocking hard against its lines, the great sails secured tightly. The dock is otherwise deserted—

Except for a small, black-robed figure, head tilted back, arms spread wide, screaming into the storm.

I am down at the dock in a moment, my feet making squelching noises in the freezing mud as I run, my toes already going numb. I come up slowly behind Wren—the last thing I need to do is startle her when she's like this. It's like when she made that tornado at the School of the Silver Flame, that first major manifestation of her powers. This time it is a gale—black clouds sparking with green lightning, winds whipping the harbor in towering white-capped waves. I guess we are finally far enough south that the sun actually sets, or close enough, and her magic is alive again for the first time in weeks. She is completely soaked—and doesn't care. Somehow she senses me approaching, though, and turns.

Her eyes are glowing with green fire, the light of her magic dancing along her sleeves and gathering at her fingertips, wrapping her in the radiance of the god of night. The look on her face isn't one of fury, like it was at the school. She is letting her magic speak for her, give voice to the grief and anguish of these past few days, letting the rain be the tears that she cannot let fall. This is her eulogy, one that will be spoken of here for generations. *Do you remember when the great Shield Dimitra Gataki fell to the dragon behind the obsidian door? Even the sky wept, in the greatest storm Abelon City has ever seen. Green lightning streaked the sky, the blessing of the god of night on her sacrifice.*

I don't try to stop Wren.

Instead, I shift and roar my own pain into the screaming wind, right beside her, where I belong.

The storm rages for an hour, leaving the streets flooded. We trudge back, spent. I try to take Wren's hand—she squeezes it once, her fingers icy, and gives me a sad smile before letting go.

The storm was the best send-off I can think of for a warrior's soul—a storm as strong and wild as Dimitra was. Despite the mud in my socks and the freezing rain in my hair, I feel cleansed. The storm was more than a tribute—it was cathartic. Dimitra would have been pleased.

As we head for our beds, Adriana catches my arm, and I nod to Wren to go on ahead. She's nearly dead on her feet after that display and doesn't argue, for once. She leaves a trail of water and mud on the floor, but the innkeeper doesn't say anything. In fact, the man is as white as snow.

"I saw Tekton while I was gone," Adriana whispers to me, like she doesn't want the nosy innkeeper eavesdropping again. Honestly, the man is too stunned by Wren's power to do much of anything at the moment.

"That's nice," I say, wrenching free of her hand. I figured my sister would still be awake, drinking and making a general spectacle of herself, but it seems she was just waiting for me to come back. There is an urgency in her voice that I don't like.

"There ... well, King Leonidas sent another letter. Seems it got lost with all of your travels," she says. She looks over her shoulder at the stairs Wren has taken, as if to make sure she is truly gone.

"All right," I say, and I put out my hand. "Let's have it, then. I'll get it to Wren."

Adriana bites her lip. "It ... um, it was already open when I got it, I swear," she says, handing me the scroll, the wax seal cracked and partially flaked off. "I, um, think you might want to read it, before Wren does."

CHAPTER 57
LEO

My Wren,

I am sorry to hear of your disillusionment. While Ismini has assured me in the past that each Mage-and-Shield pair eventually find their own way, I'll admit, I do not understand how your partnership will work. While Aris is a fearsome Shield, perhaps one of the greatest in their history, he remains at his core a man who lives only for the attention of others, intent on glory above all else. He is a notorious rake, a philanderer, and while you may trust your life to him, please be careful of your heart.

Let me be quite plain. My time here is short. My dearest wish is that you will fly home soon. I can't wait to have you sitting at my side. What a queen you will make.

Yours,
  Leo

EPILOGUE

Aris

I stand at the rail of the ship, Leo's letter crumpled in my fist. A rake, he calls me. I am no pious saint, no gentleman. I've never pretended otherwise. But knowing that this is Wren's opinion of me as well, and that all this time she's been exchanging such letters with another man about us... am I really the villain here? I have been true to her since the moment her lips first touched mine, and would have been for the rest of our lives. Now, because of her, I've lost my best friend and my country has been betrayed, and my Mage wants to rush off to play the white knight, rescuing the king in distress.

The letter falls from my hand. For the briefest moment, it settles on the surface of the sea, that damned line, *fly home*, stark against the black sea before it sinks below the waves.

I pull the band from my pocket. I've carried it with me since Basti, when I bought her the necklace. The necklace was just a ruse —I was eyeing a ring the man was selling the whole time.

I flip it over in my hands. It looks impossibly small and delicate against my calloused fingers, like it doesn't belong there, like I'm not the kind of person that should be holding something so fine. It's not flashy, just a band of silver set with a stone the same gray-green shade as her eyes. I saw it on the vendor's table and knew immediately that I had to have it, knew it like a bolt to my heart. I slipped the man a coin for it when Wren was turned around, looking down the row of shops, and I've carried it with me every moment since. I thought to give it to her after we got the Book of Silver, after we triumphed, together, finding this sacred object that we'd all thought lost to the tides of time. What a story that would have made.

What a queen you will make.

I cock my arm back and throw it, watching the fading sunlight catch the stone as it soars—before it, too, sinks beneath the waves. The symmetry of the moment is not lost on me—I once threw Wren's manacles away in a similar fashion.

But I have to go with her. She is my Mage, and I am her Shield. If something happens to her on this fool's errand, I will go gray. If something happens to her, despite everything, I will not survive it, going gray or otherwise. I make a fist and pound it against the ship's railing.

A rake, am I? Things *were* simpler before Wren. I glance over my shoulder and see Loren leaning against a mast, balancing a knife point on her finger, all the while keeping her dark eyes trained on me. I flash her a grin.

A rake, Leo said. Someone not to be trusted when it comes to matters of the heart, as if I did not possess one of my own.

Then a rake I will be.

Acknowledgments

None of this would be possible without the support of my family and friends. Firstly, my husband, who supports my quirks and nerdiness and who willingly reads everything I write – I love you and this life we've made together. Thank you for everything.

For the Bad Ass Book Club, who regularly drowns my imposter syndrome with good drinks – y'all are amazing. None of this would have ever gotten off the ground without you.

For my editors, Ben and Leonora – you have taught me so much, and my stories are infinitely better for your help.

For the artists who have supported me along the way, including Gabrielle, Salome, Christin, Elena, Aiphos, Amai, Mica … thank you for bringing my characters to life.

For my bookstagram community – I've met (and read) so many amazing new authors. I am indebted to you all for your knowledge, kindness, and experience along this journey.

And for my readers – every like, comment, post, and review means the world to me, and I am immeasurably grateful for your support. I hope you enjoy reading about the world of Wren and Aris as much as I enjoyed writing it!

About the Author

E. M. Leander lives in the American South with her husband, two children, and a grumpy old cat. A life-long lover of all things literary, when she's not spending free time with family, she can be found devouring books and coffee in equal measure.

Also by E. M. Leander:
    Space Camp:
    -The View from Ganymede
    -Daughters of Jupiter

Game of Gods:
    -Wren and the Tarnished Tiger
    -Aris and the Obsidian Door